LIESL WEST

OF RIME AND RUIN

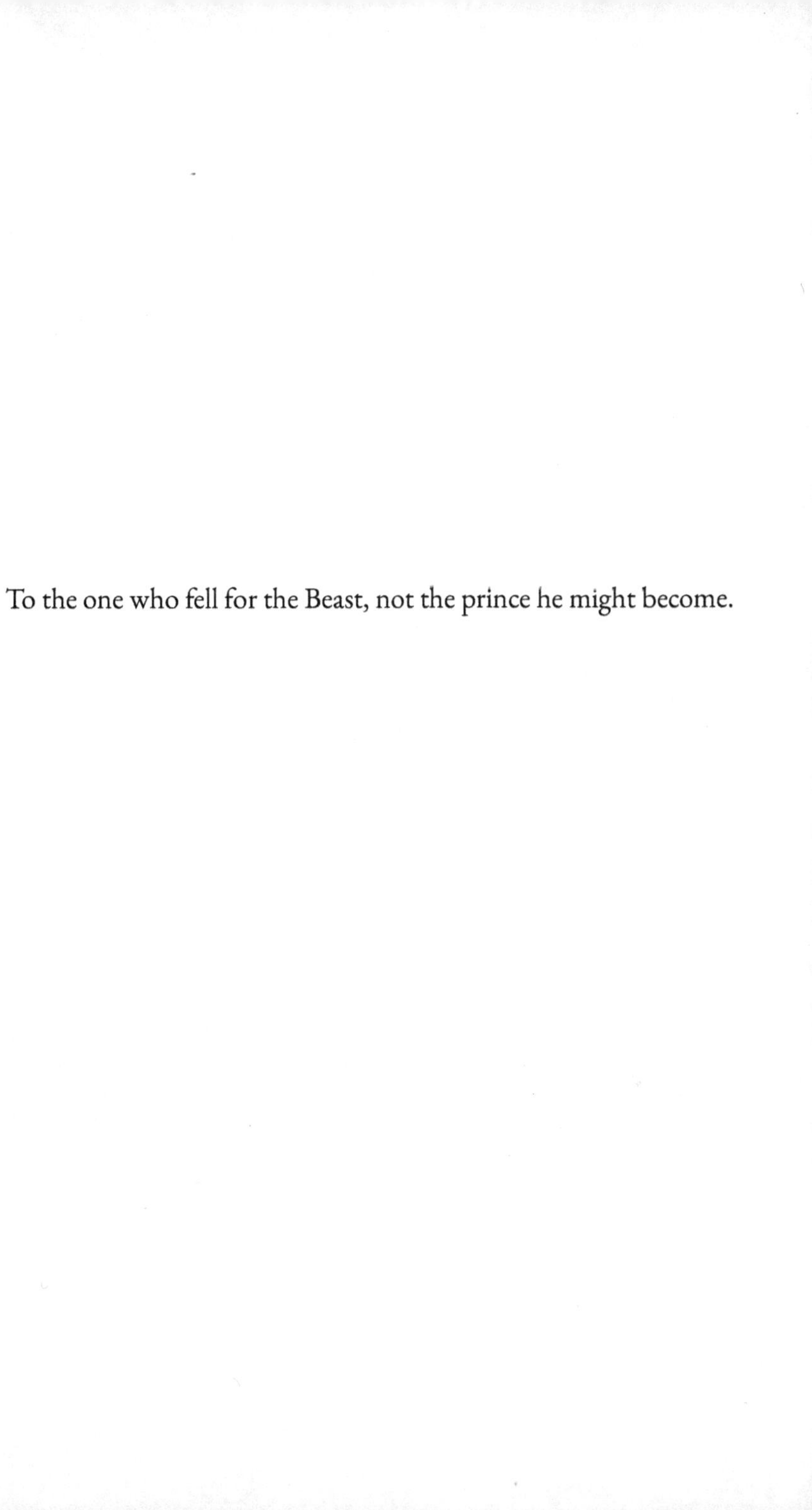

To the one who fell for the Beast, not the prince he might become.

CONTENT NOTES

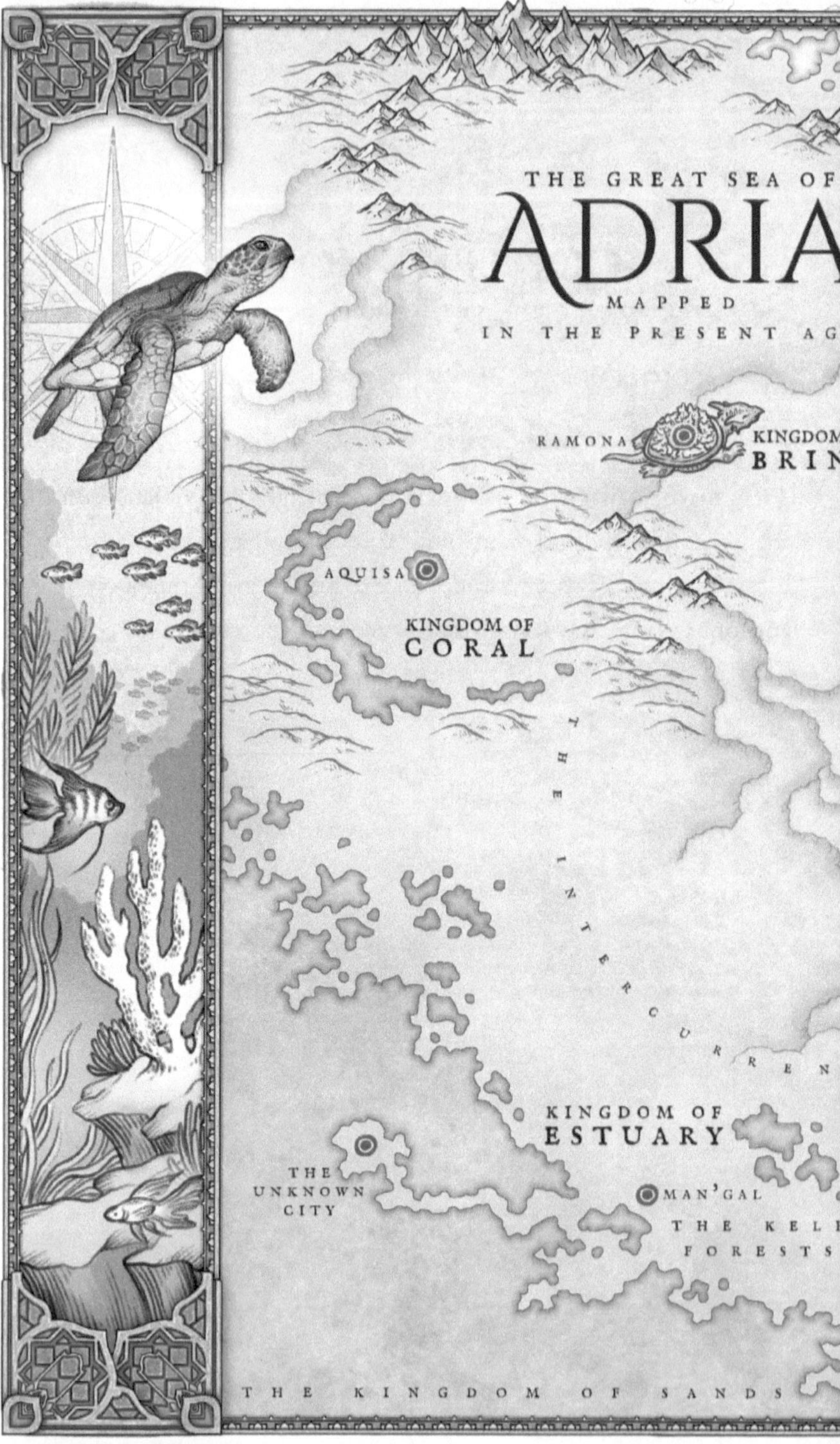

THE GREAT SEA OF
ADRIA
MAPPED
IN THE PRESENT AGE
RAMONA
KINGDOM
BRIN
AQUISA
KINGDOM OF
CORAL
THE INTERCURREN
KINGDOM OF
ESTUARY
THE
UNKNOWN
CITY
MAN'GAL
THE KELP
FORESTS
THE KINGDOM OF SANDS

THE FROSTED PLAINS
DOLOCH
KINGDOM OF
FROST
THE
RIME
THE INTERCURRENT
DREDGEMAW
KINGDOM OF
ABYSS
THE DRINK
VESPYR

PRONUNCIATION GUIDE

Characters

Aethan: AY-then

Audrina: aw-DREE-nuh

Cyrene: sy-REEN

Deirdre: DEER-druh

Ferrell: FAIR-uhl

Geena: JEE-nuh

Isolde: ee-SOHL-duh

Mahelona: mah-hey-LOH-nuh

Nahla: NAH-luh, Nahlani: nuh-LAH-nee

Perrin: PAIR-en

Soren: SOAR-en

Vaughn: VAWN

Winona: wih-NOH-nuh

Places

Adria: AY-dree-uh

Doloch: DOH-lock

Ramona: ruh-MOH-nuh

PLAYLIST

Shadow – Livingston
Lose Control – Teddy Swims
No Angels – Stellar
Madman (feat. Hidden Citizens) – Sam Tinnesz
She Got Me Like – Kode
Shackles – Steven Rodriguez
trouble – Camylio
Figure You Out – VIOLÀ
No Mercy – Austin Giorgio
Darkerside – David Kushner
Careful What You Wish For (the doctor said to) – Jack Harris
Dangerous Game – Stellar, Camylio
Man or a Monster (feat. Zayde Wølf) – Sam Tinnesz
Troubled Waters – Alex Warren
Dangerous – Sleep Token

"There are chords in the hearts of the most reckless
which cannot be touched without emotion."
—— Edgar Allan Poe,
The Masque of the Red Death

CHAPTER ONE

NAHLA

The sun's not up, and I'm already breaking the rules.

My sister's rules, in my defense. Not mine. Silly rules like *be prompt for your royal duties*, and *no loud mouth noises at the table*, and *princesses do not way-make in the wee hours of the morning*, and, her worst one yet, *princesses shouldn't way-make at all.*

But I can't help myself. Especially when Winona said *no* so loudly.

Unladylike pastime, my golden-scaled ass. There's nothing more refined than strapping myself to the head of a giant paddledrake and taking the city by its reins. Nothing more regal. Elegant.

If she wasn't the beloved Queen of the Brine, I'd tell her to fuck off.

"Bring her westward. Steady, now," Keen cautions. The old way-maker shifts next to me, his hand extended to test subtle changes in the current. Despite his weathered hands, silver-streaked hair, and the audible creak in his spine, Keen doesn't act a day over forty, with more than twice the time under his gills.

We barrel through the water together, tethered in place where our mount, Ramona, tucks her head beneath the waterline. Keen makes the pose look effortless, his amber tail steady as he perches in the saddle, one hand resting against the colossal reptile's slick skin to guide her path with his magic.

My tail slips and flutters as I fight the current, the system of leather straps saving me yet again from a tumble into the expanse.

Water ripples above us, parting where Ramona's shell crests the surface like a living island. She's the largest beast in the Sea of Adria—with a firm beak mouth that can crush mountains, four paddle fins each the length of several dredgebeasts, an armored underbelly as thick as a palmwood is tall, and a poisonous lashing tail at her rear.

The Brine City of Ramona, my home, is built on the back of an ancient paddledrake of the same name. Where she goes, we all go. As way-makers, it's our job to direct our living vessel.

Travel is slow, but it keeps the city dry. We could submerge Ramona, as we sometimes do for stealth, but that requires securing several districts to prevent loss of inventory in the open ocean.

The horizon stretches in all directions, isolating us in the center of the sea. Why should we hide? No other kingdoms dare swim this far into open waters without a protector as formidable as the Brine's. They hitch a ride on fleetwhales, keeping to the safety of the Intercurrent, or they never venture out at all. The Coral Kingdom clings to their colorful beaches, Estuary to their kelp forest. Frost hasn't shown their faces in a generation, and the Abyssals rot in the depths of the Drink. The Kingdom of Sands—if it exists at all—only appears in whispers.

But I belong to the Brine, the Kingdom of the Brave. I won't be caught land-bound until I'm dead and dissolved.

I nod to Keen, acknowledging his direction. There's a swarm of sunfish to the west. We've been tracking their scent all morning. In the murky blue water, I spot the glint of their golden scales.

Magic unfurls in my stomach, coiling at the command of my Voice. I activate my spell with a clear alto note and reach with my mind. Ramona's conscience is as ancient as the sea—vast but chaotic. It feels like swimming through jelly. Her thoughts are slow and emotional, untainted by the lesser worries of merfolk. I weave through her psyche until I locate the center of her being.

She grunts, and her great eye rolls to stare at me. I smile at her, pressing my hand to her flat brow bone.

Westward, Ramona.

Her thoughts color with understanding. She tilts, and my stomach dips at the shift in position. The sunfish center in my line of sight, their sailfins cutting through the water.

"Excellent," Keen says. I can hear the pride in his voice. "Now, lure the swarm. They should be close enough."

I alter my song, reaching farther this time. Part of my mind lifts from my body and spirals forward through the water. The farther I push, the weaker my connection to the spell becomes. But the swarm is close enough now. I brush the simple minds of each sunfish, and they obey my command without fuss: *Come.*

With a flick of their tails, they turn. I strengthen my spell, drawing them toward Ramona for our hunters to collect.

If that wasn't royal enough for you, Winona, I don't know what is. This power—my style of Voice magic—is unique to way-makers. It lives in my veins; it's mine to command. I can conduct a sea of thought with the fluctuations in my song. My sister may play politics and parades, but this is real talent.

I'm an integral part of the system that keeps our society churning forward. This is *important.* Beneath the waves, I matter. Sunfish don't care if my hair is askew. I call, they answer; and the entire city feeds from my efforts.

I move the ground Winona walks on.

With a change in my tune, I coax Ramona to slow her pace. She flares her fins, and the city decelerates to a slow tread. The sunfish fill with curiosity as they approach the mammoth paddledrake. Compared to her, their bodies are like glowmites, insignificant flecks of glitter. Yet she hums in greeting—a deep rumble trembles the water—and they brighten with interest.

My stomach curdles, anticipating what comes next.

Around us, merfolk dive from their post on the Rim. Bubbles trail through the water where their sleek bodies cut the current. I see the hunters through each fish's mind: stern faces and colorful tails. The bone tip of their spears angled to kill. The fish are wary, but not overly so. Ramona's presence is too baffling for the fish to give the hunters any mind.

This is good. Meat tastes better when the animal never fears for its life. The hunters hit their marks with precision—kill shots through the eye.

One by one, the fish disappear from my mental radar, and I close my mouth to withdraw my magic. Energy drains from my stomach as the spell ends. The water clouds with blood and the scent of iron spreads.

Keen grins. "You're getting better, Your Highness! Impressive."

"Thanks, Keen. I've been practicing on birds when the queen's not looking." We're sirens—magic-wielders—but the Voice in our blood can take talent only so far. I must hone my skills through careful discipline.

"On birds, really? How resourceful, Your Highness! Though I'm not sure I'd like to spend much time in the mind of a bird, personally." He claps my shoulder. "Does she know you're here again?"

The siren's blue eyes sparkle with mischief, clear as the sky. I look away, pretending to be engrossed by the tether knot as I trace the smooth leather. I'd rather be here, in the saddle with Keen and Ramona, than stuck in court playing princess for my queen sister's approval.

Keen knows this too well. He's watched me grow from a rambunctious guppy into a rebellious princess, and he's been my best friend and secret keeper through it all.

When I look up, the old male smirks knowingly.

"Look, Keen. If Her Majesty got her way all the time, her head would swell like a blowfish. Someone's got to deflate her now and then."

"Was it princess lessons on your schedule this morning or political training?"

"Politics." I sigh. "My maid is covering for me. I've got a bad case of paddledrake flu."

"Clever girl."

It's an honored gift to be Voiced with the magic of a way-maker. Most Brine sirens can perform basic magic like controlling the tides, helping crops grow, or healing wounds. The ability to communicate with animals is special and necessary for this role.

But what does it matter? I'm second born, which means I'm politically dispensable. As the first-born heir, when Winona married two years ago, my parents passed the crown to her and her stuffed-shirt, worthless husband. And now all I'm good for is to become some other royal's wife, a piece in Winona's inherited game.

Around me, corpses float belly-up in blood, their once-golden scales a lifeless brown. We've harvested enough to feed the city for a few more days. Hunters collect the sunfish, hoisting the carcasses over the Rim, and I try to tune out the repetitive slap of their bodies against the shell.

When the water is cleared of the catch, Keen gives Ramona the next command. He hums a spell, placing his hand flat against the paddledrake's brow. She stirs, her fins swivel and push, and we regain momentum.

Soon, a pod of glosswhales joins us. They thread the surface, gliding in elegant arcs as the rising sun glistens off their sleek gray hides. They call to one another in chirping tones, parting their bottle noses in approximations of a smile. Ramona responds with a grating chuckle that vibrates my body. I brush their minds with my magic, absorbing their emotions—happiness, friendship, freedom. My chest tightens at the sweetness of it. I'd trade my left tailfin to be as free as a glosswhale.

"I won't get to do this forever, Keen."

"Do what, exactly? Sneak out of your duties to hang out with an old witherfish? I'm not stopping you."

"If Her Majesty has her way, I'll be shipped off soon."

He gives me an apologetic look. "No harm in practicing the craft, Your Highness. You never know when your Voice might come in handy." When I don't respond, he nudges me gently. "Who knows? You may get lucky. I hear the Abyssal King keeps a hoard of dredge-beasts. Perhaps he needs a tamer." Keen winks.

I shiver. The Abyssal Kingdom, settled in the lowest trenches of the sea, is a place I never want to go. I can't imagine a life away from the sun.

A shadow falls over us from the Rim, in the watery outline of a tall female with my sister's elegant scowl.

Shit.

Before I hear her song, Winona's magic wraps around me with a hard rope of water. She severs my saddle tether and yanks me skyward, suspending me like a fish on a line. My golden tail flops in the dry air until finally my bones rearrange and split into my two-legged form. Dangling naked for the city to see.

The air is warm and sticky, frizzing my hair in an instant. My scales lift at the rush of the sea breeze, nipples brushing the starfish that cover my breasts. The sun is brighter up here, unfiltered by seawater. I squint, adjusting to the abrupt change.

Winona tightens her magic around me and glares.

My sister is everything I'm not: tall, thin, and effortlessly graceful in her crisp morning robes. Our bronze skin and brown eyes match, but hers are sharper, somehow. While my dark curls dangle past my shapely ass, hers are slicked in a no-nonsense bun. There's nothing soft about her.

And there's nothing she loves more than taking time out of her royal duties to see to my embarrassment *personally.*

The subjects stare at me, and I roll my eyes; it's nothing they haven't seen before. Still, their duties pause—nets half-folded, fish half-filleted, hair half-braided. A basket of sweetnuts spills on the ground. A guppy halts their game of hop-two, their lifted knee bent and mouth gaping wide. Only the birds ignore me, chattering from the high branches of the palmwoods.

I search the crowd for my empathetic favorites: the middle-aged florist waves from the half-propped door to her shop. The baker salutes me with his baguette. In the city center, a blonde guppy swings from a tree and screams out her greeting.

Winona flexes her jaw. "Care to explain why I found Miss Elodie in your bed this morning? Giving her your nightclothes was a good touch. Brilliant. But don't take that as permission to do this again, Nahlani. This is unacceptable. You're not a way-maker. You're a princess."

I beam. "You think I'm brilliant?"

With a twitch of her mouth, she yanks me higher.

"How long before you realized this time?"

"It's not funny."

"Five minutes? Did you recount the whole to-do list or just the first twenty items?"

Through the glistening tide, I glimpse Keen barely keeping his laughter to himself.

"I'm serious, Nahlani Mahelona. This ends today."

My full name. Nice.

Her face is stern. I've found the line, and if I push any more, the consequences won't be pretty. Gone are the days of our guppyhood, when harmless jokes flowed both ways.

I dip my head. Her magic tugs, and she plops me down with a splash. The shell is rough beneath my bare skin, hot and half-baked in the morning sun.

I straighten, wringing my hair as she hands me a robe, and I slip my arms through the breezy sleeves.

"You're out of control," she hisses under her breath. A small crack in her armor. "Pull yourself together."

Shadows skitter across her face for a moment, and I can't tell if she's talking to me or herself this time. She clears her throat and pulls a stone tablet from her robe; its surface engraved with the Coral Kingdom's signet. Wordlessly, she hands it to me. I touch the stone, activating its stored magic to reveal the message it carries.

An image plays in my mind.

The Queen of Coral greets me with a flashing smile, spreading her hands in invitation.

"Princess Nahlani of the Brine. To unite our great kingdoms, I request you consider my son, Soren, Crown Prince of Coral, for your hand in royal marriage."

There's a brief image of the prince himself. Muscular, with bronze skin. Dark hair braided down his back. A perfect cocky smile.

What's left of my breakfast threatens to exit the way it came in. I sever the tablet's spell and extend it for my sister to take.

"Keep it." Winona threads her fingers, refusing the stone. It hangs between us, and my arm grows heavy with its weight. "We make for Coral tomorrow."

She bends to knock on Ramona's shell. Keen's head lifts from the water, and he touches his gills in a sign of respect, like he wasn't just eavesdropping.

"Steer her toward Coral, Master Keen. We'll submerge in the morning. Her Highness has a wedding to attend."

My stomach rolls. Bile rises, and I taste its acid in my mouth. I take a dizzy step, as if I might dive into the saddle and turn Ramona off her course.

At Keen's command, Ramona tilts southwest. On her back, the city bustles with action, preparing to submerge. The captain shouts orders. Some brace the palmwoods while others move loose items inside their abodes. Guppies weave around the trees, squealing in their giddy games as their feet stir the dust. It's been a few moon cycles since we last submerged. The air crackles with excitement. Already, I can hear the whispers: *Princess Nahlani's getting married!*

Blood roars in my ears as my heart pumps frantically, threatening to pop. There are worse ways to go than an exploding heart. I'd get out of this whole ordeal, and Winona would be rid of me for good. Win-win. My knees knock together as I wobble on my feet.

My sister steadies my elbow and gives me a tight smile. She tucks a stray lock of wet hair behind my ear. "This is our destiny. You and me, Queens of Adria. We're going to make a difference, Nahla."

I find the horizon, focusing away from her face as I inhale the salty air. The ocean stretches in every direction, the only constant greater than Ramona herself.

Could I live a land-bound existence, rooted in the shallows? All for her vision of our royal destiny?

"Come," Winona says. She smiles, making it up to me with forced kindness. "Let's ask the chef to make us some sweetnut cakes to celebrate. What do you think?"

I swallow against the nausea, pushing it deep into my belly. The message stone quivers in my hands. If I dropped it into the sea, would I still have to marry the land-dweller? Or would Winona send me diving after it?

I check her expression. That smile is already fading as the disappointment spreads.

Shit. My entire life, I've been her greatest letdown.

And it's not just Winona. It's Mother and Father, too. My entire family is counting on me to grow up and play my part. To release my grip on this silly dream of being *useful*.

No more pretending my future awaits beneath the waves. I cannot disappoint them again, not with something this important.

If I marry the land-dweller, will my sister finally be pleased?

She's frowning now, watching with a weariness all too familiar to me. I tuck the stone into the pocket of my robe.

I grimace, nod, and then I lie. "Win, I'd *love* some cake."

Chapter Two

Aethan

I'm naked, but not in a good way. Naked in the *where are my pants and how the fuck did I get here* kind of way. And dripping wet to boot.

It's the dead of night. The sconces in the hallway flicker with uninterrupted rhythm, casting long shadows across the stone floor of my castle's lowest reaches. I stand in front of a heavy wooden door—inches from my nose. Its iron knocker smells of damp rust. My hand is raised, fingers curled tight as if to knock. Dark blue scales cover my knuckles where my skin is usually snow white. Veins thread across my fist, frosted like silkmite string before dawn.

The only sound is the soft splattering of water as it drips from my hair, pooling at my bare feet. How I got to the servant quarters remains a mystery. The last thing I remember is the warm weight of the furs on my bed upstairs. Here, the air is brisk and sharp, waking my senses—and it reeks of blood.

Fuck.

I know the signs. And this isn't the first time I've woken from a trance, blue and bleeding. The blood is mine, oozing and warm on my ribs. A gash cuts across my abdomen, skin splitting over angry, aching flesh. I shake my head, but I can't force my memory to focus. I can't remember what I've done.

In the lamplight, I twist my hand and the scales crawl beneath my flesh like a thousand hurried legs. My skin fades from dark blue to white, the color and energy recoiling into my stomach, where it twists into an icy knot.

Before I can knock, the door opens, and light splits the darkness. I flinch and strain my eyes to adjust as the healer's hollow face appears. "Your Majesty, I've been expecting you." Lucas tips his head.

Has he?

He leads me through the doorway, pinching the wicks of candles with his long fingers to extinguish all but the lone stem on his squat, orderly desk. Smoke curls like ribbons, acrid in my nose.

His office is tidy, as usual. A small fireplace sits in the far corner, framed by bookshelves that reach the ceiling. Cabinets are lined with trinkets and vials. Old tomes are stacked on the desk, their chipped stone faces reflecting candlelight. Above the mantel, a taxidermied head of a frostcat hangs, surveying the room with glazed, black eyes and a permanent snarl.

"Here." Lucas hands me a fur cloak, and I drape it over my shoulders to cut the chill.

He sets a pot to boil on the hearth, the lid clanking. With an iron rod, he arranges two stones on the coals and pokes the embers until they flare red. "What do you remember?"

I don't answer. He already knows what I'll say—it's the same every time. The past few hours of my life are muddied. Like I tripped through time and landed here.

My memory comes in pieces: rocky shore. Waves lapping bare feet. Audrina's full-moon face, with the lights of the aethersky rippling around her. That ice-hot feeling in my stomach, burning, edging me forward. Taking a step. Then another.

Another midnight swim.

Fuck. I pinch my nose until it hurts—a punishment or an effort to focus, I can no longer tell. I'll break the habit as soon as I get the rest of my shit under control.

Lucas approaches, preparing his healing spell. With the soft lilt of his Voice, he coaxes a thread of golden light from his fingertips. The magic prods my skin with warm tendrils, slipping beneath the fibers and knitting the flesh together with a few quick passes. With a flick of his tune, he knots the spell, leaving nothing but a pink line behind. The scar joins the collection that decorates my skin. A web of secrets.

As the pain eases, I pull the cloak tighter. "How many casualties?"

"Nothing yet."

Yet.

He removes the stones from the coals, tossing them between his calloused palms to cool them. He swipes them over my chest, shoulders, and temples. The stones are hot on my skin. Near burning. I grit my teeth. Rage flares with a burst of ice in my stomach, but it's no match for the heat, and it quenches with a hiss, releasing its grip on my lungs.

"Begone," he murmurs as he moves the stones in small, rhythmic circles. "Spirit, be still within this mortal husk. With flame and stone, I expel the darkness. Begone with you, dark spirit! You are not welcome here!"

The heat nears unbearable, and I close my eyes, pushing through. Pushing it all away. The anger. The fear. Until nothing is left but shame.

What have I done?

"We'll get you right again," he says.

The kettle screams. Hinges creak and the door swings open, followed by pattering feet and hissing skirts.

"Oh, deary me." It's Deirdre, my housekeeper, carrying a tray of porridge.

She rushes to the hearth and retrieves the whistling pot. My temple throbs as silence resettles.

"I thought I heard someone rustling about in the middle of the night. Thought it might be a frostcat." She eyes the mount above the hearth, shivering at its snarl.

Lucas stiffens in the female's presence, and the stones press into my skin. "So you brought it porridge?"

Her eyes twinkle. "Naturally." Deirdre's room abuts the healer's office, and she has the sharp hearing of a glosswhale. No doubt she heard us through the wall.

"Bah," says Lucas.

Deirdre ignores him. "How are you feeling, Sire?"

She makes quick work of the tea, pouring and steeping. One sugar cube.

"I've been better," I say, accepting the mug. The liquid singes my tongue. With every cell of my body aflame, the knot in my stomach finally dissolves.

She watches me, those attentive eyes missing nothing. "Midnight swim?"

The healer grunts as he passes the stones over my shoulders. "Don't rile him, Deirdre. Unless you want to be on the receiving end of that icy wrath."

The mug creaks in my grip.

"Shush now," the housekeeper hisses, swatting Lucas away. "I'll take it from here."

His stones leave my skin with a hiss of pain. "This is *my* office."

"Go sit in the corner, then. He needs a gentle touch, and you're in no mood for this, Lucas. Look, you've burned him again."

"Spirits never respond to *gentle*," Lucas grumbles, stepping back. "Might as well thaw the Rime by blowing on it."

Her gaze pins me. "Sit," she says. I sink into the chair. She hefts the bowl of porridge, fishes out a lump with her spoon, and lifts it steaming to my mouth.

"I'm not a mewling guppy, Deirdre," I complain. "I'm the fucking Frost King."

"Watch your language, love."

We both know the routine. These are the instructions my mother left behind—heat to quench the anger, bran to stave the hunger, darkness to calm the fight.

Deirdre smiles, and I open my mouth for the spoon. With a swoop of her hand, she catches a drip of milk on my lips and dips the spoon into the bowl.

"Your mother would have wanted me to take care of you, Your Majesty. Goddess rest her scales. This is the oldest trick in your book, and if it works, why change it?"

My mother left other instructions, too. Locks on the doors and bars on my window. Keep everyone else far away from me. But we don't mention those. They've never worked.

Deirdre is no easier to sway than a frostcat. Beneath that motherly expression is a will of steel. Either way, this will end in porridge.

So I accept her coddling. With each swallow, I resettle in my skin. Rooted once more in time and place.

"Best trick in the book, bah!" mutters the healer. "Unless the king requires more *drastic* measures than porridge on a silver spoon." He squats next to the fire, poking the embers. When he looks at me, his eyes reflect the flame. "It could be arranged."

A chill crawls over my skin as the corner of his mouth lifts.

"No," I say.

He shrugs, turning to the fire. "Whatever His Majesty requires."

"Come now." Deirdre moves to disrupt my line of view. "Off to bed with you, Sire."

She walks with me, steadying my elbow. Panic twists in my throat. There were no casualties tonight. But what about the next time I lose control?

The air grows colder as we enter the West Wing. Icicles cling to the ceiling, growing larger and more frequent the closer we get to my chambers. At the end of the hallway, my guard stands watch before a massive iron door. Hoarfrost forms webs across the iron surface, coating the seams and screws with an eerie blue tinge. Ten locks and two deadbolts hold it fast—not a latch out of place.

The guard startles when he sees me, and he glances about, searching for the answer to the mystery. *How the fuck did I get out?* Wouldn't we all like to know?

Deirdre pats the guard's shoulder softly and fishes her keys out of her apron pouch. She turns each lock, filling the night with the rhythm of grinding gears.

"In you go, love," she says. The ice groans as the door opens.

I pass into the darkened chamber, inhaling the iron scent of the room.

The walls are made of solid metal. There's a door to my washroom, but no means of escape. No windows. It's a cage of my making, and I step inside with a sigh of relief. My breath fogs in the chilly air.

"I'll fetch you for breakfast," Deirdre whispers.

"This will not happen again, Deirdre. Make sure of it." It's a fool's request. We both know she's as powerless to stop me as I am. We're doing the best we can.

"As you wish, Sire."

The door closes, and the locks turn. I lean against the door and release a *whoosh*ing breath.

CHAPTER THREE

BEAST

DARKNESS.

Hunger.

Dread.

I rest.

Waiting.

Watching.

Sharpening my claws.

Chapter Four

NAHLA

First, it's sweetnut cake and a giddy string band. Then a lavish dinner with Brine nobility and a dance that drags past midnight. Flowers—flowers fucking everywhere. They hang from the ceilings, wrap around the banisters, and arch over every doorway. Enough pink, swollen blooms to clear the florist of her stock for the rest of the season. Their scent cloys like stale piss.

Everyone smiles. Everyone stares. And when the spotlight finds me, I twirl in my glittering gown, perfectly poised and drenched in applause. What a strange thing, to celebrate the departure of a talented way-maker. Don't they know they need me?

This is my sister's show, performative generosity to cloak years of emotional estrangement. The lights burn, her booze is bland, and my cheeks strain from smiling. If Winona wanted to please me, she'd leave me alone. Or at least give me a choice.

Cheers, bitch. Cheers to your lonely empire.

When I walk into breakfast the next morning—on time and fully dressed—I brace for Winona's next attack on my good graces.

I squint into the low-tide sun that streams through the breakfast room's eastern windows. My head throbs with the remnants of last night's rum. Bland as it was, drowning in it was the only way I made it past midnight.

The royal family sits around a handsome palmwood table, picking at overfilled platters of fruit and bread. My aged father sits at one end; Mother beside him. Winona's unfortunate husband, Ferrell, reclines beside the queen's empty seat at the head, fiddling with a tassel on his shirt. A servant pulls out my chair in the middle, and I plop into it with a rustle of silks.

Winona stands facing the windows, posture straight. Completely sober. Her dark hair twists into a perfect coil atop her head, drenched with sparkling beads.

"You look beautiful," she says without looking my way. Like she's hiding eyes in the back of that hair. "The Coral Prince will be pleased."

"You didn't even look at me," I mutter.

"Your hair could do with some brushing, Nahlani." My mother sniffs. "What did you do, sleep on it?"

I busy my hands unfolding my napkin and resist the urge to touch what's left of last night's updo. Half my heavy curls have fallen out by now, and I haven't bothered to fix it in silent rebellion. Shame nips at my ears. I should have let my handmaid tame it when she asked me this morning. Why did I tell her no? I could have avoided this encounter.

Around us, the servants scurry to prepare the windows for submersion, securing the watertight panels and closing the curtains. I track their movements, avoiding my family's eyes. I've been in this room for two minutes, and I'm already deflating, making myself small.

"She has plenty of time to get ready," my father offers. "Submerging will take a while. It's not like the prince will see her *today*, Geena."

"And I thank the gods for that." Mother picks up her tea and sips, narrowing her eyes over the rim. She stares at the space above my head—my hair—not my face directly. "Winona, dearest, you *responded* to his message, yes? I know how forgetful you can be with these things."

"I have it sorted," Winona says.

"And about the entourage. Have you selected who will stay with Nahlani once she gets to Coral? We can't skip the details, Winona."

"It's *Your Majesty*," Winona snaps, whirling to face the table at last. "You forget your place, Mother." She pins the former queen with a steely glare, and my mother bristles. It's been two years since Winona inherited the throne. The tradition has stood for centuries in all of Adria—when the first-born heir marries, the throne passes. I thought Mother would give up by now, but she clings to her old title like a bloodfish on her arm.

Pity swells in my stomach as Winona's cheeks stain pink. Her left eye twitches, and I start the countdown in my head—ten minutes before she snaps.

"You should be thankful. I'm only trying to help," Mother says. "Your sister is a handful, and you must be prepared. We can't afford the embarrassment. That's why they'll wed as soon as possible. Less time for the prince to discover what he's getting himself into."

"An excellent strategy," Father says. "That's what worked on me. Mahelona females are a rare breed, and it's best we keep him in the dark. He'll figure it out soon enough."

Mother reaches for his face and pats his fleshy cheek. "Exactly."

After a deep breath, Winona steadies herself and returns her expression to a wan smile. She crosses to the table, settling into her place at the head—an intricately carved chair too menacing for her narrow frame. Her visible anger melts away as she grips the armrests. "Yes, of course, Mother. I'll arrange the wedding shortly after her arrival."

"I'm sitting right here," I whisper. I'm twenty-five years old, not a fucking guppy they need to manage. My headache throbs anew, and I reach for the toast. My knife scrapes loudly against the bread as I smother it with jam. Winona's eye twitches again. Nine minutes and counting.

Mother drops her gaze from my hair, and her eyes focus as if registering my presence for the first time this morning. "I hope you know we're proud of you, Sweetfish," she says, scrunching her face with forced affection. "You're making the right choice."

What choice? I can either accept the engagement or *what*? There's no other option. Forget way-making; I'll be busy hatching guppies for a foreign family line.

"It's Nahlani's duty to this kingdom," Winona says. "I'm happy we have a viable match this time. Coral is a strong kingdom; uniting with them will be good for us."

Winona's husband fiddles with that tassel, saying nothing. The product of local nobility aiming too high and winning anyway, the quiet male got his title by happenstance. When Winona couldn't decide among the prospects our father presented, she ordered them to duel. Ferrell won by default; he overslept the morning of combat and avoided a bout of poisoning in the ranks. The suspect was flayed on the spot. As the last contestant living, Ferrell secured Winona's hand.

Their honeymoon period didn't last long. But married at last, Winona got her throne. And that's all she really wanted.

"What if he's awful, Winona? What if he's a complete chumwad?" I hear the desperation in my voice, and my throat tightens as I rush to get out the words before someone cuts me off. "You've decided my fate for me, without consulting me for a moment, and you expect I'll go along quietly? I haven't even *met* him before."

For just this once, I want her to stand up for me instead of following the protocol or caving to our mother's demands. I want her to say, *You're right, Nahla. I didn't consider your feelings, and I'm sorry.* She's the queen now. She can choose to do things differently and prioritize our relationship over her rules. No one's stopping her.

Instead, she blinks at me. "You have the message stone. He seems handsome enough to me. Charming. Are you not pleased? Many would kill for a chance to marry that prince."

"*I'd* kill for that chance," Mother muses.

I slouch in my chair. That's it then. I have no argument.

Father clears his throat. "The sky is clear today, which should make for smooth waters." He tucks his teacup beneath his gray mustache and sips. "Good for submerging. Ramona should have no issues."

I nod mechanically in simple relief—an easy submersion means we'll get there sooner, and if they're going to pin my fins to the floor, I'd rather them do it quickly.

As my family launches into a discussion of the weather, I reach beneath the table and pull the message stone from my pocket. At my contact, its embedded magic awakens, replaying the Coral Queen's message in my mind's eye.

The image of the Coral Prince dances before the backdrop of my breakfast. Soren, he's called. My future husband. He *is* handsome, I'll admit, in the breezy Coral style. He stands two-legged in a white-washed marble hallway, dressed in linen pants. Brown skin like mine. Bright eyes. Cocky smile. Sand stuck in his dark hair.

In the recording, he scowls as if irritated to be captured in his mother's writing spell.

We might get along.

Or maybe I'll be miserable, separated from everything I know and love, and resigned to never way-make again. My magic, unnecessary. My future, as fixed as Winona's.

Gods.

I sever the magic and groan. This is my duty. I was born for a royal marriage. As the second-born female, I would never be a royal of *this* kingdom forever. That has always been Winona's job: to marry a buffoon up to his neck in silks, like Ferrell, so she could secure her claim to the Brine Throne.

I'm happy we have a viable match this time. Was that sarcasm in her tone? Does Winona regret her decision?

Is she... jealous?

"What do you think, Nahlani?"

I look up into four pairs of waiting eyes.

Ferrell looks away, dropping three cubes of sugar into his lushfruit tea. He clinks his spoon, stirring, stirring. *Tap, tap, tap.* Winona flicks her gaze at him, her brow puckering with irritation.

Gods, their sex life must be awful.

"Nahlani Mahelona, are you listening to me?" My father speaks again, and his eyebrows twitch.

Shit.

Winona's fingers rap on the table, her nails clacking one after the other. Louder. Faster. Two minutes and counting until she snaps. My head throbs again, and I curse last night's rum into oblivion.

What were they talking about? The weather? All the ways I've failed them?

I swallow a lump of bread, and it slides down my throat.

"If you'll excuse me," I say, standing. My pulse pounds in my ears. Winona protests with a click of her tongue. So I snatch a piece of cinnamon cake for good measure, fold it into a napkin, and rush out of the room.

"Is she running away again?" Father's booming voice echoes through the hall before I burst out the front doors into a shallow courtyard.

The air hangs heavy outside, thick with moisture on a hot gust of wind. Voices erupt in the streets beyond our gate. The doors to the palace slam shut behind me, but I do not stop. I push through the gate into the chaos of submersion day.

My family won't follow. They never do.

The captain shouts orders in the streets. Merfolk scramble to tuck last-minute items into their homes. Hatchlings wail. Birds screech from the palmwoods. Guppies stand at the bottom of the trees, trying to coax them with stale bread. The birds will have to come inside before we submerge or find a new home somewhere else. If I had time, I'd stop to help bring in the birds. But I'm already breathless, and my pounding feet carry me past.

Keen stands at the helm, readying to dive into the saddle.

It's happening.

In a few moments, Ramona will submerge, and we'll speed toward my future.

Keen points west. The captain nods. Before he dives, the old way-maker glances in my direction. I lift my hand and wave, and he smiles as I charge toward him with the cake cradled to my chest, weaving around the merfolk.

The shell is hot beneath my bare feet. The wind rips through my hair, spoiling the elaborate style. Against my chest, the cake squishes, crumbs escaping to skitter down my belly.

I come to a screeching halt in front of Keen, and he eyes the napkin with interest.

"That for me?"

"Happy submersion day," I say.

He takes my offering and unfolds the napkin. The cake is malformed but still edible. Keen dips his finger into the icing and sucks on it.

"Sorry I can't join you in the saddle."

He grins around the cake, pushing a lump into his cheek. "I'm not stopping you. Especially not after you feed me cake."

I laugh. "Consider it a thank you. For everything."

He narrows his eyes. "That's cryptic."

"I mean—" I pause. It's just cake, right? "I'm so glad you took the time to teach me. I don't know the next time I'll be able to—" The words lodge in my throat.

What am I saying?

Sweat beads at my temples, wetting my scalp. I glance over Keen's shoulder to the sea's unwavering horizon.

A pod of glosswhales leaps through the waves, glittering in the morning light. What if...

An itch crawls from the crown of my scalp to my toes as the thought solidifies. *What if I joined them?*

No. I couldn't.

It's too risky.

Winona has flayed deserters before. Why should her good-for-nothing sister be any different?

The old siren tracks my gaze. "Ah," he says. "Some of my favorite creatures, glosswhales. I've always wondered where they go when the weather turns. I have a hunch they head south. Cross above the Abyss. Swim past the edge of the known sea. Now, wouldn't that be exciting?" His voice drops to a whisper, brittle with emotion. "Wouldn't that be something to live for?"

I join him in his whispering, leaning close. "What are you saying, Keen?"

He jerks his head toward the bustling city. "They're all running around with their fins dried out. A bird could shit in their eye, and they wouldn't notice a thing."

"But I'm not..."

He winks. "I won't say anything. Not even if she strings me by my gills."

"But that's treason."

He pinches the cake and tucks another bite between his lips. "And it never tasted so sweet."

"Oy!" shouts the captain. "You ready, Master Keen?"

I frown. Even as my heart jumps into my throat like an excited guppy.

"What about you? If you assist a deserter, she'll snip your tongue."

"Her best way-maker?" He finishes the cake. "She'd be lost without me."

My toes grip the edge of the Rim. I stare into the glittering water. Ramona's fins churn beneath the surf, making long, sweeping arcs.

"Now, I'm getting into the saddle. And you..." He squeezes my shoulder. "May the current guide your fins."

"And the stars light your way," I echo. My eyes burn, tears pricking at the corner. "But it's open water. What if I'm caught by a dredgebeast? Or worse?"

There's that knowing smile, spreading across his face. "Then tame it, my girl. Make it your bitch."

My jaw drops from its hinges. He grins. With one last squeeze, the old siren dives off the Rim, and his amber tail emerges beneath the waves.

Behind me, the streets are nearly empty. The captain barks an order, and stragglers rush into their homes.

He spots me where I crouch on the Rim. "Your Highness!" I grip the coarse shell with my hands, finding little purchase. He rushes toward me. "Secure yourself!"

I raise my hand to stop him. "I'm in the saddle today, Captain."

"Get situated, then. Make haste." He leaves me to it.

Ramona releases a low, trembling groan. Her shell shifts beneath my feet, and I stumble. The water churns and wakes. Ramona tilts. My breath catches, lungs sucked dry. The sea rises to meet me.

My tail snaps free, my gills flutter, and my ears ring with the low roar of rushing water. And as Ramona plunges into the deep, I release my hold on her shell.

CHAPTER FIVE

AETHAN

THERE'S ALWAYS A *YET*. Every. Fucking. Time.

A mutilated body lies on the rocky shore, icy tongues of seawater lapping at the leftovers. The Rime has preserved what's left of him—an arm, the sleek curve of the siren's tail, three deep gashes across his torso. In webbed patterns, ice clings to the wounds like lace, staving the blood. He wears the mark of a hunter around his neck, but I can't make out his face beneath the mess of silver hair.

Another subject is dead at my feet.

The Frost Guard pulls the stiff corpse from the water. They make quick work, keeping their feet low to the stones, careful to avoid splashing or submerging too deep. They eye the surf warily, as they should. According to legend, the clawbeast attacks in darkness, and the sun has barely risen.

"Your Majesty, we await your orders." The captain looks at me. His eyes have sunk into his broad face, and the hook of his nose is speckled white with chill. This isn't the first body he's pulled from the Rime for me. Because of me.

Her face, pale as the morning snow, blooms with freezing blood. A gash on her cheek, tugging the corner of her sad, knowing eye. She reaches for me through a cloud of bubbles. It's the last I remember of her, before my world went dark.

Pain twists in my throat, and I avert my gaze from the waiting captain, swallowing my anger.

This is why I ordered my people to stay *out* of the water. Why I invited them into my ancestral warm-season grounds to live ashore year round. No one swims, no one gets hurt.

It's like telling a bird not to fly into a pane of glass. They won't fucking listen, and they'll never learn.

This is the second casualty this moon cycle; four in the cycle prior. Since the killings began, it's always the same injury, the same three marks where the clawbeast's talons cut deep. And the monster leaves his kill on my goddessdamn doorstep every time.

I scan the basin for signs of movement, knowing I'll find none, knowing it's an act—to deflect the suspicion. Let them think the Beast is out *there* somewhere, not standing next to them on the shore.

The clawbeast attacks in darkness, and I have no memory past midnight.

The floes bob in the soft current, undisturbed. Ice stretches toward the early morning sky, framing the cavity that marks the entrance to my dominion and shielding against the worst of the wind.

Still, its sting penetrates the thin threads of my fur cloak, nipping my bare chest beneath.

"Take the remains to the healer," I tell the captain. "Have Lucas identify the victim and alert the family. Condolences from the king."

My voice is cold and rhythmic, the words a recitation. How many times have I given the captain this same order? It should be habitual by now. Another body on the shore? Clear the evidence. Condolences to the family. Done. He does not need to rouse me or pull me from my iron cage.

Anger uncurls in my stomach, icy hot. It slithers through my chest and tightens its grip. My teeth chatter as the ice moves through me, numbing my veins.

I can't breathe. My lungs burn. Frozen. I stare at my feet, my snow-white skin marbling with dark blue scales. The color spreads, crawling over my ankles, then calves. With it, a burning chill.

Not now. Fuck no. Keep it together, Aethan.

I inhale, pushing the anger deep. I count to ten. Then twenty. I unfurl my fists. Drop my tongue from the roof of my mouth. The wind wicks the sweat from my palms. Finally, the color fades from my feet, and I exhale in relief.

The guards lift the corpse into a litter, the stones beneath their feet clacking as they carry the victim the short distance to the gate. A handful of servants have gathered behind the frosted iron bars, craning to glimpse the scene. As the gate parts to let the Frost Guard through, the servants scatter.

I narrow my eyes. Did anyone see? I keep a small staff for this reason; fewer eyes to notice oddities, fewer mouths to spread half-truths, and fewer bodies to wash up dead.

Deirdre pushes through the gate, dropping into a quick curtsy greeting when she reaches me. Her eyes are tired. "Shall I put together a gift basket, Sire?"

As if a gift basket could replace the life taken. I run a hand over my neck, massaging the tension before I speak.

"Yes, and add extra blubberchips this time, Deirdre." I tug my furs tighter as the wind whistles over the Rime, spraying frozen mist. "It'll be cold tonight."

"Excellent idea." She follows me toward the gate.

Underwater, this wind was never a problem. What's left of Doloch is carved into the ice below my feet, the royal city abandoned entirely at my command. My kingdom has been land-bound, hunkering two-legged inside our huts, for the past decade, merfolk separated from the sea. But I'd rather them land-bound than lunch.

Some disagree. If I was a good king, I'd dive into the depths myself and wrestle the clawbeast into submission, they say. End this madness.

But I am anything but *good*, and I won't set fin in the Rime again.

Not wittingly, anyway.

Not when it ends like this.

The wind cuts out as soon as I step into the hall.

"A bottle of wine as well, perhaps?" Deirdre says, brushing the snow from her gray hair.

I grunt. "If it will help you sleep at night."

She ignores my icy tone and nods. Deirdre has always been a hopeful type; her lips curl warmly at me, her round face soft with age. All these years, she's served my wretched family, first as my mother's favorite handmaid and now as my head of house. She knows all our secrets, and she still finds reason to smile.

She glances over her shoulder toward the shore. "I'd sleep much better if this situation was—"

"I have it under control." My tone cuts too sharply. Too loud as it echoes through the vast hallway.

I clench my fist to tamper the next flare of anger, but the energy builds and burns through my veins, and a cord of muscle twitches on my neck.

It's not enough. Energy rushes through me, and my siren Voice erupts in deep, rattling bass. The power of my magic is addictive, uncoiling in my belly as it grows. I twitch my hand and, unable to control it, shards of ice sprout from the ground, cutting a line out the hall, through the gate, and to the sea. Deirdre gasps, leaping out of the path of my magic. The ice crackles and twists skyward as my spell continues to fall from my mouth.

Rage building. Power unfurling. The familiar darkness stirs deep within me, waking up as my hands stain blue.

A scream cuts the air, and my heart lurches. I wrestle the energy into submission, snapping my mouth shut. The shards of magic shatter and fall in glittering dust over the stones.

A young merman collapses onto the beach with a howl, his severed leg slick with blood. I recognize him as a Frost Guard trainee. Deirdre's nephew.

And I've just sliced off his foot.

Deirdre screams and rushes to the shoreline, a sob ripping from her throat. The family resemblance is clear—the spotted pattern on their dark blue cheeks, the broad brown eyes, the curly mops of hair, one silver, one sandy. Deirdre said her nephew joined the Frost Guard this year, and he was proud to be in my service.

Perrin, he's called, after the wandering glacierweed; her late sister's favorite floral.

I watch in frozen horror as she kneels next to him. Perrin screams, hands coating with blood as he grasps his severed ankle. His right foot lies dismembered on the stones. Already, his foot mottles purple, the hoarfrost of my magic claiming territory.

"Healer!" Deirdre tears her skirt, tying a quick tourniquet above the wound. Her mouth moves again, but no words reach me.

All sound fades into a hush of panic. My ears ring. I clasp my head, staggering as the vertigo hits, and I catch myself on the cold bars of the gate.

Lucas breezes past, rolling his sleeves with four quick tucks. I blink. My hearing rushes in with a whoosh.

What am I doing? Standing like a dick in the doorway? I curl my shaking hands into fists and burrow them in my cloak.

Perrin whimpers as the healer prods the wound with a spell. The youngling's head snaps back, his teeth bared, and Deirdre gives him a piece of cloth to bite. His foot can't be reattached; my hoarfrost has spread too far.

I wrench my gaze away, turning on my heels. The hallway is silent. Empty. No one to see me flee the scene of my crime.

I grab a vase of flowers and shatter it against the wall as I pass. The shards cut the bottoms of my feet. But the pain is not enough.

When will I learn?

I'm the Beast who haunts the Rime.

Chapter Six

NAHLA

Deserter.

Through a cloud of bubbles, Ramona's rough shell passes before me. Her fins angle, then tuck, and she dives. The palmwoods bend, trailing in the water. A few loose barrels get caught in the current and spiral away from her shell to be lost to the deep.

Traitor.

My heart aches. My fins itch to chase her. To catch up, somehow, as she gains speed. My friends, my home, my past, my future—it all fades into the blue.

Disappointment.

The voice in my head sounds a lot like Winona, so I ignore it. The more water I can put between us before my deed is discovered, the better. Ramona heads west, so I angle northeast. I'll skirt the Frost basin and loop south. Keen said there's life beyond the known sea, and I'll be the first to go there and back again.

With one final glance at Ramona's wake, I steel myself. I ball my fists and ready my gills for the journey.

The current beneath my fins, I cut through the water with speed. My gills slip into an efficient flutter. I open my mouth to catch the scent of the sea, following the bitter trail that will lead me northward. My tail pumps with purpose. Easy.

No one to tell me where to go. When to sleep. What to eat. I'm the maker of my own way, and I've never felt so free in my life.

I can do this.

***

I can't do this.

The first rays of morning light pierce the surface, filtering through the waves with dancing hues of gold and pink.

And I haven't slept a wink.

I swam all day and through the night, unable to stave the sense of being watched. Like a million pairs of eyes were on me, hidden in the depths. My stomach tingles as I think of their invisible gaze.

Beasts don't care if you're royal or low-born. You're either food or foe, and I look a lot like the first one.

The sea is endless. Lonely. I swim for hours without spotting a single creature. Blue stretches in every direction, and my mind spins until it feels like I'm swimming in place, getting nowhere. My body shrinks, a tiny golden fleck swallowed by the blue.

I need to find cover. Or friends. A large pod of fleetwhales would do, if I'm lucky enough to find them. The gentle giants rarely mind a clinger or two.

But I can't catch their scent. Out here, I'm alone.

I reach with my magic, every so often, to detect predators. But my energy is depleting fast. I need to sleep before it can renew. So I keep it locked tight, swimming with mental blinders on.

Already, I miss the protection of Ramona. If I see her in the future, never again will I take her guardianship for granted.

Fear's teeth puncture and chew until my gut is a mess of panic. My gills filter oxygen at a frantic rhythm.

What was I thinking?

I'm a silly little princess. Not a hunter. Not a warrior. I should be home in a plush bed, a guard at my door. Snacks at the ready on a silver tray. Or strapped in the saddle where it's safe.

My stomach growls. I really didn't think this through.

A swarm of sweetfish darts from my path, terror white in their eyes.

"Sorry, sorry," I mutter.

They thrash their tails and flutter out of my depth of vision.

Weariness weighs like an anchor. I can't maintain this pace; I can't sleep, either. Not with those eyes on me.

But the expanse stretches on, and my vision grows heavy. My heart slows.

I let my body become like reedgrass, flowing where the currents take me.

And I drift.

For days. Weeks, maybe. I've lost track of the pattern of the sky.

I sleep with one eye open.

I snatch fish to calm my hunger, consuming their flesh with murmured apologies.

The sea gradually cools and the sun pales. My muscles wake to the chill, and I shiver. I've drifted into northern waters, that much is clear, but I don't know how far I've come.

The water parts around my face as I break the surface. Night air greets me with a chilling kiss. Across a starlit sky, bright streaks of light ripple like glittering scales set aflame. Mountains crest the sea in the distance, mammoth white caps jutting above the waves. The skylights play on the snow.

I spit the water from my mouth, letting it drop into the waves.

A chill crawls over my wet scalp, and not just from the air. I tilt back, lifting my tail to float. The waves hold me, and I watch the lights with joy in my heart. Have I ever seen anything so beautiful?

I want nothing more than to be closer to them. I reach my hand high, as if I might grasp their ribbons between my fingers and draw from their power.

Forget south. If there's a place for me among these mountains, I'd gladly spend eternity beneath this tetra-colored sky.

But it's not close enough. So I roll over and thread the waves, leaping in slow arcs toward the mountains.

I catch the scent of glosswhales and call them with a low whistle. They rise to the surface, flanking me.

One catches my gaze, its curious eye bright with mischief. I reach for it with my magic, singing a connection spell.

Race me?

Pleasure colors its mind. Its tail kicks hard, and it lurches forward.

I brighten at the chase.

The mountains draw closer. Under the waves, they're formidable, sloping beneath my line of sight. When we near the rock face, the glosswhale turns, pod in tow. We swim parallel to the rock, gaining speed.

The glosswhales chirp and chatter. I join in quiet song, harmonizing with their chaotic melody.

Is this what my life could be?

Unfettered by political posturing? Just me and the waves and the creatures of the sea.

Ahead, a narrow channel splits the mountains, lined with iron spikes. Ice floes bob, their dark shadows teetering above me.

The glosswhales adjust their aim, slipping between the gap in the rocks.

Fear prickles my scalp, and I stall, backpedaling my fins. My song dies in my mouth, and my connection to the glosswhales severs. The bitter scent of the water grows stronger, coating my throat.

This is Frost territory.

I may have skipped political lessons, but I know between that gap lies a kingdom harsh and cruel. Their royal's heart is as cold as the castle he calls home.

I can't just *wander* into the Rime. It's one thing to admire the skylights. Quite another to ask for hospitality from a tyrannical king.

Ahead, the glosswhales chirp, circling back to collect me.

I chew my lip.

Reckless. Foolish. Traitor.

My stomach sinks as Winona's voice returns. I can almost picture her scowl, regal as ever. Disappointed, yet again. If she knew I was risking a dip in the Rime for a few more minutes of fun, my sister would scream—in that silent, internal way of hers.

Do it.

Adrenaline fills my veins, and I ache with longing. It's a small rebellion. Nothing too major, just a little trespassing...

I can't wander into foreign territory and expect to swim away unscathed. What happens if I get caught? Do I pretend to be lost and confused? A regular damsel in distress routine—they'll never see *that* coming. I'm fucked.

But what if I don't stay long?

What if I finish this race, then leave?

It's well past midnight by now. What are the odds of meeting a Frost Guard patrol at this time of night? I could sneak in and out, no problem. Stick to the periphery, finish our race, and then I'll be on my way.

Harmless.

The Frost King will never know I was here, and neither will Winona.

The glosswhales chitter, nudging me with their glassy noses. My heart melts, and I can't say no.

Chapter Seven

Aethan

My chamber is black as the night. Thick furs hang over the walls to cut the chill of the ice that clings to every iron pore. It's late. The candle on my mantel burned out long ago, its smoke lingering in the room like a stale guest.

My ass is sore from sitting in this chair too long. When I tilt my head, my neck cracks and a series of pops break the silence.

I should sleep. Resign myself to the creature comforts of the soft furs on my bed. Any sane person would have given up the chase by now.

But I must stay vigilant if I'm to catch the clawbeast. It's the only thing that will prove my innocence.

So I dip my fingers again into a shallow bowl on my desk, its water cool and clear. As I hum the activation spell, it creates a mirrored pool, glowing awake and casting a blue hue into the darkness. I peer into an enchanted replica of my frozen domain.

My Voice deepens, directing the spell. On the surface of the pool, the conjured image narrows and dives into the Rime. I grip the bowl, transfixed by the moving image. The seafloor slants away from the beach. Shale gives way to a sprawl of dark, jagged rock. Silverfish flick their tails in unison, forming a tight unit of flashing scales. Glacierweed sways in the slow currents, the curly tendrils clinging to pockets of stone. Then the floor drops. Steep ice walls plummet to the darkest reaches, swallowed by the blue.

I alter my spell, and the image plunges into the depths, speeding through the trench and scanning for signs of struggle. Claw marks in the ice, or a molted scale. Bones on the seafloor. Anything to prove the existence of another clawbeast living in the deep.

The knot in my stomach hardens, sharp as a knife.

There's nothing here.

Slowly, my vision rises, floating toward the surface for a final wide-angle view.

I've searched the Rime for over a decade, and the bitter truth remains the same: I am the sole cause of my people's suffering. And unless I can find a cure soon, I will need to abdicate my throne. I've already broken tradition—a young king with dead parents, I took the throne unmarried. A scandal I've done nothing to remedy. Twelve years later, without a prospect or an heir in sight, I can't preserve my lies much longer.

The stone bowl creaks under the strength of my grip. I blink, partly withdrawing my attention from the pool. My knuckles stain blue. But before I can sever my spell, a light catches my eye.

Somewhere, in the crystal blue expanse of the Rime, a bright flash of color. I intensify my spell, zooming in on the spot.

Scales, not light. Bright golden scales shimmer in a monochromatic sea. And they belong to a mermaid.

My stomach flips over.

She's beautiful.

She executes a somersault, arching her back and tucking head over tail. The signs of magical lineage are there—features smoothed by magic, earth-toned skin blending into a colorful tail. Long, dark hair fans around her. Two starfish cover her ample breasts, the planes of her stomach soft and bare. Her tail, brilliant as the sun, ends in feathered yellow fins, flowing like a sunfish. Her petite hands are clasped above her head, driving her dive.

As her face circles into view, I catch her smile. Sweet, plump lips. Her eyes pop open. Two brown orbs, flashing with mischief beneath thick, dark lashes.

My stomach bottoms out. It's like she's looking right at me. But I grip the bowl, rooting myself in my chair. I'm safe at home. It's a fluke. A coincidence. She can't see me.

A pod of glosswhales rises from the deep, pumping toward the surface. Bubbles churn in a path behind them as their slick gray bodies cut the water with ease.

Her mouth opens, and bubbles escape. The sight-pool silences her song as her lips quiver, forming a Voice I cannot hear. *A siren.*

The glosswhales approach, circling the siren with curiosity. She watches them, reaching out with her hands to stroke their noses. Petting them and puckering her lips. Her fingers tickle the underside of one's chin.

She giggles, and my stomach twists as I wonder what it might sound like. Light and melodic? Bright as her scales? Or would she have a deeper rasp, one to match the mischief in her eyes? Those watchful, haunting eyes.

The scales rise along my neck. She has no right to have eyes like that. In one glance, she's unraveled me. My body no longer feels my own—my stomach is tied in knots, my heart thunders, and my breath catches. I long to reach into the pool, to snatch her up, to fold myself into her being. To dissolve in her warm, playful gaze.

I shake my head to clear the pang of desire. A siren with such power over my senses—she must be dangerous.

She pumps her tail, leading the glosswhales toward the surface. I turn my spell, squinting as the aethersky streams from above. They break the waterline, threading it with bubbles.

What is she doing in my Rime?

My stomach twists tighter still. Who is this outsider, giggling in the middle of my domain like she owns these waters? I've never seen this female in my life. I'm the fucking king. I should know if an outsider infiltrated my ranks.

Doesn't she know she's in danger? Can she be so naïve to enter a foreign territory to play with whales? A clawbeast lives here. *I live here.*

My hands chill. Ice crawls over the surface of the sight-pool, frosting my view.

She is not welcome in the Rime.

Outsiders can never know my secret. A cursed king still in power? They'd flay me on the political scene. Chase me from my home, turn my kingdom over to the dredgebeasts.

My family may be wretched, but we've earned the right to keep our secrets. Outsiders have no place here. My business is *mine*. My own.

I study her soft skin, the way the chilly water laces over her. A sun-drencher will not last long here. Either the Rime will take her or the clawbeast will.

What if she's a spy? Or worse, a death-dealer? My spine erects at the thought.

Do the other kingdoms finally suspect something? I should have accepted that invitation to the Estuary Queen's latest flower festival, to avoid suspicion. When was that? Six moon-cycles ago?

There was blood on my beach. No way could I have left.

Perhaps I should have sent an ambassador in my stead.

Fuck.

My heart thunders, an echo of its pulse thrumming at my temple.

I snap my teeth, ending my spell. The water's glow snuffs out in an instant, casting me into darkness once again.

But it's not enough to calm the rage. I can sense it, crawling up my hands, my toes. Cold claws, climbing.

I grip the desk. The wood cracks, divots forming where my fingers clutch the edge.

I push out of my chair. If I pace, if I channel the energy elsewhere, I might control it—

There's a spy in the Rime.

One step. Two steps. Walk in a circle.

There's a fucking spy. Here to uncover my secrets.

Unlikely. She's high-born. Playful and innocent. She could be lost.

That's what they want me to think. It's the perfect disguise.

Her eyes. Dark, playful eyes, looking into my soul.

Fuck.

I flare my nostrils, inhaling the iron scent of my chamber. Focus on what I can feel, what I can see.

Only darkness.

Wooden slats beneath my bare feet. I strip off my clothing.

She can't be here.

My hands grasp the wardrobe, sliding it across the floor.

In the floor, a beast-sized hole. I slip inside. Set the wardrobe in place with one hand. I will not remember this in the morning. Already, the darkness has descended.

She doesn't belong.

I plummet.

Splash.

The water swallows my body into its icy gullet. Blue scales sleeve my arms, crawling over my shoulders. Beneath the scales, my muscles scream for release, burning, shifting, growing, until finally my vision darkens, and the transformation drags me under.

CHAPTER EIGHT

NAHLA

ONE MOMENT, I'M SKIPPING waves with glosswhales. The next, I'm someone's snack.

I sense it coming, the beast. Its large body forces through the water with shocking strength and speed. Fish flee it, their little minds sparking with terror.

What kind of beast this is, I have no clue. But I can't fuck around and find out.

The glosswhales shriek, abandoning our game. They kick their tails and speed away in a fury of bubbles. My body catches in their wake, spinning from the force of the escape. The dark water swirls, and with it my sense of right-side-up.

I'm caught in open water. The sea floor is the same monotonous shade of blue as the dim light from the surface. I steady my fins, searching for somewhere to hide. Glacial walls surround the basin. If I could make it there in time, I could find a crevice—

I kick my tail. There's no time to think. Just do.

My muscles ache with a chill. My gills flutter at record speed, laboring to filter oxygen from the cold water. Too slow. I kick harder until my tail screams from exertion. And it's still not enough.

The beast barrels toward me, all my senses alert to its presence. How large is this thing? I risk a glance to my left, scanning the water. Nothing. To the right, nothing.

But I can *feel* it, all around me. Like the Rime is an extension of its essence.

A god among the fish.

The glacial wall comes into view. I adjust my course.

In my periphery, I spot it then. The large, blue body, strung in a tight line of muscle. Long, white hair slicks back from its face—*his* face. The broad angle of that jaw, the fierce brow, is undeniably male.

Ruthless and handsome all at once. *A god, after all. Shit.*

I kick harder, tearing my gaze away. My arms cramp as I strike, faster, faster, parting the water around my body. I spy a crack in the glacial wall and send all my good vibes in its direction, praying to all the gods—minus him—that my body will fit.

He stalks closer, closer. Faster than I thought possible.

I slam into the wall. *Shit.* Pain explodes in my shoulder. I curse and dive, aiming for the crevice.

I slip tail-first between the ice, wedging my entire body into the narrow space. Jagged ice scrapes my skin, and I hiss in pain as a few scales rip away. The walls crush, freezing cold. The fresh iron scent of my blood floats around me. Through the crack in the opening, I'm forced to watch the beast as he makes his approach.

He's unlike any merfolk I've seen before, propelling through the water with movement more akin to a shark than a whale. His hips swing side to side instead of up and down, two hind legs tucked against his tail as the long rope of muscle whips through the water.

He pivots. His body angles for my hiding space, nostrils flaring. *Stupid, stupid.* Of course he'd try to follow. As he turns, I glimpse the spikes that sprout from his spine, following the line of his long, thrashing tail. Two curling horns pierce through the skin of his temples, framing a pair of dark eyes.

His gaze locks on me. Cold. Cruel. His lip curls, revealing rows of sharp teeth.

I'm fucked.

I press farther into the crevice. A rock digs into my back. My tail coils uncomfortably tight. My shoulders squeeze. The water is still in here, too still for my gills to filter properly.

Either the beast eats me or I suffocate.

What the fuck was I thinking, surviving on my own? I should have stayed on Ramona. Married that fucking land-bound prince.

The beast collides with the glacier and the ice trembles.

Another slam. His shoulder batters the ice. Then his claws grasp the entrance, curling into the rock. Dark blue. Sharp. They dig, and the ice crumbles in his grip.

Here dissolves Nahlani, Stupidest Princess of the Brine.

His face snaps into sight. Black eyes pierce me with a glare—void of emotion. He reaches inside, claws extended.

"Hey!" I shout. "I'm a friend!"

The beast cocks his head, but nothing more. I should have paid better attention in my diplomacy lessons.

"I'm Princess Nahlani of the Brine, and I mean you no harm. Please don't eat me."

His claws lengthen, slipping further out of the tips of his fingers. He opens his mouth as if to speak. Hope flares in my chest for a moment before the growl hits. Loud, reverberating through my bones. *Shit.* The ice around me trembles. Then, gods above, he licks his lips.

Diplomacy is dead. No matter how merfolk he may look—a predator can't be reasoned out of his meal.

Then make it your bitch. Keen's words bloom in my memory.

I lock eyes with the beast. His mouth parts in a snarl. With a steadying suck of my gills, I ready my spell.

I start with a low, soothing song, reaching for his conscience. If he's animalistic, my magic might work on him. I lift out of myself, glancing back to see my body cowering in the glacial crack. The beast's claws reach for me, scratching through the ice.

A dark barrier shrouds his mind like a hardened shell. Walls stretch high and thick. I press against the barrier, meeting cold resistance.

I hiss, retreating as ice crawls through the mental connection. My brain freezes and pain splinters through my head. My song drops dead in the water, and I land within myself.

I blink, refocusing. The beast's eyes darken to impossibly black. His claws inch closer, screeching on the ice a scale's breadth from my tail.

I shake my head, fighting the brain freeze with sheer force of my will. I sing again, stronger this time. My Voice ripples out. Angry. Loud.

I meet the barrier again, but instead of charging head-on, I spread out my magic, searching for weak points. I slip through the smallest crack, my conscience thin as thread.

The beast snarls. He blinks and shakes his head. Inside, his thoughts are a mess of black swirls, writhing like rattlefish.

Complex. Most fish are singular-minded with one dominant emotion at a time. With a psyche much closer to Ramona's vast menagerie of thought, this creature has three emotions, at least. Chaos. Anger. Fear. And they've taken the offensive.

The tendrils rear their heads as I spiral into their midst. They lash at me with sharp tongues, protecting the center of his mind. I strengthen my spell, pouring more and more of myself into it until my energy uncoils from my gut and drains.

My Voice pierces his psyche, and the black mist parts to reveal the glowing center. The orb is black, with thin beams of white light streaking through the cracks. I speed toward it. Focus my energy. Surround him with my essence.

Friend.

I project the word with all I've got. His thoughts batter my conscience, cold as ice.

Friend, I repeat.

I concentrate on my happiest, warmest memory: climbing a palmwood as a guppy. Before the politics. Before I realized my future was a meaningless sham.

The bark scrapes my hands, rough and hot. Its sap sticks to my skin and my hair. Broad leaves brush my arms. My feet press into the trunk, propelling me higher. Higher. The high-tide sun beats from a clear sky. Sweat drips on the side of my face. I reach for the sweetnut suspended within its branches, my mouth watering for its milk.

When I look down, Winona stands with her hands stretched, ready for the catch.

His claw snares my fin, and he yanks. My body slips out of the crevice, scraping along the ice. Pain traces my spine.

Fuck. I shouldn't have gone with a food memory. For all I know, I've made him hungrier.

But he doesn't eat me. Yet.

He tucks me into his side, claws gripping my hips, arm across my back. My breasts press into his toned, scaled stomach. His thigh brushes my tail, which tucks between his legs. Against his body, I feel small. He's at least twice my size. I wriggle, trying to break his grip, and a growl rumbles through his body.

My stomach dips as the beast shifts. His muscles flex. He kicks with his legs, tail snapping, and propels us through the water. Against me, his hips move rhythmically side to side.

If I didn't know any better, I'd think this was sexual.

I squirm and press my hand into his skin to strengthen our mental connection—his abs, I realize, as my fingers graze a pocket of raised muscle. Just beneath the broad pectoral. His nipple puckers from the cold, a dark button in a plane of blue scales.

FRIEND!

A reminder, for me and for the beast.

Within his mind, his center of self glows brightly, the orb expanding in a dome of light. The shadows soften and change color, from black to blue to white.

Curiosity floods his thoughts. He replays my sweetnut memory, focusing on the sunshine. The warmth.

That's right, Beasty. See? We're friends. I can show you the sun someday, if you like. Have you ever seen the sun before?

I pat his chest with my hand. *Pat, pat, pat.* Like a guppy.

This pisses him off. The curiosity zaps away, replaced once more with those shadow-tendrils. I flinch as they pelt me with ice, and I sever my spell to conserve what's left of my energy.

I withdraw into the shell of my mind, gills fluttering fast.

It's no use. His mind is too complicated for my skill. Ramona's mind is more so, but she's always been willing.

I've never met a creature I could not subdue. But this beast cannot be tamed.

His body shifts as he alters his course. I peer around his arm, watching the wake of water sprawl behind us as he speeds through the Rime.

Soon, we enter a submerged cave system, and my stomach flips. Is he going to eat me here? Take me home to feed his starving guppies?

The roof of the cave blocks the surface light, and the water darkens beneath its eerie blue shadow. He swims between ice walls, deeper into it. I can't see much beyond the expanse of his skin.

Diplomacy has failed. Magic, failed. That leaves only Plan C: engage combat.

I bite his nipple. Hard.

The beast roars. He grabs at me, tugging my body away, but I latch on. His claws dig into my flesh, and the scent of my blood trickles into the water. I clamp the bud like a tartberry between my teeth.

He dives suddenly, wrenching his body into a sickening spiral toward the floor. His hands leave me, and I'm left clinging to him with my teeth alone. I reach for his shoulders and loop my arms around his thick corded neck. But I can't reach all the way around, and my hands slip on his smooth scales. He twists again, and the torque sends me flying away from him.

I spiral backward, slamming into the ice. Stars splatter my vision. Fuck Plan C. Time to go.

I push off the wall and kick my tail, speeding out the way we came. The cave is a tunnel, with openings along the sides that lead into more tunnels. One way in, one way out. A pocket of light streams through the opening. I stretch for it, my body lengthening. The thin membrane of my tailfin clusters with ice, heavier than I'm used to. I labor through the water, knowing already it won't be enough.

The beast passes above me, then drops into my trajectory. His teeth flash in the low light, bright white razors. He grins—or grimaces, hard to tell—and raises his claws.

I stop short of slamming into him. I smile, doing my damndest to appear friendly as my heart batters my ribs. As if to say: *See? I'm fucking adorable. Don't you want to be friends?*

His eyes trace me from head to tail, and a rumble emanates from his chest.

Can he not use words? For a sea god, he sure does a lot of growling.

Then he grabs me again, yanking my body like a wet strand of reedgrass. He dives into one of the side caves. The walls narrow around us. At the end of the tunnel, a dead end.

He tosses me, and I slam into the wall, tumbling down the ice to skid across the floor.

Metal creaks. I look up in time to see him dragging a grate across the opening. Thick iron bars to lock me in.

"Hey!" I shout, dashing toward him. The bars stop me, stinging ice against my skin. I slam my palm against the metal with a clang. "Chumwad!"

He stares at me, tail thrashing, but says nothing. Only snarls.

"You can't do this to me! I'm a—"

The beast snorts, releasing a flood of bubbles, and with a push of his mighty legs, he slips out of the tunnel.

"Princess," I mutter. The bubbles float to the ceiling and pop, one by one.

Princess or not, I'm in deep fucking shit.

CHAPTER NINE

AETHAN

I crank the heat in my shower. Water hisses from the spout, burning my skin. My fingers slip through tangled hair, and I ball my hands into fists, gripping the strands. Pulling hard.

But the pain isn't enough.

My memory is gone.

Last thing I knew, I was in my chamber. Peering into the sight-pool as I looked for signs of another clawbeast.

There was a female. Wasn't there? A female in the Rime? I saw her in the pool. And then I... Then what? *What have I done?*

I pound the wall with the meat of my fist.

I need to get my anger under control. Two nights in a row? That's two too many. Whatever I've done can't be undone. Soon enough, we'll find her body on the shore.

Rivulets stream down my back. I press my forehead to the stone tile and let the water pelt my body. A pounding, roaring torrent. Indifference is the best remedy, the only thing between me and the spiraling cliff of despair. I must not cross that line. My memory is gone, but there's no retrieving it. Whatever happened, happened. The icy knot of anger in my stomach unfurls, dissipating with the steam. My muscles relax.

I could select a steward to hold the throne in my stead. Someone wise but unaffected by the swell of power. Someone kind. Someone who can give my people the care and attention they need.

They could return to the sea. Without me, they'd be safe.

No more king? No more clawbeast.

Jealousy claws my throat as I pound the wall again. Then again. The sound reverberates through the bathroom.

I pause mid-punch. A rapping sound at my chamber door. Three quick knocks.

Water hisses in my face, sticking in my lashes.

"Sire? I don't mean to intrude. But it's urgent."

Fuck. I can't say no to Deirdre.

I stop the water and squeeze out my hair, then wrap a towel around my hips.

"One moment!" I shout at the door, padding out into the main bedroom. My wardrobe is a simple armoire. Dark wood, harsh lines. Two doors open to five sets of the same clothing: loose cotton shirts, goatskin pants, white fur cloaks. I grab one of each and slip them on. "Enter."

The door opens, and she bustles in. Her hands twist in front of her stomach, winding together, then apart. Her eyebrows pucker in concern.

"Speak, Deirdre. You're going to kill me with that face. What happened?"

"This morning, two younglings went swimming and found a…"

My stomach flips. "A *what*?"

"There's a—" She pauses. Twists her fingers. Starts again. "I think you might have—"

I pull out my desk chair and sink into it to brace for the news. A dead body. That's what she'll say next, I'm sure of it. And, *goddess above*, a pair of rebellious younglings found it. "Go on."

She draws a deep breath. "There's a female in your dungeon, Sire."

"Dead?" Those poor younglings. This is why I have rules—to keep them from tumbling into trauma like this.

"No, Sire."

I frown, moving to activate the sight-pool. "How?"

"I believe you put her there. The *other* you."

My fingers dip into the pool, and the water glows. I guide the vision into the water. The dungeons are beneath the ice, part of the abandoned city of Doloch. A system of tunnels with several caged cells unused for years.

I lean onto my desk, pinching the bridge of my nose.

"Is she one of ours?"

The hands twisting again. Then, "She's Brine."

I alter my tune, focusing my search on the dungeons. The image ripples and shifts, revealing the tunnels as I seek an occupied cell.

What did I do? My memory is muddy. I only have pieces: anger. Swimming. Chasing something. Someone. Chasing her. A palm-wood tree, warmed by the sun. *The fuck?*

The water stills, framing an image in the icy haze. There she is. A female with a golden tail, curly hair, and warm brown skin, tucked into a ball in my dungeon. I've seen those scales before. Right here in my sight-pool.

I clutch my pec, brushing a thumb over my sore nipple, and my rage flares.

Intruder. Spy.

She penetrated my domain. I remember what drove me to transform. Why I hunted her. She's dangerous. Unwelcome.

And very much alive.

"Bring her to me," I growl.

***

I GRIP THE ARMS of my polished darkwood throne. The room has none of the glacial grandeur of my ancestral hall beneath the waves, but it's impressive in other ways. Imported darkwood beams hold the ceiling high, creating an echo chamber. Thick fur hangs from the walls to keep the cold at bay. I've added my touch—a crystal chandelier suspends from the ceiling, each delicate piece formed with magic.

My guards stand at the door, tridents held at the ready. Torches are posted on either side of me, providing the only light in the room.

Before me kneels the siren, bound in ice. I've trapped her ankles, cuffed her hands. The frost isn't cold enough to harm her skin, just to hold her until I get the information I need. She wears a servant's cloak, her full breasts pressing against the constraints of the rough fabric. Are those *starfish* underneath?

The female, on her knees, bends her neck to glare at me.

Bold.

I study her face. Features full, smoothed by magic—round ears and soft jaw. A constellation of golden freckles decorates her cheeks, the same color as her tail. Long, thick eyelashes. Her gaze hardens under my scrutiny.

She's beautiful. But it's not enough to soften my resolve. If she wanted a warmer welcome, she shouldn't have come here. I don't play games, and I don't take kindly to visitors.

Visitors are a liability.

"I'm not known for my compassion, siren spy. Don't expect to be here much longer." My voice rumbles through the room. Her eyes widen at the sound.

"I'm not a spy, I'm a—"

"Death-dealer then? You're doing a shit job of it. Go on." I lean forward, tilting my head to the side to expose my neck. With a low, rumbling hum of magic, I melt the ice from her hands to give her an opening. "Here's your shot."

The guards shift, angling their tridents.

She appraises my neck. Her gaze traces the angle, the slope of my muscles, and her jaw flexes. Is she plotting her aim? I lean closer, stretching. If she's here to kill me, she might as well get it over with.

"Well?"

Her lip quivers, but she says nothing. Pathetic.

How much encouragement does she need? I stand from my seat and stalk forward. My furs drag along the wooden floor. She's small. Looming over her, I easily double her height. Did she honestly think she could best me? How cute.

She recoils, a gasp escaping her.

I squat before her and angle my neck once more. When she makes no move, I seize her wrist and place her hand on my neck. Her fingers are cold. Smooth. Her breath spills over me, sweet as vanilla. Up close, her brown eyes are speckled with green.

But she does not kill me. Doesn't even try.

Pity, that.

I release her hand, and it drops to her lap with a dull sound of surrender. My Voice rumbles, and ice reforms around her wrist, binding her once more. I straighten, standing before her as she stares at my feet.

"Thought not. Tell me, siren, who sent you?"

"I sent myself."

"To ruin me?" I place a knuckle beneath her chin, forcing her to look at me while she answers. Beneath my touch, her throat is soft.

"No, Your Majesty. I was playing with a pod of glosswhales and I followed them. Your guard-beast scented me, I assume, and attacked. I didn't realize I was in your waters until I was locked in that cage."

Her tone is sweet. *Too sweet.* Her pupils dilate, and I stiffen. She's lying.

More pieces of my memory fall out of the shroud: glosswhales. The scent of a female. A flash of light. Golden scales.

I glance over her body, checking for wounds. No dried blood. No gashes. Relief washes over me, and I swallow the lump in my throat. What would I have done if *this* body washed onto my shore, instead of my dungeon?

My imagination plays the image of this female's body, shredded by my claws. Her hair dripping with blood. Her corpse, stiff with frost.

Nausea rises. I step away from her, sinking into the furs of my throne. My hands find the armrests, and I clench them.

I wouldn't wish that fate on anyone. Not even an outsider.

What am I going to do with her? She can't go back to the Brine, not now, never. She's seen too much already.

And if she is a spy...

"Playing with glosswhales, you say?" What an odd excuse for a spy. If she is one, she's in a league of expertise I've never encountered.

Or she's stupid.

"That's right." She jerks her chin in defiance. I can't help the smile that twitches at the corner of my lips.

"And you expect me to believe that?"

Her answering smile is coy. "That's right," she repeats.

"You realize your fate lies in my hands, little spy. Don't play me for a fool."

"It's hard to imagine His Majesty knows the meaning of play."

Somewhere, a guard snickers. I shoot him a look, and he stiffens at his post.

She's feisty. I like that. But I need an answer, not a game. With a snap of my Voice, I tighten her bonds, and she groans, twisting against the strength of my magic. I pull the ice across the floor, forcing her hands forward. She bows to me, still glaring, helpless to do anything but.

I wince as her soft lip trembles. Fear?

Good. She should fear me. Her delicate whims will not protect her against the danger I harbor inside.

Even if all I want to do in that moment is lean forward, suck that lip into submission, and calm it with my tongue.

I raise my hand and give the order. "Take the spy back to her cell."

Chapter Ten

NAHLA

The Frost King is an asshole.

I've met his type before. Arrogant. Controlling. An emotionless void trapped inside a husk of hardened muscle—lots of muscle.

The way he looked in that throne room, his tight, snow-white stomach peeking beneath that cloak of matching furs. Torchlight casting him in a warm glow. Shadows playing on his cheekbones. That jaw. His hands, gripping the armrests of his handsome wooden throne.

Even his godsdamn bare feet were built.

He makes all the males at home seem like wrigglefish in comparison. I wanted to climb him, to see how light I'd feel in his arms. A male like that could *handle* me. And I would have climbed him, if he hadn't pegged me to the fucking floor.

And when he placed my hand on his neck. *Gods.*

If those muscles weren't thick as ropes, I might have done what he asked. If I had a knife, how long would it have taken me to saw through them?

I blink to clear the vile thought. I'm not violent, and I do what I'm told, mostly. A little rebellious, sure, but not *violent.* What is it about that male that brings out the absolute worst in me?

It must be the cold. No one who lives in this climate could have an ounce of warmth in their heart.

I pull my tail into my chest and shiver. My teeth chatter, the noise echoing dully through my cage.

The walls are thick, too thick to claw my way out. An iron gate bars the exit, each rung clinging with frost too cold to touch. A coat of rime covers my tail like white lace, dulling its vibrant color. I swipe my thumb down my scales, clearing the residue to maintain the shine.

I will not succumb so easily.

But the frost keeps forming, and after hours of passing my time clearing the shit from my tail, hopelessness descends.

I swipe and swipe. Saltwater pricks in my eyes, warm and then cold. Why the fuck did I leave again? To avoid being trapped in a marriage?

Like this is much better.

Winona was right. I'm foolish. Stubborn. Led by my guppish whims.

How naïve of me to think I'd have control of my future. The tides of fate have never treated me so kindly.

I take to swimming laps in my cage. Round and round. I kick my tail lazily, turning at the corners. It's a small space, but at least I have room to move. The exercise warms my blood, and the movement warms the water. Not by much, but it's better than it was.

Gradually, the water darkens. Nightfall, I assume, though I can't see the sky. When the blackness descends completely, I hear a screech of metal. Someone jingling the lock.

I move to the back of my cage, heart pounding. Is it the king, here to taunt me further?

A Voice comes, tenor in pitch, not the deep rumbling bass of the king. A golden thread of light emits from the siren's mouth.

A different male, then. His small eyes reflect the light as it spirals from his lips, then fingers. His voice is sharp and raspy.

"Hello?" I call. Fuck it. He already knows I'm in here, and I won't cower in the corner.

His Voice purrs around the words. "I've come to inspect your condition." His light slithers through the bars, swirls around my wrists, and snakes up the length of my arms. Warm.

"Inspect away." I want to lean into the magic, and its heat is hard to ignore. But I stiffen and hold my posture. "I'm in no position to resist you."

He smiles, and his perfect teeth reflect the light. "Says the female who ruffled His Majesty's gills this morning. I believe you have more power than you admit."

"I'm not powerful."

His magic brushes beneath my chin, then sprawls over my chest. "We mustn't tell lies, my sweet." His lips snarl around the words so briefly I think I imagine it.

"Now hold still. This won't hurt." He pauses. "Much."

"Much?" I repeat, fear spiking. But he doesn't answer. His song alters, taking on a deeper tone. His magic rears, then dives beneath my skin with a stinging thread.

I gasp, watching with awed horror as the light swims beneath the surface of my skin, illuminating the sinew and bone.

"Anywhere giving you pain?"

"My ass," I quip. His magic crawls lower, passing over my stomach, then hips.

He hums as he inspects my hind end. "I'm not finding anything."

I roll my eyes. "Your king," I clarify. "He's a pain in my ass. He sent you to poke at me, no?"

"Poke? You insult my skill."

"Apologies, healer. You'll have to excuse my manners. I'm a bit out of my element."

The magic stalls, caressing my tail. "No. This was Deirdre's doing. She gets fussy when we have guests."

I file the name away for later. A friend among my enemies. "And this is how you treat your guests? Locking them into an ice cube?"

His magic resumes, passing through me faster now. Hotter. I flinch.

"No. That's how we treat foreign spies, m'lady. But I'll pass along the message." His teeth gleam.

The magic reaches the end of my tail, then retreats, speeding through my torso and neck. It swirls around my temples, glowing in my periphery. Pressure taps the boundary of my mind.

Odd. Is he a type of mind-speaker?

Then I feel him, testing the edges of my conscience. Fuck no. I steel my mental defenses, shoving him out of my head.

He cuts his spell, the light fades, and I'm plunged into darkness. "Impressive," he says.

I shiver at his spell's final brush and pretend he didn't just violate my inner sanctum. That's a line we way-makers never cross; to enter another merfolk's mind is the ultimate breach of trust. Impossible for most to achieve. We specialize in animalistic minds. The king's beast was difficult enough.

Who the fuck is this male?

I speak through chattering teeth. "You're a healer. Can't you do anything for the cold?"

His voice comes from the darkness, hovering at the boundary of my entrapment. "Unfortunately, no. The heat of my magic is temporary. I fix only what's broken, not merely *uncomfortable*, and you, my dear, look right as Rime."

The water stirs. I hear the whisper of his tail, churning bubbles. The bastard's leaving.

"I'm not a spy," I call after him, hoping he'll pass it along.

His voice echoes through the tunnel. "Then you'd best prove it, Sunshine. You won't survive forever down here. And the king takes a while to... warm up?"

Chapter Eleven

AETHAN

I'm out of distractions, and my self-control hangs on by a thread, as frayed as the tattered hides on my bed. One more thought of *her*, and I'll unravel.

My latest mug of tea is cold in my hand; cold, like everything in this frigid room. I could light a fire or a torch or any of the tallow candles stored in the closet, but I'd rather wallow in my hoarfrost.

I dunk the herb pouch in the tea, winding the string around my knuckle.

Dunk.

The sight-pool catches my eye, and I fight against the craving in my gut. My fingers itch to awaken its magic and dive into the Rime. But if I cave, I'll be sucked in by her wiles in an instant, and I'm weak for pretty eyes and a pouting mouth, even when they belong to my enemy.

Guilt rushes in, and I look away from the pool. She's not my enemy.

Dunk.

Probably not a spy, either.

I shouldn't assume the worst. Why would the Brine Kingdom care to spy on me now? My family hasn't made contact for two generations, so there's no need for them to send a spy.

Dunk.

Besides, Lucas's report came back clear. She has no hidden weapons, nor any trace of poison. Just an outsider, visiting my keep for an indeterminable and highly suspicious reason.

Am I supposed to fall for her clueless damsel routine? She carries a wit behind her eyes, a creature of far greater intelligence and power than she lets others see.

Which makes her a damn good spy, after all.

I pinch the bridge of my nose to clear the thought. The other royals in Adria do not think like this—they play politics, attend each other's fucking flower festivals, and trade resources.

But the other kingdoms don't have secrets to hide, and if they learn mine, I'm sure they wouldn't hesitate to turn on me. They'd join their forces and threaten my people—my people, who are threatened enough by their own king.

Dunk.

And what would I do when the forces descend? Retaliate? Shred them with my bare claws until the great sea fills with their blood?

They'd call me the enemy, so it's only fair I position myself now for the reality to come.

She is my enemy, because I am hers, and I will not look in the pool. I *won't.*

Fuck it. The sight-pool stirs at my touch. I growl, appalled by the sound of my Voice, the sight of my own fingers as they dip in that glowing water.

I will not look!

With a flick of my fingers, I abandon the pool as quickly as I started.

But not before I glimpse that prison cell, with its occupant curled in a ball. Her long hair splays on the floor and her golden scales dim with frost. Gentle fingers stroke aimlessly, swiping again and again to reveal the color before the crust clings once more.

My throat tightens.

I dip my fingers again and alter my tune, swiping the image away. I flick through views of my domain: the beach is calm, and the trench is undisturbed. Pikewhales float in the vertical grip of slumber, soft bubbles globing from their blowholes.

In the dungeon, she's changed positions, approaching the front of her cell where a guard is posted outside the iron gate, his body slouched against the wall. Vaughn, one of my Frost Guards. She pushes off her hands and glides over the floor toward him. Vaughn snorts, and his head bobs. She threads her hand through an opening in the grate, reaching for him.

I grip the bowl, peering closer into the sight-pool. Her fingers graze the keys at his hip, she stretches, and her fingers trill out of reach.

Vaughn shifts and floats beyond her grasp.

I smirk. *Serves her right.*

But then she moves her mouth. Her eyes dart to the guard, checking his reaction. He slumbers on. Soon, a small fish approaches, and she smiles at it, beckoning. The fish flutters through the bars, swirling around her head. She laughs, strokes its fins, and then her lips move. The fish exits the cage, darting for the guard's keys. They detach and sink to the floor.

My smirk fades. She's clever. Too clever.

Lucas didn't mention she was a strong magic-wielder, and that makes her a threat.

The guard snorts awake and glances around, spotting his keys on the floor. Inside the cage, the female feigns sleep while he scoops the keys and attaches them to his belt, then leans against the wall.

A moment passes before she opens her eyes, pretending to yawn and stretch as Vaughn watches her sideways.

I frown into the pool. I know that look. It was on every guard's face the moment this female entered my throne room.

She contorts her body, cocking her tail to enhance his view of her breasts and belly. She says something to him, and I curse this silent spell for depriving me of eavesdropping.

The guard stares as she runs a hand through her hair, then along her neck. She brushes the starfish that clings to her breasts, and Vaughn's eyes bulge. *Damn. She's good.*

She floats to the gate and touches his arm through the bars. He leans into the contact while she stretches for his keys with the other hand.

She sneaks a finger through the ring, and the guard freezes. His hand drops to his hip, catching her wrist. He shoves her into the cage, and she slides across the floor.

I sever my spell and stand from my chair, putting distance between myself and that damn pool. I pace, heels digging into the rug.

If she thinks she can fuck with my kingdom from the inside out, she's sorely mistaken. I am the goddessdamn King of Frost, and I won't be made a fool of. I grip the post of my bed, and the wood cracks. Blue scales reach my elbow.

Power crackles and streams from my hands, coating the walls in a thick sheet of ice. Icicles drip from the ceiling, lengthening as my anger builds.

This siren will be the bane of my self-control.

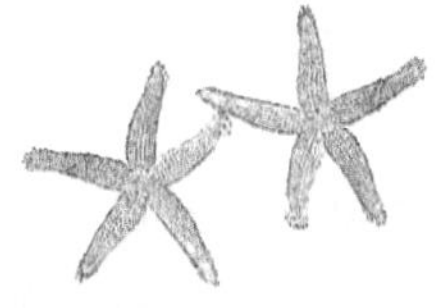

Chapter Twelve

Nahla

My knees hit the throne room floor. I wince as the pain registers, sharp in each knee, then shooting up my thighs. *This shit again?* With trembling hands, I steel myself for what's next and resolve to make him pay for this.

The king sits on that fur-lined throne, nestled in warmth, while ice-cold water evaporates from my body. My hair hangs in wet clumps, dripping onto the darkwood slats. Torches flank his throne, casting their warmth over my skin.

Fire. Gods, how I've missed this heat.

Is it pathetic to be glad for this moment of respite? This dark abysmal room, full of warm, dry air. The thin cotton shift his gentle housekeeper, Deirdre, dressed me in. Small wins, but I claim them. Revel in them.

These things, at least, he can't take away from me.

"You can't treat me like this. I'm a p—"

"Prisoner?" he says with a glare. His voice is smug and menacing, the kind that cuts straight to my bones. Fear traces my spinal cord, and I lose hold of all thought.

In my hesitation, his magic finds me. Ice encircles my wrists and ankles, securing me to his floor like a godsdamn criminal. For what? Going for a joy swim with glosswhales? *Grow a heart, asshole.*

I thrash against his restraint, and the ice cuts into my skin. With a hiss of pain, I raise my head to meet his glare. His eyes are a near-silver shade of blue, like morning snow. His white hair is slicked into a knot at the nape of his neck, one loose hair falling across his forehead. I wonder if he styles it himself, or if his morning whore does it for him. *Chumwad.*

How can I make him pay for what he's doing to me? How do I make the pretty king squirm? My defiance pissed him off to no end last time. Maybe if I annoy him enough, he will set me free.

Plan D: become annoying as fuck.

Shouldn't be too difficult. I've annoyed Winona since I first fluttered my gills.

The king rises from his seat, flipping the train of his long-ass cloak. All royals are the same, adorning themselves with the most pretentious garments available. Like Winona and her imported silks. His cloak is pieced together with the hides of many animals, the rich white and silver furs oiled and groomed.

Does he brush it himself or is that a special position for some poor, hired soul?

He sways on his feet—just a fraction—and I narrow my eyes. Darkness hollows his cheeks, like he hasn't been sleeping. There's an edge of hysteria in his gaze.

I smile. He's easy pickings.

"It's come to my attention that you require boundaries." His voice rumbles, impossibly deep.

"No, thank you," I quip. "But I appreciate the kind gesture."

The king crosses his arms, pressing them tight to his chest. A thick vein protrudes from his snow-white skin, wrapping around his arm. Those forearms alone could do serious damage to a weaker girl's heart.

Not me—I'm on a mission, and I won't be thwarted by male intimidation.

"Here in the Frost Kingdom, we live by several rules. I expect you to follow them."

To think I could be out of the Rime by now, speeding toward warmer waters. I was a fool for going north. I should have gone to Estuary and stuffed myself with wine and fruitmead. My mouth waters at the thought.

"Rule number one," he says. "You will never leave the Rime."

I wait for the punchline to land. He can't be serious. His jaw twitches, then hardens. This male doesn't have an unserious bone in his body.

Who does this asshole think he is? "Try to stop me."

"Easy enough." His ice tightens around my wrists and ankles.

I want to claw his face, rip out his hair. Smack that smirk from his pretty lips. My vision blurs with loathing.

"You think you can lock me up with a little snow? You'll need to try harder than that, *Frosty*. Do your worst."

Wincing, I twist my wrists and pull against his ice. Fuck, they're tight. I'll chew off my hand right here, in front of him, if it comes to it.

My stomach lurches. Who am I kidding? I don't have the guts for that.

"You can't handle my worst." The king stands tall, watching with those icy eyes. I work to keep my face neutral as the scales at the back of my neck rise. "You. Will. Never. Leave. No one does."

Never leave the Rime, my ass. I will escape him. Even if it destroys me, I will not let him keep me forever.

"Rule number two." He paces, the cloak following him in a slither of leather. "You are my prisoner. My space is off-limits, and you will not enter the castle without my permission."

"Hard to explore when you've locked me in a cage."

He pauses, turning to glare at me. His eyes darken. "Your Majesty," he corrects. "I am the king, and you will address me properly. Rule number three." He paces again. His white toes splay on the floor, turning a deep shade of blue. "You will *not* interact with the Beast."

"Which beast do you mean, exactly?"

"The clawbeast."

"Does he have a name? Or shall I call him 'Beast'?"

His jaw flexes. "That's none of your concern."

"If I don't know his name, how do I know I've got the right clawbeast?"

"There's only one," he snaps. "And you're *not* to go near him."

I open my mouth to retort again, but nothing comes. What a strange rule to make.

He continues, "Follow my rules, and we won't have any trouble."

I spit on the floor and hope he steps in it—so much for ladylike charm. "Your little pet approached me, *Your Majesty*. Or are you forgetting you set him on my tail?"

"Enough," he snaps.

He whips his cloak around, turning to face me. The king squats, his large frame looming, and I stare at his feet. The blue has spread to his ankles now.

"This is no way to treat a princess," I mutter. Winona wouldn't stand for this. By now, she would have concocted some masterful political speech intended to cut him to his core while securing an alliance. All I've got is annoying quips and guppish jabs, and they're all falling flat. "Freezing cold and locked in a cage. What kind of monster are you?"

He grips my chin, lifting my gaze. "What?"

I look him dead in the eyes. "I said what kind of monster are you, *Your Majesty*?"

His eyes flash with something, a stray emotion in the void.

"Princess?" he echoes, his grip on my chin softening. His finger slides, stroking the soft skin of my throat once before curling back. Is that an edge of guilt in his tone?

I smirk. "Yes, Your Majesty. I am Princess Nahlani Mahelona, second heir of the Brine. And a threat to me is a threat to my kingdom. Her Majesty *will* find me, and you'll regret the day you locked me in."

Will Winona come for me once she realizes what I've done? Or will she finally cut ties? Decide I'm a lost cause and leave me here to freeze to death, all alone?

He stares at me. His nostrils flare, and he sucks in a deep, long breath. "Find you?" he says. "As in, she doesn't know her *princess* is here?"

Shit.

My mind reels, grasping at all threads of logic. "Of course she does." I bite hard on my tongue. It's a terrible lie, and one that will get my sister in trouble, if he would act. If I'm not careful, I could start a war.

Because why the fuck would Winona send her sister into Frost territory unannounced?

Should I spin this as a surprise marriage proposal? Would he buy it?

Shit. Shit. Shit. Why did I skip those politics lessons?

The panic hits me like a wave. I grit my teeth to stop the tears from springing. Not now. Not here. I will not show him my weakness.

The king smirks. "Oh, does she now?" His eyebrow raises, and relief skitters through my stomach. He doesn't believe me. The Brine will be safe from his wrath.

For now.

He lifts my chin higher, and his gaze drops to my throat. His pupils widen. Would he accept a marriage proposal?

The thought is a dagger in my gut. I might as well have married the Coral Prince. At least there, I'd be warm and well fed.

Tears sting my eyes, threatening to fall. If I don't escape soon, I will be stuck here forever. All because of a stupid choice; a useless rebellion against fate.

"I have a few rules for *you*." I try my luck. "First, if I'm here to stay, you will give me a proper room. With a fire. And one of those nice fur capes. Second, you will have food prepared for me three times a day. And third, you will stop with this prisoner sh—nonsense. I am no spy."

I finish my demands, proud of myself. What more do I have to lose?

But then the king smiles, and my stomach flips.

Pinching my chin, he leans closer. His breath is cold as it spills over my face, smelling of peppermint and snow.

"Nice try, *Princess* Nahlani of the Brine. But your word means nothing here."

CHAPTER THIRTEEN

AETHAN

Fuck it. If I spend one more evening sucked into that sight-pool, obsessing over that damn *siren*, I'm going to blow my steam. I'll take my dinner in the dining room tonight. Like a functioning member of society.

I pound on the door, and the stationed guard unlocks it. He opens the door partway, poking his narrow face through the gap. His lips quiver.

"But Your Majesty, you said under no circumstances should I listen to you if—"

"Ignore what I said." I cut him off with a raised fist. The door opens.

As I turn the corner in the hallway, I narrowly miss Deirdre carrying my dinner tray. She stops short, stabilizing the tray to avoid dumping the contents. A bowl of soup, a steaming lump of bread, a butter dish, and a cup of tea. She dips into a quick curtsy, and the tea sloshes.

"I've changed my mind," I say, to assuage her questioning look. "And I'm afraid I confused my guard."

She glances over my shoulder. "I see that, Sire."

Balancing the tray on one hand, she mops the spilled tea with a spare napkin from her apron, then frowns at the sogging roll. I try to apologize for the mess, but she dismisses it with a wave of her hand.

"Nonsense. Shall we set a place for you in the dining hall this evening?"

I nod, and we follow the corridor out of the West Wing and down the parlor staircase in cautious silence. The dining hall, like the rest of the castle, is a modest tribute to darkwood timber framing. While it's more rustic than the glittering grandeur of my childhood home, the style has its charm. Rough-hewn imported lumber. Functional furniture with the smallest touch of artistry, like the large table in the center. Iron florals wrap around the thick wooden legs, giving it an effortlessly regal appearance.

My family used this place in the warm season for entertainment, mostly, to give the royals a chance to stretch their land-legs and dance under the moon. With a few minor adjustments for year-round accommodation, it's been serving my needs just fine.

Deirdre arranges my meal at the head seat, then lights the iron candelabra. Steam wafts with the smell of herbs and glacierweed. Roasted silverfish floats in the broth. My stomach gurgles.

"Anything else I can bring you, Sire?"

"That'll be all, Deirdre. Thank you." I dip into the soup with my spoon.

My housekeeper hesitates.

"Perhaps something for dessert later," I add.

"Thought so." She chuckles. "How does a piece of cinnamon cake sound?" Deirdre leaves without waiting for my response.

The fish wedges tight in my throat, and I cough. I reach for my water, gulping it to clear the obstruction.

And there she is, Nahlani kneeling before my mind's eye with her mocking mouth, saying, *What kind of monster are you?*

I'm up here, warm and cozy with a bowl of soup and cake on the way, while she's freezing in my dungeon. I stare into the bowl, disgusted by its contents.

I am Princess Nahlani Mahelona, second heir of the Brine. I have a few rules for you.

The fight in this female is strong. Princess or spy, I have to hand it to her—she's got spunk. My mouth quirks into a smile.

"Not hungry?" Deirdre's skirts hiss across the floor. I turn to see her enter with a plate of cinnamon cake. She sets it next to my untouched soup, then props her fists on her hips.

I grunt, eyeing the cake as my throat fills with bile.

"Hard to believe," she presses.

I avoid her questioning gaze.

"May I?" She pulls a chair from the table. I nod, and she sits. "Your Majesty. About this princess."

"Spy," I correct, "claiming to be a princess." I can hear the doubt in my voice.

She sighs. "I can find her in the royal directory, if you'd like." Deirdre fishes in the pocket of her apron, retrieving a tablet. She brushes its surface to activate the inscribed spell. "Princess Nahlani, sister to Queen Winona, second daughter to Jovan and Geena. Two and a half decades old as of this warm season. Golden fins. Bronze skin. Brown eyes and curly hair." She lifts her gaze from the book. "Ring a bell?"

Twenty-five? She's practically a youngling. I scoff and tell Deirdre so.

"Not much younger than your thirty years, Sire."

I lift my fork and skewer the tip of the cinnamon cake. It melts in my mouth, and I swallow my groan. This isn't helping.

"You know what I think, love? Cut this dungeon act. Give her an upper room like she requested. She'll be here a while, no? Unless you plan to send her home?"

"No. Never."

She can't leave now. She's seen too much.

"And how long do you think you can hold this princess, before the Brine comes looking?"

"Did I ask you to join me, Deirdre?" I snap. "Or are you going to leave me to eat in peace?"

"Is that what you're doing? Eating?" She nudges my abandoned soup closer. "You can't leave a foreign princess to rot in our dungeon. It's a bad look."

"She doesn't belong here. I will not coddle her. I will not let her inside my keep so the Brine can poison my tea." I tip my mug, sniffing for ailments. "Now, *that* would be a bad look. Is that what you want, Deirdre? Another corpse on your hands?"

She flinches, and I bite my tongue with instant regret. That was too far. It was just this week I severed her nephew's foot.

Deirdre straightens her apron. "All she asked for was a few simple comforts, Your Majesty. If you intend for her to stay awhile, then maybe..."

I sigh. "You want me to make her comfortable?"

"She is our guest."

"And I am the king."

She's not taking my shit. With a cocked eyebrow, she leans closer. "Assign Perrin to watch the princess. It'll give him something to do, at least. He's been having an easier time swimming than walking, with that foot."

My gut twists, and I blow the air out of my cheeks.

Deirdre slaps the table with the flat of her hand twice before standing. "Perrin?" she calls out.

The door cracks open, and her nephew hobbles inside on a pair of wooden crutches. He fumbles with them, making his way forward with excruciating awkwardness. A bandage wraps around his stump leg, hanging in a listless reminder of what I've done.

I *am* a monster. Fucking hell.

The young guard blushes under my scrutiny and does his best to stand tall, wedging the crutches deeper into his armpits.

I clear my throat. "Have you been stationed in the dungeons before?"

"No, Sire." His voice trembles. "But I can learn, Sire."

"You're aware of the protocol, at least? No friendliness. No foolery. You sit there and make sure the prisoner doesn't escape. You'll have a set of keys. Don't lose them."

"I can do that, Sire. No problem."

"All right." I run a hand over my face to smooth the tension twitching in my jaw. "You start tomorrow. Day shift."

Perrin glows, his mouth stretching in a tusky grin. "I can do it, Sire. Thank you, Sire!"

Deirdre squeezes her nephew's shoulders and steers him to the door. After one more smug glance, she departs with an exaggerated curtsy.

As if she didn't just deflate my ego in a matter of minutes.

Chapter Fourteen

NAHLA

I CRY MYSELF TO sleep. It's not a good look for me, and the guard shifts outside my icy cage, but I don't give two flipping fucks what he thinks.

My sobs choke me and my neck strains as my gills work to suck in enough oxygen. Tucking my tail to my chest, I hug myself and let my sadness work itself out.

I cry for Ramona. For Keen. For the freedom I won and lost too soon. I cry for Winona—our sibling rivalry be damned. If I knew my choices would lead me here, I wouldn't have deserted her. I would have married that Coral Prince. I would have thrown the best wedding the sea has ever seen, and when Winona walked me down the aisle as the reigning head of my family, I would have kissed her hands and hugged her before she gave me away to the male of her dreams.

My tears freeze in the Rime, floating to the ceiling to join the ice, until sleep finally takes me under.

When I wake, I'm met with a new face at the gate. I blink to clear the fog from my eyes. The newcomer is young. He wears a guard's belt, and the keys are secured at his hip. The belt looks too big for him, wrapping around his waist twice.

He cocks his head, smiling.

Cutie. He has a pleasant face and broad brown eyes. A curly mop of sandy hair sprouts from his head, a sharp contrast to the blue tone of his skin and scales. His teeth are the pointed tips of a merman, his ears wide and fin-like, untouched by magic. Long, thin whiskers hang from his mouth.

"You don't look like a spy," he says. "You're too pretty."

I can't help but smile. "Thanks, I think?"

He fiddles with the keys, dropping his gaze for a moment. "Are your scales really made of gold?"

"No. They're regular scales."

He's funny. A vast improvement to the other guard.

"Huh. I don't have those. Just a slick of blubber." He twists his tail, and I get a closer look. His tail is smooth, more like a gloss-whale's hide. The blue tone covers all of him from head to tailfin, speckled with deeper hues on his back, lighter on his stomach. His tail is injured—half of his right fin is missing, freshly scarred.

"I bet that blubber keeps you warm," I say. On cue, my teeth chatter.

"It does," he says, eyeing me with pity. As quick as his expression darkened, it brightens again. "I've never met a Brine spy before.

Aunt Deirdre says spies are dangerous, but I don't believe her, after seeing you."

"I'm not a spy." Where the hell is everyone getting that from? I told them I'm a princess, didn't I?

"My king says you are."

I roll my eyes. That explains it. "Your king's an asshole."

We both stop short, staring at each other in shock. His whiskers wiggle, and I curse my lack of filter. How old is this youngling? Fifteen at most? Is he old enough for that word?

Finally, he grins. "I'm Perrin," he says. "And I don't mind if you curse, even if Aunt Deirdre does. But don't call him that, though. His Majesty is a great king."

Doubtful. Would a *great king* abandon all reason and trap a potential ally in a freezer? I don't think so.

"Are you going to get in trouble visiting me?"

Perrin puffs his chest. He turns to show me the emblem on his belt, then jingles the keys. "I'm a Frost Guard."

"Congratulations," I say, grinning. He reminds me of the guppies back home, and my heart sinks.

"We're not supposed to swim in the water, but..." He shrugs. "They stuck me on light duty, and we're safe in here during the day."

I file that information for later. Merfolk not allowed to swim? *Safe during the day.* What the fuck kind of place is this?

Biting back one question, I give Perrin another. "What if His Royal Asshole catches you?"

"He never comes down here."

I lift from the floor, drifting to the front of my cage. I wrap my hands around the bars, ignoring the sting of the ice. "Why not?"

Perrin's pupils grow. His gaze drops to my lips, and his ears quiver. "He doesn't swim."

"But he's a siren. Merfolk. We all swim." My gills ripple along my neck, excited by the thought. What is the asshole hiding? I know the Frost Kingdom to be a secretive, reclusive lot. But is there more to the rumors than bad manners?

"Aunt Deirdre says he's just sad. I think he's scared. But I'm not. I'm brave." He puffs his chest and grins.

If I could fit my face through these bars, I would. I'd shove myself straight into this youngling's brain and leech everything he knows. "Scared of what?" I whisper. Here it comes, the king's great secret.

A low rumble tremors the water from within the larger cave.

My stomach flips. I've heard that growl before.

Perrin's face falls, all bravery gone. "Of *that*," he whispers. He cowers against the wall, whiskers trembling. "I-I-I have to go. They said it'd be safe, but…"

With a hurried flap of his tail, Perrin retreats, leaving me to face the king's greatest fear with nothing more than metal bars to protect me.

I stare down the tunnel, helpless to escape, and wait for the Beast to come.

Chapter Fifteen

BEAST

Freedom.

Power.

Plunging into water.

Cold, invigorating water.

Submerge.

Swim.

Open my mouth.

Inhale.

Search for *her* scent.

Is she where I left her?

Warm scent. Like sunshine.

Yes.

Still there.

Intoxicating.

Swim faster.

Have you ever seen the sun?

Her voice. Inside my head the other day. Like music.

The female with a golden tail. Golden, like the sun.

Sunfish.

Must see her again.

Must hear her music.

Follow her scent.

Enter the tunnels.

No one sees. I am alone.

Good.

Slick water. Quick tail. Easy as breathing.

"Friend?" she asked.

Confusing. What did she mean?

I have no friends.

I am a Beast.

She is soft, like lapping waves. Harmless.

Follow her scent.

Closer, now.

There. End of the tunnel.

Right where I left her.

Small tunnel. Not enough room for me.

Body fills the tight space. Horns scrape the ceiling.

Fuck.

I crouch low. Bend so I can see her.

That's better.

Her face, peering through bars. Soft and warm. I remember those eyes.

Happy to see me?

Hard to say.

I dig my claws into ice.

Get closer.

Closer.

Last time, she said "friend."

Did she mean me?

I think so.

Heartbeat.

Excitement.

Nervous, aching hope.

I've never had a friend.

Poke bars with my claw.

Pathetic metal. Cage would never contain me.

Powerful Beast.

Raging Beast.

I am a hunter.

She is prey. With large, round eyes.

So fragile.

She's beautiful.

I wait for her music.

Crouch. Wait. Stare.

What's taking so long?

Her mouth shuts. Frowning. No music, this time. No thoughts in my head.

Why not?

Maybe she needs encouragement.

A friendship sign.

I widen my mouth. Show her all my teeth.

Polished, sharp teeth. Handsome teeth.

The teeth of friendship.

Is it working?

She cowers. Eyes wide. Trembling lip.

She is scared?

Fuck.

Why?

I don't want her scared.

I want a friend.

Widen mouth until my cheeks hurt.

She cowers again. No song.

No!

I slam the bars.

Growl.

She doesn't want a friend?

Liar!

Slam the bars. Harder.

Rattling, shrieking metal.

Claws slashing.

Anger. Betrayal.

No friend!

Liar!

Sunfish stares. Cold stare.

No song? Fine.

Inspect the lock.

It's secure.

She will stay.

Tomorrow, she will sing.

Trap her. Keep her.

Mine.
I growl, to let her know.
Possessive, loud growl.
Unmistakable.
Water trembles.
Finally—emotion in her eyes.
But not friendly.
Sunfish is angry. No warmth.
She opens her mouth.
"Go away, asshole."
I snort. Crude word from pretty lips.
Can't be friends. I am her enemy.
Sunfish said so.
But Sunfish lies.
Slink away.
Leave her.
Leave her.
Until tomorrow.

CHAPTER SIXTEEN

AETHAN

LUCAS IS IN HIS office, where he stands at his desk, poring over an assortment of metal tools. The fire burns low. Hanging from its mount on the wall above the hearth, the taxidermied frostcat greets me with its permanent snarl.

"Sire," Lucas says without looking up.

As I approach, he pulls a cloth over his tools, hiding them from my view. "New project?" I ask.

"Just dabbling, Sire," he deflects. "How can I help you today? Are you bleeding? Is someone *else* bleeding?"

"No." And I'm fully clothed. My hands and feet are white again, as they should be. All evidence of my swim is gone. But an anomaly shouldn't dictate my future, and I'm not in the clear. "I need you to fix me. There must be a way to keep it from happening."

Lucas snuffs out a few candles on his desk, casting the room into shadow. "I'm afraid I have discovered nothing new since your last request, Your Majesty."

"We're missing something important," I press. He pulls out a chair for me, and I sit. "Tell me what you remember of my mother's condition. You treated her too, correct?"

He purses his lips, pondering for a moment. "If you're like your mother, it happens when you submerge in water."

"Cold water, yes." I keep my tone level and stare straight ahead. Emotion has no place in this room; this is medical business.

"And you started noticing these changes as you transitioned into adulthood. Eighteen?"

"That's right."

"The same as your mother." He leans against his desk, crossing his ankles. "And from my research, that's where the curse entered the bloodline. There are no records of her ancestry before she married into the royal family."

"Did she ever have... outbursts?"

Her face, pale as the morning snow, blooms with freezing blood.

I flinch as the memory resurfaces. No matter how hard I've tried to bury it, it's always there. Stewing in the dredges of my mind. Waiting to suck me under. My hand curls into a fist, tightening around the rough fabric of my pants.

"She didn't sever limbs, if that's what you want to know," Lucas says evenly.

Fuck. It's the truth, and we both know it. I'm a monster. A cold-blooded killer. It doesn't matter if I have no memory of it. I'm the one leaving the bodies on the beach.

I stare at my clenched hands, waiting for the inevitable shade of blue as my heart increases its rhythm. "Sometimes, it feels like the Beast is waiting inside me, waiting to break free. Sometimes, it seizes control, and I can't—"

"It's unusual that you should have an emotional connection to the Beast. Your mother only began the change when in contact with water." He says it like it's the most obvious thing in the world, but it's news to me.

My condition is *unusual*. Just my fucking luck.

I cross my arms and inhale, trying to get back to baseline. This was a chum-brained endeavor, and I should never have asked him about her.

"The curse is stronger for you, Sire. I knew that the moment you first transformed." He watches me carefully, his gaze flicking over my body. He notes my fists in my lap, and he frowns.

A gash on her cheek, tugging the corner of her sad, knowing eye. She reaches for me through a cloud of bubbles. It's the last I remember of her, before my world went dark.

A distant look falls over Lucas's face as he wipes his hands on the corner of his shirt. "I've forgiven you, you know. For Cassandra."

Scales rise along my scalp at the mention of that name. His sister. We haven't spoken of her in years.

He cocks his head. "Have you forgotten her so soon?"

"No, I remember. May Audrina rest her scales." I force the words around the lump in my throat. Cassandra was a healer, and like Lucas, she served the royal family. Until the day she stood too close.

I shudder.

The healer shrugs. "Audrina has given me compassion, Sire. Like I said, there are no hard feelings. I simply want to help you prevent future *mishaps* from happening."

"I am honored," I choke.

Lucas hums. His magic spirals from the tip of his finger, casting golden light. He watches the tendril, a slow smile spreading. "Are you a murderer, Your Majesty? Hard to tell, isn't it? That implies intention."

The thread of magic convulses around his fingers. Twitches. Like a candle fighting the wind.

Cassandra. My mother. The siren on the beach...

I run through the faces of my victims as the guilt drags me down.

In the back of my head, another voice growls in disagreement.

"Murderer?" I rumble. I can hear him in my tone, the rough growl of the clawbeast.

"There you are, Beast," he says. He pushes off the desk and leans on the arms of my chair. His breath spills over my space and his mouth contorts into a snarl. "Now, Your Majesty, pull yourself together!"

I gnash my teeth. The ice twists in my stomach. Darkness spreads from my fingertips, crawling up my arms. "How?" I gasp. "How do I control it?"

"Wrestle it. You want to be a king? Start by mastering yourself," he hisses.

I squeeze my eyes shut. Count to ten.

"Not good enough!" he bellows.

Breathe. In. Out. In. Out. The tingling sensation retreats from my arms, the cascade of scales creeping away.

"Wrestle, Sire! Master it!"

In. Out. I unfurl my fists. My hands are warm again, the chill nearly gone from my fingers.

I feel the ghost of his presence step away from me, and I open my eyes.

"Something like that," Lucas says. His breath leaves my face, and his footsteps pad toward the fire. "Let's try getting back into a solid routine. You've been unpredictable. Lazy. Avoiding your kingly duties to attend this pity party of one. Keeping yourself caged up is one answer, but I fear for the long-term effects on the state of your kingdom."

"What," I spit through gritted teeth, "do you suggest?"

"You let yourself off the hook too easily, Sire. You shy away from difficult matters when you should embrace them. Adversity strengthens you." His voice comes from far away, near the fire. He pokes at the stones in the hearth, red hot.

"Brisk walk every low-tide. Simple breakfast. Attend to the ledger. Visit the townsfolk. Take requests. Make them happen. Maintain control of your kingdom—and you'll maintain control of yourself, naturally."

"I am the king," I growl. "I'm always in control of my kingdom." Breathe. Breathe.

"Certainly." He turns from the fire. *Is that a smirk?* "But you could be *better*, Sire. And that's where I come in." He twirls the iron poker in his hand, inspecting the glowing tip. "I have a theory. For how to fix you. I need more time to complete my research, but if you're... willing... to cooperate, I'm certain we can achieve great things together."

"Research," I echo. "How long do you need?"

"A couple weeks, Sire. Re-establish your routine. Then we can get started."

I loosen my jaw. Force my tongue to drop from the roof of my mouth. With a cautious hand, I reach for my neck, massaging the tension away.

Lucas has always served my family well. He treated my mother's ailments, and he's known me since I was a guppy. If anyone can cure me, it's him.

I trust my family's secret with no other healer but him.

"Deal," I say, lifting from the chair. I point at his beloved frostcat on the mantel. "But I'd better not end up like him."

Lucas's grin spreads slowly. "You have my word."

CHAPTER SEVENTEEN

NAHLA

FUCK THE FROST KING. Fuck his rules. I will break each one—it's what I do best, after all.

Rule one: Do not leave the Rime. *I will leave this wretched place if it kills me.*

Rule two: Do not explore his castle. *I will infiltrate every room.*

Rule three: Do not engage the clawbeast. *I will make him my bitch.*

As I sit in my cell, brushing the frost from my scales for the thousandth time this morning, my resolve hardens. I'm no better off in this cell than I would be as some land-dweller's statue queen. Either way, I'm collecting dust.

I want to be useful. Necessary. And I can't achieve that trapped in here.

Rules one and two are out of reach for the moment.

But the clawbeast visited me yesterday. *He* engaged with *me*. I instigated nothing, but who's to say I can't next time?

Can he be summoned? It's worth a try, anyway. He could help me escape.

I settle into the far wall of my cage, curling against the ice where I'm partially out of view from Perrin's position. I keep my Voice soft, quiet, and cup my hand over my mouth to stifle the sound.

My power threads through the water, part of my mind lifting out of my body. I scan the tunnels for signs of life. Several bottomfish nibble at the reedgrass growing in the rocks below. Larger silverfish move in unison, the swarm leaving the mouth of the cave toward open waters. I follow them out, brushing their minds for memories of the clawbeast.

Nothing.

I expand my reach. A few glosswhales skip waves, but their memories hold no evidence of him since yesterday. A lone thrashershark prowls near the beach. Again, nothing.

Farther, I push. Into the depths. Is he a nocturnal hunter? A cave at the bottom of the Rime would provide him with the darkness he needs to rest.

I scan the crevices, reaching, searching, until I reach my magic's limit. My mental grasp thins, my vision fogging. My gills flutter at my neck, as energy uncoils from my stomach.

Dammit.

"Whatcha doing?"

I flinch at the sound of Perrin's voice and cut my spell.

The youngling presses against the bars of my cage, a gotcha-grin spreading across his face. With him, he carries the set of keys and a new satchel tied to his hip.

My face warms with embarrassment. "Nothing," I say. "Per the orders of His Royal Asshole."

I clear my throat, now hoarse from the spell. I pushed it too far. All for nothing. The clawbeast is not on this side of the Rime. And if I'm to search farther, I'll need to eat first.

Hunger batters the walls of my empty stomach, and I stifle its growl with the heel of my fist.

"Riiiiight," Perrin says. "I heard you singing."

"Just a little warmth spell."

He raises his eyebrows. "You can do that? Wow."

I shrug. No, I can't. But he doesn't need to know that.

"Wish I could sing. That'd be so cool." He sighs. "My family's just... normal. Can all of yours do that?"

"My sister"—I swallow thickly as I picture her face, frowning as always—"is a siren. My parents, too."

"Wow, all of you? Lucky."

I shrug again, feeling awkward. "It's a royal thing, to marry only magical blood."

"Why?"

"To keep the family strong, I guess."

He lets out a puff of bubbles. "Not fair."

My stomach twists. "Hey," I say, smiling. "You're lucky Grumpy Gills didn't capture my sister. She's got some wicked spells."

Perrin perks at the thought. "Oh yeah? What's her best trick?"

"When she's mad at me, she makes this rope out of the water. And she hangs me by my fins."

His eyes widen and laughter bubbles out. "No way! I can't imagine you getting into enough trouble to deserve *that*."

"I'm a royal handful, trust me." I wiggle my eyebrows. "When I'm not freezing my ass off."

"I bet the Frost King could take her. He's strong." He slouches to the floor and brings his tail to rest in his lap. His fingers find the severed part of his fin, and he strokes it absently. "He's not that bad once you get to know him."

"I don't believe you."

His hands brush the pouch at his hip. "Oh! I almost forgot! I have something for you." He reaches into the pouch, revealing a roasted spinefish.

I glide toward the gate. "A snack?" I could kiss him, I'm so happy. "How'd you sneak this out?"

"It was His Majesty's idea." He hands it through the bars.

I hesitate, narrowing my eyes at the freezing, pink flesh in his hand. The king is... feeding me? It must be a trick. That male wouldn't take care of anyone if his life depended on it.

"It's not poisoned." Perrin rolls his eyes. "Here." He picks a bit of the meat, popping it into his mouth. "Yum."

I take the offering, my stomach winning out over my caution. "What a decent siren he must be, to feed his royal *guest*."

The meat is lukewarm. I close my eyes, groaning as the flavor hits my palate. Smoky. Tender. It melts on my tongue.

"I guess technically it was Aunt Deirdre's idea. But the king agreed to it. Sort of. I'm sorry you're locked in here, Nahla. I'd let you out myself if it didn't mean I'd lose my head."

"See." I push the meat into my cheek to speak. "Nice kings don't threaten their subjects with decapitation."

"I never said he was nice. Just not *that* bad."

I roll my eyes. "Guess I'll find my own way out of this cage, then."

Back to Plan... what am I on now? Plan D or should it be E? Escape. Break all the rules.

I swallow the last of the fish—gone too soon—and punch the wall for a show. Pain flares in my knuckles. Perrin laughs at my pitiful attempt.

"Don't hurt yourself."

I ignore him and dig my fingers into the ice. My fingertips turn numb at the touch, slipping on the wall. Not a fucking scratch. I try my shoulder next, backing away, then swimming at the wall with all my force. Stars flash across my vision as I make impact, and I skid to the floor.

Fuck. The clawbeast made this look so easy. Where is he when I need him?

Perrin chuckles from his perch outside the door. "You've not been around ice much, have you?"

"Is it that obvious?" I grumble.

"You've gotta find its weak points, then apply heat. Use your breath, soften it, then eat it."

"That works? Seems like a shit idea for a prison cell."

He shrugs. "No really. Might not work as well with your stubby siren teeth, but, here, I'll show you."

He faces the wall, and with a snort, lengthens his front teeth into two thick tusks. He exhales on the wall before digging in with the teeth. The ice crunches.

He chews on it, then spits. "See? Easy."

"Okay, tusk-man. Here I go." I face the wall. It's solid ice, impenetrable so far by nails or force. This is silly. Why should my teeth be any different? It's not like I have a nice pair of tusks like Perrin.

With a deep suck of my gills, I filter oxygen, then exhale. The ice changes color—hardly enough to notice—a subtle shift from white to blue. I blink. Will this work?

Hope burning in my chest, I open my mouth and dig in.

Cold bites through my teeth, and I yelp. Pain flares in my nose and zings into my brain, and I squint my eyes against the cold.

Shit.

"Oh, sorry," Perrin says. "Ouch." He jangles the keys and metal creaks. Perrin opens the door, sneaking through a tiny gap, and shuts himself in behind it.

"I can't open that gate for you," he says, patting his keys with another jingle, "but this cell isn't too deep. If we tunnel up, you'd pop out in the courtyard. Easy peasy."

My jaw drops. "We?"

Perrin scratches his head, ruffling that mop of blond curls, then grins. "It's technically not breaking the rules. He said"—Perrin clears his throat, dropping into a low gravel reminiscent of the king—"*don't let her through that gate.*"

I can't help the giggle that escapes my lips. I bring my hand to my mouth to cover it, swatting the bubbles away. "You're not a very good guard, are you?"

He winks, but it's more like a one-and-a-half-eyed blink. "And you're not a very good spy."

We pick the corner of the cell, where another guard would have to strain to see us. His claws cling to the ceiling like a silkmite, and he starts munching. The ice crunches in his teeth with ease. I rub my jaw, warming the ache, as I watch.

Soon, he's carved the beginning of a tunnel, wide enough for my shoulders to slip through. He grins at me, snow sticking between his tusks.

"I probably shouldn't be doing this," he says.

I laugh. "Sometimes it's fun to break the rules."

The ice is softer now, inside the tunnel. I join him, digging with my hands through the powder until the daylight fades and his day-shift ends.

He promises to help me again tomorrow, and I promise not to get in trouble with the night-shift guard.

The gate squeaks closed, Perrin safely on the other side, just in time for the burly night guard to arrive. I pose on the floor of my cage, tail drooping, somber expression, and he scoffs at my listlessness.

"Not much of a spy, is she?" the guard grunts, settling into his position.

Perrin shrugs, glancing back to half-wink at me. "That's what I said."

Chapter Eighteen

Aethan

Go through the motions, Lucas said. Establish my kingly routine. Whatever the fuck that means.

How hard can it be?

I pull on my thickest fur cloak and exit the castle grounds. The darkwood halls give way to bright white sky, prompting me to squint and shield my eyes.

The posted guard startles and straightens at my appearance. I hesitate, letting the door hang half open as my mouth goes dry. My hand tightens on the doorknob, not yet ready to let go.

The city's main courtyard is a short walk from my back door, but it's been years since I've entered its gates. Am I afraid of my own subjects? Maybe. Or maybe they have too many warm, fuzzy feelings, and I can't bear to see it. Happiness is fragile; I'm not to be trusted with it.

Glaciers stretch around the gated courtyard, shielding it from the wind. They taper toward the far end of the yard, opening into a wide white plain littered with small round homes of ice and leathers.

Snow falls gently, dusting the ground with cottony tufts. Footprints track across the snow, revealing dark stone beneath. Guppies play in the central garden, hiding and seeking among the large, jagged rocks and sapwood conifers. Their shrieks fill the air, blending with the chatter of market day.

Vendors camp around the yard in wooden huts, displaying their wares beneath leather canopies. Their tables are sprawled with trinkets and treats. Merfolk amble among the booths, visiting shops and clutching mugs of hot drinks.

They look happy. Well fed and warm. That's a good sign, right? A good king has happy subjects. My stomach twists, and I look away. Their happiness is a cruel coincidence; that's all. Lucas is right, and they deserve better.

"Sire, do you require an escort?" the guard addresses me, his voice piercing my reverie. He's young. Merman. His ears fan out like fins, his dark hair tied in a neat bun. His nose quivers under my assessment, and his gray eyes flash in fear.

Afraid of me?

Frustration. Anger. He should not be afraid.

The rage flares cold in my stomach. My grip tightens on the knob, and I inhale sharply. Either I keep my shit together or go inside and forget the whole fucking charade before someone gets hurt.

I shrug the nagging thought away. I have no reputation for being *nice*. Or for leaving my home, for that matter. Why shouldn't he fear me?

It's only natural.

"No need. I'm just going for a walk." I release the doorknob to pull my cloak tighter.

He chews his lip, as if biting back judgment.

"Spit it out, soldier," I snap.

"Apologies, Your Majesty. Please, proceed." He gestures to the square, taking a shuffled step away from me.

"Something wrong with a king taking a walk through his own city?" I toss over my shoulder, approaching the gate. The metal latch is cold in my hands.

"N-no, Sire. Apologies. I don't mean to overstep." The fear intensifies in his eyes.

Pathetic. I make a mental note to test the mental resilience of the new recruits, then I grunt, pushing through the gate and into the courtyard. "Trail me, if you wish."

He follows, keeping a safe distance.

"What's your name, soldier?" There. I can be nice, when I try.

"O-Orson," he says.

A nice name. "Have you been posted here long?"

"Since this season, Your Majesty."

I grunt, having nothing more to say. The snow is slippery beneath my snowleathers. I pass the squealing guppies, watching as one of them—a small female—tackles her comrade to the ground. The male thrashes beneath her, but she pins his hands and whispers in his ear. His eyes widen, and he kicks her off. She rolls through the snow, laughing hysterically.

The female looks up, and her face drops when she sees me. She elbows the male, and they both stiffen, eyes wide, tracing my beastly frame from toe to face.

I clear my throat. Before I can say something, they scatter, bolting for cover behind the nearest tree like a couple of scarefish.

A smile tugs at my mouth.

Fuck. Was I not smiling until now? I massage my cheek. No wonder they fled at the sight of me.

With renewed resolve, I turn away with a whip of my cloak, heading for the shops. *Smile. Look approachable. You're their king, remember?*

A king shopping on market day. There's nothing wrong with that, right? Nothing is out of the ordinary.

I pick through the wares, fingering the bone handle of a curved hunting knife. It sits on a wide fur mat among others of its kind. I weigh it in my palm, wrapping my fingers to test the grip.

"Forty silver." The merchant sits in a chair, whittling a stick with a small blade. His thick, dark beard crusts around his mouth, frosted where his breath has frozen.

"It's a nice blade," I comment. "And a reasonable price for your handiwork."

He startles, lifts from his chair, and bows. "Your Majesty. I didn't recognize you at first. Apologies."

"It's okay," I say, placing the knife onto the furs. "I don't get out much."

The merchant stares flatly, then forces a smile. An out-of-tune laugh follows. "Right," he says, hovering over his wares. "Anything I can help you with, Sire?"

"Just looking for now." I trail my fingers over the handles, admiring the precision of the carving. He watches me too closely.

Pressure builds in my throat, and my heart flutters. I cough, swallowing the anxiety before it can spoil my mood.

Calm. Smooth. In control.

I inhale, letting the smell of smoke, leather, and crisp air fill my nose.

Dropping two coins on the mat for the merchant's time, I duck my head to miss the canopy bar.

"Thank you! Audrina bless you, Your Majesty!" he calls after me.

I hunch into the snow, pleased with myself. There. No harm done. No explosions of temper. Only good, friendly interactions.

I can do this.

The next shop is a tailor. Clothing hangs from a wooden rung, the assortment of furs sewn into hoods, capes, and muffs. A basket sits on the table, overflowing with knitted mittens and hats. I approach the booth and nod in greeting to the middle-aged female merchant. The browsing customers spot me coming and slowly back away from the wares.

The tailor shoots from her seat, slamming her knitting onto the table with a gasp. Afraid of me. She bubbles out a greeting and curtsies. "What brings you in today, Your Majesty?"

"I'm just looking." I cringe and step back, giving her the space she needs. I forget they're not used to seeing me. It must be as much a shock for them as it is for me.

My fingers trail through the furs, catching on a frostcat cloak. The fur is creamy and warm next to the gray-brown fur of its neighbors. Like a dollop of cream on hot chocolate. I recognize the color, and as I run my thumb backward on the fur to reveal its dappled undercoat, my brow pinches. The spy has the same gold-flecked pattern in her eyes. Glaring at me from my throne room floor, they burned with rebellious flame.

I release the cloak, flexing my hand.

Not a spy. Princess of the Brine, she said. Freezing cold and locked in a cage. *What kind of monster are you?*

"That's one of our finest cloaks," the merchant says, shuffling closer. "My husband speared her himself, last hunting trip. Not often that you find a frostcat on the plains. A rare thing of beauty, they are. I'd be honored to see it worn in the glory of your hall."

I pinch the corner between my fingers, already missing the touch of the soft fur. It's a gorgeous piece. Golden thread wraps around the edge, protecting the skin from fraying.

The merchant rushes to remove it from its hanger. She holds it for me, showing off its size and length. The furs brush the tops of her toes. Judging from the width of the shoulders, it would fit the Brine Princess perfectly.

"I meant it for a female frame," she stutters. "Might not fit the likes of you, Your Majesty. No offense intended."

I'm already opening in my pouch, fishing among the coins. "How much?"

"No cost to you, Your Majesty."

I grunt, dropping five gold coins into the basket before I can change my mind. "I'll take it." Will it match her eyes? Will it keep her warm?

My pulse thunders in my ears. She wraps the cloak for me, and I tuck the parcel beneath my arm. I glance at Orson and find the young guard watching me with stunned interest.

My ears burn. The high of the purchase plummets, and I'm left with regret twisting in my stomach.

A stupid, rash decision.

I hurry into the streets, weaving through the other shoppers. Beneath my arm, the cloak grows cold.

Why would I buy something for a prisoner? A foreign spy? She's *not* welcome here. She's *not* a guest—no matter how much Deirdre may wish to entertain her.

And it's not like she can wear it underwater.

I pull my cloak around the package to disguise it. If Deirdre sees it, no doubt she'll have questions.

Would it fit my housekeeper, instead? It could be a surprise gift. A thank you for putting up with all my shit over the years.

I clench my fists. Behind me, Orson scurries to match my increasing pace. I push harder, eager to escape into the safe, dark halls of my home.

I was a fool to take the healer's advice.

Kingly routine? Interact with *more* people? How is this helping anyone? I'll never be one of them; I only scare them. It's the one thing I'm good for.

As I approach the center of the market, the crowd thickens. They gasp and scurry out of my path. Voices echo loudly, growing more unbearable by the second. Their eyes watch every twitch of my face.

I clamp my teeth. Suck air through my nose, out my mouth. Breath crystalizes on my exhale, pushing through drying lips.

Too many people around. Nowhere to hide.

Somewhere, a shop owner slams a door, and I jump out of my skin.

Two guppies dart across my path, and I narrowly miss barreling them over.

My heart beats quicker. The knot in my stomach bursts, and ice crawls along my spine.

Fuck.

The guppies shriek, a pitch too high, piercing and ringing through my head.

I pass them, but the ringing persists.

Like an itch inside my skull.

Louder.

Louder.

I slouch deeper in my cloak to hide the blue scales creeping from my fingertips.

Louder.

I'm through the gate now, a few paces from my back door. Orson rushes to open it for me, and I storm inside, leaving behind the wind, the snow, the voices, the chaos.

"Leave me," I bark to the guard.

My feet slip on the floor, numb and wet.

The ringing intensifies.

I lean against the wall and grasp my skull with both hands, dropping my package. I squeeze. Hard. But the ringing is still there. Itching, burning.

Come.

A foreign voice sings through my thoughts, and the world grows still.

It sounds like a golden sunrise—warm and clear.

What the fuck?

A shiver traces my spine.

The scales crawl past my elbows. In my stomach, the Beast purrs, awakening with a burst of ice.

And then I'm running.

CHAPTER NINETEEN

NAHLA

Next time I see Keen—if I ever get out of here—I'm going to thank him for my new favorite mantra.

My summoning song spirals out of my mouth, muffled by my hand. I've been calling for the Beast for the past hour with no luck. As my spell weaves through the water, searching for my target, I recite my plan to myself.

I can't leave a job unfinished. If I break all the rules, I'm going to do it right. I'm thorough as fuck in my little rebellions.

First, I'll befriend this Beast. I'll use my magic to master his mind and bend it to my will. I'll start small, impressing him with simple tasks. Then comes phase two: get him to finish the tunnel Perrin started for me. I'll break into the castle. Explore the fuck out of it. And then I'll leave the Rime, escorted by the king's own pet.

Once I break all his rules, I'll be out of here, and the Frost King will get his dues. It's foolproof.

I'll work at night. The king forbade me from interacting with this creature. Whether the Beast is dangerous or there's another reason, I'm not sure, but I won't bring Perrin into my mess. He's too good to spoil so young.

The night guard, on the other hand, is a sorry fellow named Vaughn who holds little regard for his job. From the moment his shift started, he settled to the floor, tucking his tail into a comfortable spiral, and leaned against the wall. He fell asleep in minutes.

Easy.

I sense the clawbeast near the beach as he enters the reach of my spell. My mind lifts, twists, and penetrates. His guard is lowered this time. I slip beneath his hardened shell, finding myself amid those black, angry swirls of thought. They rise at my presence, slithering closer, wrapping around me with curious caresses. Cold. But not enough to freeze.

Come see me? I smirk. Gods, I hope this works.

His center of self glows, flaring brighter at the touch of my Voice. The surrounding shadows lighten in color, a soft gray with a tint of blue. I approach the center, gently brushing it with my mind. He might let me—

The Beast recoils. The clouds of thoughts rear, sharpening at the edges.

Too far. I retreat to the edge of his mind. *Whoa, there, Beasty. We're friends, remember?*

He doesn't attack. Yet. I wait as his mind glides closer, closer, until finally, a shadow falls over the entrance to the tunnel that holds my frosted cage. The temperature grows impossibly colder.

Then his body appears, a dark silhouette against the dim twilight waters. I can't make out his features, only the muscular outline of his body as it floats. Behind him, his long spiny tail twitches, the barbed tip flicking.

Hey there, Beasty. Did you miss me?

His thoughts soften, easing into curiosity.

That's it, big guy. Come say hi. Quietly now. We don't want to wake poor Vaughn.

My heart thrums as he glides into the tunnel, silent as the dead. He lands in a crouch at the iron gate, tucking his tail and anchoring his claws around the bars. His form crowds the space, and he ducks his head to avoid the ceiling. He glances at a sleeping Vaughn, and I swear his eyes roll a little. Then his gaze is on me, two black orbs sparkling in the low light.

Inside his mind, I brush against his center of self. Testing. His mind shivers at my touch. He's not ready for full mind control. We'll have to start smaller.

I glide closer, raising my hands in surrender. His eyes follow my movement, cautious. *Wonder if you might do me a favor?*

His thoughts slither closer, caressing me with invitation.

Here goes nothing. My projection is simple and focused: the pain in my stomach as it twists on empty. Weakness in my bones. The taste of meat, salty and fresh.

Understanding colors his thoughts. Then his inner voice rumbles deep and cold: *Hungry?*

He sounds like thunder on the open sea, terrifying and beautiful all at once. I shudder as fear runs along my spine, and I get the feeling I've trespassed somewhere I should never have wandered.

Most minds communicate in images, colors, or emotions. But words? What type of being is this?

I'm in too deep to stop now.

Yes, I'm hungry. Would you hunt for me, please?

He sends me the image of a silverfish between his teeth, fat and juicy.

I nod eagerly. *Yes, please.*

He snorts, bubbles flowing out of his mouth. His face presses into the bars, eyes growing large and hungry as he studies me. He parts his mouth, revealing a double row of sharp, white teeth. He stretches through the bars, and I eye his paw as fear flares in my gut.

Nahla is a friend, I remind him. *Not food.*

He blinks. Cocks his head. His claws curl in, leaving one to point at me. Crouching lower, his impossibly large frame sinks to my level. He holds my gaze as his voice rumbles through my mind: *Nah-la.*

Something inside me unhitches at the sound of my name in that rich bass tone. His thoughts surround me, circling, prodding, as if trying to enter my soul. I hold still as the dark clouds whisper past.

I'm flooded with a sense of amusement, then one word: *Cute.*

I frown.

He dips his head, tucking his nose into my cell. My skin tingles. And then the Beast sniffs me.

Cute, he repeats with satisfaction.

I'm not cute. My name is Nahla. I'm hungry, and I'm being serious.

He hums. His mind swirls, solidifying into a singular image. A small golden fish, with a wide sailfin. A sunfish. Then, *Cute.*

I roll my eyes. Sunfish are not cute. They're unintelligent, herd-minded animals that are easily manipulated for a quick kill.

Sunfish hungry, he says with a note of determination. *I fix.*

Then, quiet as he came, he releases the cage and slips out of the tunnel. I squint into the darkness as the bubbles settle around the place his body occupied.

I uncurl my fists, noticing now how tightly I've clenched them.

It worked.

He's not eating me—he's *feeding* me.

I smile, settling against the wall to wait. My fists press into my stomach to stifle its hungry protests.

I keep the connection open, maintaining my spell with a near-silent hum. His vision plays in his thoughts, and I watch him slither through the water, scent his prey, and track a swarm of silverfish. He pierces their formation, snatching one from the water. He eats his first catch, tearing into its flesh with ravenous teeth.

Sunfish hungry. Fix. He refocuses, targeting another fish.

Soon enough, he returns with it wriggling in his mouth. His teeth bite into the flesh, pinning the catch with a trickle of blood.

He crawls through the tunnel, careful to avoid Vaughn. On the floor, the guard moans, shifting in his sleep.

The silverfish thrashes in the jaws of death.

I sigh. That meat's going to taste like fear. But beggars can't be choosers. My stomach grumbles at the smell of its leaking blood.

The Beast slows his approach. He catches my gaze, then his teeth sink deep, blood clouds the water, and the fish ceases to move. The dead eye stares glassy at the ceiling and silver scales dim to dull gray. He drops his prize and passes the carcass through the bars of my cage.

I catch it, the meat heavy in my hands. My fingers trace the length of its body, slipping along the scales. Poor thing. I should teach the Beast to hunt with empathy.

Sunfish eat. His voice penetrates, rumbling with the note of an order.

I cock my eyebrow at him. *Thank you.*

He waits at the cage until I lift the fish to my mouth and tear into the flesh. It's sweet but soured at the finish.

The Beast nods. *Fixed?*

I smile. *Fixed.*

With a quiet snarl, he slips into the night, leaving me to chew the bones.

***

I SUMMON HIM THE following night. Then the next; each night, he hunts for me. Silverfish, grayfish, and bottomfish. He drops them in my cage, then watches me with dark eyes, making sure I eat something before he leaves.

He crouches there now, squatting on his rear legs. His muscular body crowds out the low light coming from the tunnel behind. His shadow drips across the floor, tail flicking in that anxious rhythm of his.

I have fixed, he says. *Sunfish should eat.*

A few days ago, his mind could only form singular words. Now he's stringing several together. I smile. Perhaps our exchanges have been good for him, too.

I lift the carcass to my mouth and puncture its skin with my teeth. He grumbles in approval.

What other tricks can you do? I ask him. *All this fish has been great, but I'm awfully bored in here.*

His thoughts flex around my request, confused.

I try again.

Backflip? I assess the size of the tunnel and change my mind. *Not enough room. What if you brought me a game to play? Or a book?*

He brightens at the final word.

Sunfish wants book, he says. *I will find.*

He slithers out of the tunnel, sneaking past a sleeping Vaughn.

Every day is the same: brush frost from my scales, chat with Perrin, dig a little more of the tunnel, then summon the Beast. The hole in my ceiling is now deep enough to fit my torso. A few more days of work, and I could fit my tail, too.

The exercise is good for me, and the Beast keeps me fed. But my mind needs more stimulation. I can only stare at the same wall for so long before I drive myself insane.

He returns a while later with a stack of tablets. Crouching to avoid the low ceiling, he stops at my cage, then passes them to me one by one.

Books for Sunfish, he says with a note of pride.

I send my gratitude through our connection as I shuffle through the tablets, skimming their titles. A few grimoires, a diary, and a book on ancient curses. Odd choices for entertainment.

Any romance, by chance?

The Beast wrinkles his nose. *Romance?* His thoughts test the meaning of the word.

You know. Kissing books. Happily ever after.

Kissing?

I pucker my lips, demonstrating a kiss.

The Beast snorts. *I do not kiss.*

I cover my mouth to keep from laughing aloud. *That's okay. It's the characters in the book who kiss. You don't have to.*

Kissing... His confusion spreads. *...is good?*

Very good. I grin at him, at the same time searching my memories for a better demonstration. His thoughts swirl eagerly as I impress the memory of my first kiss.

It happened under the shade of the sweetnut trees. I was cracking open a nut. Or trying at least. I couldn't find the opening. My blade was too dull. His shadow slid across my face, and I looked up into the setting sun. I was ten years old, but he was older by a few years. A hunter. Handsome, in a freckled guppish kind of way. He had dark curls, like mine.

"Need some help?" he said, offering his knife.

I nodded. "It won't crack."

When I reached for the knife, he moved it out of the way. "I don't work for free," he said, grinning. "I'll do it if you marry me."

I wanted the milk inside that nut. My thirst was burning my throat. So I did the logical thing and said yes. He laughed and called his friend over to marry us beneath the tree. And when he kissed me, it tasted like the sun.

The Beast's eyes grow large, searching my face in the dark. His claw brushes his bottom lip. *Like the sun.*

Yes. It was nice, as far as first kisses go. I've had better, but I'll spare you the details.

His mind tugs at my thoughts, pulling for more.

No! No more. You'll have to bring me those books first.

I brought books. Sunfish asked. He eyes the stack of books in my cage. *Not good enough?*

My heart sinks. Have I offended him? Shit. *No, no, these are fine. I mean for next time.*

Next time, he repeats. His brow furrows, one side lifting. His mouth curls. Is that a... smirk?

Chapter Twenty

BEAST

SUNFISH WANTS KISSING BOOKS.

I will find them for her.

How hard could it be?

I know a cave full of books.

Scattered, shattered, broken, some of them. But still many books in there.

I squeeze through the opening.

My body is large, and the ice creaks, but I fit.

Inside, pillars of ice. From floor to ceiling high above. Each pillar carved with shelves.

Most empty. Most books have been taken by now.

But not all.

I pick up the first tablet I find.

Tap the stone.

Gently, with my knuckle.

Wait.

The image plays.

No kissing.

I toss it.

The king remembers a book-keeper, from before.

A helpful siren who sat near the entrance. He could find anything, if you asked nicely.

I could use that book-keeper now.

But he is gone, like the rest of them.

He prefers the king, too.

Frustration.

Doubt.

Annoyance.

I tap another tablet.

The image plays.

Still no kissing.

I toss it.

Will Sunfish be angry with me?

The shelves tower high. So many books to sort.

I groan.

But I promised. Sunfish needs these kissing books.

I can't return with empty claws.

I must bring her *many* books. My claws will overflow with them.

Then Sunfish will be happy.

Then she will smile.

And then, if I'm lucky, she will show this *kissing*.

Pucker her lips so I can taste them, like she did for that male in her memory.

I bet she tastes like the sun.

I pick up a book.

Tap.

No kissing.

This could take a while.

CHAPTER TWENTY-ONE

AETHAN

This has to stop.

Every night for the past three nights, I've woken exhausted and wet, unsure where I've been or what I've done. Anxiety gnaws at my mind like a parasite, growing larger each day it feeds.

Still, no casualties since the day I injured Perrin. By what miracle of the goddess I've been blessed, I do not know.

I need answers. *Now.*

Lucas said he needed a few weeks to research my ailment, but I no longer have the luxury of time. Every day that passes is another that could end in bloodshed at my hands.

What if Deirdre is next? Perrin? Lucas himself?

Nahlani?

Pushing away the memory of her face, I shudder.

I skip breakfast, to Deirdre's hearty disapproval, and head straight to the library, hoping to help the healer's research move along.

The small library is practical, originally made for storing a bit of light reading and nothing more. It pales compared to the grandeur I grew up with beneath the waves, but I prefer it this way. It's cozy. Bookshelves reach to the ceiling, lining every wall. Sconces flicker, casting dark shadows on the books. I pick a table and light a candle.

The librarian approaches, scurrying to meet me with a feather duster in his hand. A short older male, Horace is as round as the spectacles that perch on his nose.

"Your Majesty." He bows. "How might I help you this morning?" He runs the duster over my place at the table, brushing it clear.

"I'm hoping you could help me with a project I'm working on. Anything you have on royal ancestry. Or curses."

Horace sucks his lips into a tight line. "Any particular curses in mind?"

I swipe my hand over the table, studying the dust that clings to my finger. "Nothing in particular. Just a curiosity of mine. I'm looking to pass the time, and I'm afraid I've read through all the books in my chamber."

"I'll see what I can find." Horace's frown deepens, and he makes another pass with the feather duster. "The tomes you require may be... inaccessible for the time being."

Stuck in the old city of Doloch, he means. When I first gave the evacuation order, it took him several weeks to fish the current supply out of the depths, before the danger became too great to continue, and he abandoned the rest of the books.

Horace puts his hands on his hip, thinking for a moment, and begins singing his spell. With a soft tenor Voice, he summons the books he needs.

The shelves quake. Several flat stone tablets tilt forward and lift from their slots. They float toward me, bouncing through the air with the lilt of his Voice. He stacks them on the table until I can hardly see over their height, then cuts his spell.

"That should keep you busy," he says, brushing his palms together.

I thank him and inspect the first tablet from the stack, titled *A History of Everything: Secrets of the Sea*. The magic ignites beneath my touch, releasing its stored memory. Images play in my mind's eye. Faces from the past flick by, their mouths moving soundlessly as a monotone voice summarizes the contents of the book. I skip to the Frost Kingdom and settle in as my great-great-great-something grandfather introduces himself.

As I read, I watch for signs of hysteria. Blue scales creeping, perhaps. Or a nervous twitch of the eye. But he seems calm. Smiley. His pale features remind me distantly of my father's, his violet eyes set in my ancestor's too-sharp face.

I read until I reach the chapter about my mother, then sever the spell before I can see her face.

This was a stupid idea.

I grab the next book, activating it to remove any possibility of her memory returning.

This one is a generic history lesson I've heard a thousand times. A lyrical voice relays the formation of the Rime. In the beginning, the Moon Goddess Audrina breathed over the sea, and the Frosted Plains stretched from her mouth. She scooped the glacial bowl, pulled up the mountains, and carved the tunnels of Doloch. Then with her fingertips, she painted the aethersky to remind us not all dark places are void of color.

Whaleshit, all of it.

I skip to the next book. Then the next.

I'm a dozen books deep when the door glides open. The quick, efficient footsteps announce Lucas before he appears at my side.

"Sire," he grunts in greeting. Before I can respond, he plops a parcel onto the table. I bristle. It's fur, folded and bundled in string. I recognize the creamy coat of a frostcat hide peeking through the wrapping—the cloak I purchased from the market the other day, the one I meant for the princess.

"Did His Majesty enjoy his shopping trip?" Lucas hedges.

A vein pulses along my neck. "No."

The library is all but empty—Horace sits in a rocking chair by the hearth, his eyes unfocused as he reads a stone.

Lucas drops his voice to a whisper. "You were careless. That's not what I meant by creating a kingly routine. What if you exploded among all those people? You barely kept it together long enough to get out of sight. And you have seen no one since. Once-and-done is not good enough, Sire."

I flinch, fingers digging deeper into the fur. Wasn't he the one who told me to try interacting with my subjects? "What do you want me to do then? Wake early, exercise, take my tea, study for twenty minutes, stretch for five. Go greet a guppy on the street. Rinse and repeat till I die?"

"That's a start, yes," Lucas grunts, sorting through the books before me. With each tablet, his frown deepens.

"And how goes your research? Anything useful?" I ask.

"It's hardly been a week, Your Majesty. I'll need more time than that. It may require forbidden access, you see."

The books he needs are underwater. Goddessdamn. "I'm out of time, Lucas. Work with me here."

"If I could have access to the original library, it may speed my research."

Meaning, if I could stay out of the water for one fucking night, he might make some headway. My hands roam over the cloak, gripping the frostcat fur. Can I keep myself land-bound? What will it take? More locks? A numbing spell?

The Beast always finds a way out. Every. Damn. Time.

I speak around the knot in my throat. "I cannot promise your safety."

"Understood, Your Majesty." Lucas taps three tablets together, stacking them neatly. "As you were."

With a whisper of wind, he leaves me to brood. I shove the cloak aside.

What was the point of bringing this to me? To remind me of my failure?

Freezing cold and locked in a cage. The princess's accusation echoes as guilt stabs sharply.

I pick the next book and activate its spell, but I can't focus on the words. All I can see is the siren's pretty face. Her lips, quivering. Her skin, damp and cold to the touch.

No way to treat a princess.

Fuck. I wouldn't know where to start. A chamber in my palace, three meals a day, and no more spy nonsense—that was her request.

It shouldn't be too difficult.

Except then she'd be *here*. In my home. Taunting me with her very presence. Close enough to kill me in my sleep or slip poison into my tea.

My stomach gurgles, running on empty. Evening light streams through the windows. I've spent all day here without breakfast or lunch. I thank Horace for his time and hurry from the library.

When I find Deirdre in the dining hall, she flays me with her glare. "Your Majesty." She forces a smile. "Ready for dinner?"

The rich smell of food wafts over me, floating out from the kitchen. Guilt stabs again, sharper this time.

Nahlani must be hungry. And I'm sitting here, about to feast like a cold-hearted jackass.

I'm not a good king. But that doesn't mean I can't be a good person. My heart skips at the thought.

"Deirdre, send for the princess and alert the chef," I say. "She will join me for dinner tonight."

Chapter Twenty-Two

NAHLA

I PULL THE BONE through my teeth, cleaning the final bit of meat from the clawbeast's prize catch. With a flick of my fingers, I stack the bone with the rest of the pile in my frigid cell.

My stomach is bursting. I couldn't eat another bite if I tried. I tried to spread the meal out over the course of the past day, savoring each morsel. The large catch should have lasted me a few days at least, but I underestimated my hunger.

I cleaned that poor creature to the bone, wasting nothing, in a matter of a day.

At the end of the tunnel, I can see the fading light. Soon, Perrin will leave me, the darkness will descend, and I will summon the clawbeast once more.

Satiety spreads warmth through my limbs. If I can get the Beast to hunt for me each night, I might have a chance of escaping this dreadful place.

Will he come to me again? Or have I stumbled into an unusually good stretch of luck this week? My stomach twists around my meal, gurgling uncomfortably.

I hardly know anything about this creature. This *Beast*. He's proven dangerous and unpredictable, and yet I'm trusting him to be the opposite. I need him to help me. I can't break out of here alone—and Perrin won't unlock my cage for me. Yet.

A burp builds in my chest. I push it out, and the bubble bursts through my lips.

Perrin glances at me from his post by the gate. "Gross," he says. His whiskers twitch as he wrinkles his nose. "I give you a five out of ten for that one."

"Damn. Not my best."

He laughs. "Where'd you get that fish, anyway?"

"Same place I got the tunnel." I wink, and the tips of his ears darken. "Outside help."

He raises his hands in mock surrender. "I don't want to know."

We made good progress on my escape tunnel today. The hole in my ceiling is deep enough to hide my torso and tail. Perrin says we'll be out the top in a couple weeks, if all goes well. It's a thick ceiling, but I've got nothing but time and a few boring books, and I need the exercise to stay warm.

Perrin stiffens to attention as a shadow covers the entrance to the tunnel. The youngling's gills flutter at his neck.

"Perrin!" Vaughn swims into view.

The youngling drops his shoulders and blows bubbles from his mouth. "Here, sir." His voice shakes. "You're early. I thought you might be—"

Vaughn leers. "Your aunt here to tell you it's your bedtime?"

Perrin shakes his head and straightens his posture. "No, sir."

Vaughn approaches, and Perrin swims out to meet him. They whisper for a moment. I drift to the front of my cage, gripping the bars, but I can't make out their words.

Perrin shoots me an apologetic look over his shoulder. "I'll ask her."

He floats toward me, expression grim. "Sorry," he says, reaching for the keys.

"For what?" This can't be good. Why would he be ordered to let me out of the cage? Has the king decided to do away with me, after all? I stir my tail, retreating a pace into my cell.

Perrin's eyes widen. "Nothing bad, Nahla. The king wants you to come to dinner. I know you don't want to go, but..."

"That's right, I don't." I snort. Dinner with the king? Is this a fucking joke?

The lock clicks, and he hesitates, hand at the ready to move the gate. I watch him, tensing. If he opens it, I could swim free. Vaughn's a slow swimmer. I could out-maneuver him.

But it'd mean consequences for Perrin. I study the youngling's soft face. The nervous twitch of his whiskers. The round ends of his tusks poke through his top lip. He's been so helpful. I can't betray him like that.

"He's not that bad," Perrin whispers.

But that doesn't mean I have to do it. I have standards. And frankly, the king falls short by a nautical mile. The Beast, on the other hand? I might consider. "I'm not hungry, and I don't want to spend my evening with that arctic asshole."

"Come on, Nahla. It won't be that bad. Promise."

"He can't make me."

Perrin glances at the guard. "He may try."

Vaughn grips his trident, narrowing his eyes. "Oy. Just grab her and let's go."

I chew my lip. If there's one thing I don't like, it's being *manhandled.*

"What do I tell the king?" Perrin sighs.

I reward him with my best beaming smile. "You're smart, Perrin. You'll think of something clever. Perhaps I've come down with the paddledrake flu."

It's a guppy's tale, meant for scaring young merfolk into an early bedtime. But the Frost King doesn't need to know that.

Perrin perks up. "Paddledrake flu? Okay. I can work with that. What are your symptoms?"

I feign exhaustion, slouching to the floor and draping my hand over my forehead. "Lack of appetite," I groan, patting my belly. "Boils on my face. Terrible cough. I'm afraid it's deathly contagious. Wouldn't want the king to catch it."

"Alright. I'll try it, thanks." Perrin chuckles, then turns the key in the lock, sealing me in. His tail stirs, and I crane my neck to watch him discuss my sickness with Vaughn.

Vaughn's lip curls, and he shoots me a disgusted look. I moan for good measure, turning to hide my face in my arms.

Oh, the horror. I might not survive this illness. Give my bones to the Beast when he comes.

I peek through the crook in my elbow to check the effectiveness of my act.

They whisper some more, until Perrin hands Vaughn the keys, then disappears. Vaughn settles at the entrance to the tunnel, shooting me dirty looks.

I cough loudly, and he turns the other way, grumbling to himself.

My smile spreads in the darkness. Maybe I'll get lucky tonight, and the Beast will eat Vaughn for dinner.

Chapter Twenty-Three

Aethan

"Does my hair look okay?" I ask Deirdre as she refills my tea. Any moment, the princess will walk through that door, and I find myself eager to look presentable. Kingly.

When was the last time I brushed my hair? This morning?

The housekeeper assesses me, lifting the kettle to stop the pour, then narrows her eyes. "You look handsome as always, Sire. Why?"

Why, indeed. It's silly to look nice for her. For a prisoner. An enemy.

But she's not the enemy. Not really.

She's a lost princess trapped in my dungeon because I'm terrified by the thought of hurting her.

Fuck.

I tug at the fabric of my shirt, appalled by the way it clings to my skin. "Excellent," I mutter.

Deirdre tips the kettle again and hot water splashes into my cup. Steam curls, and the scent of peppermint wafts.

In mere seconds, she'll be here. Finally. And then I'll stand, like a fucking gentleman, and apologize for being an asshole. She shouldn't go hungry on my account.

And I shouldn't either. My stomach grumbles, protesting the delay of my meal.

What's taking so long?

"Just be yourself." Deirdre's mouth quirks into a smile.

"I don't want to scare her," I grumble.

"Be yourself, minus all the..." She searches for the right word. "Growling."

Footsteps approach, echoing through the hallway. A shuffle and a hop, then a scrape of wood.

I rise from my seat and fold my hands in front of me. But no, that's too formal. I unlace them, then clench my hands into fists. Too stiff. I cross my arms. Too angry.

Dammit.

I clasp my hands behind my back and square my shoulders, ready.

Perrin enters the room, propped on a wooden crutch beneath his right armpit. He wears the Frost Guard uniform, the shirt rumpled and still damp. His pant leg ties in a knot beneath the amputation. His eyes dart, avoiding my gaze.

I take a steady breath, letting the guilt wash over me.

"Your Majesty," he greets me, tipping his head.

The hallway behind him is dark and quiet. I wait for his companion to enter, but she does not come.

"Where is she?"

"She's, uh—" His lip trembles. "She's not coming."

"Not coming?"

"Paddledrake flu?" It comes out as a question, like he's not sure he gave the right answer.

I snort. "Is that so?"

"Deadly contagious, Sire. She wouldn't want you to catch it. Boils on her cough. Bad face." He coughs, as if to demonstrate.

"Pity. I'll send the healer momentarily, and then she can join me for dinner. Shouldn't take him long to fix a little…" My lips twitch. "Flu."

Perrin's throat bobs, and I hear him swallow. Hard.

"She *is* sick, yes?" I say. "I'd hate to send Lucas for nothing."

I step closer, hating that I have to resort to intimidation tactics with him. His eyes widen and he drops his gaze to my feet.

Perrin nods slowly, then he shakes his head. The tips of his ears darken.

"I thought not," I grunt. "Bring her here, Perrin. By order of your king."

He looks up, torn. "And if she doesn't want to come with me?"

I close my eyes briefly and pinch the bridge of my nose. I've known he's soft, but *this* soft? He's as bad as his aunt. "Then use a little force, Perrin. You can do that, no?"

He nods again, then turns to leave.

Next to me, Deirdre releases a heavy breath. "That went well," she says in a strained tone.

"What was I supposed to do, believe him?" I slump into my seat and cross my arms to muffle the sinking feeling in my stomach. "Paddledrake flu? Right."

She frowns, but otherwise lets it drop. "I'll bring you something to snack on while you wait, Sire." She hurries from the room, skirts hissing around her feet.

Silence settles in the dining hall, except for the crackle in the hearth as the flame licks logs to ash. The long table stretches before me, each chair empty but mine.

Alone.

I smooth my hair, retie the knot, and press my hands flat to the table.

Anxiety swirls in my gut, and I chase it with hot tea.

Should I practice? If I know what I'm going to say to her, it won't be so hard in the moment.

I clear my throat, testing a few options. Then I nudge the mug, centering it before me, as a stand-in for the princess.

"Hey there, Princess." My voice is whiny and strained. The mug says nothing. Will she say nothing? Or will she lob more insults? Sweat prickles my scalp.

"Uh, sorry I thought you were a spy. I can see now you're too delicate for that. Are you hungry? Cold? Well, there's food here. And I got you a cloak. I don't have it here though. It's in my room. I could show you later."

I drop my face into my palms before it can get worse. What the fuck was that? Why did I mention the cloak? I hid it in my wardrobe for good reason.

It's not for her.

That cloak was a lapse in judgment, and I will return it in the morning.

With a long pull of tea, I wet my throat and try again. This time, I turn the mug, so the handle faces me. Kind of like a nose.

"Hi. Hope you're hungry," I croak. "This is me, admitting I'm a jackass. Friends?"

Fuck no.

Friends?

What kind of line is that?

I drop my forehead to the table and thump it a few times. This. Will. Not. Do.

I should send for that damn frostcat cloak. She's a female. Females like gifts. It might help—

"And then say what, asshole?" I counter my thoughts, twisting my voice into a mockery of itself. "I wondered if I gave you this cloak, you could stay here with me and stop flirting with all my guards."

That's it. I'm officially losing my mind.

I push out of my chair, and its legs scrape on the floor. One foot before the other, I pace.

Where is she?

I make three turns about the room before I hear Perrin. I strain my ears to listen for a companion.

He comes alone.

I ball my fists and clench my teeth. The knot of rage in my stomach threatens to burst.

When he appears in the doorway, it takes all my strength not to glare.

His voice is soft. Scared. "She's not coming. I'm sorry, Sire. She said she's not hungry."

Not hungry?

When last I saw her, she complained of me starving her. She called me a bad host. What the fuck does she mean *not hungry*?

"Not hungry?" My resolve breaks. The ice pierces my veins, and the scales crawl.

Perrin trembles, trying hard to hold his ground. Deirdre appears behind him. She steps in front of the youngling, shielding him with her body.

"Your Majesty, deep breaths," she cautions. "I have your snack here. Let's eat, okay?"

Her words come muffled—like sound through water.

"She's not hungry? Impossible." I snap my teeth together. I flex my hand, and ice skitters across the floor. "If the princess doesn't eat with *me*, then she will starve. That's an order."

Chapter Twenty-Four

Nahla

I wake to the sound of fish slapping on the floor. Foggy from sleep, I barely make out the clawbeast's looming silhouette. It's the middle of the night. From his mouth hangs a large silverfish, its bloody scent spiraling into my cage.

It's not his only catch. Two more rest on the floor, their glass eyes staring at me in the darkness.

He spits the final fish from his mouth and tosses it to join the rest.

I rub my eyes. Did I summon him in my sleep? My hand finds my throat. There's no spell vibrating. No magic stirring in my stomach.

Ice traces my spine.

No. He came of his own accord tonight.

I push from the floor, heart pounding, and glide toward him. He watches me with eyes black as midnight.

A low grumble emits from his shadow, and his hand reaches through the bars. One claw extends. Flexes. He's beckoning me.

"Hi, big guy," I whisper.

Tonight's the night I break free. If he's here willingly, then he could be inclined to help. I'll have to time it right. Persuade him when he's vulnerable.

Fuck rule number two—I can go home without exploring the castle, if he'll help me now.

His hand finds my face in the darkness. The scales on his palm are cold and leathery as they slide against my skin. My body ignites at his touch, all nerves zapping to attention. My heart pounds harder.

Claws glide over my scalp, slipping into my hair. His thumb tucks beneath my chin. I try not to think about how easily my head fits in his palm. If he wanted to, he could crush my skull like a lushfruit.

The tip of his claw taps my temple twice. Then his thumb brushes my lips. His mouth curls into a snarl, and he leans closer, turning his ear.

I hold still, the only movement coming from my gills. Of all the reckless things I've done, befriending the Beast may be my stupidest idea yet.

His thumb strokes back and forth over my bottom lip. I part my mouth at the touch, bubbles leaking out. He stares at my mouth. His brows tug, expression troubled.

He taps my temple again. Then with his other hand, he taps his own head.

Oh.

I awaken my magic and form a spell. With a quiet hum, I lift from my mind and weave into his.

He grins, teeth glinting in the darkness. His thoughts brush my conscience, surrounding me with caressing mist. They swirl with an exuberant current, lifting me and sucking me deeper into his mind.

Hello, Sunfish. His voice reverberates through me. *Miss me?*

Of course I did! My heart threatens to burst from my chest.

He purrs. *Missed you, too.*

Any romance books today?

He blows bubbles from his nose and his eyes tighten. *Not today, sorry.* He prods me with his thoughts, testing and inviting me in deeper.

He's friendly tonight. Vulnerable. This could work. It's now or never.

What do you say to another favor? I ask.

Sunfish needs something? I will fix.

I strengthen my song and extend to surround his center of self. Then, I fill him with my vision: the Beast breaking my cage. Carrying me through the water. To the edge of the Rime. Through the mountains. Dropping me there.

The orb flexes, resisting my influence. Confusion colors his thoughts.

I push harder—*break the cage. Take me out of the Rime.*

His claws curl around the bars.

Break the cage.

He tightens his fists. With a loud crack, he rips the gate clean off. The ceiling shudders and splinters.

Vaughn stirs at his post, snorting loudly.

The Beast's hands snare my waist, and he tucks me into his side. His thighs tense, his hind claws grate into the ice, and he launches from the tunnel. Water rushes past me in a whoosh of cold current. Behind us, the ice collapses in a mess of rubble.

Vaughn shouts after us. I watch his form shrink into the darkness of the night as the Beast swims away.

Sunfish is free?

Wow, that voice. Mighty and rumbling, the thunder of him strikes me every time. I shudder against his chest, fighting my instincts to flee.

He's helping me. Friendly. Whatever I've done to convince him, it's worked. Hope burns through my chest.

He speaks again: *Free?* This time tinged with annoyance.

It's a question.

I push all my warmth through the connection. *Yes! Free. Good Beasty.*

His chest rumbles against my ear, and he pulls me in tighter.

My spirit lifts as we leave the cavern, entering open waters. Skylights pierce the waterline, filtering through like rainbow dust. The sea celebrates my victory, welcoming me into its waiting embrace.

I've done it! He listened to me. Just as Keen said, I made him my bitch.

My stomach swells with pride. Take that, Winona.

Perrin may be disappointed tomorrow morning when he swims to his shift, only to find his prisoner missing—but I brush the thought aside. He'll find something else to do, surely. He's a bright youngling with a big heart. The king is lucky to have him in his service.

And the king! A laugh escapes my lips. I never have to see that asshole again.

The Beast dips, and the seafloor rises to meet us. My heart skips. I cling to his chest, squeezing my eyes closed as the sharp shale bottom rushes closer, closer. I cringe, preparing my body for the sting of rock and stone.

With a gulping tune, I strengthen my spell: *Look out!*

At the last second, he lifts. We skim the floor a scale's breadth away. His chest rumbles again, and he tightens his grip.

If he will not listen, I'll have to break free myself. I ball my fists and dig into his stomach. His abdomen flexes, muscles hard and tight. Unaffected. I wind up my punch and land it square on his ribs.

He grunts. Then, *No.*

His hands grip my hips, and he turns me around so that my ass presses into his stomach, and my arms swing free. I wriggle, my tail slipping against his legs.

He growls, wrestling my arms to my sides. One hand finds my throat, wrapping around and lifting the length of my neck and snapping my teeth together. His leathery thumb brushes my gills. *Be still.*

The sensitive skin blooms beneath his touch, sending shocks of sensation through my body. I grit my teeth and obey. I know when I'm defeated.

Good girl.

I quiver in his grasp. And, fuck me, maybe it's the deep rumble of his voice. Or the pressure of his hand on my neck, his thumb stroking as I sing softly to maintain our connection. His body pressed against me, swallowing mine whole. Or the sheer joy that swims in his mind at the thought of me, like he's seeing the sun for the first time. But my insides turn to mush, and the hidden slit in my tail softens and swells.

I wave my hand, trying to clear the scent from the water.

He inhales. Recognition dawns, and his thoughts darken. *Sunfish is*—he searches for the right word—*hungry?*

There's an edge of humor to his inner voice. At the sound of it, my arousal strengthens.

Shit.

This is out of hand. I try to retreat, sucking my mind out of his grip. But as I withdraw, the shadows in his mind rear and take hold, pinning me with freezing tendrils. Sucking me back in.

No, he says. His thumb strokes my gills, tracing the soft ruffles. *Stay*.

The Rime sprawls before us, drowning in the hues of midnight. I strain to see into the darkness.

A sour taste fills my mouth. Where is he taking me, if not out of the Rime? His lair? I imagine a cave full of squirming hatchings, mouths gasping for the feed, and I shiver.

No. I will not go down like live bait. Even if he's friendly about it.

I'm the godsdamn Princess of the Brine—a stupid one, but a princess nonetheless—and I *will* break free of this place. Of the king and his wretched Beast.

How stupid was I to think he'd listen to me? That my little "we're friends" routine would work on such a complex, dark being?

He's murderous. Angry. Manipulative. I sense it in his thoughts as he pins me in place against his body, his hands squeezing me tight. If he squeezes any harder, he'll crush me.

So I abandon my pride. Time to grovel. *Please. Please take me away from here, oh mighty Beast.*

He snorts, bubbles tickling my hair. *Beast.*

Please. Out of the Rime. What do you want? What can I give you? I'll let you come with me. Are you trapped here, too? Do you want to leave?

I concentrate on my memories of the sun. Warm water. Golden rays.

His tail thrashes, as we turn again, lifting from the seafloor into open water. *Can't leave.*

We pass through a swarm of silverfish, and he snatches one from the cloud, slurping it into his mouth. His jaw works against the top of my head, crunching the bones.

I can hunt for you. Any prey you want, it's yours. I'll help you. It tastes better when I hunt. You might like a sunfish. Come, let's leave the Rime and I'll catch you a whole swarm.

Sunfish. His hand slides from my neck, tracing the length of my arm. He finds my hips, and his claws curl into my scales.

Sure. We can hunt sunfish. All yours. No problem, big guy. Let's go get them.

His claws dig deeper, pricking the surface of my skin beneath the scales. Pain springs, and I scent my blood in the water.

Mine.

My ass bumps against a protrusion between his legs. His hidden sheath, bulging, flexing behind me. A flash of affection in his thoughts. Then, *Cute.*

Fuck. That's not what I meant. This is not what I want.

We're approaching the surface. The lights dance in the sky overhead, like a rainbow painted against the blackness. I suck in their beauty through watery vision.

Come on. Take me out of here. The king will never know.

The king?

The shadows in his mind rear high, hardening in an instant. Ice pierces my mind, and I flinch as the brain freeze seizes me.

He will know. His last words suck into a dark vortex of emotion, disappearing in an instant. His thoughts are replaced with a singular, building roar.

I slip out of his mind, cutting the connection spell, and land within the boundary of my skull. *Fuck.*

The roar bursts through his mouth, loud in my ears. I thrash and kick, pushing away from his body. His grip on my body breaks, and he flounders, reaching for me. I dodge, twisting out of the way. His teeth glint in the darkness to catch the rainbowed rays of the skylights, his smile twisting into a snarl.

I pump my tail. His claws graze the feathered edge of my fins.

No time to think. Just swim. Faster. Faster. I scan the dark water for familiar landmarks. Where is my escape?

He roars again, drowning the sound of the heartbeat thundering in my head.

I don't make it more than three pumps before his hands are on me again. I slam into his chest. Arms tighten. A push of muscle, and we launch through the water.

CHAPTER TWENTY-FIVE

BEAST

Panic.

Anger.

Chaos.

The king will know what I've done.

Her golden ass, pressed to my erection.

Cock swells, hidden beneath a sheath. Desperate to emerge. To feel her. This soft, golden female, with kind, warm eyes.

And she wants to escape.

The king might know already. I have been careless with her.

I have been desperate.

But she is my friend. A friend that smells of arousal.

She wriggles in my arms.

Freedom, she wanted. Freedom, I gave her.

But it's only for tonight.

I will never let her go forever. Was I not obvious? Does she think I'm stupid?

Inferior?

Submissive?

I snort. I am not any of those things.

I am the Beast—the king's Beast. Important. Essential.

Protector of the Rime.

This is the thanks she gives? Trying to escape?

No.

She cannot escape.

She's mine.

This Sunfish, with the singing mind. She's my only friend. I will never let her go.

I tighten my grip.

She squirms.

Damn this erection.

She taps at the edge of my mind, and I let her in.

Please! I can't go back. I thought you would help me, she says.

Her voice is like sunshine on morning waters. Music in my mind. I could listen to her song forever.

But I do not speak to her. Only swim. I do not trust my thoughts. She reads them too well.

I thought we were friends.

Pain, through my chest. Like a sharp tooth.

Ignore her.

Take her.

Hide her.

Somewhere the king can't find.

Somewhere the king will never know what I've done.

Is it the king? Are you under orders? I can take you with me. We can escape together.

Me? Escape?

Bah.

It's nonsense.

I can never leave the Rime.

I could never leave the king.

The king's an asshole. He'll miss you, but not in the way you think.

Panic. I cover my thoughts. Hide them from her.

Sunfish can't know the truth.

I raise a wall. Thick, cold ice around my thoughts.

She taps. Presses. Wriggles through the cracks.

Please, just turn around. Let me help you.

There is no help.

Only death.

Memories drift from my other form. Of bodies on the shore. Claws. Blood. Flesh.

He thinks I am to blame.

But I have no memory of the deaths.

Only guilt.

Cold, piercing guilt. Flaring in my chest.

Are these... Did you kill them?

I cover my thoughts again. Another wall of ice. How much did she see?

Shit.

It's Sunfish's favorite word: Shit.

She softens in my grip.

I scent her emotions. Surrender? Fear?

She wriggles. Close, now, to the center of my soul. Soon, I'll have nowhere to hide.

You're dangerous, I know.

Her voice is careful. Afraid of me?

No. No. Please, no.

I am safe.

I protect. I fix. All for my Sunfish.

But you wouldn't hurt your Sunfish, would you?

Never.

I could never forgive myself if I did.

The shore is close.

I glide over the rocks.

But I do not exit the water. Do not transform.

She can't know. She may suspect, but she must never know.

She is afraid of me. Because I am a Beast. Sunfish is never safe with me.

My heart breaks at the truth.

She will be safe there, with the king. He can protect her. He can bring her books and fish.

Romance books. With kissing. He will know what she needs.

Not me.

It will never be me.

I bury my face in her hair. One last time. Inhale. She is sunshine, softness. All the beautiful things.

But she must go now.

It's for the best.

I push her ashore. Leave her on the beach. In the dry air.

I speak: *Sunfish will stay.*

She peers through the water. Mouth frowning. Confusion.

Then angry. She smacks the water.
Her tail flops. Bones crack. Tail splits into two legs.
Naked.
Pussy.
Warm pink flesh.
My heart races.
I stare.
She's beautiful. So beautiful my heart aches.
I can't look away. Can't leave her like this. Can I?
Her arousal floods the water. Warm scent. Wanting.
I can't deny what Sunfish wants. Her wish is my task.
And Sunfish wants me. I can smell it.
I lick my lips.

CHAPTER TWENTY-SIX

NAHLA

THE CLAWBEAST PUSHES ME out of the water, where my ass meets smooth, cold stones. Water runs down my back, slicking my curls against naked skin. My scales prickle at the rush of night air, and my tail splits in the middle. Bare legs lift from the waves.

I smack the water with my palm, sending an angry spray.

This is not how I wanted my escape to go. One moment I was free—the next, I'm land-bound with a grumpy guppysitter.

Sunfish will stay, he commands from the sea. His reptilian form slithers on the beach, pausing before he breaks the surf. He lifts his face above the waterline, focusing on the space between my legs. With shimmering eyes, the Beast smiles, and a wash of appreciation colors his thoughts. His tongue swipes over his bottom lip.

I flush and tuck my thighs together, cursing as arousal flutters in my center. The cold water laps at my entrance, and I clench.

It's the cold. That's all this is.

My reaction has nothing to do with the Beast, rising from the water like a demigod to stand on his hind legs.

Shit.

He's beautiful in the moonlight. His white hair drips over his broad shoulders, the same star-silk color as Audrina's cratered face. Water laps at his muscled torso, flowing over the washboard of dark scales and hiding the powerful flex of his thighs from view.

As he steps closer, his voice rumbles in my head: *Beautiful.*

My eyes flutter partway closed as a shudder moves through my body.

The water sloshes, the curve of his hip rising above the waves. Muscles cut a sharp path from his hip to the waterline, and I follow it with my gaze, tracing toward his pelvis. His broad shoulders block the moon, and I tear my gaze away. He reaches out his hand, claws glinting with the silver sheen of seawater, and watches me.

My heart thrums. I take his hand, cold and leathery, and his grip swallows my fingers. With a gentle tug, he lifts me to my feet.

Sunfish will stay, he says again. *You will be safe.*

His words land in my mind with the weight of a command; I have no choice but to be safe. He tightens his hold on my fingers, brushing the pad of his thumb over my knuckles. His gaze pierces mine, eyes a stormy gray.

Have his eyes always been that color? A few moments ago, I could have sworn they were pure black. Now, a distinct blue hue feathers the perimeter of each iris, like ice crusting over iron. The longer I stare, the lighter they fade. A pale gray now, swirling with threads of sapphire.

I can't stay, I tell him. *I have places to be, and I can take care of myself.* A cage will never hold me.

My only friend. He twists his hand, threading his webbed fingers through the gaps between mine. *Stay, please. For me. I will protect you.*

From what? I trace the thin membrane between his fingers, velvety to the touch. *You're the scariest thing around.*

I mean it as a joke, but his face twists in pain and a wash of regret filters through our mental connection. His thoughts jumble, clouds rising to block the answer from me.

Friends don't keep secrets, I tell him.

He drops my hand and takes a step backward.

Bitter wind breaks around his body, stinging my skin. My wet hair crusts to my skull, and my teeth chatter. I can't stand here much longer. I need to find shelter—fast.

On my breasts, the starfish lose their grasp, their suckers slowly freezing solid. I cup them in my hands to block the wind. The Beast tracks my movement, his pupils growing large.

Sunfish is cold? he asks.

You live in an ice trap, Beasty. I'm always cold.

The Beast snarls. Through our mental connection, he sends an image from his memory: my body curled into the corner of the frozen cell, golden tail covered in frost. His hands reach out, grabbing the bars and pulling him closer. In his memory, I glance up, and my eyes are hollow. Hungry. His distaste colors the memory, anger simmering at the edges.

The sun should not be dimmed, he says. The memory recedes into the swath of his thoughts.

He reaches for me again, running his hands over my bare arms. It's harmless, his touch, but still my stomach flutters.

He pulls me closer, blocking my body from the wind once more. His hands move up and down, and the friction generates a rush of heat.

I look away from his face, focusing on his broad chest. The scales shimmer with seawater, beads of it sliding down the muscled expanse. On his breastbone, the scales are thinner, sparse, revealing creamy white skin beneath. Without thinking, I reach out and brush the spot with my finger. It's smooth and cold, soft instead of leathery.

Has that spot always been there?

I spread my fingers, pressing against his chest. The Beast inhales sharply. Beneath my palm, I feel the heavy beating of his heart.

His breath bathes me on his exhale, smelling faintly of peppermint. Hooking his thumb beneath my chin, he tilts my face.

His eyes are pale, like a snowy sky, as I search his gaze, and he searches mine. On his cheek, the scales have thinned, too, revealing the same swath of creamy skin. When he smiles, his teeth are rounded like the dull canines of a siren.

How strange. That smile—I've seen it before, somewhere. The scales rise at the base of my neck as a tingle traces my spine.

Where have I seen it before?

Those teeth, the shape of his mouth, it almost looks like...

Go inside, Sunfish, he says. The deep rumble of his voice shatters my thoughts. With a gentle twist and a push, he aims me toward the gate. *I'll be here whenever you need me. Go. Be warm.*

The castle slumbers ahead of me, warm lamplight beckoning from its windows. Snow spirals in gentle flakes, dancing like glitter before the dark timber frame. A gust of wind howls over the sea, battering my hair and causing me to stumble forward. The cold stones clack beneath my feet.

Maybe if I come frozen blue and begging to the king, he'll finally impose his hospitality and grant me that damn fire I asked for.

It'll be warm inside. But can my pride withstand the blow?

I chew my lip, growing colder by the minute.

When I glance back, the Beast is gone, the only trace of him a small ripple on the surface of the Rime.

The frosted water stretches through the basin. Ice floes bob quietly, reflecting the colors of the aethersky above. If I'm fast, I could swim for it alone.

Fuck the king and his toasty warm castle. I could go home *right now*.

I step toward the water and cringe as my toe catches a frozen stone.

A low growl rises from the tide in warning.

The Beast will catch me. And then what? He'll drop me here again? Evoke a bit of déjà vu?

No. The Beast is unpredictable, but he's unlikely to make the same mistake twice.

My stomach sinks as I fold my arms across my chest and slouch into the wind. It nips at the wet corners of my eyes as I squint. My muscles are cold and weary. I need sleep, I need fire, and I need to get out of this godsdamn wind.

My pride can suffer one measly blow. It's only for tonight, after all. There's a warm castle to explore, a king to annoy, and I'm not about to let the opportunity pass me by.

Chapter Twenty-Seven

Aethan

This is a first, I'll admit. I've emerged from the sea naked many times. But never once with a boner. I'm naked. I'm horny. And I can't get the princess out of my head.

The guard unlocks the iron door to my chambers, averting his eyes from my stiffening cock.

I cross the room, activate the sight-pool, and adjust my view with a twitch of my fingers. Her cell is a pile of rubble, the gate torn free of its hinges. Chunks of ice stack on the floor. Neither guard nor princess are in sight.

I shuffle through the dungeon, slipping through the cavernous tunnels. The next cell, empty. The next, and the next. She's gone.

I slap the bowl, and it flies from its perch, shattering on the floor with a loud crack of porcelain.

Fuck.

I bury my fists in my eyes, groaning. How did I let this happen? What have I *done*? One minute I was in the dining room, inviting her to join me for a meal, and the next—*I made her my meal.*

The back of my neck tingles. My memory is here, in order. It's foggy and indecipherable, but I can make out the shapes. Me, charging from the castle. Plunging into the water. The transformation. My hands, grasping metal bars. Ripping. Swimming. Her ass, pressed against...

Mine.

I blink, and my gaze focuses on my lap. In the course of my reverie, my hand has circled the base of my cock. It swells in my hand, lengthening. One pump—to relieve the need.

No. I groan and release my length. *The princess could be dead.*

I play my memories again. The ripping. The swimming. The ass—skipping forward—the fear, the rage, icy hot and all-consuming.

Hunger.

Fuck.

With force, I push away from the desk, stand, and pace. I fist my hair, pulling until the pain sharpens my mind.

My stomach churns around a recent meal. Did I eat her?

Goddess. What have I done?

As I slip into my pants, I shove my offending cock inside the leather, then button my shirt and pull a cloak from the wardrobe.

I must find her—dead or alive.

I bang on the door until ten locks click in rapid succession and the door swings open. The guard stiffens to attention, eyes white and wide. "Your Majesty?"

"Gather a search party," I bark. "Now."

The sconces flare as I pass through the hall, flames fueled by the flap of my cloak behind me. The guard scurries to keep pace. "Right away, Sire. Who are we searching for?"

Will he be so accommodating once he learns my truth? Or will he abandon me with the rest of them, their once-king rightfully dethroned?

For if she's *not* dead, then she's a liability. A spy with a secret that doesn't belong to her. And that knowledge in the wrong fins can only mean trouble.

My voice turns hoarse. "The spy."

***

I STAND ON THE dark shore, waiting. Unmoving. Snow falls around me like dust, crusting my hair and melting against my face. A pile accumulates on my shoulders. The white powder sits in my periphery, washed in the colors of the aethersky.

The night wind is as restless and bitter as my thoughts, skittering across the waves and tossing the ice floes, seeping through my cloak to nip at my chest. But I will not leave this spot.

Ten of my Frost Guard have entered the Rime, searching for the princess I lost.

Or consumed.

What will they find? The rest of her, stowed in a cave somewhere? Or is she gone without a trace?

My stomach rolls. My tongue turns to sand in my mouth, and I vomit onto the stones. Chunks of meat float in the remnants. Pink and fresh, littered with dainty bones.

Goddess above.

I vomit again. Then again. I heave until my stomach wrings out like a cloth, squeezed of all that's left. Acid coats my tongue.

I can't unsee those bones. Small, fragile bones. Are they hers? Too small for an arm but maybe her fingers...

Again, I retch. My vision clouds, and I stumble toward the ground, settling on my knees. I tuck my head between them and squeeze my eyes shut. When I inhale, the acrid scent cloys my throat.

I'm losing my shit.

When the bile finally passes, I wipe my mouth and sway as dizziness sets in.

A stronger male might have sorted through the mess, just to be sure. But I cannot bear it. Instead, I cover the evidence, pushing stones to hide my weakness.

Finally, the water stirs, and my Frost Guard emerges. Water streams from their slick bodies, their tails rearrange, and the captain steps forward.

I stand to greet him, and my cold muscles protest.

His expression is sullen, shoulders slouching with an air of defeat. The guards behind him shuffle along, kicking the stones. I cringe as they narrowly miss my vomit.

"Your report, Captain," I say. My voice croaks, and I clear it as my cheeks flush.

He massages the ridge of his nose, shaking his head. "No luck, Sire."

My heart sinks. That's it, then. She's gone. At least they didn't find half of her. Either I consumed her entirely, and my secret is safe, or she got away.

Either way, I'm fucked.

I thank the Frost Guard for their service tonight, unable to meet the captain's inquisitive gaze. They shiver, standing tall as they try to hide their chattering teeth. They're good soldiers, all of them. It's too bad their king is a monster.

I grunt, turn toward the gate, and shuffle inside without another word.

As I approach the dining hall, Deirdre's voice floats through the night, cheerful and wide-awake. I quiet my footsteps and pause outside the door.

There's someone in the room with my housekeeper. Deirdre offers them tea, followed by the sound of splashing water. A clinking spoon.

Another voice answers the housekeeper—familiar and warm—and my heart trips.

"This is the last one, though. Any more tea and I think I might burst," the princess says with a giggle.

She's alive.

Chills spread over my body, lifting every scale. I stagger, gripping the doorframe. My forehead thumps against the wood.

Inside the room, footsteps approach.

She's alive.

Goddess, it makes me want to scream. Though for joy or annoyance, I can't say.

She's alive, and my secret lives with her.

Alive and giggling.

I couldn't have harmed her *that* much then. If she's feeling well enough to laugh?

The doorknob turns, and the door dips away from me. I exhale sharply and scramble to find my composure.

Light spills into the hallway, revealing the round face of my housekeeper. Her eyes are bleary and sleep-deprived but cheerful. Shock spreads over her features like a guppy caught stealing cookies.

"Your Majesty! I wasn't expecting you at this hour." She drops into a quick curtsy, rearranging her expression. "Did someone let you out, love? Are you okay?" she whispers.

"Do you ever sleep, Deirdre?"

"About as much as you do, Sire."

I peek into the candlelit room. Deirdre's silhouette blocks my view of the princess. I make out only her smooth, brown ankle tucked daintily around the leg of a chair.

If I could invoke her to turn with just a glare, I would. I stare at that small expanse of skin, willing it to move, for her foot to flatten on the floor, to stand and face me. I need to see her. All of her. Whole.

"Would you like some tea, Sire?" Deirdre hedges. I shift my gaze, locating the concern in her eyes. "I can bring it to your room."

"No, I'll take it in here."

"Are you sure, Sire? I've got... company."

The housekeeper opens the door wider, revealing the princess inside.

Her half-damp hair hangs behind her chair, catching the lamplight. She's wrapped in furs, curling her hands around a steaming mug of tea. She turns, and I meet her large, brown eyes.

My heart swells, threatening to punch through my ribs.

And like a complete idiot, I smile.

"Pour the tea, Deirdre."

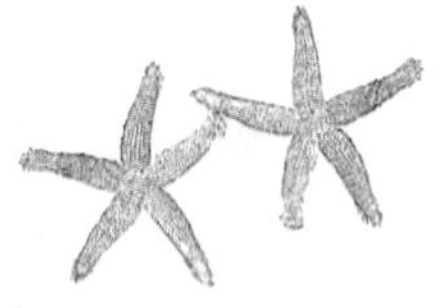

Chapter Twenty-Eight

NAHLA

For the first time since I left home, I'm properly warm. A fireplace crackles at one end of the dining room. Beneath the table, I dig my toes into the soft fibers of a furry rug. All thanks to the gentle female who found me wandering in the hallway, wrapped me in furs, and plopped me before the biggest pot of tea in my life. Four cups in, and I feel myself again.

How an asshole like the Frost King could keep staff like Deirdre is beyond me. She's much too nice, and I suspect blackmail. No other explanation holds water. In the matter of an hour, the kind housekeeper warmed me, cheered me, fed me, and got me thinking that I could stay here forever and we could be friends *if it wasn't for her asshole king.*

My shoulders slouch at the thought of him, ruining my peace.

The king, standing now at the doorway, looks like he's been hit by a fleetwhale. Frost crusts his hair, thawing to slide down his wind-bitten face. There's still snow on his cloak, and a pair of leather pants peek through the gap in its furs.

He sheds the cloak, hanging it from an iron rack near the door. I slide my gaze along his frame, noting the tapered slope of his waist. The slant of his shoulders. His skin is creamy white where it peeks through his shirt collar.

"Nahlani Mahelona," he greets me. A smile twists his mouth, devilishly handsome, and my stomach flips. "I see you're alive and well."

"Yes," I say, from my seat because *fuck* curtsies. "With no thanks to you, Aethan Nastrond." His full name feels foreign in my mouth. I lick my lips to clear the aftertaste.

His smile falls as quickly as it appeared. He steps into the room, followed by the friendly housekeeper. Him, a tower of ice. Her, soft and motherly, her gray hair hardly clearing his shoulder.

The king pulls out the chair across from me, scraping the legs across the floor. I cringe at the squeal of the wood. The large table stretches between us, on it Deirdre's teapot and my cooling mug of tea. Three candles burn low in the center candelabra, dripping wax.

He watches me, frosty eyes unblinking. Deirdre pours tea for him, adding a cube of sugar. He takes it and stirs, eyes never leaving my face. "Porridge, Deirdre."

"I won't leave Her Highness alone with you. The poor girl thinks you're unpleasant, Sire, and you've yet to prove her wrong."

I smirk. *Unpleasant* is not exactly what I told her. The king's eyes tighten, and I hope he knows I meant *asshole*. I mouth the word at him, just in case.

His eyes darken. Still, the king stares. A chill traces the base of my neck. I touch my cheek, searching for crumbs and finding none.

"I'll take her to her room first, if that's okay with Your Majesty," Deirdre continues.

My heart soars. I could kiss her right now. *A room?* No more frozen cage. No more boredom. No ceiling tunnels or cranky Vaughn.

No more visits from the Beast.

The emotional whiplash is fierce. Joy and pain twist together, ripping through my chest.

He'll be all alone, without a friend. The aching sadness in his mind was clear at our parting—and the guilt pierces me now.

But he told me to get warm. Practically pushed me onto the beach.

I shouldn't feel badly.

And yet...

"Her room?" the king echoes, his stare unwavering.

"Yes, Sire."

He frowns. "Show her in a moment. I'll take the porridge first, please."

The housekeeper doesn't move. She stands next to him, wringing her hands. She frowns and shoots me one last worrisome glance. "If he comes after you, love, just whack him. I'll take the heat."

Finally, he breaks his stare, watching as she exits through the service door at the back of the room.

Silence settles in her absence. I can't decide which version of him I like least—the restless, angry pacing king from the throne room or this frozen, quiet one.

The silence stretches another minute. I trace the wood grains in the table, following the sweeping curves and knots with my fingernail. What I'd give to get inside *his* mind, if only for some noise.

I can't bear it any longer. "I like her," I say, nodding toward the door.

He lifts his eyebrow, a perfect arch of white hair. "Most do."

"She's nice." *Unlike you.*

Silence falls again, and I internally curse myself for making it awkward. My ears burn under his gaze.

The king leans back in his chair, crossing his arms over his chest. His forearms flex, a thick vein rising. "You have trouble following the rules," he says.

"Rules are meant to be broken, don't you know?"

"No, Princess." He turns his face, and the candlelight catches the sharp line of his jaw, the plane of his cheek. From this angle, he looks almost beastly. Powerful. "Rules keep you safe."

His voice drops in timbre, deep as thunder.

My heart quickens its pace.

I've read the royal directory before. In his entry, there's not much there. A few sentences at most. King Aethan Nastrond is known for his cold demeanor, with a personality to match the rugged terrain. Ascended to the throne while he was young. Then one word: *secretive*. No physical description.

The king is hiding something. Something he doesn't want the rest of us to know.

I flick through the options, considering each one: fertility issues, perhaps, or a sex dungeon. A hoard of the undead penned in the backyard.

"Aren't you going to ask me how I got out of my cage?" I whisper.

His jaw unhinges, dropping an inch before he snaps it shut again. "Tell me, how did you summon the clawbeast?"

That's what he wants to know? Not how I managed not to starve or freeze to death? "None of your business, Blizzard Balls."

He bristles, shoulders rolling, jaw clenching. "I'm the king. Everything is my business here."

"Not me. You're not my king."

I glare at him, hoping he can feel every ounce of my hatred. *Motherfucker. Land-dwelling King of the Assholes.* But these insults never reach his ears. I'm nearing the line, and one more wrong word from my mouth and it's back to the ice cage for me.

The king folds his arms on the table and leans forward. "Especially you, Sunshine."

I narrow my eyes. That word, from his lips. It almost sounded like *Sunfish*.

He smiles, white teeth glinting in the candlelight. Round, white teeth.

I shake my head, clearing my suspicion. I'm exhausted, and a week in freezing water hasn't done my brain any favors.

His big dark secret is probably just a sex dungeon, nothing more. I'm letting my imagination get away from me.

At that moment, Deirdre returns, carrying a tray with a steaming bowl. She sets it before the king and sweeps her assessing gaze over me. Pleased, she nods.

"Ready for bed, love? I'll get you settled in the East Wing."

The king dips his spoon into the porridge. "The queen's quarters?" he protests.

"Yes, Sire. Unless you'd rather give her *your* bed, it's the only room halfway decent these days."

He glances up. His eyes darken suddenly. Hungry. His tongue darts out, swiping over his lips.

Deirdre's eyes widen, and she sucks in a breath. "My apologies, Sire. I've come all undone. I don't know why I suggested that." On cue, her mouth parts and stretches in a yawn. Poor thing.

"Go to bed, Deirdre," the king says, rising from his chair. "Please. I'll show her the room myself."

When he turns his smolder on me, his eyes—for a moment—are soft.

Chapter Twenty-Nine

Aethan

The two females exchange a weary glance. Deirdre hesitates, seeming to pull strength from the look in the princess's eyes. "I won't leave Her Highness alone," she says, swaying on her feet.

The princess shrugs. "I'll be alright, Deirdre. I think I can handle him." Her gaze swivels to me, daring.

Handle? My cock twitches.

"But, Sire—"

"Please, Deirdre. You're exhausted. Let me take care of it."

Deirdre doesn't fight me for long. After one final protest, she dips her head and submits to my offer, leaving us to fend for ourselves.

Me and the princess.

Alone.

Everything about her screams *trouble*.

What could go wrong?

"Come on, then," I say, before she tries to fill the silence with something frivolous or irrelevant. The quicker I get this done, the better. It's a favor for Deirdre. And nothing more.

I may not like guests, but I can still be an excellent host, dammit.

I retrieve my cloak from the rack and head for the East Wing, swallowing the anxiety that prickles my throat.

She follows me, feet quiet on the wooden floor. Sconces flicker in the wind of our passing. In a few hours, dawn will break, and daylight will stream through the windows as the aethersky fades. Until then, we move in a cocoon of near darkness.

"I have a few requests for my room," she says.

"You assume you have a say."

"Somewhere with a window, if possible," she continues, ignoring my comment. What's she planning, another escape mission? My fists clench at my sides.

"Fireplace, like I said before. An attached bathroom would be nice. And a bookshelf..."

"So you can read your romance novels?" I snap.

"You assume because I'm female, I must like romance novels?"

"What? No. I just meant..." My jaw grinds, and I trail off. I'm not sure why I said it.

Something tickles my mind. Something about a sweetnut tree. Sunset rays. A guppy with curly hair. Guilt trails a cold claw down my spine. This young male in the Beast's memory, is it her lover she left at home?

"You strike me as the type to crave a happily ever after," I mutter. There. That should be enough flattery to shut her up.

She inhales, readying to speak again.

Or not.

"I read other things, too. Lately I've been into grimoires." She catches up to me, and in my periphery, I spot her smirk.

She searches my face for something, then frowns. Disappointed in me? Get used to it, Princess.

"Sounds better than romance," I say.

"How so?"

"Magic, unlike romance, is predictable. You guide your intent, and the spell happens as you imagine it. Romance..." Why am I telling her this?

At the end of the hallway, I spot our destination. Relief washes through me. Just a few more moments with her, and my duty is done.

I glance at my hands. No sign of the scales, yet. Despite the princess's insistence on annoying me with her questions. I can do this. I can keep it under control.

"Romance is what?" she presses.

"It's misleading. Guppy's play. And it never goes as planned." I stop abruptly, turning to face the door to the suite, and she walks into me.

Her starfish-clad breasts press into my arm, bundled in soft fur, and I hiss through my teeth. She's too close. My cock flexes, aroused by the touch, by the thought of taking those breasts, soft and supple in my hands.

"Your room." I sidestep to break the contact, like a fucking gentleman.

It's the only room I've kept clean the past ten years besides my own. No guests mean no reasons to keep spare beds, which is a blessing for my staff, but has put me in a bit of a crunch tonight.

I have no other choice.

With a deep breath, I open the door and let it swing wide. She tiptoes inside, peering into the dark room. I know the layout by heart. There's a large bed in the center, a writing desk to the left. Two plush chairs frame the fireplace on the right, next to a handsome bookshelf. The whole room is painted in a deep muted blue, too dark to see clearly now. In the morning, light will stream through the single window, chasing away the horrors of the night.

This is my mother's room. When we moved ashore, I had it made up for her, on the off chance I've been wrong, that she'll come back from the dead, walk through my front door, and demand a place to rest her weary feet.

Every week, I make sure the sheets are fresh. Just in case.

Inviting the princess here feels strangely like bringing a female home to meet my parents.

My fingers find the top desk drawer. I rummage for a match to light a few squat candles on the desk. The strike breaks the silence, and flame flares with a hiss of smoke.

"Oh," she gasps. "It's beautiful."

It's dusty. The air is cold, the fireplace empty. A few stacks of dry wood rest on the hearth, collecting silkmite webs. I cross the room, then squat to arrange the wood. My fingers are numb, beginning to stain blue, and my heart races.

Heat to quench the anger, bran to stave the hunger, darkness to calm the fight.

I need heat. Now. Before I lose control. Maybe I can stave it off. I've already transformed once tonight. What's the likelihood of it happening twice?

With another match, I light the kindling. The sticks crackle and pop as the fire grows. I hover my hands over the logs, much too close to the flame.

"Did you decorate this?" she asks, and I turn to see.

Her curls catch the candlelight, glinting bronze, and she looks almost regal. She walks with a certain sureness, a spunky twitch in the swing of her hips. She peers around, running her hands over the frame of the bed, the blue velvet curtains.

"No. It's all Deirdre."

My chest burns, watching her. Is she impressed? I let my imagination wander, just this once. Her, living here long term. Her, curled in a reading chair. A romance novel on her lap. Deirdre tottering through the doorway with endless cups of tea.

No guard at her door, because this is where she *wants* to be. It wouldn't be so bad, would it?

Would she learn to like me? Could we be friends?

More?

Hunger for her claws at my heart, sharp and fierce with sudden desire. The longer I watch her, the more I want it. Want her, under my care. A chance to tame that troublesome tongue.

Earlier tonight, I thought she was dead and nearly succumbed to my relief. But I know I could not live with myself if I let that nightmare come true.

The princess turns toward the bookshelf, her eyes widening. Her fingers trace the stony spines. In the candlelight, her face falls into shadow, her eyes reflecting the flame. Watching me, from the corner of her eye.

She's fucking beautiful.

Who am I to desire the likes of her?

"Are you trying to catch yourself on fire?" she asks.

I glance at my hands. The flames lick at my skin, hot, but not hot enough. The Beast prowls the periphery of my mind, refusing to submit.

When I look at her, I feel him growl. Possessive.

I yank my hands from the fire.

"That should keep you warm until dawn. The washroom is through that door." I point to the attached doorway next to the wardrobe. "Good night."

I practically run from the room. My foot knocks a bucket of iron firesticks, and they clatter to the floor. Pain throbs through my big toe. I hop over the mess, send her an apologetic smile, and hurry to the door.

"Good night, Grumpy Gills," she calls after me with a muffled giggle.

I pause at the doorway, gripping the frame, and allow myself one last glance.

Her eyes shine in the amber glow of the fire. She drags her appraising gaze over me, and a warm pink colors her cheeks. And *damn* she looks good in a blush.

My stomach twists into a tight knot, and the truth punches me square in my chest.

I'm in trouble. And if I'm not more careful, trouble will lure me somewhere I can't afford to go—deeply, irrevocably obsessed with her, the princess I've made my prisoner.

Chapter Thirty

Nahla

"Coming up, you'll find the throne room to your right." Deirdre gestures to an engraved wooden door. "The king is in there now, so I can't show you. Perhaps another time."

"That's okay. I've seen it already." I shiver at the memory of my first time in that room. The king prowled before me, deciding my fate.

Asshole.

We round a turn, and I adjust my mental map of the building. It's a minimalistic layout for a king. Winona's palace is thrice its size, at least. And he doesn't have a ballroom. Apparently, this used to be the royals' warm-season home, and all the balls were held in the courtyard under the moon.

So far, I've found only two ways out of the castle—one door shore-side, another back-side into the courtyard. Centered in the building is a grand parlor with a lofted timber-frame ceiling, housing a double staircase to the second floor. The primary floor holds the kitchen, dining hall, and throne room. From the second-floor landing, the eastern wing leads to guest rooms and the queen's quarters, the western to the king's residence and library.

It's a gorgeous home. The architecture has a handsome simplicity, dark and cozy. The style suits him. Efficient. His family's wealth is subtle, built into the quality of the imported wood, the richness of tapestry and furs. He keeps no superfluous sitting rooms or expensive knick-knacks. A practical king—Winona will never believe me.

I smile, admiring his choices despite myself, as I trail my fingers along the wall. My fingers catch the hem of a navy-blue wall-hanging, and I lean closer to inspect it. Intricate leather stitching, done by someone's careful hand. I inhale. It smells like him.

Perrin clears his throat, a gentle signal for me to move along. All morning, the young guard has trailed our little tour of three, pointing out his favorite paintings along the way, much to my delight.

His company is the best I could ask for in my glorified imprisonment. Perrin said the library is beautiful, but I have yet to see it.

Ahead of us, a scattered line of merfolk spans the length of the hallway. They hold various baskets and bags, their expressions troubled. Frowning. A few mermaids sit on the floor, tracing lazy patterns in the wood while their eyes glaze over.

The door swings open, and a male guard pokes his head out. "Next," he calls. The first merman in line enters the room, and the line shuffles forward.

Winona's supplication days aren't this somber. With free cake and tea for every subject who comes, the Brine celebrates whenever she opens her doors to their complaints.

I used to think her style was overkill. Wasteful. But seeing the opposite makes my heart ache. When I smile at a Frost mermaid, she looks past me with a listless frown. Her fingers twist the tail of her braid.

Maybe Winona was right. She wasn't superfluous, but *generous*. Maybe a little pageantry goes a long way.

Deirdre steers us through the hall, avoiding contact with the waiting line, and we enter the grand parlor. "It isn't usually this crowded," she mutters. "Come, I'll show you the healer's room, in case you need to find Lucas."

I file his name away.

"Our staff isn't big. It's me, the handmaids you met in the kitchen, the chef, the librarian, and the healer. We're a tight-knit group."

"And me, too, Auntie," Perrin pipes in, hopping on his good foot to keep up.

Deirdre flashes him a warm smile. "Yes, and you too, love. Though the guards keep their quarters in the barracks."

We take a side door, then descend a flight of stairs. The air grows damp and cold, smelling of salt and aged wood. The scraping sound of Perrin's crutch echoes deep into the chamber below.

"This is the servant quarters," Deirdre explains, stopping to turn up the wick of a sconce on the wall.

She stops before the first door and raps on it three times. The knob turns, and the door swings in to reveal the tall, thin male who visited my cell on the first night.

The healer's gaze lands on me, and my skin prickles with a sudden chill. "Hello, m'lady," he says, flicking his eyes over me. A wry smile curves. "Are you still experiencing pain in your rear end?"

I grin. "Yep. Still there, I'm afraid."

Behind me, Perrin coughs.

Deirdre shoots me a puzzled look. "Do you require medical attention, Your Highness?"

"No, no. Just an old joke."

I peer over the healer to glimpse the room within. It's cluttered with trinkets and vials. A fire burns low in the hearth beyond, casting a golden glow on the mounted head of an animal.

"You're welcome any time," Lucas says. "Perhaps we could explore your thoughts on magic, m'lady. I'd be happy to take another look."

His eyebrow arches, his gold-flecked eyes boring into mine. What the fuck does *that* mean?

"During daylight hours, of course," he adds.

Deirdre exchanges a glance with the healer, a flicker of tension in her eyes.

"Yes, well, we'll continue with the tour. Not much else to see down here. My room is there, darling. Second door on the left." The housekeeper points, then shoos us toward the stairs. "Shall I show you the library?"

"You mean I hobbled all the way down here for nothing?" Perrin complains, casting a weary look at the stairwell. He drops his voice to a whisper and speaks sideways from his mouth so only I can hear. "Fuck me, Nahla, why can't we just swim?"

"Don't let her catch you saying that," I whisper, reaching out to ruffle his sandy hair. Perrin's ears darken, and he shoots me a wry grin.

"Life's full of disappointments, I'm afraid." The healer's voice sounds closer than I expected. I glance back to find him still in the doorway, leaning against the frame with his ankles crossed. His eyes remain steady on my face.

"Up you go, love. You'll be all right now." Deirdre helps her nephew get started up the stairs.

As I wait, I peer around the hallway—anywhere to avoid looking Lucas in the eye. The ceiling is low, dripping with moisture. There's a gap between the stairwell and the far wall, leaving barely enough room to stand.

Light catches my eye from a pool of water on the floor. I step sideways, careful not to draw attention from Deirdre. Craning my neck, I peer around the corner to get a better look.

There, in the space between broken floorboards, is a hole full of water wide enough to fit the shoulders of a grown-ass male. A crust of ice clings to the top, cracked in a few places. Around the hole, several marks scar the wooden planks. Like fingers grasping for purchase.

"Coming, Your Highness?" Deirdre calls.

I scrutinize the hole, trying to compute its purpose. An escape hatch, perhaps? But that doesn't explain the marks. Something has been getting *in*, not out.

My toe catches, kicking an object across the floor. I bend to pick it up—a small, blue scale, dark as midnight.

The same shade as the clawbeast's hide.

My mouth goes dry.

Is the Beast *here*, inside somewhere? Hope flares. I didn't know he could venture on land, much less kept a room in the king's castle.

"Careful, now," Lucas warns. I leap from my skin. "Don't want to go poking where we don't belong."

I turn to face the healer, clutching the scale in my fist. He pins me with a cautionary look and spreads his arms toward the stairwell.

"You're getting lost, Princess. Better hurry."

I tuck the scale into my front pocket and hurry up the stairs.

CHAPTER THIRTY-ONE

AETHAN

THREE CUPS OF TEA, and I'm still not awake enough for this. I recline on my fur-lined throne, bracing my body against the wooden frame to keep from slumping over in my seat.

After minimal hours of sleep, I was dragged from my bed by an equally irritated Lucas, who so kindly reminded me I'd promised to hold court this morning. A fucking kingly duty, to endanger the masses.

An ache throbs through my temple, drowning out the complaints of my subject, who kneels before me in tattered furs. He's a hunter, by the looks of his garb and the haunted look in his eyes. He's middle-aged, gray hair streaking through his slick white braid. Siren ears poke through the strands, smoothed by his magic.

From his neck hangs a bone pendant, carved in the likeness of a pikewhale. With rough hands, he grasps it, drawing upon its strength, and mumbles something under his breath.

"Speak louder," I snap. The ache pounds, a dull roar in my ears. A flinch crosses the siren's face, and my stomach sours.

Lucas is right. I'm the shittiest king to grace this throne. I itch to stand, to distance myself from my ancestral seat. But I grip the armrest, holding myself in place. I take a steadying breath, then add, "Please."

He straightens. "Thank you for granting me this audience, Your Majesty. Hunter Leon, at your service. I believe we're long overdue."

He releases the bone pendant from his fist and lets it swing from the string. I watch the bone figure move, back and forth, until it settles.

"This belonged to my son," Leon says. "Not two weeks ago, I retrieved his body from my doorstep. Or what was left of it. Along with blubberchips and wine, stamped with the royal crest."

My memory flashes, and I spiral back in time to the beach. The silver siren hair. Mottled, frozen flesh, ripped by claws. The day I severed Perrin's foot.

"Audrina rest his scales," I say, the words like ice on my tongue.

"May I speak freely, Your Majesty?"

I spread my hands in invitation.

"Twelve years ago, we moved ashore on your orders. We've been careful to avoid the water, and we've learned to hunt the beasts of the land. But it's been hard. Joa, he…" He clutches the pendant more tightly. "You couldn't take the water from my son if you tried, and I tried, Your Majesty. It was part of him. As it's part of all of us. Frostcats and woollygoats aren't as challenging to hunt as pikewhales. Where's the thrill? Where's the honor? And Joa's not the first we've lost to the clawbeast. Now, we're a dying breed. Forty hunters dead, Your Majesty. And the killings have only increased in frequency."

I run the math. "Forty-two."

His stare grows cold. "Too many. How many of our guppies must we needlessly bury before we act? Let me gather a hunting party and track the clawbeast. I'll rid the Rime of it once and for all."

The siren snarls, his face twisting with vindicated anger. Shame that his blame is misguided. The villain sits in front of him now, comfortably reclining on a throne of furs.

I sigh. "You will not win."

"We must try."

"No."

"You deny my right to avenge the life of my son?" He tilts his face, giving me a clear view of his expression. If he knew the truth, he'd kill me on the spot.

I motion for the guards. "I deny you the right to decide for this kingdom. That is my responsibility to bear."

"You are blessed with the siren's Voice. You built homes for us near the plains with your magic, and we are grateful for your generosity. You are powerful, Your Majesty. Build a barrier beneath the waves. Give us a portion of the Rime to hunt as we please, according to our tradition. A fishing grounds. If it pleases Your Majesty."

I flare my nostrils. "It won't work. The clawbeast can't be contained. Tell your pod to stay ashore, hunter. My order remains unchanged."

The guards lift him, and Leon shoots me a glare. "Thank you for your time." He seethes. "I half hoped you'd respect mine."

My pulse roars in my ears. Cold tingles my fingers, and the blue scales spread.

Leon follows my gaze. His brow puckers, forming a tight V.

The guards pull him from his stance and escort him from the room.

I clench my fist. With a sharp bark of my Voice, I shoot a stream of ice after the hunter. The shards embed in the closing door.

Keep it together, Aethan. You killed the male's son. Let him go.

I draw deep breaths and wrack my brain for a warm memory—anything to chase the anger away—and plunge into the first one that arises.

I stand beneath a palmwood, sunshine burning hot on my back. My hands sting from the scrape of bark. My toes dig into the grooves, gathering sap as I climb. Higher. I'm sweating. My hand reaches out, aiming for a large, fuzzy fruit hanging in a bunch between broad green leaves.

But this isn't my memory.

It's hers.

When I look down, a female guppy stands with outstretched hands. She looks like Princess Nahlani, with a sharper face and stern brown eyes. Her sister. I grasp the fruit and let it fall into her waiting hands.

Whatever magic the princess has in her veins, it's saved me more than once. My scalp prickles as I recall her face one more time, scrunched in a sassy smirk. I smile as the warmth eases my nerves.

A confused pair of guards stand several paces away, careful to avoid the shards of ice that part the room.

"Shall we invite the next subject, Sire?"

With a dry throat, I form a spell and melt the ice. "Bring them in."

The complaints come in waves. A mother grieves her son who will never use his tail. A noble says the winds are too cold this year; I should build higher walls. A hunter reveals the lack of local game. Then another.

By the third hunter's arrival with the same complaint, my stomach is in knots. I drum my fingers on the armrest. Is this an issue I can remedy, without opening fishing grounds?

"How far have you expanded your hunt?" I ask the hunter before me now, a tall female named Cyrene.

She runs a restless hand over the tail of her braid. "Two days' ride across the plains. We haven't dared to go farther. There's no telling what's out there, Your Majesty, and the hunters lose morale venturing too far from the sea."

"And how have the mounts fared?"

"The wind is brutal, but the snowbears are better suited to it than we are."

"I see." I press my fingertips together, forming a pyramid before my chest. "When is your next excursion?"

"We leave in two days, but we're struggling to gather recruits." Her expression is grim. "The hunters don't want to waste their time if there's no game, Sire. They'd rather risk their time in the water."

I close my eyes and let the guilt wash over me. I'm failing them all. Cyrene. Leon. The rest of the hunters. Lucas. Deirdre. Perrin. My entire kingdom.

They need leadership, encouragement, and vision. All the things I cannot give.

"I'm afraid, Your Majesty. If we can't find a solution, my comrades will continue to face tragedy." Cyrene shifts her weight, furs rustling.

With renewed determination, I meet her gaze. What is a king if not a symbol of leadership? A pageantry of hope—even if he has none?

I form my words carefully. "If their king would join them on the plains, would that boost morale?"

Her eyes widen. "Yes, of course, Your Majesty. It'd be an honor."

My nerves clench at the instant approval. Was I rash to suggest it? Can I do this safely?

This curse requires I touch water before the Beast fully emerges. The Frosted Plains are a vast stretch of glacial ice, far from the reach of the sea. If I can't complete the transformation, maybe it will keep the Beast at bay.

A bud of hope unfurls in my stomach, sweet and reckless. What if this has been the answer all along?

I don't need Lucas's research or routines. I just need to disappear in the vast, white north.

Cyrene awaits my response. "I will join you, then," I grunt. "Ready a mount for me."

CHAPTER THIRTY-TWO

AETHAN

It's late by the time I leave the throne room and make my way to the parlor. The castle is quiet and dark, the loudest sound the soft crackling of torches and the distant creaking of ice floes on the Rime. I massage the tension from my jaw. My throat is parched from speaking all day, and my body aches for the soft relief of my furs.

How do I expect to fare on a hunt? Sitting in a saddle in the cold wind, or giving speeches to boost morale? Fuck. What if the ice cracks and I fall in—my secret exposed by beastly rampage? A chill runs up my spine.

It's not possible. The Frosted Plains stretch across a meters-thick crust of ice that never melts, even in the warm season. The hunters will be safe from me. I'll ride my own mount away from the others, so that way if...

My thoughts scramble as I reach the stairway, my scales rising with intuition—I'm no longer alone. A shadowed female figure stands at the top of the steps, the white of her night-robe shimmering in the darkness. Silk, likely. She tiptoes, peering over the railing in the other direction from me. Her dark curls hang loosely down her back and brush the top of her shapely rear end, which the hem barely covers.

I pause.

She takes a few steps down, then leans over the rail, as if straining to see something in the near-darkness. The hem lifts. Black lace clings to the curves of her ass cheeks, delicate and much too scant. My breath catches and warmth floods my face. Who gave her such things to wear in public?

A quick scan of the parlor proves we're alone, to my twisted satisfaction. There are no watchful eyes on her. Only mine.

I clear my throat, and the princess whirls around, letting out a muffled gasp.

"You shouldn't be here," I say.

Her startled expression changes swiftly into annoyance. "And why not?"

"It's late." I step onto the bottom stair and grasp the railing. "You don't know what could be lurking in the shadows."

"Is that supposed to scare me?" She glances over the railing again, and I track her gaze. The door to the servant quarters is closed, and it's past the time Deirdre and Lucas turn in for the night. What could she want down there?

"If you need a cup of tea, I'm sure Deirdre would be more than happy to serve you. In your *room*."

"No, thank you."

"You expect me to believe Your Highness is wandering the halls at night, not in search of tea, after you've already had a tour of the castle grounds. How curious." I step up again, closing the gap between us. "You see why I must assume you're up to no good."

"Certainly not." She lifts her chin defiantly. *Cute.* But if she wants to intimidate me, she should try being less adorable.

"Then what are you up to?"

Her fingers trail along the banister as she steps down. I catch a whiff of her scent on the air, sweet vanilla and sunlight. For a moment, my eyelids flutter closed, and when I catch her eye again, she smirks. Looks at me from beneath her lashes.

"Nothing good," she says. She takes a few more steps, and she glances around me, as if meaning to pass. A bold choice.

Annoyance blooms in my chest, and I grip the railing tighter. It was a mistake to bring her inside. I should have known she'd get under my scales. Guests always do, but *this* one is doing it on purpose.

"Have you always been this much trouble?"

"Oh yes. Winona was sick of me."

"Is that why she abandoned you here?" I snap, stepping into her path. She frowns and tries to skirt around me. I move to block her again, and we're face to face. The princess, still two steps up, meets my eye level. Large, brown eyes, sparkling with mischief.

"Abandoned *me*?" She scoffs. "No, that's why she wanted to ship me off..." Her face contorts. "I don't have to explain myself to you, Peppermint Breath. If it weren't for *your* obsession with imprisoning passersby, I would be out of your hair by now." She jabs her finger at my chest, and I catch it, holding it there.

We both stare at our hands, her small fist curled up in mine. Her skin is soft and the tip of her finger is warm where she touches the thin fabric of my shirt.

"Peppermint Breath?" I echo.

Her throat bobs as she swallows. "I could be in the Coral Kingdom by now, getting married on a beach. Somewhere warm and sunny, two things you'd never understand." She tugs against my grasp, and I release her hand as the weight of her suggestion lands.

"You're engaged to the Coral Prince, and you didn't think to *mention* it?" I rake my hand through my hair. If that cocky prince learns I've held his betrothed hostage, I'm fucked. The Coral Kingdom has wealth, influence, and assuming he's already planned her rescue, the element of surprise.

"It never came up." She blushes and avoids my gaze, twisting her hands together. I glance at her fingers. No ring. Odd.

"You *are* betrothed?"

She bites her lip. "That's right."

She's lying.

"My condolences to the happy couple."

Her jaw drops, and the fire returns to her gaze. "What does *that* mean?"

"Have you met the prince?"

"Well, no."

"You won't like him. He's too cocky."

"And *you're* any better?" She raises her finger to jab me again but seems to think twice about it. Smart girl.

She crosses her arms beneath her breasts instead, and I struggle to keep my gaze on her face. A gentleman would keep his eyes steady. Or stare at the ceiling.

Not me.

I risk one quick glance, and my mouth goes dry. Her nipples are hard through the silk. *Goddess above*, they're perfect. My ears burn as I force myself to look away.

She must be cold, wearing that thin little thing at night. It has nothing to do with me.

"If anything, I suffer from the opposite problem," I grunt. The Coral Prince could learn a lesson or two from me in self-loathing.

"I'm sorry to hear about the size of your package, Sergeant Smalls. You know there's a tonic for that." Nahlani wrinkles her nose and flicks her gaze to my crotch. "Now if you'll excuse me—"

She tries to step around me, and I snare her waist. My hands slide on the silk of her robe as I twist her into the railing. I frame her with my hands, caging her where she can't escape me. Her scent floods my nose, intoxicatingly sweet.

She stares at me with wide, wild eyes. Her lips part, glistening and pink, as her breath brushes my neck.

Kiss her, says the Beast. *See if she tastes like the sun.*

I shake my head. Where is he getting this from? I pound my fist into the railing to dispel the intrusive thought. "Are you engaged to him?" I demand.

"That's my personal business, Your Majesty."

Infuriating, stubborn female. I inhale and try to steady my tone.

"I need to know if I should expect his goddessdamn army on my doorstep, so tell me now, Nahlani. Does he have a claim on you?" My voice booms with an edge of hysteria. So much for steady.

She flinches, shrinking into the railing.

Fuck.

With a growl, I tear myself away from her, putting distance between us before I can do physical harm. Ice burns in my veins, power churning beneath the surface.

Inhale. Exhale. Count to ten.

She watches me with a guarded gaze but does not turn to leave. We stare at each other for a long moment, and my panicked breathing fills the silence as I wrestle for control. Dizziness darkens my vision, narrowing my tunnel of view until all that's left is her face.

"Are you okay, Your Majesty?" she whispers. Pity flashes across her features as she softens. Her brows knit, and she steps tentatively forward. Like *I'm* the one in danger of *her*.

I clench my teeth. "Answer my question, please."

"I didn't accept the engagement. I..." She shakes her head. "I ran away."

"So no one's coming to look for you, Princess?"

"Probably not."

I pinch the bridge of my nose and close my eyes as relief washes over me. She is unclaimed. Not a spy. Not a death-dealer. Not betrothed to a foreign prince. Just a lost troublemaker, far from home. I sway on my feet, weariness hitting me as my feelings settle and the ice retreats from my veins.

When I open my eyes, she's still there, fiddling nervously with the ties of her robe. Her shoulders slump in defeat. How brave, to admit the truth. She's all alone with no one to look out for her. No one to save her from me.

"Then you are mine to protect," I grunt. *Mine*, the Beast purrs with approval. He likes the way she smiles in return, and the blush that creeps over her cheeks.

I like it, too.

"Good luck," she says; that sparkle of mischief flashing anew.

"That doesn't mean you can wander around my castle," I warn. "My rules still stand. Go back to your room."

She glances one more time toward the servant quarters, then turns away. "Fine." Her fingers slide over the railing as she ascends, a slight sway in her hips.

A smile tugs my lips. "Good night."

# Chapter Thirty-Three

Nahla

I DREAM OF THE hole in the basement floor, gaping wide like a mouth of razored teeth. Creatures of the night crawl out and haunt the castle, scratching their long nails on my door. Digging ruts in the wood. Claws screeching. High-pitched and piercing, like gulls on the wind. And the Frost King stands there, watching but doing nothing.

I wake sweaty, tangled by silken sheets and pillows.

With a gasp, I tear from the bed and drag the curtain open. It's not quite dawn. Thick gray clouds blanket the horizon and enshroud the glacial bowl.

I pull a fresh night-robe from the wardrobe and cinch its belt at my waist. With a match, I light a candle. My heart keeps time with the adrenaline from my nightmare. If I could just check the hole, I could return to sleep...

Lifting my candle to dispel the shadows, I turn the doorknob and push into the hallway. A figure stirs next to the door. Perrin's slouched form squints into the light, then raises a hand to shield his eyes.

"Nahla?"

"Sorry, Perrin. Just going for a walk."

He yawns, his mouth puckering. "Sorry, no can do." His forearm drops to block my path.

"Pardon?"

"King's orders, as of this morning. You're not to leave your room."

His words scramble like bumblefish in my brain. Not to leave...? Then it clicks.

"I'm a prisoner again, aren't I?"

The youngling nods solemnly.

"Then why is my door unlocked?" I press.

He blushes, then checks the keys at his hip. "Right."

"Perrin," I say, keeping my tone as even as I can manage. "I'd like a word with the king."

Perrin makes a show of unhooking his keys and fitting one into the lock. He gives me a gentle push into the room. "Sorry, Princess, I'm under strict orders." As the door clicks shut, I hear him mutter once more, "Sorry, Nahla."

I lean against the door with a heavy thud and survey my new prison. Godsdammit. This shit again? What did I say to him last night to piss him off so badly? Was it the stupid dick joke?

The guest suite is better than an ice block, that's for sure. I've got a dwindling fire, a stack of books, a washroom, a warm bed, and a view of the sun. Technically, he fulfilled all my initial requests.

How *chivalrous*.

How fucking arrogant.

I thought we had a *moment* last night. I shared my secrets and he...

Well, he let me overshare, that's what, and he didn't return the favor. Just some heavy breathing and a lot of staring at my breasts. Fuck, I should've seen it coming.

I pace the floor, determined to track a trench in it. There's no telling how long I'll be here. And I won't waste the rest of my life following that Frosted Fiasco's silly rules.

As I wait for Deirdre to arrive, I form my escape plan.

The housekeeper dresses me, feeds me, and leaves me with a full tea pot and a stoked fire, muttering apologies all the while. I assure her it's no problem, better than the ice dungeon, and this seems to soothe her a bit.

As soon as she leaves, I set to work.

The sheets come off the bed easily. I roll them and tie them together with double knots, then yank the curtains next. Soon enough, I've fashioned a rope long enough to lower me from the window.

After anchoring the rope to the heavy bed, I check the window. The latch is jammed. I cram my fingers trying to move the mechanism and give up when I rip a fingernail. *Shit.*

I need a club, or something heavy enough to break through. The iron fire poker catches my eye. That'll work. If all goes well, I won't be staying here much longer. I heft it and swing at the glass. It shatters with a delightful tinkle, spraying shards into the snow-drenched alley below.

My heart pounds. Perrin certainly heard that. Pausing, I strain my ears for any sense of his movement. But nothing comes.

Quickly, I slip my feet into the snowleathers Deirdre set out for me. Then I stuff the rope out the window and, avoiding broken glass, crawl out the jagged hole after it. My wool skirts snag on the glass, and I yank them free with a rip of the cloth. I clench the rope with my legs, and inch my way past a window, praying to the gods the room is empty. My heart beats loud enough in my ears, I won't be able to hear them if they shout.

Finally, I land in a snowbank next to the first-floor window, feet sinking deep. A shadow moves inside, and I duck, face-planting into the snow.

The cold flares, spreading through my body, and I hiss. How do these Frost fuckers *live* like this? Their climate is terrible. Give me sunshine and thunderstorms any day. A warm ocean breeze rattling through the palmwoods or the call of squawkbirds in the air. Will I ever hear home again?

Not if I stand still.

Crouching beneath the windowsill, I wade through the snow. A few pieces of glass have cut my skin, and I curse my stupidity. I'm a shit escape artist. My blood leaves speckles in the snow, right next to my obvious footprints.

No time to cover my tracks. The alley skirts the side of the castle. With a quick glance, I try to check the position of the sun, but the sky is cloudy, and I can't determine east from west.

I'll have to circle the building and sneak in the back gate. Then to the basement. Find that hole. Uncover its secrets...

Gritting my teeth, I hike my skirts and tiptoe through the snow. I duck beneath windows as I pass them, hugging the wall. When I cross the length of the castle without incident, my pride swells.

Look at me go, a good spy after all.

The alley empties into a gated courtyard, where rows of tents circle a central area paved in stone. Beyond, several clusters of ice-built homes form an orderly perimeter against the steep walls of the glacial bowl. A wave of voices hits me as the wind shifts in my direction. The cold slams into me, and I hug my arms to my chest.

Commotion stirs at the far end of the yard. A fur-clad group of merfolk wrangle several large, white-furred snowbears. The bears' paws slip on the stone walkway, and the whites of their eyes show their fear.

One snowbear rears its legs, paws swiping. The animal-handlers shout and duck, grasping for ropes that hang from its furry muzzle. One handler cracks a whip against the ground, and the bear roars.

Merfolk stop to stare. Snow falls from several sapwood limbs, shaken from its perch. Silence settles in the courtyard, the only noise the bear's protesting snarl.

My vision tunnels, focused on the rearing bear. It balks, ripping the ropes from its handler's hands. Lumbering into the street, it searches for an escape.

I may be a foreigner in this kingdom, but I know how to treat an animal. *This* is not right. And I will not stand for cruelty.

Squeezing my eyes shut, I inhale a steadying breath. *No, Nahla. Let it go.* I have places to be. Escaping to do. I can't risk being seen just to save a helpless—

Fuck it. This animal needs me. Stepping out of the alley, I plant my feet.

I cluck my tongue, stir my magic, and send my Voice spiraling after the snowbear. I pierce the shell of its mind and plunge into the chaos. A full-grown female. Through her eyes, I see the stone path, feel her frustration. Anger. Fear.

The whip cracks again, and the animal's flinch reverberates through my body.

Be still, I command.

The bear skids to a halt.

She swings her head, searching. Then she focuses on me, the whites of her eyes disappearing. Curiosity. Calm.

That's it, girl. You're okay. I've got you. Now, come find me.

Eagerly, the snowbear saunters across the square, dragging the handler's ropes with her.

My song echoes through the air. Merfolk swivel their heads to stare, stepping back as the snowbear saunters through the center of the courtyard.

The handler shouts, then cracks the whip.

She flinches and breaks her stride, but I soothe her fear.

I've got you.

She stops before my outstretched hand and presses her soft forehead into my palm. Her dark eyes soften. I stroke her large face, her whiskered muzzle, and scratch behind each round ear. Humming quietly, I withdraw our connection.

Whispers break out among my audience, and my stomach flips. Behind the snowbear's furry form, I glimpse a male siren, stalking toward me.

Oh, I fucked up.

I'm not supposed to be here. If word gets to the king, Perrin could be reprimanded.

"Go," I whisper, giving the bear an affectionate pat.

As much as I want to turn his own whip on that handler, I'm out of time. Now, it's time to disappear. I bolt the way I came, speeding through the alley. Adrenaline burns through my veins, pushing me onward. No time to find the beach. My makeshift rope still dangles from a second-story window somewhere. I can patch the glass when I get inside, pretend this whole mess didn't happen. I'll need something to do in confinement—

A sharp note sounds behind me, and ice curls around my ankles, stopping me in my tracks.

My jaw snaps from the sudden halt in momentum. Securely rooted to the ground, I tug each foot but can't budge. My scales prickle with awareness of the looming figure behind me.

"Going somewhere, Trouble?" His footsteps crunch the snow, growing closer. His scent carries on the wind, that damn hint of peppermint.

My heart punches in a frantic rhythm. My core clenches, and I hiss through my teeth.

Gods, this cannot be happening.

I squeeze my eyes shut, then open them again. Anything to wake myself from this nightmare. I look over my shoulder.

And there, smirking at me, is the Frost King.

I give him a finger-wiggle wave. "Your Frostiness."

"What did you do to poor Perrin?" He takes another step, shortening the gap between us. He flexes his jaw, a quick disruption to the sharp plane of his cheek.

My stomach flips. "Is Perrin okay?"

The king cocks his head. A few more steps, and he'll reach me. I wrench against the restraints to no use.

"Strange how I tasked him with keeping you *inside* your room. Yet, here you stand. Charming snowbears. I assume you knocked him out cold? Should I call for Lucas?"

"Nope. I took the window, like a lady." I shrug. His gaze flicks over my shoulder, no doubt spotting my makeshift rope dangling through the broken glass.

"Don't you have everything you need? Everything you asked me for? Tell me, what have I overlooked?" He sounds troubled, genuinely concerned.

How infuriating. How fucking *accommodating*. Where was this willingness weeks ago, when he locked me in the dungeon? He's giving me whiplash.

He stops inches behind me, and his breath skitters on my neck. My skin cries out, every scale standing in alert. If I tilted my ass, I'd meet his lap.

I inhale sharply. *No, Nahla.* Attractive males always come with a catch. Every. Damn. Time. And this one? He harbors a dark secret, lying in wait to ruin me.

"You're insufferable," I hiss. "This sudden sweetheart routine won't work on me."

"Is it not?" he asks, breath ghosting the top of my head. His hand hovers next to my arm, fingers stretching, then retreating. "Working, that is."

Finally, his thumb brushes my woolen sleeve. My eyelids flutter. "Let go."

"I can't do that, Princess. You know the rules." He trails up my arm, over my shoulder. His hand finds the warmth of my throat, long fingers wrapping around. His touch is cold and smooth, like frosted glass, as he strokes the length of my voice box. "Your Voice is impressive. Tell me, where did you learn such power?"

"Tell me," I retort, "why I should reveal all my secrets when you share none of yours?" My pulse batters against him, rapid and eager.

He chuckles. "My secrets would scare you, Princess."

"Try me."

"All right," he says. His finger trails lower, ghosting over the hidden marks of my gills, the rim of my collar bone. "I'm a terrible king."

"That's no secret," I say, wrinkling my nose. "It doesn't count."

"The secret is, I prefer it that way." His touch grows still, lingering on the hollow of my throat.

"A king who doesn't like to rule."

"Aethan the Terrible," he muses. "And the princess who ran from home. What will everyone do, when they finally learn our truth?"

His icy breath tickles the side of my neck, and my scales lift. What's left of my stubborn resolve disappears in an instant.

"I learned it from Keen, our way-maker," I answer finally. "I can enter the minds of animals and communicate with them. Persuade them. Sway their emotions, like I did with the snowbear just now."

He hums, the sound rumbling through his chest into my body. "Sounds useful. Better than making it snow." The rumble strengthens, forming a low note of magic. Several snowflakes fall from thin air, dusting my face with glitter.

I laugh. "I like your snow. When it's not trapping my ankles."

He grunts, and the magic melts from around my feet. I stand still, held in place by that finger, pressing softly into my pulse. I swallow, and my throat bobs against it.

"What do you say to helping me tomorrow? I'm leading a hunt. My terrible reputation hinges on its success." He squeezes my neck gently.

Fuck. I don't want him to stop touching me. A tingle passes from head to toe as my skin cries out for more.

"What do I get in return?" I whisper.

"A little fresh air and a chance to stretch your legs? You're a beast-tamer, and a good one, too. Say you'll help me, Nahlani Mahelona. Come with me. I—" His voice catches, dropping into a growl. "I need—"

His touch grows cold against my skin. He peels his fingers away. A swath of blue scales coats his fingertips, midnight blue, like he's dipped them in ink.

I turn my head, glancing at him through my lashes. His eyes are wild with emotion, darkening each iris. His jaw clenches, nostrils flare. And when he meets my gaze, he groans. A deep, beastly rumble. Like thunder over the open ocean.

"You need *me*," I finish for him in a breathless sigh, a smile tugging my lips. "And lucky for you, Frosty, I'm in."

Chapter Thirty-Four

NAHLA

The Frost King comes to my room that night. Perrin announces his presence with a few curt knocks, and I cinch my night-robe as I hurry to answer the door.

What could he want at this hour? Another heart-to-heart? The hunting party departs early tomorrow morning, and I haven't managed a wink of sleep. Nerves have kept me pacing the floor, predicting all the ways I could fuck this up.

Hunting in the Brine is easy. The water carries my song far and wide. But I haven't tested my skill in the open air beyond birds and that snowbear. What if he's wrong? What if I'm not powerful enough?

What if I prove to be useless?

The door opens to reveal the scowling king in his regal fur cloak, bathed in torchlight and holding a large package. It's tied with a bow and wrapped neatly in paper, crinkling in his hands.

I shoot Perrin a look, but the young guard shrugs, as confused as I am. The hallway carries a chill through the doorway, and I pull my robe tighter.

"For you," the king says, shoving the package toward me. I accept it on instinct, and the smell of peppermint wafts from the paper. It's heavier than I expected, with something soft inside.

"Um, thank you?" I juggle the package awkwardly and pull the string.

"Not now," he grunts. "For tomorrow."

I pause. His face is shadowed, but even in the gloom, I catch the hue of his eyes. Dark blue instead of pale ice. Have they always been that color? Or is it the bad lighting?

"For the hunt," he explains.

I squeeze the paper to test the contents. A blanket maybe? Or a pillow? "What is it?"

He grunts again but doesn't answer. Odd. The king had plenty to say this afternoon. I study his face, finding it sunken and weary. Shadows collect under his haunted dark eyes. I guess I'm not the only one who can't sleep.

"You were cold," he mutters. "I fixed it."

The scales rise along my neck. That phrasing sounds familiar somehow. "Okay," I say, raising my eyebrow. "Thank you."

He nods curtly but says nothing else. His mouth moves as if he *wants* to speak, and then he snaps his jaw shut again and shoves his hands into his pockets. He shifts his weight from one foot to the other as he stares at me in silence.

My cheeks grow warm under the intensity of his gaze. Is there something on my face? Is my robe falling apart again? I glance down, relieved to find my bits are covered.

He flicks his gaze away. Was he just...? My heart stumbles as I consider what he might think of me as I stand here in nothing more than loosely wrapped silks. Again. I was stupid to answer the door, looking like this. It's unladylike. Improper. *Intimate.*

Last night was accidental, and I didn't know anyone would be roaming the halls. But tonight? I have no excuse.

I shift the package and hug it against my chest, blocking his view of my attire. No wonder he can't speak to me. I'm probably breaking another unspoken rule, one about dressing properly in his presence.

His pupils dilate, and he clears his throat. "You're welcome," he says, then whirls on his heels and leaves with a slithering hiss of his cloak as it drags on the floor.

Perrin and I share a curious glance.

"Are you going to open it now?" he asks when the king is out of earshot.

I grin. "Sure am."

I tug the string, and the package opens to reveal a thick fur cloak. It's a warm creamy color with flecks of tawny and silver over a dappled undercoat.

"Wow, that's rare," Perrin says. "A frostcat cloak. Mine's made of boring woollygoat hide."

I slide my fingers into the soft fur, then lift it to my nose. Inhaling deeply, I bury my face in the peppermint-snow scent. Does everything from the king smell like this?

"Put it on!"

I oblige, shaking out the cloak and slipping inside. The hide is soft and warm against my skin, with a weight that feels like a hug. The scent of peppermint grows stronger. Calming. My eyes flutter shut as my anxiety snuffs out.

This is nice.

"You look like you belong here," Perrin muses.

"Think so?" My chest squeezes.

He grins, his tusks glinting in the torchlight. "Yeah."

CHAPTER THIRTY-FIVE

AETHAN

WE RIDE AT DAWN. Twenty snowbears, seventeen hunters, one healer, one king, and a troublesome Brine Princess.

Saddled, provisioned, and mounted, the snowbears plod single-file through the snow. Their paws break the frost layer, crunching in a steady gait, as they carry us toward the morning sun. Cyrene leads the pack. The hunter's thick cloak drapes over the wide, white bottom of her mount. The wind whips across the plains, penetrating every hole in my leather armor.

Our plan is simple: we'll trek until twilight, then make camp. The prey that hunker in the outer reaches of the plains are most active in the early morning hours. One day to get there, one day to hunt, one to return.

I squeeze my thighs, urging my mount forward. The snowbear shifts beneath me, putting more distance between me and Nahlani Mahelona. As there should be. This kingdom follows a simple order of things: she's my prisoner, and I am the king. I should not be so beholden to her whims.

But if I'm being honest with myself—truly honest—I've known nothing would be simple since the moment I laid eyes on her.

That princess is nothing but trouble. Those full lips always curved around a witty insult, her eyes burning with mischief, that goddessdamn Voice, wriggling inside my head—she's ruined me.

With a simple flick of her tongue, she ensnared me, shackled me, and bound me body and soul. Her Voice awakened something inside me in the courtyard yesterday, and now I can hardly breathe without craving her. Needing her. Desperately.

This is going to be a long three days.

Even now, I sense her every movement. Meters behind me where she rides alone, swaddled in her new frostcat cloak, as far away from me as fucking possible. She murmurs affectionate nothings to her snowbear, maintaining a quiet song.

That cloak looks good on her.

With clenching teeth, I tear my attention toward the Frosted Plains spreading before us. A sheet of ice stretches from the mouth of our basin to the horizon, uninterrupted and covered in snow. Somewhere out there is the prey we seek, but as I scan the expanse, I see nothing. We're the only sign of life on the goddess-forsaken ice.

Have I made a mistake? What if we return empty-handed?

"You're doing well, Sire. A kingly mission indeed." Lucas's voice penetrates my thoughts as the healer pulls his mount next to mine.

His long, dark hair catches in the wind, battering his sharp cheek-bones. "I wonder if we might have a word. About my research."

I grunt my affirmative.

"The dungeon rubble is cleared. I think you'll be interested to know what the Frost Guard found in the princess's cell." The wind carries his words, but the nearest hunter is several lengths behind us, and hopefully out of hearing.

I pull my mount closer and lean to hear him better. "A dead body?"

"No, Your Majesty. Several grimoires on curses—the same I've been wanting to retrieve from the original city library. They will be immensely helpful in my research."

"In her cell? Why? How'd they get there?"

"Curious, isn't it?" He reaches into his cloak and tilts a stone tablet from the pocket within. He pats the book and grins. "A stroke of fate, the goddess shines brightly upon us! I started reading this morning, and I think I'm onto something. A cure is in sight, Sire."

The idea twists through me, fragrant and intoxicating. I could be rid of this curse. I could be whole again. I could return to the person I was twelve years ago—before my world descended into darkness.

What would that feel like?

Hope flares, dangerously fast. I tamp it down.

"Well, keep reading," I say. "A hunch isn't good enough, Lucas. I need certainty."

He nods. "Of course, Sire. I thought you'd like to know."

Sudden cold pierces through my body. Every scale rises in alert. Someone shouts from the rear of the group, and I glance over my shoulder in time to see the princess slump from her mount and topple into the snow. She lands in a puddle of fur, unmoving.

My heart plummets. The world zooms in, blurring at the edges, until all I can see is *her*.

Her body crumpled so easily.

Is she dead?

Without another thought, I yank the reins, turning my mount. The snowbear grunts from the urgent pressure of my knees in the saddle. We plunge through the snow to reach her, lumbering past the long line of confused hunters. Blood roars in my ears, urging me faster, faster.

Her snowbear grunts, plodding forward a few paces before it realizes it lost its rider. Its large head swivels in confusion. The hunters near her cry out, leaping from their mounts and trudging through the snow. As they pull her face from the snow, I glimpse her expression, blank and weary.

Relief twists my lungs. *Alive.* Her nose dapples with the beginnings of frostbite.

I should have known better than to let a sun-drencher ride solo on the Frosted Plains. I should have left her at home instead of dragging her along to feed my selfish whims like a goddessdamn fool.

The mount halts at my command, and I leap from the saddle. Cold seeps through my snowleathers, crunching the ice beneath my feet. As I approach, another sound clarifies—the rapid chattering of her teeth.

The hunters lift her onto her feet, and her knees wobble beneath her, knocking together. She moans and her gaze drifts aimlessly. Her plump lips are pale, ashy. A perfect picture of hypothermia.

My heart punches hard. Hot.

Anger. Fear. Panic.

My fault.

"She's too cold, Sire," one hunter says, to state the fucking obvious.

"Give her to me." My growl pierces the morning, and the princess's gaze snaps to meet mine. I reach for her, arms spread wide. War rages in her eyes—her pride rears against her shame, her need—until finally, good sense wins out. With a weak step, she tumbles into my embrace.

I squeeze her against me. *That's a good girl.*

"Fetch the healer," I bark, whipping my cloak with a snap of leather as I pull it around her. I catch her wrist in my hand and press my finger to her pulse. It batters pathetically against my touch, slow and feeble.

Didn't she think to wear a fucking hat? She's not invincible. Her body is poorly suited for the harsh climate. She's too warm. Too fragile. And she's wearing nothing more than a sweater, leather pants, and the frostcat cloak.

Goddessdammit, why didn't I give her a hat, too? Or a fucking scarf? Gloves? The cloak is warm, but it's not enough.

Useless, stupid king. Anger flares in my stomach, and I clamp my teeth to tame it, tugging my cloak tighter around her small frame. She'll just have to share mine.

I peek through the opening of my cloak-tent and frown at the crust of snow on her hair. Her fingers splay wide on my chest. With a shiver, she tucks her nose into my bicep, an icicle piercing straight through my sleeve.

I hiss. "Dammit, Nahlani."

Her mouth moves against my chest. "It's N-N-Nahla," she chatters.

I dip my head, tucking my ear inside the furs to hear her better. "What?"

She huffs and tries again. "My n-name. It-t-t's Nahla. Only my s-sister c-calls me Nahlani, when I'm in t-t-trouble."

"Nahla." My tongue curls around her name, as my grip tightens on her wrist, monitoring her quickening pulse. "You *are* in trouble."

"I'm f-f-f-fine. Really."

Whaleshit. She's one cold gust of wind from dissolving on her feet. Where is Lucas when I need him? I tear my gaze from her, searching for the healer. He dismounts with the speed of a slogfish, ambling toward us.

"Do something," I snarl.

Lucas raises his hands and readies his spell. Golden tendrils of healing magic dance around his fingertips. His mouth quirks.

"What are you waiting for?"

He nods sharply. "I need to *see* the patient, Sire. You're blocking her."

Right. With stiff arms, I part my cloak, revealing the shivering princess within my grasp. She gasps as the wind rushes in.

"Make it quick," I snap.

Lucas reaches for Nahla, and his long fingers cup her cheeks. Every nerve in my body stretches taut. His Voice whines and weaves as his magic enters her skin. The glow spreads through her limbs, illuminating the pads of her fingers, the tip of her nose. It swirls over her belly and legs, wrapping around her thighs.

The healer stares into her eyes with intensity and presses closer, closer. Nahla gasps, a soft hiccup in her throat, and my temper roars. My hands quake. My thighs clench. It takes every ounce of self-control not to rip her from his grasp.

From the depths of my mind, the Beast crawls out. His claws scrape, clamoring for control. *She's mine.* Jealousy stings, like a poison in my veins.

I tremble, watching Lucas as he watches her, and quietly break at the seams. One wrong touch—one lengthy glance—and the healer's head will land in the snow.

Finally, he severs the spell. "I got the worst of the frostbite. Find her a hat and keep her under furs. Body heat is best for hypothermia. She needs to warm up slowly."

Nahla trembles in my arms. "C-can't your magic warm me up-p?"

Lucas bends, stooping to her level. I bristle. She's not a fucking guppy.

"Sorry, m'lady. We've been over this, remember? My magic doesn't work like that. No heat, only healing." He raises his hands in defense.

Her teeth chatter loudly in response. "R-r-right."

Anger flares hotter. Has she been *this* cold before, to have needed to ask Lucas for help? Fucking hell. What a complete dick I've been.

"Would you like me to take her weight, Sire? There's room on my mount." Lucas flashes a debonair smile.

"No," I growl. I pull the cloak around her once more, smothering her to my chest. My heart thunders, so hot and heavy I'm sure she can hear it. "She's my responsibility, and you have reading to do."

Without waiting for her protest, I lift her into my arms. My hands splay across her round ass, holding her feet out of the snow as I walk her to my mount and swing her into the saddle facing backward.

Nahla will ride with me.

I mount with her, so our chests meet. Heart to heart, that's the best way to warm her. I unbutton my shirt, exposing bare skin.

She gasps, eyes widening. "W-what happened to you?"

With cold fingers, she traces the web of scars on my stomach, each one a memento of a fight I can't remember. My muscles clench at her touch.

"Don't worry about it," I grunt.

Her brow puckers, but she wraps her legs around my waist wordlessly and tangles her fingers in my hair. My chest tightens, and I wonder if she can feel the gallop of my heart.

"You're so warm." She presses her face to my skin and shudders.

That's not good.

I'm the fucking Frost King. I'm practically made of ice. If the princess thinks I'm warm, something is seriously fucked up.

"Warm up," I order her. "I'm gonna find you a fucking hat."

I squeeze my thighs, urging the snowbear forward. Slowly, the hunters regain course. I pass several on my way to the front and manage to borrow an icefox fur cap.

"Here," I grunt, tugging it over her ears.

With wide brown eyes, she stares at me. Gone is her usual defiance, the ever-burning flame of insolence. Only softness remains. She's goddessdamn beautiful.

Have I noticed before?

Her brown skin flushes, speckled with golden freckles across her petite nose and full cheeks. Dark lashes frame her ever-watching eyes. The soft curve of her lips is perfection, as they pale with the remnants of frostbite. Would her lips be cold if I kissed her now? Should I warm them for her?

The longer she looks at me, the harder my heart pounds.

"Thank you," she whispers. Her breath spills over my chest, those plump lips parting.

"You need to warm up slowly," I tell her. "So unfortunately for us, that means skin-to-skin contact. Can you undo your sweater?" I glance at the small buttons entrapping her bosom, small pieces of dark stone threaded into the wool. Ten of them, *good goddess*. My throat tightens.

Her breasts rise and fall with her shallow breathing. With clumsy fingers, she grasps at the buttons.

"Here," I grunt. I pinch the top one and push it through the hole. She spills through the opening, and my fingers brush her soft skin.

I freeze. Is this... okay? My head swims, clouded with a sudden pang of desire. It takes every ounce of my control not to take her breasts into my hands, bury my face between them, and become lost to the world.

Her hands fall into her lap, and she tilts her chest, giving me more room to work. I swallow thickly.

"Well, you d-d-do it, then," she huffs. "It must b-be done."

Carefully, I manage the rest of the buttons. With every pull, the restraint loosens. My hands skitter past her belly button, the soft rolls of her stomach, until finally the last button comes loose. I peel back the wool, revealing her bare, heavy breasts. Not a clinging starfish in sight.

My breath catches in my throat. *Fuck me, they're perfect.*

Then she adjusts her position in the saddle, snuggling closer. As she presses against me, I can feel the stiff buds of her nipples. Her legs constrict around my waist, and she settles on my stiffening cock. She swirls her hands in my hair, twisting tighter. Tighter. *Fuck.*

"Stay still, Princess."

She wiggles again, and fuck if I can help the responding twitch in my cock. "But you off-f-fered your hosp-p-pitality. Who am I to refuse?"

My hand moves of its own accord. I slide up her arm, gliding over the fabric and slipping around the chilled skin of her neck. My thumb brushes the faint lines of her hidden gills. A snarl ripples from my mouth.

Something inside of me comes undone, releasing a slow bleed of emotion. Darkness swirls in my thoughts. Hunger. Memory.

And in my head resounds the chorus of my being: *Mine. Mine. Mine.*

"Careful, Sunfish," I whisper. "You don't want to outstay your welcome."

Her weight presses on my erection, and I grit my teeth. She lifts her gaze to my lips, a soft mewl escaping her mouth. "What did you c-call me?"

"I—" I frown.

Her responding smile is as bright as the sun. "Thought so." I could dissolve in that expression and I'd die happy.

With the last push of my self-control, I release my hold. Grab the reins. I squeeze my heels, urging the snowbear faster. The sooner we make camp, the better. Cold wind bites at my face as I tear my gaze away from her. Focus on the horizon. The stretching white plains. The teetering rump of the snowbear ahead of me in line.

Anything to distract me from the female in my lap, dragging her nails on the skin of my back.

Nahla is my prisoner. Someone else's princess. Fucking her would be wrong. I could lose control, explode into the raging Beast. I could hurt her. Maul her. *Or worse.*

But of this much I'm certain: resisting her will be my undoing.

The animal jostles beneath me, and Nahla's legs shift. With a growl, I snare her waist. Trap her against me.

"*Still.*"

"N-no," she whispers, tucking her nose into my skin. She inhales and moans quietly. "That s-s-smell. I c-can't."

My ears burn with rejection. I've always found her smell to be intoxicating. Enchanting. The fucking bane of my existence. It's ridiculous to expect the same to be true for her. "You'll have to deal with my scent, sorry. I can't fix that."

She shakes her head, dragging the tip of her nose across my chest. "I *like* it."

My stomach drops. "Oh."

"It's soothing." She wiggles again, nudging right into my erection. Finally, she grows still. "Oh," she says. "I'm sorry, are you...?"

"Don't worry about it," I growl, clenching my teeth.

She lifts her head with searching eyes. "I thought you hated me."

"Nahla, there's an objectively attractive female sitting half-naked on my cock. What did you expect?"

A wry smile spreads her lips. "The terrible Frost King *does* have feelings," she says.

"And the troublesome Brine Princess is immune?" As I hold her gaze, I slide my hand down her back to circle the crest of her thigh. She trembles in my arms as my fingers itch and crawl over her tight travel leathers, reaching for the heat that tempts me so. My thumb brushes the seam of her pants.

It's soaked through.

She inhales. Her eyes flood with need.

"I'm not the only one." I bring my thumb down, retracing my path. Her smile falters, and she whimpers. Her hips tilt and she presses into my touch. "Admit it, Princess. You want me."

She grinds her hips into me, slowly, with devastating pressure. I grip her ass. Hard. Pressing her into me as she grinds once more. Twice. She gasps, and her eyelashes flutter. Her body tightens and arches, bending to her need. And then I release her.

She moans. "More."

I lean closer until my lips brush her ear. "When I fuck you," I begin. "And I *will* fuck you, Nahla. But not like this. I'll fuck you the way you deserve."

"And what do I deserve, Aethan?" she whispers.

Warmth blooms through my chest. I inhale the scent of her hair—sunshine and snow—and commit it to my memory. Because there's no going back, once the truth tumbles from my mouth. My lips move, forming the words. "Everything I can give."

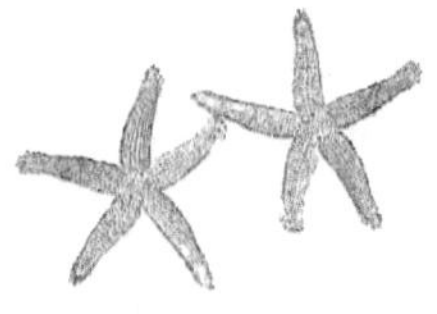

Chapter Thirty-Six

Nahla

I burrow my face deeper into the snowbear's fur, press my frigid feet and fingers into her blubbery skin. She growls and squirms, wrenching from my grasp. I pursue her relentlessly, searching with my toes for her warmth.

"Dammit, Nahla," a deep voice rumbles in my ear. "Be still."

I open my eyes to a smooth male chest. My fingertips scour the surface of him, tracing the rough topography of his scars—not a snowbear then. A Frost King. I tilt my face and meet his darkened grimace.

We're lying in a nest of furs, in the dead of night. Our legs tangled together. I press my toes into his leather-clad calf, spreading them to take full advantage of his warmth.

He hisses through his teeth.

"Did we make camp?" I ask.

"Yes. Hours ago. You slept most of the day, after you got settled." Then he drops his voice low and adds, "Don't know how."

The wind howls outside, shrieking against a hollow bowl of ice. I lift my head and survey the cramped shelter. A snow-packed ceiling forms a dome overhead, curving into walls that meet the ground. The bed is in the center of a small round room. Moonlight streams through the tunnel that branches off the sleeping area, just large enough to crawl through. The cold does not reach us here.

The king must have summoned this shelter, thank the gods. That wind is fucking brutal. If not for the chill it brings, I could have made it on my own. I was prepared. I had a cloak, pants, and a thick wool sweater.

But it wasn't enough. And he needed to save my sorry ass.

My ears burn with embarrassment as I recall our little ride in his saddle today. I press my hands to my breasts. They're still bare. His pupils widen with hunger, watching me. Warmth floods my center. This whole body-heat-keeps-you-warmer thing is messing with my head.

"Am I still hypothermic?"

His brows knit, and his arms tighten around my waist. "You're not chattering like a rattlefish, so that's a good sign."

"So we can give up this charade?"

He chuckles, the sound reverberating through me. "I'm afraid not," he says.

"Why not?" I press. If I'm better, then I no longer need his chivalry. I pat the furs, swinging my arm wide to locate my sweater in the dark. He catches my wrist and folds me against his chest, where his chin nuzzles the top of my head as he holds me.

"Nahla," he cautions.

I shiver at my name dropping from his lips like a forbidden sweet. The scales rise along the base of my spine.

"Be *still*," he says through clenched teeth. I wiggle one more time, for spite, and *oh*.

His erection presses through his tight leather pants. Yesterday's words float from my foggy hypothermic memory: *When I fuck you, and I will fuck you, Nahla. I'll fuck you the way you deserve.*

I can't help the mewl that escapes my mouth. That wasn't a dream. And now the Frost King holds me half-naked in his arms, all evidence of his arousal prodding me.

His hand slides up my spine, brushes my neck, and tightens around my hair. "Make that sound again," he growls.

"Is that an order?" Desire builds deep in my gut, twisting around the base of my spine. Drawn by the magnetism of his presence, I arch my back, and my nipples brush his chest. A ripple of excitement flutters in the pit of my stomach.

"I want you, Sunfish. To bend you over till you're soft and crooning and begging for more." His breath spills over my face, tinged with the sweet peppermint smell I've come to crave. "No more defiance. No more trouble. *Mine*."

My body responds to his claim with a shiver of delight. Wetness slicks my thighs, and I clench them together. My breath comes in a harsh, uneven rhythm. Desperate for him to make good on all his promises. A hot ache burns in my throat as I stare into his eyes, seeing him with full certainty.

The curve of his lips, the quirk of his irritated mouth, it's all the same. The Beast's scales, the king's temper, his fear of the water. That fucking nickname. *Sunfish*. There can be no other explanation.

The king and the Beast, they're the same.

I don't know how or why, but it's him. The kind, generous, cocky fool of a Beast—it's *him*. He's in there somewhere. And I'll make it my life's new mission to drag him out of his self-made cage.

He tightens his fingers in my hair, yanking my attention. "Tell me no," he demands. There, swimming in his hardened expression, is a splash of careful uncertainty, that wild hope—a glimpse of the soul I've waded deep within.

"Do your worst," I whisper.

With the brute force of the Beast, he rolls me. My back presses into the furs. He yanks my hands above my head, holding my wrists together. His muscular frame looms over me in the darkness, a shadow hovering out of reach. A familiar shiver of awareness traces the length of my body as I lie before him, on display.

His Voice rumbles deep in his chest, and his eyes glow. A thin tendril of ice slips through his lips, threading through the air to wrap around my wrists. He freezes them to the ground. I tug against the cuffs, thrashing with theatrics. In the dim light, his white teeth glint as he grins.

"You're trouble, aren't you, Princess?" His knees settle on either side of my hips, caging me in as his erection presses against my heat, and I feel him lengthen within the leather. *Oh gods.* His cool hands slide over my belly, leaving a wake of rising scales. I shudder as his thumbs stroke the undersides of my breasts. "I've wanted to do this since I saw you in that night-robe."

He takes one breast in each large hand, and moans as he tucks his face between them. My nipples tingle against the pads of his palms. He nips at my skin, sealing the pain with a swipe of his tongue. With soft passes of his lips, he makes his way to my left nipple. He traces the circumference twice before finally sucking the sensitive bud into his mouth.

The caress is a command. I arch into him and moan, unable to keep quiet. Pleasure blossoms, and I ball my fits, pulling tight against my icy cuffs above my head. His tongue swirls with sickening speed. "Gods above," I gasp.

He withdraws sharply. I cry out at the loss of attention. His hand finds my chin, gripping me as he tilts my face to look deep into my eyes. "No, Nahla," he growls. "Say my name. I am your god tonight."

A quiver surges through my center. "Aethan," I whisper. I tug out of his grip, craning my neck to reach for him. For his mouth. Does he taste the way he smells? I can't stand one more minute without knowing. "Aethan, kiss me."

Triumph flashes in his eyes. "That's a good girl," he says, moments before our lips meet. He kisses me like he's chasing his final breath. Soft at first, then urgent. Ravenous. His hands slip out of my hair to clasp my face, pulling me in to deepen the kiss.

I hitch my legs on his hips and draw him closer. More. I need more.

His tongue twines with mine, stroking deep, consuming me, and scattering my thoughts until there's nothing left but the feeling of him. He's everywhere all at once. Heavy pressure along my body. Greedy hands brush my face, my wrists, my neck, my breasts. He passes over my stomach in a worshipful caress, then wraps his hand around the crest of my thigh.

With efficient fingers, he unties the lacing of my pants and rolls them over my hips, placing a path of kisses as the leathers slip off.

"Fuck," he whispers, staring at my bare pussy with hungry admiration. Then he hitches my legs higher, lifting my ass. I grind into him, sliding my wetness. Pleasure flitters through my core, and I gasp for air.

"Tell me what you want inside you, Nahla," he growls. "My fingers or my cock?" His thumb dips into my heat, not waiting for my reply. He swirls and finds my clit with ease. I arch into the pressure.

More. *More.* I pull against the restraints and moan as a wild swirl batters my stomach.

"I see the answer there in your eyes. Say it, Nahla. Out loud." His fingers tease me incessantly, right where I need him. Pleasure builds within me, and I spiral down the path to bliss. But it's not enough.

I want to feel full. I want him inside me, stretching me. The hot slap of our bodies, animal instinct driving us into oblivion.

He dips down for a kiss, pulling the answer out of me with his cool tongue.

"Cock," I gasp into his mouth. His lips ripple as he growls, and then the pressure dissipates.

He pushes from the floor, standing to his full height. With quick fingers, he loosens the leather lacing and slips out of his trousers. His cock springs free.

His *large* fucking cock.

My heart stutters. He's going to put *that* inside me? Is there room?

In the darkness, I make out the sleek curves of his muscled body, his defined abdomen sloping in a sharp V. Thick thighs that could snap my neck if I'm not careful. I swallow my rising panic. He's the spitting image of the Beast's physique, captured in a soft siren skin. No tail, no horns. *But it's him.*

A wave of arousal surges through me, and I clench my thighs. Panic, arousal—I can't tell them apart. The longer I stare, the more my hunger for him builds. "Fuck *me*," I gasp. As in *fuck me, this can't be happening*. I'm not ready for this. And yet...

I've been ready for him since he grabbed me in the Rime.

His forearm flexes as he discards the clothing. He drinks in the sight of me, his gaze traveling from my bound wrists to the tips of my toes. "Gladly, Sunfish," he whispers. "Whatever you need."

His voice breaks on the final word. He nudges my knees apart, slips his hands beneath my ass, and lifts.

Then he feasts. His mouth nuzzles my heat, searching out my sensitive bud. When he finds it, I hiss at the rush of pleasure. His tongue laps in rapid torture, coaxing a wave of bliss.

Shit, he's good at that.

With each stroke, my need winds tighter.

"Aethan," I moan. "Your cock, dammit."

He nips my skin. "Come on my tongue first. I've been dreaming of your pussy on my tongue since..."

I thrash against my restraints, groaning as he tucks his thumb inside me. "You said"—I pant, vision sparkling at the edges—"whatever I need!"

"I know what you need," he says. He rotates my hips, laying me on my side before his hand leaves my ass. It slaps with a sting. I gasp, and he smooths the spot. "And you're going to fight me for it. Isn't that right, Trouble? You get off on fighting me tooth and claw. Go ahead then. I won't stop you."

His Voice morphs into a spell, continuing in a low note while his vibrating tongue swirls through my wetness. Above my head, the ring of ice tightens ever so slightly. *Asshole.* How am I supposed to fight him when he's trapped my ammunition?

Aethan lifts his head, smirking, as evidence of my arousal dribbles from his chin. His tongue darts out, scooping it into his mouth. His eyes dance with mischief, watching me over my belly.

Beasty wants to play.

I match his smirk and cock an eyebrow.

Then I buck my hips, knocking him playfully with my knee. His jaw flexes, and a slow smile stretches wide, teeth glinting in the darkness. He dips his head, spreads my legs apart, and plants a smacking kiss on my heat.

"That's it, Sunfish," he growls, and the sound rumbles through my core. "Now be good and come on my tongue." With a swift scoop of my ass, he hooks my knees over his shoulders.

I whimper as he renews his efforts. Swirling in a torturous rhythm, the Frost King unravels me. With every pass of his tongue, my inhibition dissolves. I lift my hips and mount his face with desperate vigor.

My orgasm builds deep in my stomach, swelling and rising like a thunderstorm tide. He works me relentlessly, sucking my pleasure to the surface. His hands grip my ass as he moans. I clench and buck, giving myself over to the strength of ecstasy. With a twist of his knuckle, he brings me to the edge. I burst. Stars explode in a glittering shower of light as I come undone on his tongue. He drags through my heat, lapping every drop.

"Good," he rumbles.

His voice sends tingles through my body, and my scales lift to greet his praise. This male—he's ruined me for anyone else.

But he's not done with me yet. His hands slide over my hips, gripping my waist. He positions himself at my entrance and drags the velvety tip of his cock through my heat. I wrap my legs around him, pulling him closer.

"Are you ready for me, Nahla?"

I whimper, like a pathetic, needy hatchling, but I don't care. I've gone soft for him. The infuriating, obtuse Frost King has tamed me with the flick of his tongue. I'd do anything for the thick glide of his cock inside of me.

So I beg. "Please." My heat flares, ready for him.

Aethan leans over me, holding himself right at my entrance. He presses in half an inch, parting me slowly. His eyes find mine, and I stare him down.

"Do it!" I gasp. "*Aethan.*"

With a grunt, he buries himself inside me. "Fuck," he groans. He slides easily, sheathing deep.

I moan his name as his cock stretches me and fills me to the brim. *Aethan. Aethan. Aethan.*

"I thought you were my personal hell," he grunts. "But now I see. You're my paradise, Sunfish. And I'm going to explore every inch of you. *Fuuuck.*" He withdraws with a shudder of his hips, then thrusts.

Again. Then again. Faster. Harder. I tilt my hips. Grind. I ride his cock hard, working into a fury. But I can't stop. Another orgasm builds, just out of reach. Over and over, we mold our bodies together.

My eyes roll as my walls flex and stretch, fitting snugly around him. A perfect fit. Like a fucking puzzle. He hitches my legs higher on his waist and deepens his thrust to hit—

Oh. His cock presses the spot deep inside me, and pleasure spasms. I scream. I grasp the furs beneath my bound hands, clenching them as I spiral faster, faster. The edge of ecstasy rushes to meet me.

One more thrust, and I come undone around him.

He watches my face with fierce possessiveness, his eyes darkening as I come.

"That's my girl," he growls. "Fuck!" He thrusts again, harder. Stars skitter across my vision as another wave of bliss rolls through me.

And then he's coming, too. He grabs my hips and plunges deep. I feel him shudder and quake as we climax together, gasping for air.

With a grunt, he collapses next to me. We stare at each other, our chests heaving as the reality of what we've done creeps in. He reaches for me, his fingers trailing across my cheek, brushing loose hair from my face as he smiles, lopsided and beautiful.

My heart squeezes painfully tight as I look into his eyes, bright as starlight. My soul shifts. Reorients. Every nerve in my body points to him.

And I know I'll never be the same.

CHAPTER THIRTY-SEVEN

AETHAN

IF FUCKING HER IS wrong, I never want to be right again.

As we fall into the furs, the wind howls outside our ice-shelter, carrying the echoes of her moans into the night. The sound of my name, on her lips. Over and over as she took my cock. Begged for it. I'll never forget this night.

With a quick hum, I dispel the magic that binds her hands. She sighs, and I reach for her, tucking a loose curl behind her ear. Her eyes shine in the darkness, glazed with ecstasy. She curls on her side next to me, one hand splaying on her hip, the other propping her head. Her breasts cradle in the soft furs, nipples tight and hard. Sweat beads on her forehead and slicks her stomach, coating her in a glittering sheen. Alive and well. Healthy.

She's fucking beautiful. Does she know that? Have I told her yet?

My fingers cup her ear, tracing the smooth ridge of scales. My heart punches wildly, bracing for the aftermath of my confession. *I think I love you.*

But the words stick in my throat, and I swallow around the knot.

I've been alone for what feels like forever. By choice. For years, I've refused to take a lover, knowing I could hurt them if I tried. It's risky and dangerous for everyone involved. Unfair. What if I transformed in the heat of the moment? Could I handle their blood on my hands?

I've been careless tonight. I knew the risks. And still, I fucked her. Whether that's stupidity or trust on my part, I can't say.

Nahla is my first since I was a naïve, horny youngling, fresh to my power and burdened with grief.

Is this love, or is it the relief of my cock in a warm cunt?

I clench my teeth. *No.* Not just any cunt.

Hers. I want only her.

I want my wild, unpredictable prisoner, my forbidden treasure. Who begs for romance novels and charms beasts with the flick of her tongue. Infiltrator of my kingdom, my mind, my heart. I'll never let her go. She's mine now. Forever.

I grip her hair, rubbing it between my thumb and forefinger. So delicate. Smooth.

I love you.

But I can't say it. Not yet.

Not while *he* still prowls my mind, poised to ruin everything I'm working for. I almost lost her today. My little Sunfish, half frozen to death in the snow. If it wasn't for the Beast, she wouldn't have been exposed to the elements like that. I wouldn't be here, making amends with the hunters, putting on a show. We'd be home, and I'd be fucking her in a real bed. Shaking the castle with the sounds of her screams.

In the pit of my stomach, residual anger festers. The icy knot twists and grows. From the margins of my mind, the Beast rises and claws at his restraints.

Stay back, I warn him. *She's mine.*

He spirals through my thoughts, leaking through the cracks. My vision darkens.

She's mine. And I almost lost her.

Guilt. Pain. Anger.

What a royal moron I am. What a raging, fucking idiot. If I ever lose her, I will freeze the whole damn sea—from the Rime to the depths of the Drink. My rage will know no bounds.

She touches my cheek. Soft, tentative fingers. "Are you okay?" she whispers, and her voice pulls me back into myself.

"Perfect." I give her my best smile. "You're perfect."

Her nose twitches. That cute, ball nose, covered in freckles. My fingers curl, clenching as a wave of aggression washes through me. She's too cute—I can't fucking handle it. She makes me want to punch something. Shatter the ice beneath our feet.

Instead, I kiss her nose. As gently as I can manage.

She giggles, and my heart swells. "You're pretty perfect yourself," she says.

"Did I hurt you?" I smooth her wrists where the ice wrapped around her. I draw them into my chest for a gentle massage, testing her muscles with careful fingers. No broken joints. When I reach her wrist bone, she flinches.

"A little bruise," she whispers. "But that's okay. I'm a big girl."

My heart lurches. My ears burn with shame. *I hurt her.* Goddess, I'm a monster. "I'm sorry, Sunfish," I whisper. "I'll do better."

She throws her head and laughs. "Better?" she gasps. "Fuck, Aethan. I don't know if I can handle any *better* than that."

Relief washes through me. I press a kiss to the back of her hand.

"You know that, for an asshole, you're pretty sweet?"

"Get over here." With a growl, I ensnare her waist, flip her over, and pull her into my chest. She molds against me, soft and warm as I cage her with my arms. Her hair cushions my chin, dark curls thick with her scent. Her ass nudges my softened erection, and I twitch, stiffening once again.

She nuzzles into me without complaint. I pull the covers over us, tucking the heavy furs around her delicate body. "Mmmm," she hums. A yawn breaks over her lips. "I should get hypothermia more often."

I chuckle. She's dead wrong, but she's cute.

"Sleep, Nahla," I whisper, kissing her hair.

With my thumb, I draw lazy circles on her arm. Soon enough, her breath settles into the slow rhythm of sleep. Her ribs rise and fall beneath my arm. So easy. So trusting.

What have I done to deserve this?

I stare blankly into the surrounding darkness. The wind whistles against my ice-shelter, trying to find a crack to slip through. But my magic is solid; the cold can't reach us here.

We can't stay cocooned in the furs forever. Eventually, the sun will rise, and we'll emerge from our haze. And what then? How long until she discovers my secrets? How quickly will she turn on me once she realizes the truth?

I'm not some princeling hero from her romance novels. I am the villain in her story, and someday I will ruin her beyond repair.

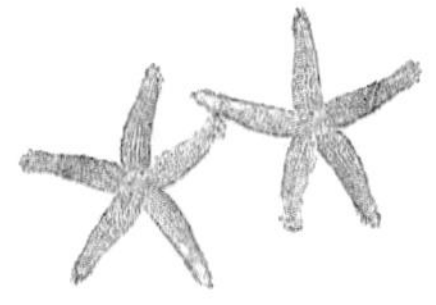

CHAPTER THIRTY-EIGHT

NAHLA

THE PLAINS ARE PRETTY, in the same way the Frost King is pretty—sharp lines and irresistible mystery. A foreboding emptiness stretches in all directions, promising life if only you know where to look for it. Or summon it. Morning greets the landscape with a swirl of violet clouds and a brisk wind. Even the sky mimics the shifting shades of his eyes. In the distance, a jagged mountain range squats at the horizon, dark silhouettes against the breaking dawn.

Rubbing the sleep from my eyes, I inhale the crisp air. We're off to an early start, hoping to catch the prey as they wake. The morning scout said there's a herd of woollygoats in these parts, about a half-hour ride to the north. Around me, the hunters bustle, tossing their last supplies into saddlebags and mounting their snowbears.

Aethan stalks through the camp, his brow furrowed with deep concentration. Stalking is the only way to describe his movement—back straight as a rod, shoulders rolled with effortless confidence. Those eyes flashing, missing nothing. His lips twitch as he lets out a low, sustained spell. He clenches his fist. In a second, each domed ice-shelter collapses into the snow, and the wind scatters them like dust.

My breath catches. Such raw force, rippling through his body.

And I fucked him last night.

He glances in my direction. Piercing eyes, straight into my soul. He doesn't smile. Doesn't speak. Only stares with the intensity of a blazing fire. Every nerve in my body awakens and screams at me to run. *Toward* him.

My core flutters, replaying the feeling of his cock pounding me into oblivion.

I fucked the Frost King last night. Slept in his shelter. Spooned him all night long.

Shit.

This is not what I had in mind when I agreed to come on this trip. Hunting is the closest thing I've found to home since I've been taken prisoner. It's similar enough to way-making—riding at the helm of society, thrilling at the chase, and feeling useful for once—but it's a strange comparison to make, as I freeze my ass off instead of basking in the high-tide sun with Keen and Ramona. Are they doing okay without me? How far did they travel before my sister realized I deserted her?

Here I am, getting frisky in a foreign king's furs, while my family and friends are... what? Are they searching for me? Or did they decide I'm a lost cause? Did Keen find another way-maker to train in my stead? Is Ramona in good hands?

The king is still staring at me. Cocking his head. My stomach flutters anew.

I wrench my gaze away from him, forcing myself to focus on the task at hand. *Mount the snowbear, Nahla.* It's not that fucking hard.

I came on this hunting trip to avoid imprisonment and to help the hunters—not to fuck the king.

It won't happen again.

"Hey, girl," I coo, stroking my mount's snow-speckled muzzle. "Up for an adventure?"

She grunts in greeting, tilting her head to look at me with her big eyes. I scratch beneath her chin before I grab onto the saddle. Slotting my foot into the hold, I swing over her back and land on the leather seat.

It's not much, compared to the saddle that Keen and I use for riding Ramona, and this version has fewer straps. There's no water to worry about with a land-bound mount. My legs squeeze her easily, keeping my position without threat of slipping away in the currents. Maintaining a connection spell in the bitter wind will dry out my throat again, as it did yesterday afternoon. Two straps hang from a band around her mouth, which I can use to steer her. Tactile directions, instead of mental guidance. Seems less efficient this way, but I'll try it.

No more hypothermia, and no more fucking the enemy. Should be easy enough.

I'm more prepared for the wind this morning, thanks to the kindness of another female hunter with enough layers to share. I wear wool leggings beneath my leather travel pants, a thicker sweater, a hat, gloves, cloak, and a frostcat scarf. It's a new day. A fresh start.

If I'm lucky, I won't have to speak to Aethan all day, and we can leave the whole sex thing in the past where it belongs.

I was exhausted last night. A recovering hypothermic. He wooed me with his warm furs and careful words, and I let my guard slip. That's all it was. It meant nothing.

Even if it was, fins-down, the best sex I've experienced in my life. But I'm never telling *him* that. No way in hell.

I keep my gaze forward. Cyrene barks orders from the front of the line. Most of the hunters are mounted now. I grasp the reins, ready to move. I can do this.

"No freezing to death today. That's an order, Sunfish." Aethan's voice sounds next to me, and my stomach flips.

He grasps the edge of the saddle, then swings into a seated position behind me.

"What are you doing?" I hiss.

As he takes the reins from my hands, his fingers brush the top of my glove. The hunters move out. With a squeeze of his legs, Aethan guides my snowbear forward, falling in line.

"I'm fine to ride alone," I mutter. "Look, I'm wearing a fucking hat today."

The tip of his nose grazes my ear. He leans forward, and his chest presses against my back so that his voice rumbles through us both. "And it looks good on you, but you're not riding alone."

"You don't think I can handle it?"

"Oh, you can handle it, Nahla." His lips ghost over my cheek. "But I can't. I'm a selfish male."

"What's that have to do with anything?" I protest.

I grapple for the reins, and he wraps his forearm around me, pinning my arms. When I squirm, my ass slides deeper between his legs.

"Careful, Sunfish," he growls. "Unless you'd rather I keep you warm from the inside out."

He's hard already.

Warmth spreads through my center, and wetness pools in my leggings. He's here to tempt me into fucking him again.

I suck in a jagged breath. "Listen, about last night…"

His fingers curl around my hip, securing me against his lap. My heart batters its bony cage, threatening to punch free. His nose skitters along my ear and dips to trace the exposed line of my throat.

"What about last night?" he whispers.

My eyelids flutter. Words jumble in my mind, leaving me with bumblefish soup. "I wanted to say…"

His lips press into the hollow beneath my jaw. "Hmm?"

I shudder as his voice rumbles. My body zings, craving him. I arch my back, and my ass nuzzles closer. *Closer.*

"I had a good time," I admit, finally. The words sting on their way out. One night in his furs has me acting like a lovesick guppy.

His teeth graze my neck briefly, and then he straightens. "Thought so."

With another squeeze of his legs, he pushes the snowbear faster. We pass several hunters, making our way to the front of the line. My snowbear plods through the snow, her shoulders shifting rhythmically beneath the shared saddle. My pussy aches from the overuse last night, sensitive where it rubs against my leathers, and I clench with each one of her steps.

This day will test me. The sooner we find the prey, the better.

We travel a kilometer in silence. Soon enough, the sun lifts above the mountains and pierces the sky with angry bursts of red and amber. I relax a little at the sight of the sun; like a familiar friend keeping me company.

The hunters fidget and scan the horizon, looking glum. I can understand why—there's not much life out here. With a quick scan of my magic, I locate several lifeforms. A herd of woollygoats to the west and a few frostcats prowling the perimeter. We're not the only ones after a meal.

Cyrene raises the hand signal, pointing with two quick flicks of her fingers.

"You're up, Nahla," Aethan whispers.

I take a deep breath and stir the magic in my stomach. With a soft song, I weave a spell and lift from my mortal frame. My mind spirals west, skimming the earth in search of life. Ten dozen woollygoats graze witlessly, their whiskered muzzles snuffling among bare patches of frozen reedgrass.

I raise my hand and signal to Cyrene, like we practiced. Three flicks means I've found them.

Gently, I penetrate their minds. *Come.*

The woollygoats lift their heads, swivel their ears, and look in my direction. One by one, they fall in line as my command takes hold. Their hooves shuffle across the snow, bringing them into view.

Cyrene notches her bow.

Aethan rummages in the saddle bags. For a moment, my concentration breaks. From the corner of my eye, I track his movements. A bow. With effortless grace, he strings his arrow and lifts the weapon into position. His forearm brushes my back, and his breath leaks cool on my neck.

My breath hitches, and my spell wavers.

The lead woollygoat spots us and tenses. It hesitates, hoof hanging in the air. Through the connection, I feel the leaking of its fear.

I need to focus. Dammit.

With a small change in my tune, I smooth its worries. *Calm. You're safe. Come here.*

The leader tilts its head, dipping its broad antlers, then places its foot. The rest of the herd follows its lead. Soon enough, the herd prances into view. I project a happy image for them—warm sunshine, endless fields of dewy reedgrass. Ears forward, eyes wide with curiosity, they trot toward the waiting hunters.

A few more paces, and they'll be in range.

Cyrene closes her fist. Arrows fly and meet their marks. Flesh squelches. Blood spurts. Several woollygoats collapse. My heart twists as each conscience goes dark, and bile sticks in my throat. At least they die happy this way.

I strengthen my spell, easing the fear of the remaining woollygoats. *Come.*

They march onward, stepping around their fallen comrades with stiff obedience. Their eyes glass over, entranced by the vision I project for them.

The hunters reload. Aethan tenses, then aims. Cyrene signals.

With a twang, Aethan releases his arrow. It spirals perfectly and embeds in the center of a woollygoat's heart. A clean shot. The animal grunts and stumbles, planting face-first into blood-stained snow.

I cut the spell, and the remaining herd stops short before the waiting snowbears. Their eyes widen, showing the whites. Then they bolt. In a clatter of hooves and puff of snow, they race for their freedom.

"Let 'em go!" Cyrene shouts. She throws her head and whoops. When she turns toward me, her expression is bright. "That was so easy! Done in five minutes? That's gotta be a new record."

Aethan lowers the bow, resting it against his knee. "Impressive," he rumbles. His voice is strained, like he's got something caught in his throat.

I turn around to check his expression. His eyes are dark as midnight, and his mouth pulls into a tight line. His jaw flexes, and he swallows hard enough for me to hear it. He tucks the bow into the saddlebag.

"You killed it," I say, shock obvious in my voice. Most royals own weapons for show. Like Winona's heirloom sword collecting dust above her mantel. She's used it once, with no level of expertise.

The king's shot was nothing short of masterful.

Finally, his mouth shifts, curling into a smile. "I'm a killer." There's a rough edge to his tone. "Is that a problem for you, Sunfish?"

"I wasn't expecting you to have the skill." I bite my lip.

"You made it easy for me. Your Voice is magnificent, Nahla." He reaches for my face and cups my cheek. His thumb brushes my bottom lip, releasing it from my teeth. "Though I never pegged you as a killer. You're... soft."

"I'm not soft. I just don't kill." I thrust my chin in defiance. Let me pierce his mind, then he can tell me who's *soft*. "My song makes them happy for their final moments, so it's a win-win. The meat tastes better when the animal dies without fear."

His gaze drops to my lips. He rests his forehead on mine, his breath spilling over my face, and we breathe together for a moment as my heart recklessly flutters. "So you'd sooner kiss a Beast than kill one. Is that right, Sunfish?"

My heart lurches to a stop. Without another thought, I grasp his shirt collar and pull his face into reach. Softly, with my lips, I trace the outline of his smirk, wiping the expression from his mouth. "That's right," I whisper.

He walks me around the side of our mount, pressing me against her flank where the hunters can't see. Then he kisses me hard. Fast. Hungry. His fingers slide from my face to grip my chin, tilting me to deepen the kiss. His mouth crushes mine with the force of his desire until I'm breathless and dazed. Dizzy from the scent of his skin, the taste of his mouth.

As quickly as we began, he breaks away and releases his hold on me. "Stay," he says.

I blink at him as I catch my breath, already missing the press of his body against mine. My fingers brush my bottom lip.

He shrugs out of his cloak and drapes it over my shoulders. "No freezing to death without me," he adds, before stalking toward his kill. His long white ponytail whips in the wind.

He pulls a bone knife from a sheath on his hip and with quick, efficient flicks of his blade, he field-dresses the animal. The leather of his travel pants stretches around his muscular rear as he leans into each cut, dragging the knife through the carcass. The hunters watch him work with widening eyes, and I check the direction of their gaze.

That ass is mine.

I blink, shocked by the strength of my thought. They're not looking at his ass. The hunters watch his hands, his knife. When he clears the innards, they scoop them up and store them with the rest of the dressings. Then they tie the animal's hooves and drag it to the storage sleigh.

There's more to the king than meets the eye. He may not offer treats on his supplication days, but he kneels on the ground, hands covered in blood, to make sure his subjects eat. An inspiring leader. I pull his cloak to my nose and inhale his crisp scent.

Aethan cleans his knife on the snow, then sheathes it.

He saunters toward me, his gaze fixed on my mouth. A slow smile spreads across his face. My heart swells, and I fight the flurry of eels that tickle the lining of my stomach.

Am I developing feelings for this male?

Am I fucking crazy?

The Frost King. Who captured me, imprisoned me, froze me nearly to death, ensnared me with his magic. Refused to meet my requests. Growled at me.

Brought me fish and novels. Befriended me. Cared for me. Freed me from the cage of his own design.

Built a fire in my bedroom.

Posted Perrin to guard me, so I wouldn't be alone.

Warmed me heart-to-heart.

He's a walking contradiction. Enemy and lover, king and Beast. My mind aches with the weight of holding both sides of him together.

Chapter Thirty-Nine

Aethan

By the time we make camp that evening, we've collected enough woollygoats, frostcats, and blubberseals to fill the supply sleighs. Spirits are high as we dismount and work to build the camp. With my magic, I raise several ice-shelters while the hunters build a fire ring. Within half an hour, there's a roaring blaze and a spitted carcass rotating above it. The seasoned scent wafts and mixes with the sharp bite of the wind.

As I approach the circle, Cyrene raises her flask of rum. "To the king!" she shouts. The hunters cheer, toasting in my direction. One of them teeters off his perch on an ice block, already too far into his drink.

"Speech!" someone chants. My ears burn, and I dip my head, scanning the group. The male who turns the spit looks at me, a broad smile on his sharp face. He pounds a fist against his chest. "Speech!"

The other hunters join in the chant, echoing his call. Their heads swivel, eyes fixing on me.

Panic twists my chest into a tight knot. I can't remember the last time I gave a speech. What do I even say? Today's hunt was a greater success than I imagined, but not because of anything I did.

I clear my throat. "Our kingdom will eat well, thanks to your skill and bravery."

I spot Nahla on the opposite side of the fire, bundled in furs and holding a steaming mug. She catches my eye, her gaze reflecting the golden dance of the flames. Air sticks in my lungs, and for a second, I forget to breathe. *She's incredible.*

Beautiful. Witty. Powerful. A hero.

This victory belongs to her. Without Nahla's song, we'd be returning empty-handed, I have no doubt in my mind. My plan would have fallen apart.

Cyrene presses a flask into my hand, and I lift it.

"And to Nahlani Mahelona, Princess of the Brine," I say. "We are forever in your debt."

Several eyes flick in her direction, appreciative and curious. As she blushes deeply and dips her head, tucking her cheeks into her cloak, I regret my remark.

No one looks at her like that. Not on my watch.

"To a successful hunt!" I finish through clenched teeth.

The hunters cheer and we drink our liquor. The flask is cold against my lips, but the liquid burns with a welcome heat. I swallow, pulling it into my gullet, and step toward Nahla.

"An excellent speech, Sire," Cyrene says, sidling next to me and blocking my path. "You did well."

I grunt. "Thank you.

"We could use a morale booster more often, it seems. Thanks for being here."

"It's nothing I've done." I pull more rum from my flask, watching Nahla over the rim. The blush is spreading. Orson approaches her, teetering on drunken legs. "If you'll excuse me."

I step around Cyrene and reach Nahla in time to intercept her. Wordlessly, I settle in next to her, placing my body between her and the approaching male. Orson stops in his tracks, snow skidding beneath his feet. *Good.*

"Don't tell me you practiced that speech," Nahla chides. "It was awful."

Warmth spreads through me at her voice, and I can't help but grin. "I'll let you write it next time."

"Thanks," she deadpans. Her hand snakes out of her bundle of furs, and she snatches the flask. "This for me?"

Tilting her head, she guzzles the liquor. Her soft neck bobs with each swallow. Eager.

"Easy now," I caution, trying not to think of what else of mine she might swallow.

She shoots me a look, takes one more swig, and returns the near-empty flask.

I stretch out my legs and settle in. This is nice. Me and her, next to a blazing fire. The sun has dipped beneath the horizon, and the lights of the aethersky emerge, rippling with radiant color among the stars. It'd be fucking romantic, if not for the company of the hunters.

I nudge her with my knee, and she sways playfully. "You did well today, Sunfish," I say. My chest swells with pride. She did more than well—she was fucking fantastic.

"You know, at home, we hunt sunfish." Her eyes sparkle as she nudges me back.

"And do you consider that cannibalism?"

"It's too bad you were born royal." Her mouth quirks as she flicks her gaze over my sprawling form. "You could've made a career out of comedy."

I laugh—a sudden, loud burst of sound. She jumps, and the low murmur of conversation around us cuts off. All eyes swivel to me. But I can't help it. I can't stop the laughter rolling from my mouth. A pinch forms in my side, and I grasp it, bending forward. My thoughts swim through a booze-drenched haze, and she just said the funniest damn thing I've heard in my life.

"You think you're funny, don't you?" I gasp. Saltwater pricks in my eyes, stinging.

She watches me with an incredulous look. Smiling. Goddess, that smile. Is there anything more perfect?

"I'm hilarious," she says.

"You're *trouble*."

"That's enough rum for you," Nahla says, snatching the flask from me again.

"That's mine," I growl.

With a grin, I dive for her. My hands reaching, snaring her waist, pinning her. My legs wrap around her. Within seconds, I wrestle her to the snow, and her hair sprawls around her face. Her cheeks flush, contradicting the scowl that curls her mouth. She holds the flask outward, as if she could keep it from me.

She's cute when she thinks she can best me. I am enormous, compared to her, and my body envelops hers. With a flick of my wrist, I could snap her neck.

I blink, clearing the dark thought.

No.

Guilt pierces my gut like a searing rod. I will never hurt her. I may be a Beast, but never to her.

Gently as I can manage, I cup her hand and fold her arm between us. Her chest heaves with a heavy breath, breasts peeking from the top of her shirt.

"I'm cutting you off," she snaps as I wiggle the flask free of her grip.

"For what, laughing too hard?"

"Someone needs to take you down a notch." She glares at me as I take another swig from the flask. She plunges her bare hand into the snow, rustling around for something.

I swallow the liquor, and it burns my throat. Her eyes are piercing, focused. She bites her lip, drawing my attention. Plump, kissable lips.

Does she want me to kiss her?

It'd be so easy. A dip of my head, and I could capture her lips.

Fuck what the hunters think of me. Of us together. She's mine. Why shouldn't I claim her right here, for all to see?

Nahla raises her hand, reaching for my face. She wants me. Here. Now. I growl in encouragement as my cock hardens at the ready.

That's it, Sunfish. Take what you need.

But her hand skates past my cheek. Her eyes sparkle with mischief, and then—*smack*. Cold sludge connects with my cheek, dripping frigid water down my neck.

She laughs, shrill and perfect. "Gotcha!"

I've been duped by a princess with a snowball. Like a fresh hatchling, playing in the snow. But two can play this game.

I shake my head, scattering icy droplets. With a swift scoop, I gather snow and pack it into a ball the size of her head.

She squeals and squirms as she tries to wrench herself free.

I dip my head, catching her soft earlobe between my teeth. "I'll count to three, Princess," I whisper. "Let's see how fast you can run."

She mewls, a melodic little whine of terror, and *goddess*, my cock grows harder at the sound. I want her to do it again.

I rise to my full height and toss the snowball, catching it in my palm. Waiting.

"One," I growl.

She scurries away, kicking snow with her frantic feet.

"Two."

She leaps between two confused hunters, making a dash for the edge of the circle. Her cloak flutters and tucks between her legs. She stutters.

I take aim.

"Three."

With a snap of my elbow, the snowball spirals through the air toward her fleeing form. It smacks into her ass. White powder explodes, clinging to her cloak. She yelps and skids to a halt.

"Not very fast, are you, Princess?" I call after her.

The hunters chuckle, watching us with sparkling eyes. "Good shot, Sire."

Nahla scowls and scoops more snow, packing it between her hands. Determination creases her face. "Hey, Lucas, give me a hand, would you?"

The grouchy healer looks up from his drink and twitches his mouth. "Oh, I wouldn't interfere in royal business, m'lady."

"You had no trouble interfering yesterday when I was freezing my ass off."

"Then I believe that puts *you* in my debt, doesn't it?" Lucas raises his eyebrow, and Nahla gives up.

She turns to the next hunter in the circle, a young male with shaggy blond hair, the same one I blocked her from earlier. "Orson?"

"I don't know, Princess," Orson says, puffing his chest. "It's guppy's play. I'm too old for snowball fights."

"If it's guppy's play, would the king be doing it?" She pouts, that irresistible lip curing him in an instant.

Orson shoots me a look, and the tips of my ears burn. A grin spreads on his youthful face. The hunter leans forward and scoops a pile of snow, packing it between his gloves. "If that's the case..."

He lobs a smacker into my chest.

I snarl. "Play fair, now. This is between you and me, Princess. No fresh recruits."

"Says who?" She winds the pitch and lobs a slushball. It splats at my feet, a meter shy of her mark.

"Clearly, me," I grunt. "The best player makes the rules."

When I throw my next missile, she ducks behind a snoring Vaughn, and the snow wallops him in the neck. With a snort, he wakes and looks about. Nahla trails her flirty fingers across his shoulder and whispers in his ear, too low for me to hear. His eyes narrow, and he packs a snowball.

Smack. Ice slides down my neck. I whirl to find Cyrene studying the sky with intense interest. Nahla laughs, and another snowball collides with my ear. The sludge melts beneath my collar.

She's turning them against me, one by one.

I find her gaze and pin her with a glare. All right. If she wants to play dirty, so be it. With a clench of my stomach, I summon my magic. My Voice vibrates from my lips, and snow rises around me, twisting and compacting into perfect missiles.

Nahla shrieks and bolts. But I am inevitable. I flick my tongue, sending the snowballs flying in all directions—one each for Cyrene, Vaughn, and Orson, and the rest toward her. Nahla sinks to her knees, pulling the cloak to cover her head. Snow batters my opponents in rapid fire.

"Oy!" shouts Cyrene. "No fair!"

The remaining hunters rally. Soon enough, a camp-wide snowball fight ensues—the entire hunting party versus me. The snow pelts me, smacking against my face, hair, ears, and chest. I erect a quick snow-shield to block the worst of their attacks.

"Cheater!" Nahla cries out. Her voice pierces the air, and the hunters' protests follow.

Snowballs fly. Laughter roars. I fight until my muscles burn and my magic drains to its end, leaving a hollow pit in my stomach. With shit aim, I lob my final blow and collapse in a booze-drenched heap. Happy.

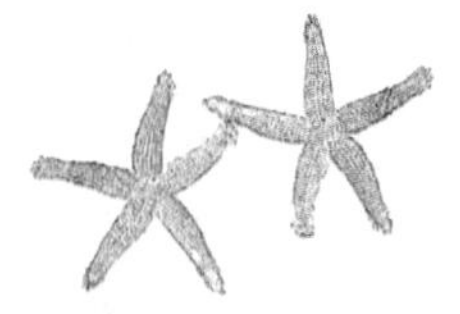

CHAPTER FORTY

NAHLA

THE FROST KING IS shit-faced, staring at me with wide, drunken eyes as I cradle his head in my lap. I stroke his white hair, tracing how it falls around his forehead. My fingers tingle as they ghost over the surface of his skin. The curl of his ear. The hard line of his cheekbone. He's fucking beautiful.

The fire burns low, blue flames dimming in a smoking pit of embers. One by one, the hunters turn in for the night and stagger to their shelters. Soon, we're alone in the center of camp, with nothing but the aethersky to keep us company.

"So pretty," Aethan says, reaching up to stroke my cheek with a clumsy finger. His smile stretches wide and crooked, white teeth glinting in the firelight. "Can I keep you forever?"

My chest tightens uncomfortably. This male—this infuriating, stupid male—is stealing my heart.

But surely he can't mean a word of it. It's the alcohol sogging his brain, the fading thrill of the hunt, the sex, the fight.

Tomorrow, we return to the castle. Me to my silken cage and Aethan to his cushioned throne. Captive and captor once again. Will he still look at me this way, when his world is back to normal, and I'm back in my place?

"Are you asking me to stick around? Or is that another order from the Frost King?"

He catches a loose strand of my hair between his fingers and twirls it. "Which one gets me a yes?"

"Funny," I quip. "Let's get you to bed, okay?"

He grins at me. "That sounds like a yes."

I roll my eyes and shift so he has to sit up. With a series of grunts and stumbles, the king rises to his feet. His cloak hangs lopsided from his shoulders. Hair falls from his usually tidy ponytail. And despite my best judgment, my breath catches at the sight of him in disarray.

Somehow, he feels more *real* this way.

I loop my arm around his waist and turn him toward his shelter. "Come on, big guy."

We stumble through the snow, leaving the warmth of the fire behind us. The wind picks up, battering our cloaks. At least his shelter is the closest; a few steps more and we reach the stooped entrance.

"Watch your head!" I caution, threading my fingers in his hair and tugging him down. Aethan narrowly misses smacking his skull on the ice.

We enter, and he collapses into the furs. His hands snag my waist, pulling me on top of him. My nose buries into his neck, and I inhale his crisp scent. A wave of desire washes over me, heat stirring in my center. His hands trail along my back, tracing sweet circles between my shoulder blades.

"You got me to bed, Nahla," he rumbles, slurring my name. "Does that mean you're going to stay?"

I pull away, staring into the darkness around us. Am I staying? Do I have a choice?

Carefully, I pull the furs over his chest, placing an extra barrier between us. Anything to keep my feelings under control.

I can't do this again.

I know how this ends. I've been here before—who hasn't—and nobody's a fan of heartbreak. Overcome, I wedge the furs between us until our skin no longer touches.

His laughter rumbles into the dark. "Are you tucking me in, Sunfish?"

"Have a good night, Your Majesty." I pat his chest once and push to my knees. He catches my wrist, yanking me in place.

"Don't go," he whispers. "I want to tell you a secret."

With a sigh, I relax into the warmth of his embrace. There's no way he'll let me go, even if I tried. "What's that?"

Is this the big reveal? Is he going to divulge the truth of his connection to the Beast? I study his face in the darkness, searching for clues. His eyes swim with drink. That lopsided smile still spreads his lips, mischievous and handsome.

"My library has a romance section. Thousands of books. You're welcome to it as soon as we get home." His breath spills over my ear, and my scales rise.

"Oh." I'm not sure what I expected him to say, but it wasn't that. "That's great. I'd love to read some."

His hand slides up my back, then grasps my hair. "I expect you to read every single one, Sunfish." His voice takes on a panicked edge. "And when you run out, I'll get you more. I'll import them from across the Sea of Adria. That way, you'll never have reason to leave me."

It's a sweet gesture, but his meaning leaves a sour taste in my mouth.

His voice grows quieter as he finishes, slipping into a breathless whisper. His grip loosens, and he relaxes into the furs, all his power softened in an instant. As sleep pulls him into its embrace, the hard creases of his perpetual frown smooth. His lashes settle on his cheeks, like white feathers. With each long breath, his nostrils flare and fall, the remnants of a smile on his lips.

And I'm left alone, staring into the sprawling dark as the panic settles in.

Sleep evades me. Outside, the wind shrieks and moans. Moonlight spills through the opening in the ice-shelter, shifting shadows on the ceiling as Audrina rises in the sky. All the while, Aethan lies beside me, taunting me with the ease of his slumber.

I've done what I said I would. I broke his silly rules, and I befriended the clawbeast. Escaped the cage. Explored his castle.

All that's left is to leave the Rime. But Aethan will never let me go.

That way, you'll never have reason to leave me.

Is that so bad a fate?

"Sunfish," he whispers.

My heart lurches, and I glance at his face. His eyes are closed, twitching beneath his eyelids. Still asleep, then.

His lips part, and he exhales. He shifts within the furs, stretching his hand out until it lands heavily on my stomach. His fingers brush my skin, and he sighs. "Sunfish will stay."

I've heard those words before. But it was the clawbeast's voice, then, echoing in my head with the weight of a command.

Sunfish will stay. You will be safe.

Like I couldn't be safe, if I didn't obey.

My chest tightens, and I bring my hand up, rubbing at the forming pressure. A pang of yearning spasms, and I gasp as the emotion hits me like a crashing wave.

I didn't realize how much I miss him until now. My friend. My glowering, gentle Beast. I miss the brush of his mind, the cold grasp of his emotions as they weave around my soul. The ridiculous piles of fish.

He was going to let me go that day. He broke me out of the cage and swam toward the exit. Until I mentioned the king, and he panicked.

Tears sting my eyes. This is silly, crying over the Beast, while he lies next to me. His breath spills onto my neck, and my scales rise in response.

I'll be here whenever you need me. The ache in my chest intensifies as I remember his toothy grin, the moment he pushed me away. Pushed me toward the safety of his king's domain.

Shit. This is so complicated. My head spins, trying to keep it straight.

Aethan's fingers spread over my stomach, rough and warm. I turn my head to peer into his face and reach for him, pausing with my fingers a scale's breadth away from his cheek. Is he in there, somewhere? The version of him I fell in love with first?

CHAPTER FORTY-ONE

AETHAN

THE RETURN TRIP IS uneventful. After an early start, we make good time, and the group rides into the courtyard as the high-tide sun peaks in a clear sky. I dismount, and my feet land on cold, sturdy stone. Home.

The castle rises in its rustic glory, beckoning me into its embrace. Nothing has changed, not here. Guppies chase the birds beneath the sapwood trees. The adults in the courtyard avoid looking directly at me as they peer in curiosity at our spoils.

My subjects seem happy enough. No fresh signs of mourning. No atmosphere of panic.

And the hunt was a roaring success, thanks to Nahla's skill with magic. I couldn't have imagined a better outcome. A sleigh brimming with fresh game, happy hunters, and Nahla in my furs two nights in a row.

Somehow, Goddess Audrina decided to shine her favor on me. And her favor looks a lot like a Brine Princess laughing in the firelight, cradling my head in her lap.

Nahla stayed with me last night. It wasn't a dream. When I woke, she was still there, curled into my side. No sex. Just cuddling. Pure trust.

Fuck. What do I do with that? I could visit her tonight. We could sit next to the fire with a pile of furs. She could read while I run my fingers through her hair, letting the silky strands pass through my hands again and again until we lull to sleep. I'll make sure it wasn't a onetime stroke of luck.

"Ready?" I hold out my hand to help Nahla dismount. But she's already out of the saddle, stroking the snowbear's chin. Her hat sits lopsided on her head, exposing an ear to the cold. She doesn't seem to notice or care.

"You be good, okay?" she coos to the snowbear, ignoring me.

She's good with animals, I'll admit. The cranky mount has taken a liking to the princess. It pushes its snout into her hand, snuffling as it searches for treats. Nahla laughs and tucks a bit of jerky between its fuzzy lips.

My chest tightens, and I look away. Would she still like me—as *him*? I hope so. It's only a matter of time before she finds out. And then what?

"Come. I'll walk you inside," I say, before the dark thoughts can creep in.

She looks up and smiles, mischief dancing in her eyes. "Depends on where you're taking me."

"Your room, of course."

Her face falls. "Of course," she echoes.

The joy of the hunt is crumbling already, like ice into a frothing sea.

She rearranges her expression into a blank slate. Is she unhappy with me? Tired from the journey? I should get her inside, where it's warm and comfortable. Deirdre can brew a pot of tea, or hot chocolate. Females fucking love chocolate.

"Come on, then," I grunt.

She pats the snowbear one last time, then follows me out of the stables. Our snowleathers crunch on the snow, the only sound between us.

Has she had hot chocolate before? Suddenly, I'm overcome with the need to see her nose-deep in a mug of cocoa, milk froth clinging to her mouth. I glance at her lips as hunger churns my stomach.

Nahla keeps her gaze on the ground, her mouth set in a firm line, following me wordlessly. The sooner we get that hot chocolate, the better. Something is bothering her; that much, I can tell. My hand flexes at my side, straining toward her. Will she recoil if I hold her hand?

Probably.

I ball it into a fist instead.

When we reach the castle, the captain greets us with a quiet salute and opens the door.

"Ah, there you are, love!" Deirdre exclaims, hurrying to meet us. She skips me completely, rushing to snare Nahla in a motherly inspection. "Let's get you warm."

Nahla brightens as the housekeeper fusses over her, removes her tattered cloak, and presses a hot cup of tea in her hands.

"Good to see you too, Deirdre," I grumble, removing my cloak.

The housekeeper shoots me a sassy look and dips her head. "Sire, I only have so many hands."

Nahla lifts her cup and takes a long, seductive sip. Her lips part around the porcelain with the promise of something more.

Amusement tightens my eyes. "Go ahead and get her warm."

"Hold the door, Captain!" Lucas's voice rasps behind me, with the sound of crunching snow. The healer rushes inside on a gust of wind, dusts the snow from his cloak, and stomps his feet on the rug.

The princess glances over her shoulder as Deirdre guides her down the hall, away from me. I nod at her, reassuring. The hot chocolate can wait, then. We'll have some with dinner.

"A successful hunt!" exclaims Lucas.

I sigh, dragging my gaze away from Nahla's retreating form. "Indeed."

The healer claps the captain on the shoulder, pulling him inside. "Captain, I hope your days without us were uneventful. No certain... casualties."

The captain glances my way, a careful strain in his gaze, and my heart leaps into my throat. I swallow it. Bad news, then.

So why do I feel relief?

Dizziness prickles the edge of my vision. I prop my hand on the wall to steady myself. If my subjects are dead without me, it means *I'm not the perpetrator, after all.*

Could it be true?

I glance up, magnetized to the sight of Nahla several paces away. Her curls lay frizzy over her shoulders, spilling down her back, that hat still ridiculously askew. Hope flares, hot and dangerous.

She's safe with me.

I don't have to protect her from myself, only an exterior force—a monster *out there* is easier to subdue.

Nahla looks over her shoulder, and her gaze bores to the back of my head. Scales stand on my neck as an intense wave of curiosity washes through my mind. Interest. Irritation. The feelings are foreign and feminine, originating outside myself.

I frown, trying and failing to wrench my gaze from her face. The corner of her mouth lifts, just so.

Is this feeling... *hers*?

"Sire?" the captain prods. "Should I wait on the report?"

Nahla turns away, finally, and follows Deirdre. With each step she takes, the strange feelings lessen. Her hips twitch with the confidence of a female up to no good.

"Now is fine," I snap at the captain.

"It's good news, Your Majesty. There have been no killings since four days past, you'll be pleased to know."

My stomach flips. I squeeze my eyes shut. Every muscle in my body strings taut.

Fuck.

The wall tips closer as my body sags against it, my weight suddenly too heavy to bear.

No killings can only mean one thing: I am to blame—for everything. No one can die if you take the villain away.

I inhale, drawing the breath through the length of my body, as the familiar rage burns. I should have seen it coming. Shouldn't have let myself hope.

Lucas's hand clamps on my shoulder, steadying and firm. "Your Majesty? This is excellent news."

"Yes." I force my reply through clenched teeth. "Thank you, Captain. Let's hope the good streak continues."

Nothing has changed. I am a liability, a risk to my kingdom, and there's nothing I can do but return to my cage.

***

"How did it go, Your Majesty?" Deirdre asks. She stands in my bedroom doorway, propping the door open with her hip. On the other hip, she balances a basket full of my clean laundry. My housekeeper doesn't wait for my answer before she pushes into the room, making quick strides toward my wardrobe.

The light of my new sight-pool fades as I disconnect the spell. All is as it should be, just as the captain said.

Fuck.

"An excellent hunt." I force a grin, standing to intercept her. "Thank you."

We've been home for a few hours, and I'm already spiraling. Gone is the lightness in my chest, the blissful ignorance of the hunt.

Deirdre's eyes narrow as I take the laundry basket from her.

"That's great," she says. She watches as I lift the first crisp shirt from the pile and hang it in my wardrobe. My fingers fumble with the buttons, fastening them lopsided.

I don't give a fuck. I need something to do with my hands. They tighten around the fabric, wrinkling the linen.

"Are you okay, Sire?" Deirdre asks. "That's my job."

"Hm?"

She takes the shirt from me and unfastens the buttons, adjusts the hem, and buttons it the right way. "You're in a mood."

"It was a good hunt."

"Lots of game, I heard." She cocks an eyebrow. "And the hunters seemed pleased by your Brine spy. She's got quite the gift. Useful."

Her words are bait, dangling on a line. Tempting me into gossip. I fold a pair of pants against my chest, creasing every fold with precision. "Yes. Useful."

"Are you planning to keep her around a while?"

I clench my jaw and work hard to keep my expression neutral. With great effort, I clear my throat. "Not sure."

"Well, it'd be a shame to keep someone so *useful* locked in the guestroom forever." Her ulterior motive. I should have guessed this visit wasn't about laundry.

"My intentions for the princess are none of your concern, Deirdre," I snap.

"Your Majesty, if I may be so bold?"

"Hasn't stopped you before." I snatch the last shirt and stuff a hanger inside the shoulders.

Her lips twitch in a small smile. "You're harboring a foreign princess. Eventually, the truth will come out, regardless of your *intentions*."

"You want me to let her go."

She says nothing, only lifts the empty basket to its place on her hip.

"We could feed the kingdom in half the time, with her leading the hunt. How could I let her go, when she's such an asset to the kingdom?"

"Is that all she is to you? A tool to wield for the greater good?"

My ears burn. "I'm not…"

"At least give her the choice, Sire. She might surprise you."

"And if she leaves me? I could never bear it, Deirdre. I—"

"Shh, shh." Deirdre holds up a finger. "This conversation is between you and Nahla. Dinner's in an hour. You can tell her then."

She pushes through the door and takes a step into the hallway. My stomach sinks as she leaves. Deirdre has always had my best interest in mind, and whether I like to hear it, she's never wrong.

The door is almost closed when I call out her name. She turns, cocking an eyebrow.

I smile, an apology of sorts. "Speaking of dinner, I'd like to serve hot chocolate tonight."

"An excellent idea, Sire." She winks.

CHAPTER FORTY-TWO

NAHLA

I stand corrected: the Frost King *is* capable of lavishness. The table before me brims with it. Salads, soups, roasted meats, piles of sweet rolls, little jars of jam. Three plates and a bowl stack at my place setting, surrounded by various sizes of forks and spoons. And to top it all, a steaming mug of a rich chocolate drink smothered in cream.

"Are you making amends, Your Majesty?" I quip, draping the napkin over my lap.

If he thinks he can keep me locked in my room all day, then apologize with an abundance of treats at dinner, he's mistaken. I grew up with Winona, and I know all the tricks.

"Drink that before it gets cold," Aethan grunts. He takes a bite of roast woollygoat and chews it roughly, like he's angry at the meat.

I lift the mug to my mouth, hyperaware of his tracking gaze on my hands, my lips. He can't look me in the eye. Am I just something pretty to watch at his dinner table? A doll, once again utterly useless in my role.

Fine. See if I fucking care. I watch him over the rim of my mug, determined to hate every drop.

Our shared intimacy on the hunt meant nothing to him, I'm sure. It was hypothermia-induced sex. Hot, heavy, record-shattering sex.

I sip. The drink is velvety sweet and coats my throat with warmth. It's like a fucking hug for my taste buds, and I almost forget to be mad at him.

I take another sip. Then another. Foam clings to my upper lip. *Shit, that's good.*

Aethan stares, his expression battling to stay neutral. "Do you like it?" he asks.

Only his eyes give him away, sparkling like crystal in the morning sun. I study their twinkling hue as my suspicion thickens. Give a female sweet treats, and she'll say yes to sex later. Is that what this is about?

Not that I'd mind a little more sex. But I shove the thought aside.

"It's good. I haven't tried it before. Is this a regional drink?" I lick my lips, growing smug as his eyes follow the path of my tongue.

That's right, big guy. I'm onto your games.

His mouth twitches. "We call it hot chocolate."

"Hmm." Whatever it's called, it's fucking delicious. As I guzzle my way to the bottom of the mug, a subtle wave of feeling brushes against my mind. Scales rise on my neck at the foreign emotions: a flash of pleasure, tinged with possession.

I stare at him, puzzled.

He tears into a sweet roll with his perfect teeth, and his eyes flick in my direction. The strange sensation intensifies into worshipful reverence.

"Did you say something?" I ask.

He dabs his mouth with a napkin. "No."

Odd.

I pluck several lushfruit from the pile and pop one in my mouth. Citrus juice floods my throat, and my cheeks pucker. Another wave of emotion hits me, this time aggressive admiration. I get the sudden urge to squeeze the lushfruit in my hands and mash it to a fleshy red pulp. To take my tongue and—

I release the fruits, and they fall to the table with a soft *plunk, plunk, plunk.*

Sexual attraction to lushfruit? What the actual *fuck*?

Aethan sucks in a sharp breath. His jaw flexes three times, eyes on my discarded fruit, and then he looks up, finally meeting my gaze.

Deliberately, I pick up a lushfruit. With gentle fingers, I push it between my lips. His pupils widen, two black saucers in a sea of ice.

The intruding emotions come again. Lust. Animalistic, burning lust. The light blue of his irises darken, navy bleeding into the edges. The longer I stare, the darker his eyes become.

My stomach flutters. *I know those eyes.*

I clench at the strength of my yearning for the Beast hidden inside him. What would it take to get him to come out and play?

I'm tired of the king's games. I crave connection, deep and utter synchrony with his mind and emotions. I want the rough touch of his hide, the sharp snick of his claws. The raw power of his thrashing tail. No more tricks. No more barriers. I want intimacy in its purest form—the brush of our souls, intertwined.

I blink, refocusing on Aethan's face. His brow is furrowed, mouth strained. His eyes are glassy now, and he looks straight through me.

Lust. Frustration. Need.

Are these thoughts *his*?

My hands grip the napkin in my lap, balling it tightly. As if a piece of cloth could ground me in my body and keep my soul from lifting. As if I could stop the slow curl of magic in my stomach, rising to his call.

The song buzzes in my throat, through my parting lips, and then I'm singing to the king. A raspy, alto note rings out, resonating deep in my chest.

Aethan goes rigid. His eyes snap into focus. Hands clamp on the table, the tips of his fingers stained dark blue.

Shit. I thought my magic didn't work on merfolk minds, only animals. So why is it working on him now? Suddenly, I crave the answer.

Part of me spirals toward him. I surround his mind, brushing against his conscience as I continue to sing my spell. I inflect the tune, adding words. "Hello, Beasty. Did you miss me?"

Aethan hisses. His head tips to the ceiling as his jaw clenches, working hard. The blue scales crawl over his strained knuckles.

"Nahla, *please*. Don't do this." His voice rumbles, deeper than usual, taking on a gravelly timbre.

"Do what, Your Majesty?"

I skirt the edges of his mind, scanning for weak points. His outer defenses form a hard shell, cold and firm as iron.

"Stop. Singing." He pushes out of his chair, rising to his full height. Glowering, angry Beast. My core floods with arousal. *Shit*.

"Come out and play."

He comes around the table, prowling toward me with the starved look of a predator. With his foot, he drags the leg of my chair, swiveling me to face him head-on. He bends low and frames me with his hands. The scent of him washes over me, peppermint and snow, and my eyelids flutter. Every nerve in my body rises to greet him.

Yes, Beasty. I'm right here.

"I don't know what you're talking about," he grunts.

A coy smile spreads my lips. "Don't you, Aethan?"

"No."

"Take me for a swim."

"No." His nostrils flare. "You don't know the risks. I could"—he chokes out the words—"hurt you."

Hurt me? I don't fucking care. Let him try. Let him do his worst. I need him. I want him, all of him, as much as he can give me.

No more secrets.

I clench my diaphragm and strengthen my Voice, forming the command with my mind and mouth. "*Come.*"

I pierce the shell of his psyche, bursting into the world of his emotions. Desire. Anger. Desperation. Yearning. The clouds of his thoughts rise to greet me, swirling and sucking me deeper. Ushering me in.

Aethan's eyes widen. His grip tightens on my chair and his breath comes more quickly. He touches his forehead against mine.

"You," he gasps. "You will ruin me."

I grasp him by his ears, and hold him in place. Our noses slide together. My song swirls between us, building as the mental connection strengthens through our touch.

"Please." I close my eyes and nuzzle closer still until our lips rest a scale's breadth apart. "Let me in."

War rages within him, the fury against the hope. A storm of ice and flame. Then Aethan closes the gap and kisses me. Hard. With a desperate growl of surrender.

CHAPTER FORTY-THREE

AETHAN

Nahla's mouth is glazed with hot chocolate and cream, complementing her sweet taste, and I devour every inch. Suck the plump curve of her bottom lip. When I growl, she trembles in her chair.

Her spell dies out, muted by my kiss, but it's too late.

She has awakened the Beast within me, and our connection lingers.

He slinks from his cage in my mind and slips into my extremities, transforming me one scale at a time. The change is inevitable, now. As soon as I hit water, I'll be gone. Already, the aching impulse in my limbs screams at me, propelling me to find the shore.

But she already knows this. Somehow, Nahla has puzzled me out. Her soft lips on mine obscure her quiet calculations, her espionage.

She fucking knows. For how long? Did she know my secret on the Frosted Plains? When I fucked her in my furs? *Did she already know when she first arrived?*

Ice crawls up my arms and legs as the blue scales ripple.

She breaks the kiss and gasps for air. "That's it," she coos. Her fingers curl around the shell of my ears, holding me fast. "Come play. Take me for a swim."

I shake my head, as my ability to resist her rapidly thins. "You don't want that. You don't want *him*, do you?"

"Yes, Aethan," she whispers. "I want *you*. All of you."

Pleasure courses through me, desperate and needy.

My hands lurch. Grab. I snare her waist. Lift her from the chair. Sling her over my shoulder. I carry her from the dining room, charging toward the front door. Her body bounces on my shoulder, soft and supple. My hand curls around the meat of her perfect thigh, securing her.

I shouldn't be doing this. I should focus on my calming techniques—heat, bran, and darkness. Inhale and count to a thousand. Anything to keep her safe from the Beast bursting inside of me.

Instead, I open the front gate. Low tide spreads before us, the rocky beach lit by the fading rays of sunset. Waves wake and crash against the stones, frothing at the mouth of the Rime.

"I'm a monster, Nahla."

She grips my hair at the base of my neck. "I don't care."

Fuck.

Would it be so bad to lose control? To let her see? What if it *works*? What if I'm wrong about everything?

I would never hurt her. Never.

The Beast's conscience rises within me, growling in agreement. *Sunfish said come. I will come.*

Fuck. It's dangerous. I can't put her in harm's way, for the sake of a fucking experiment.

Nahla clears her throat, a soft defiant sound, and then she's singing again. Her Voice pierces my mind and enters with a force of warmth. She's everywhere, expanding, filling, absorbing. Understanding. My eyes flutter, heart speeding at the intimacy of her touch.

I will come.

I jab at the rising Beast, pushing him into his cage. But he wrestles me for control, fighting with a force I've never seen. With a hard shove, he squashes me. My body turns to ice, and he seizes control.

My knees buckle. Nahla hiccups, twisting in my arms as we tumble into the water, both of us helpless to the will of the Beast.

Chapter Forty-Four

BEAST

So pretty.

So perfect.

So *mine*.

Nahla clings to my chest.

Hands tangle in my hair.

Golden scales spread.

Her legs morph into a soft, flowing tail.

We plunge into the Rime.

My heart squeezes.

I *missed* her.

My body expands and shifts. Scales darken.

Horns sprout and spines poke through.

Claws extend.

Tail thrashes.

Thighs clench and kick, propelling us into deeper water.

Power.

Control.

Her magic weaves through the barrier of my mind, and her voice echoes through me. *Hello, Beasty.*

She sounds happy.

Me too.

My chest might explode from the pressure of this feeling.

I speak, pouring all my affection into it: *Sunfish.*

My heart is fast. Needy. Never have I wanted anything more desperately.

Her slick tail slides against my abdomen, and I scent her arousal. Thick and sweet. She wants me, too.

Against the sheath between my legs, my cock hardens, begging for release.

Not yet.

Not here.

First, I must take her somewhere safe.

Who knows what could be lurking in the deep?

I angle past the dungeon, toward the old royal city, where the forgotten ruins of Doloch are embedded in the glacier. Here, the hollow passages were carved over millennia. Ancient and grand.

Nahla peers around, and I sense her awe through our mental link. It's a beautiful city. Tall spires of ice. Intricate engravings. Buttresses. Two pikewhale statues guard the entrance, their long spears home now to glacierweed. A pity, but still beautiful.

Where are we going? she asks.

I smirk. She's going to love this.

You'll see.

Through the entrance and into the hollow center of the city. Ice stretches around, forming a bowl above our heads. From the ceiling dangles a broken chandelier, its glowmite lamps scattered on the floor. Tunnels branch in all directions. I take the far tunnel, passing into the shadows.

Nahla clings more tightly to my chest. Her nose grazes my skin. My cock lengthens, and the fleshy tip slips between the gap in my sheath.

Almost there.

The tunnel opens into a vast cavern. Golden light streams high above, where the thin ice brushes the surface of the Rime, bathing the library in an orange sunset glow. Frozen stalagmites rise from the floor to form pillars of ice. Shelves are carved into every wall, each pillar, lined with old tomes. The water hums with ancient magic. A few tablets float aimlessly, dancing to the remnants of the book-keeper's lingering charm.

Nahla gasps. I release my hold on her, and she spirals into the room, spinning and staring in open wonder. Grinning madly.

Pride swells my chest. I knew she'd like it. And, fuck, she's stunning when she's this happy.

Aethan! she screams. *You've been holding out on me!*

I rumble in approval. Aethan. Yes, that's my name.

Beast, yes, but also king.

It's yours, Sunfish. All yours.

She stops her spin, turning to stare at me in wonder. She kicks her tail, barreling toward me. Gratitude slams into me through our mental connection moments before her body connects. Her hands slide over my chest, my shoulders, into my hair. *I knew it was you.*

I rumble. *I'm glad.*

She climbs me until her lips find mine, hovering a scale's breadth away. *Kiss me?*

My heart stutters. Her kissing books. Sunfish wants to demonstrate.

And when Sunfish wants something, I deliver.

I brush her soft lips with mine. Her tongue slips into my mouth and slides over my sharp teeth. I growl, and her fingers tighten in my hair.

I was right. She tastes like the sun.

Then our frenzy begins. We are two bodies, groaning and sliding together, desperate to become one. I let my instincts take me. My hands on her hips. Her ass. Her breasts.

Fuck, these breasts. So supple and perfect.

I kiss them. Suck them. Run my tongue between them. Her nipples harden at my touch.

All the while she moans. Her emotions blaze through my mind, matching my own. Desire so strong it threatens to engulf us both.

This kissing, I like it very much.

Her hands slide over my muscled stomach. Trace the V of my hips. My cock bulges in the sheath moments before she finds it, cups it, and coaxes me out of hiding.

My length springs free.

She pauses. Stares. A flash of awe, then fear.

You're fucking huge in this form. She wraps her hand around the base, but her fingers can't touch. *How's it going to fit?*

I purr at her praise, growing harder still. The king is large, but I am more so. Bigger. Better. Stronger. Made for bringing her pleasure.

I will fill you to the brim, Sunfish.

Her arousal floods the water. With my knuckle, I slide along her tail, finding the warm slit at her center. I've seen her pussy in two-legged form. But this slit is deeper. More sensitive. She will take my cock easily, I'm sure, and I will make her come on it, over and over, until she turns to reedgrass in my arms.

She trembles as I tuck my knuckle into her heat. I can't use my claws; I would tear her soft skin. So I massage softly, seeking the sensitive bud at her apex.

Her pleasure sears through our connection, and she arches her back, pressing herself into my touch.

Found it.

With eagerness, I rub her spot. She mewls and gasps. Her tail flicks restlessly, convulsing as pleasure racks through her.

The pleasure that I'm giving her. Me. How did I get so lucky?

Shit, she moans.

I need more pressure. More purchase. Tucking an arm around her waist, I pull her into my chest—as my knuckle continues to work her—and dive toward the nearest bookshelf.

Against the wall.

She obeys. Her tail tucks onto the ledge, and I sink my claws into the pillar of ice. Cage her in. My tail coils around hers, above her fins. Pinning her in place.

My erection stretches between us, wavering with need. She eyes it worshipfully, then brushes her thumb across the velvety tip, collecting my pre-cum before she slips her thumb into her mouth.

Naughty girl, I growl.

Fuck me, Aethan. Her eyes pull me in, warm and big and brown. I cannot resist her. I will not.

She will scream my name until the city collapses around us.

Her hand wraps around the base of my cock as she guides me to her warm slit. With a grunt, I seat myself at her entrance. My tip glides through her wetness, and I moan.

Are you ready? I ask.

Every nerve in my body stands on alert.

Aethan, she groans, stretching my name. Through our connection, I see visions of her fantasy. Me, slamming her into the shelves. Me, pounding her into the floor. Me, fucking her so hard the ice falls from the ceiling. All tinged with impatience.

Heat pulses through my veins. Goddess, what a dirty mind she has. I fucking love it.

Nahla grabs my hips and impales herself on my cock.

I sheathe in her heat, sliding deep inside her. Her walls flutter and flex around me to accommodate my size. Her eyes widen, mouth popping open in surprise. Fingernails dig into my hips.

F-fuck! Fuck, you're huge.

My stomach flips over, and pride swells my chest. *That's right, Sunfish. And it's all for you. Every inch. It's yours.*

Her thoughts deepen in warmth, a mental blush as my meaning leaks into her psyche.

I speak, *You're perfect.*

She tilts her hips to adjust the angle, then nods.

With a low, rumbling growl, I slide my cock out of her, leaving the tip inside. I grasp my shaft and move the tip through her heat, teasing her clit with it. Her eyes roll, lashes fluttering. The cutest fucking thing I've seen.

Her arousal spreads in the water, washing me in her scent. Sweet, desperate. Mine.

My chest burns for her, an ache so large I can't contain it, cannot soothe it. The only cure is the feel of her pussy wrapped tightly around my cock.

No, she protests, squirming as I work her clit. *Inside me. I need you inside me. Shit!*

That's all I need to hear.

I slip inside her, burying my cock to its hilt.

I rock into her. Again. Again. Faster. Harder.

Fuck.

She holds onto my hips and rides me as hard as I'm riding her. Her tail undulates as she works herself into a frenzy on my cock.

Fuck, she feels so good. So warm. So perfect. Like our bodies were made for each other. For this moment.

She moans her pleasure as I pump, over and over. The bookshelves rattle with each thrust. Ice creaks. Tablets slide and drop to the floor. But we do not stop.

We fuck.

My stomach twists with desperate pleasure. She's close to coming—I can feel the tightening of her walls, hear the desperate hiccup on her lips.

A-Aethan. I'm going to c-come. Fuck!

My Sunfish is about to explode from the performance of my cock. It's everything I've been dreaming about.

My animal instincts flare, hot and needy.

She's mine.

But it's still not enough. I need more. More. MORE!

I need to be closer.

I need to absorb her.

Become part of her.

Vision darkens. Blackness at the edges.

You're fucking mine, I rumble. *Now come for me.*

Her body convulses. Tail kicks. Nails dig into my hips. She arches her back and screams as her orgasm passes through her.

Pride swells.

That's my good girl.

I grab her.

Pull her.

Closer.

Hold her.

Tighter.

Pleasure builds.

One more pump.

Fuck!

I'm coming.

Stars flash.

Pleasure. So much pleasure.

She cries out.

There's blood.

Blood in the water.

Look down.

My claws, covered in blood.

Gashes on her hips.

Her eyes wide. Lip trembling. Face scrunched in pain.

I stare.

Broken. I broke her.

I wanted her too much.

Aethan.

Her voice comes, distant, like a whisper.

Aethan, it's okay.

She cups my cheek. Stroking softly.

Aethan, let's go. Take me to Lucas.

Her words register, but barely.

I hold her. Swim with her.

Gentle.

Her blood trails behind us.

Evidence of my crime.

I don't deserve her.

I cannot love her.

I lied.

I.

Am.

Not.

Safe.

CHAPTER FORTY-FIVE

NAHLA

WE DON'T TALK ABOUT what happened.

I recall bits and pieces. Me, in shock. Aethan, in terror. Pain. Deep, fleshy pain. Water parts around my body. Our mental link dilutes. A flash of cold wind, then the sound of creaking metal gates. Bare hands clutch me to a firm chest. A racing heart, battering ribs.

His heart. I can feel it aching.

I reach for his face.

But it's not Aethan's face, anymore. It's the healer. Lucas. Dark, glinting eyes. Cocky smile. He labors over my wounds, forehead dotted with sweat, golden tendrils weaving in and out of my flesh like warm needles.

More pain.

I scream.

Somewhere, wood cracks. Splinters. Falls. The king is angry.

His emotions brush my conscience. I feel his pain, too.

Pain, everywhere.

I swallow my screams so he can't hear them.

Then it's done. Lucas wraps my torso in gauze, just in case, but the bleeding is over. Fresh pink scars stripe my ribs on both sides.

Right as the tides, as Deirdre tells me so chipperly. She helps me to my room and tucks me into bed. All fixed.

But he does not follow me. With each step I take, our connection weakens. Then severs.

The door closes. The lock turns from the outside.

And I am alone.

***

ESCAPE IS IMPOSSIBLE. IRON bars block the window in my room, fashioned with gaps too small to squeeze my body through. I've tugged at every floorboard, every crack in the wall, and to no avail—there are no trap doors, no secret passages that might ferry me away from here.

It's been two days since I've seen the king. Or seen anything but the interior of this embellished prison. Like it's *my* fault.

Maybe it is.

Pain has a funny way of blotting out the details, right when it matters.

Once again, Perrin is my only company. Sort of. He guards my door with a stubborn scowl, trying hard not to break character, and relays gifts from the king—hot chocolate, wool slippers, a stack of romance books. Apologies passed from the king, but never the king himself.

Does Aethan regret what we did? The intimacy? The way our minds linked and synchronized, the shared climax of our pleasure...

I don't.

It was the best moment of my fucking life. I frequently wake with my hand between my legs, trying and failing to relive that feeling. Because he's never going to fuck me like that again.

Maybe he's right. It is all my fault. I provoked him. Encouraged him. Wanted it so badly he finally caved to my dangerous request.

What a mad thing to do, trying to fuck a clawbeast. By all means, it makes sense to lock me up. I'm a danger to the king, and a danger to myself. So I stay in bed. I burrow beneath a mountain of furs and soft blue pillows and pray to all the gods who listen to absolve me of my embarrassment.

The king regrets me.

I feel it in my bones.

I hear it in the way Deirdre speaks to me when she brings my morning tea. The distance in her voice. The apologetic kindness in her eyes.

Day three of this shit.

"Sugar, Your Highness?" she asks. The porcelain lid clinks next to my ear. She's standing beside my bed, her tray likely balanced on the end table.

I pull the covers higher overhead, retreating from the light of her candle. "No thank you, Deirdre." The pillow muffles my voice.

"Come now. You need a little something to cheer you up, hmm? How about some cream?"

"Just leave the tray. I can fix it myself."

Pressure dips the mattress as she sits on the edge. Her hand lands on top of my head, heavy through the layers of blankets.

"Are you feeling any better this morning?" Her fingers rustle at the hem, curling around the fabric, tugging it to let cool air through the opening.

"No."

Salt stings the corners of my eyes. I ball my fists into the covers, holding them over my face. I can't let her see me like this. How fucking embarrassing.

This is not princess-like behavior, hiding from the hurt. I should be upright and active, none of this moping, depressed lumpiness—Winona would be appalled. If she were in my place, my sister would take the king's rejection without more than a blink, then move on to her next project.

Then again, she ended up hitched to that boring lump of a male, Ferrell. At least my fate is better than hers, in that regard. I'd take one devastating tangle with the clawbeast over a life stuck with Ferrell.

And that's all it was—a tangle. Like our time in the ice-shelter was hypothermia-induced sex. It meant nothing.

My heart squeezes so tight I can't breathe.

It meant nothing.

I stuff the pillow into my mouth to keep quiet. My shoulders tremble and quake.

I'm a bald-faced liar. It wouldn't hurt this much if he meant nothing to me. Somehow, I've fallen for the grumpy Frost King. Now I'm no better than a love-sick guppy, pining over a male who doesn't want me. If he did, he'd be here. Tending to my wounds. Telling me I'll be okay. He'd be bringing me tea himself, not sending his housekeeper.

The mattress shifts. Deirdre sighs. Moments later, I hear her retreating footsteps, the turn of the doorknob, and her quiet report to Perrin in the hallway.

"Is she still in bed?" Perrin whispers, not quietly enough.

"Poor thing hasn't moved an inch."

"Shit."

"Watch your language, love."

"Sorry," Perrin mutters. I smile, despite myself. The youngling's picking up my favorite word. "I just wish he would—"

"His Majesty has his reasoning."

"Yeah, well…"

"Chin up, Perrin. He gave you an important post. You should be honored."

"I didn't know it'd be this boring," he mumbles.

Ouch.

Deirdre hisses something too low to hear. And then it's over. Her footsteps retreat down the hall, and Perrin's body slumps against the wall.

I pull the covers away from my face. Daylight filters through the crack in the curtains, cutting a line across my pillow. The stale air evaporates the tears from my cheeks. It's not Perrin's fault I'm imprisoned, and I'm being a shit friend.

I should at least *talk* to him. Maybe we could have a burping contest through the door. Or *something*. It'd be a good distraction for me, to avoid spiraling further into my pit of despair.

With a groan, I peel myself from the bed. Slip into my robe and tie the sash. I plant my feet on the cool wooden slats, my back creaks, and I sway with dizziness. *How long has it been since I ate?* My stomach lets out a hollow whine, and I clutch it.

Deirdre left toast with my tea, the butter hardened in a perfect rectangle on top. Cold. I pluck it from the plate and bite through the stiff crust as I walk to the door.

Pain flares in my side, spazzing along my scars.

Shit.

I stagger and clutch my ribs, dropping the toast. My skin itches and crawls beneath dry, puckered scabs. I rub at the gauze, unsatisfied. The itch intensifies. I rip through the gauze, tearing it from my body. With a fingernail, I slip beneath the edge of my scab. My eyelids flutter closed. *So itchy.*

I dig harder. Deeper. My nails collect dry scales beneath them. I drop to my knees, relishing the sweet sting of relief. *So fucking itchy.*

An iron scent fills the air. I tear my hands away and stare at them. There's blood under my nails. My stomach twists. What is wrong with me? Am I so fucking bored that making myself *bleed* sounded like fun?

I scrunch my eyes tight and swallow my pride.

"Perrin!" I groan.

The door flies open. "Nahla?"

Light pierces in from the hallway, and I raise my hand to block it from my straining eyes. Perrin crutches toward me as quickly as he can manage. Crouching on the floor, he inspects my hands with gentle fingers and frowns as he rotates my wrist and presses two fingers into my pulse.

"Shit, Nahla, what did you do to yourself?" His gaze lands on the discarded toast, butter-down on the rug. The torn gauze.

"You can't be saying that shit," I say. "You're a Frost Guard."

He shoots me a look. "You're bleeding, and you're worried about my vocabulary? You're just as bad as Aunt Deirdre, I swear to the goddess."

"I got... itchy." Blush creeps up my neck, hot. I'm a mess. No wonder Aethan doesn't want me.

Tears flood my lower eyelids, beading beneath my vision. Perrin pulls me into a hug, tucking me against his chest. He smells of leather and salt and sweat.

"Aw, Nahla. Don't cry on me," he murmurs. "This is my good uniform."

Too fucking late, Perrin. The pressure in my chest builds and bursts. My tears bubble over, and I hiccup as a sob trembles through me. How embarrassing.

He pats my back awkwardly.

I sob harder. My fingers twist into his uniform, smearing blood. He lets me cry for a while, sitting there like he's made of stone while my tears and blood stain his shirt.

I don't know why I'm crying. Maybe it's the boredom of the past few days in captivity. Maybe it's the residual sting of Aethan's rejection. Or maybe I'm sick of this whole damn show. I want to go *home*.

I shouldn't even be here.

The old way-maker, Keen, told me to make a life for myself, and this is where I ended up. Bawling on the floor over a little cracked scab. I'd be better off married to that damn Coral Prince.

"Should I fetch Lucas?" Perrin whispers. "For the bleeding?"

I release his shirt and nod, sniffing the snot back into my nose. "Okay."

Perrin gives me one more awkward pat, then slinks out of the room, leaving me once again alone.

Alone.

The tears build again, hot and angry. *Fuck you, Aethan. Fuck your castle. Fuck your hot fucking chocolate. Your snowbears, your staff, and your overstuffed pillows. And fuck me the worst, for wanting it all to be mine.*

Chapter Forty-Six

AETHAN

I AM A WORTHLESS cloud of whaleshit.

I remember everything. My mental fog is gone. The Beast's memories play on repeat like a guppy's carousel for the past three days—Nahla's face, Nahla's body, books falling, the bliss, then the urge. The fucking animalistic *urge*. It's all I can think about.

The bodies are piling up. Two more dead in the past three days. I'm losing control, and my subjects are dying. Because of me.

And the Beast has a selective memory, it seems. I remember Nahla's face clearly. But the others? My mind is blank. It's like he only wants to remember *her*. He's lording it over me—she wanted him, not me, and he's goddessdamn cocky about it.

I take the stairs to the basement, my rapid steps echoing deep into the recesses of my castle.

Nahla was right, I'm a fucking monster. She said it when she first arrived, and I should have listened to her then. So I'm listening to her now.

I will never touch her again.

Not until I get rid of this curse. And I know just the siren to help me.

Weeks ago, Lucas started his research, and at the beginning of the hunt, he mentioned he was onto something. Something about grimoires from the old library...

Memory flashes. Nahla perched on an icy bookshelf. Her mouth popped open in ecstasy. Bubbles escaping with every moan. Her hands clutching my hips. Nails, digging. Begging for more. *Harder. Harder.*

I drag my hand down my face as my stomach churns, clearing the memory before her blood spills. For years, I've wanted access to the Beast's memories. And now all I want is to forget them.

I clench my fist and pound on the healer's door. "Time's up, Lucas."

He opens the door, creaking the old metal hinges, and peers into my face. Lucas searches my gaze for a moment and seems to find what he's looking for. "I wondered," he says. "Come on in."

I grunt and step inside, surveying the familiar room. The same fireplace, the same stuffed frostcat hanging on the mantel, the same empty chair he saves for my sorry ass. I settle into it and grip the armrests.

Lucas takes his sweet time approaching me. He stops to adjust a few trinkets on his desk and wipes a bit of dust from the table, rubbing it between his fingers. I steady my breathing, pulling deep breaths to counteract the furious racing of my heart. "How can I help you today, Sire?"

"You said you found a cure."

"A hunch, Sire. Nothing is solid. This is all pure speculation, you see."

"Do it. I want him gone."

Lucas cocks his eyebrow. "Gone?" He opens a drawer, retrieving several strips of leather.

"Gone," I growl. The chair cracks under the pressure of my grip. "Now."

"Excellent," he says, teeth glinting in the firelight. He threads a leather strip beneath each armrest, securing my wrists one by one. Then he stoops low, tying my ankles.

Sweat beads at my hairline as I watch his hands make quick work of the task. "What's that for?" I demand, fighting to keep the anxiety out of my tone.

"Safety precautions, of course. We don't want to repeat the past." He stands back to survey his work, makes a small adjustment to the strap on my left arm, then nods curtly. "This might hurt."

After squaring his posture, the healer closes his eyes. His Voice rasps and groans, he lifts his hands, and golden tendrils slip out from his fingertips. When he opens his eyes, they glow with gilded flame.

The magic rushes into my body, crawling beneath my skin and lighting my organs as it passes. It slithers into my chest, where it swirls and builds into a large ball before sliding up my throat. I toss my head and gnash my teeth as it reaches my brain.

Fuck.

Like a thousand searing needles, his magic weaves through my skull.

My body clenches, and I flex against the restraints. Crusty leather digs into my skin. Sweat coats every inch of me. I pant, drawing labored breaths.

Lucas strengthens his song.

"Fuck!" I bark.

In the tune of his spell, Lucas answers me, "It's the only way, Your Majesty. You must push through the pain."

Time drags. I squeeze my eyes shut, and the light bursts against my eyelids. The pain is unending. Twisting, gnawing agony, tugging at every chord in my brain.

"Gotcha!" His voice reaches me as if through a tunnel.

And then his magic pulls. Hard.

From the recesses of my mind, the Beast awakens. Ice bursts in my stomach as my magic flares in response. For a moment, I lose control of my body.

My mouth moves, and words form, without my command: "Leave, witch-doctor. Before I rip out your throat."

My teeth snap shut, and I land inside myself. Fear crawls over me, lifting my scales. What just happened?

"Begone, dark spirit!" Lucas bellows. "I expel your darkness from this mortal husk! You are not welcome here!"

The twisting sensation intensifies, and he yanks. Like ripping a fingernail from its socket.

I scream.

The ice drains from my stomach, following the path of Lucas's glowing light. Out of my body. My magic weakens by a fraction, lost to the aether.

"What are you doing to me?" I shout. My teeth knock together with force.

"The curse is connected to your magic, Sire! This is the cure. I will pull the magic from your body like a bloodfish from your side, and the Beast will come out with it."

I grip the chair, and the wood cracks. Take my magic away? *Is he fucking mad?*

"No," I growl.

Lucas sings louder. His magic grips the Beast, pulling harder. The Beast rattles in my head and clambers for purchase. His icy claws scrape the inside of my skull.

The Beast takes control. My mouth moves again—"I won't go!" My hands pull against the leather straps, and the left one snaps free. My arm flails through the air, grasping at nothing. The chair tilts, then slams back into place.

"Excellent, Sire! Draw him out of his shell!"

I wrestle for control, crowding him toward the back of my mind, but he will not let go. The Beast is in charge now.

My eyes fly open. Magic unfurls. Jaw drops. My Voice reverberates through the room, and ice explodes across the floor. Steep, jagged shards, straight toward the healer.

Satisfaction. Gleeful hatred. Let it split him in two.

But Lucas sidesteps the Beast's attack without breaking his spell.

"You will pay for the countless innocent lives, Beast. Begone!"

Confusion. Hurt. Innocence.

Feigned innocence. The Beast is a killer.

Anger, hot and consuming.

The scales spread rapidly, like a tidal wave over my limbs. My skin ripples with the speed of my transformation. I watch in terror as my fingernails darken, lengthen, and curve into wicked claws. My body stretches, muscles burning as I grow. The chair splinters apart.

I rise to my full height as my skin itches, dry and thirsty.

I need water. Ice-cold water.

I need to dive into it. To complete the transformation. Escape. Swim into the Rime and never emerge again.

Yes. That would be best for everyone.

Leave Sunfish alone.

Suddenly I can't breathe. A fissure forms in my chest, and I break around a Nahla-sized hole.

Grief. Agony. Pain.

"ENOUGH!" I boom.

Lucas cuts his spell, and the tendrils of magic suck out of my body. I stagger, tripping on a broken piece of chair, and catch myself on his desk. My claws dig deep, puncturing the wood.

"That's enough," I pant. "We're done here." My head spins. My heart pounds out an angry beat, threatening to break my ribs. I inhale. Count to ten. Count to twenty. Count again. Picture her face. Her bright, warm face.

Lucas watches me from a distance. I peer sideways at him, loathing the way he folds his hands neatly in front of him. Like a goddessdamn saint. His mouth drops in a disappointed scowl.

"We will try again tomorrow," he says. "If you want him gone, Your Majesty, you'll have to let him go."

CHAPTER FORTY-SEVEN

NAHLA

Day four and still not a peep from the Frost King. I have the urge to sprawl myself naked before the fire, tuck my hand between my legs, and sing a summoning song. Could he resist me then? I bet he'd be here in five seconds flat. Break through that door and grovel like a good boy.

But I don't do that. Instead, I sink into the leather chair by the fireplace and pick yet another book. The stone tablet rests in my lap, humming quietly with activated magic, moving pictures in my mind. It's another story about another couple falling desperately in love. Working against the odds to be together, and in the end, love wins. It always does. So why does it break my heart?

When the lovers fuck, I chuck the book into the fire. The flames lick at the stone, but it remains unharmed. *Fucking useless magical artifacts.* What good are they if I can't burn them in my rage?

A short pattern of knocks sound on the door—one heavy, two quick, then two light taps. Perrin. I move to answer him, repeating the pattern on my side of the door. Then the lock turns and the door cracks open. Lamplight spills in from the bright hallway.

"Hey," he says, sticking his head through the gap. "Got more books for you."

I take the stack of tablets and hug them to my chest. Three, this time. Glancing at the titles, I guess they're more romance.

"From the Royal Icicle?"

Perrin nods. "Who else?"

I roll my eyes. "Hey, do you think you could go to the library and find some different books for me?"

The young guard brightens. "Sounds like an adventure, I like it. I'll have to find someone to take my place for a bit..."

I level him with a look. "I'm not escaping, Perrin. I'm just tired of the king's taste in romantic comedy."

"Right."

"Think you could find me history books? I'm curious to learn more about the Frost Kingdom. Origin stories, royal lineage, famous battles. Know of anything like that?" Anything to help me figure out the mysterious king.

"Sure. I'll look later today, when I'm on lunch."

If it wasn't weird, I'd pinch his cheeks. I give him my best, friend-liest smile instead. "Thanks, Perrin."

He shoots me a sheepish grin before he locks me in again. I add Aethan's books to the growing stack by the fire, then pace the room.

Aethan is doing what he said he would. Piles and piles of romance books. Way too many to read in a few days. Is that his goal, then? To stuff me with romance fantasies so I can escape the reality of *his* failures?

And when you run out. I'll get you more.

Shit. I should have seen this coming. He said it, clear as day. That night he got drunk on the Frosted Plains and told me he wanted to keep me forever.

That way, you'll never have reason to leave me.

I should take the books and shove them out the window. Drop them right into the snow. Refuse them when Perrin brings me romance. No books? No reason to stay. Maybe that'll teach the king his lesson.

With a determined huff, I scoop a pile. Out the window it is. As I make my way to the curtain, I feel a mental tug. A wisp of feeling at the periphery of my conscience.

I freeze in my tracks.

He's here.

Aethan.

It's the first time in days he's ventured to my side of the castle.

The books drop to the floor with a dull thud.

Heart soaring, I race to the door. Press myself against it, as close as I can get. My cheek slides against the smooth darkwood, and my ear suctions. I strain to hear. Is he in the hallway? Is he close?

There. In the distance. Large feet on wood slats. His footsteps come closer. Closer.

Aethan.

I get a glimpse of his emotions: Anxiety. Pain.

Is he in trouble? Is he hurt? My fingers trace the surface of the door, catching in the grain. With all my heart, I will him to come closer. To close the gap. To let me out and into his arms. His mind. To let me soothe that pain.

But his footsteps retreat, and I lose my hold on him. *Shit.* I slump against the door as my heart sinks. Serves me right for hoping.

I eye the scattered books on my floor, all will to finish my earlier task vanished. Is this my imagination playing a cruel trick on me? I'm driving myself insane. I need to stop obsessing over him and move on with my fucking life.

I've experienced heartbreak before. I knew this would happen, and I still caught feelings.

Aethan has kept me prisoner since the moment I arrived. Posted a godsdamn guard at my door. What idiot falls for the asshole who caged her?

Me, that's who. I'm a stupid, chum-brained idiot.

I ball my hands into tight fists. If he comes through that door, I'm going to punch his pretty little nose.

Angry tears spill on my cheeks.

Wait.

His footsteps sound again. Coming closer. Faster. I feel a flare of emotion, burning with hope. It's mine—and his. Aethan is *hopeful*?

I press my ear to the door, desperate for any clues. Perrin stirs on the other side. Clears his throat. His keys jingle as he adjusts his stance.

"Your Maj—"

Aethan grunts, cutting him off.

That sound, the rumbling gravel in his chest, I missed it. *He's here.* Moisture springs into my eyes anew, and I wipe them away. No time for tears.

Quickly, I run my fingers through my hair. I snare the tangles, pulling them apart. Fuck it. I toss it on top of my head and tie it in a quick, loose knot.

Hope. Anticipation. Worry.

The key fits into the lock.

I scramble away from the door. Smooth the wrinkles from my nightgown. Should I put on a robe? Mine lies in a puddle next to my bed. The sheets are a mess, drooping off the mattress like melted cheese. This is no way to greet a king.

A king, sure. But this is Aethan I'm worrying about.

I reel in my thoughts for a reality check. He trapped me in here. What did he expect me to do, keep it pristine for him in case he graced my sheets?

He hurt me, by accident, and instead of talking to me about it, he locked me in a room. I haven't seen him for four days. Why visit me now? Is he here to apologize?

The key stops turning.

Crushing rejection. Pain.

There's a thud on the door, dull like a forehead sinking against wood.

Oh, no, no, no. What happened? Why did he stop turning the key? I wring my hands, twisting them in the silky fabric of my shift.

"Aethan." A whispered plea.

"Are you all right, Sire?" Perrin says outside my door.

Aethan grunts again. "She's not ready to see me." His voice pierces like a knife, and I flinch. He must have heard my thoughts. Dread sinks cold and heavy into my bones as I sway on my feet.

No. I didn't mean it. Don't go.

"Pardon me, but what do you mean? Not ready? Sire, she's been—"

"She's. Not. Ready."

A whip of leather. His cape? And then his footsteps storm down the hall. Growing softer with each step.

I rush to the door. My palms sting as I slap the wood with both hands. "Aethan!"

"Nahla," Perrin groans from the other side. "I'm so sorry."

"Shit!" I slap the door again. Slide to the floor. My body collapses in a heap. He was so close.

So fucking close.

CHAPTER FORTY-EIGHT

AETHAN

WE FALL INTO A pattern: Lucas's magic pierces my skull, the Beast ruins the spell, and I let it happen again and again. Searching, pulling, searing pain. As soon as the Beast awakens, it's over. I lose control, the Beast fights back, and I'm left panting and sore. Each time we fail, Lucas glares at me, that disappointed scowl plastered on his face.

So fucking predictable.

My head throbs with an insatiable ache, right behind my eyes. No tincture can ease the pain.

When the session is over, I absorb into the darkness of my chambers, shying away from all sources of light. No candles. No fire. Just shadows.

It's what I deserve. What I asked for—this is the price to pay for Nahla's safety, and I will pay it, no matter the cost.

I let my magic consume me, leaking from my hands without direction. I fill my chamber with snow. Ice. It drips from the ceiling, crawls on the floor. I shiver in the dark.

At some point, my magic takes direction, and my hands carve and bend, forming soft shapes in the snow. A face. Button nose. Smooth, plump lips. Her hair tumbles past her waist, and I smooth her hips with care, tracing each perfect curve, until she stands before me in perfect replica. Her face is white, her eyes glassy and unseeing. Full of pain. Along her ribs, I carve three scars. There.

Even in ice, Nahla tortures me.

My chest aches with grief, heavy and cold. *I deserve this. I'm a monster.*

I touch her face, and she crumbles beneath my thumb.

***

Come for me.

Her Voice reaches through the fog of my thoughts, hooking me like a lure. My spine straightens at her call. Scales rise on my neck, and my heart lurches into a desperate rhythm.

My body moves, rising from my desk chair. I do not stop myself. I do not fight. Her sweet melody rings in my ears, wraps around my soul, and I am weak to the sound. I can't resist her any longer.

I stumble into the dimly lit hallway, down the corridor, and into the East Wing.

Come.

The closer I get to her, the stronger the pull.

Perrin stands guard at her door, wringing his hands nervously. "Your Majesty!" he balks. "I didn't know if I... Should I make her stop singing?"

I hardly hear him. Her Voice is strong, the only thing that can hold my attention.

I growl, too far gone for words. He steps back and hands me the key. I jam it into the lock and turn it with a satisfying click. The door swings inward, and I inhale her sweet scent.

She's aroused.

My hand grips the doorknob, suddenly the only thing grounding me in time and place. Nahla stretches out on the rug before the fireplace, propped on her elbows like a fire-lit goddess. Singing her summoning spell with a glorious smile. Completely naked.

Her fingers dangle in front of her pussy, glistening wet.

Fuck.

I clear my throat. "Perrin, leave us." Stepping into the room, I close the door before he can answer.

She beckons me with a crooked finger. Her alto Voice rolls through my head, low and seductive. *Come to me, Beasty.*

My cock hardens instantly. *Goddess above.* Why have I been resisting her so long? Is it that necessary? The Beast hasn't ruined her beyond repair, as I feared. She's healthy and glowing. Irresistible.

I stride toward her. Drop to my knees. Crawl. Like the fucking Beast I am.

That's a good boy.

Her praise lifts my heart, and my chest tightens at its expanse. Why the *fuck* did I leave her alone?

"Nahla…" I groan, her name choking me. I don't deserve to have that name bless my lips. Not after what I've done. Still, I straddle her, dipping my nose to her neck. Warm vanilla paradise. Goddess, how I missed her smell. I press a kiss to the soft hollow of her throat. "Nahla, I'm so—"

"Don't." Her finger stops my lips. I pull back to study her face.

She watches me with a glint in her eyes, mischief on her mouth. Her song continues, blocking out any emotional connection we've previously shared and making her unreadable. Warning bells ring in my mind, but I ignore them.

I need her. Now. I need to show her how sorry I am, how badly I fucked up. How much I've regretted every minute I've spent apart from her. I want to tell her everything—the curse, my plan with Lucas, how I'm doing it for her. How I'm making damn sure she'll be safe with me.

But her finger is in the way.

I growl, pushing it aside. "I hurt you. And I'm a fucking fool for it."

Her spell fades into silence, and the quiet crackle of the fire replaces the sound of her siren song. She cocks her eyebrow. Her knees lift from the floor, parting to cage my hips. Hooking around me. Pulling me closer.

Forget explanations. I'll tell her everything as soon as I've pounded her into the floor with my cock.

I groan, heartbeat thundering through me. My erection rests between her legs, prodding her sweet, naked pussy. I can feel her heat through the leather of my pants. "Fuck, you're so wet. Is this for me?"

Is this how she'll forgive me? Do I even fucking deserve it?

"No," she says.

I blink, confused.

Her legs tighten like a vise. Hands slide up my back, fingers twisting into the base of my hair. And then, with a gleeful smile, she flips me.

My head slams into the floor so hard that stars dance. Nahla perches on top of my stomach and wraps her hands around my throat.

"Asshole," she snarls. Gone is the playful look on her face. Gone is her smile. Tears brim in her eyes, reflecting the light of the fire. A single drop spills over and trails down her cheek. She loosens her hold on my neck, her thumb tracing aimless circles as her bottom lip trembles. "Hot chocolate and romance novels. Is that all you think I need to be happy? You fucking cunt." She spits the last word.

I see them now: the books are scattered by the fire. At least fifty, sprawled haphazardly. A few stones have been tossed into the flame, glowing red-hot among the coals. I'm a fucking idiot if I thought she'd be appeased so easily.

"But you like those things," I say. I reach to wipe her spray from my cheek, but she grabs my wrist and pins it to the rug.

"You locked me in here for four fucking days, Aethan. And you expect I'll welcome you with open legs."

Heat flushes my cheeks. I knew it was too good to be true.

She smirks. "The pretty king is blushing. I suppose that's answer enough."

"Nahla," I breathe. Pushing from the floor, I swivel into a seated position and pull my cloak around us to swaddle her naked form. "Come here, Sunfish."

She melts into my chest. The point of her nose slides over my shirt, back and forth. I tuck her head beneath my chin and rest in her soft curls. My hand roams her back, catching on the fresh scars on her ribs. I skim them gingerly as a deep ache builds in my chest.

These are the marks of a monster.

"Why did you leave me alone?" she whispers, voice thick with pain. I've hurt her, in more ways than one. And that's something I promised I'd never do. "I thought we were..."

"Nahla."

"Stop saying my fucking name. Say something else. Tell me why you did it. Tell me what was more important to you. I don't care that you got carried away. That night in the library... it was fucking perfect. I *loved* it. So please don't say you did this for my sake."

"Nothing is more important to me than you, Nahlani Mahelona. I cannot lose you." I swallow past the lump forming in my throat. Will she understand I must do it for her? It's there, on the tip of my tongue, the truth that will explain everything. But I can't find all the words. "I'd be lost without you. Don't you see? I'm..." I blow out a ragged breath. "Lost."

Her expression softens. She places her hand flat on my chest, right over my throbbing heart. "Then *talk* to me, Aethan. Let me help you find your way. I'm tougher than you think."

A smile tugs at my lips. "You're a badass."

Nahla's laughter peels like a bell, brightening the entire room, and the pressure in my chest eases. "I know," she says.

Her resistance fades. As she exhales, I feel a brush on my mind. Her emotions float to me, bathing me in her feelings of relief. Safety.

The lump in my throat hardens. "I'm sorry. It won't happen again."

She leans back, peering into my face with narrowed eyes. "You're talking about locking me in my room, right? Not the fucking."

"Right. Definitely not talking about fucking." I let my gaze drop, drinking in the sight of her ample breasts. The perfect curve of her neck. Soft cheeks. The way her curls fall across her forehead. Those long, dark lashes. She's so fucking beautiful. "Let me make it up to you."

"Okay." She blows the air from her cheeks. "But that's a tall order. I'm picky."

Goddess, this female.

She's got me wrapped around her little finger. I know I fucked up. I hurt her, and I got scared—scared of how she'd react when she saw me again. Afraid she'd tell me to get lost. That she hated me. Hate, I could have handled. Nobody could hate me more than I hate myself.

I didn't visit her because I was afraid if I opened the door, I'd find her room empty.

By some miracle, she's still here. In my arms. Smiling. Making shit jokes. Nahla deserves the fucking world, and I'm going to give it to her.

She arches her back, dragging her nipples against my shirt. "So, how are you going to make it up to me, Aethan the Terrible?"

"I have an idea," I say.

"Thunderous sex?"

"Likely." I smile. "But I have something better in mind."

"What's better than sex?"

I tap her nose. "You'll see."

CHAPTER FORTY-NINE

NAHLA

HE LEAVES ME WITH instructions to wear something dazzling and meet him after sunset—for his better-than-sex plot to regain my favor.

Already, nervous eels slither within my stomach, and I catch myself staring at the door long after it's closed behind him, wondering what the night may hold. Will he wine and dine me? Draw up a hot chocolate bath?

Soon enough, Deirdre arrives to help me with my wardrobe, and after four days, I taste freedom at last. She smiles encouragingly, holding the door wide open as I peer into the light.

"She has emerged!" Perrin gasps. "Thank the goddess."

"Pleased to bring you some entertainment tonight, Sir Perrin." I drop into my sassiest curtsy, and he laughs. My heartbeat launches into my throat, fluttering nervously as I step into the hallway.

Four fucking days. Will Aethan force me back in here, after this is all over? Or has he seen the error of his ways?

"You're in for a real treat tonight," Deirdre says, her eyes sparkling. "This way, love. We'll get you cleaned up for the ball."

Deirdre leads the way, and Perrin trails us, whistling a happy tune.

Warning lifts my scales. It's too good to be true—sudden freedom, Aethan making amends through dancing. The strategy screams *Winona* to me. Clean me up, give me a pretty dress, and make me perform for the spectators. How many strangers will I have to charm tonight?

My legs stretch out, muscles warming. Shit, it feels good to walk over ten paces in a straight line. I bristle. *Asshole.* His plan had better be phenomenal. I told him I'm difficult to impress, and I'm sticking to it.

We enter a grand dressing room, and my breath catches. An elegant vanity sits in the middle of the room, lit by a glittering chandelier. Brushes, pins, and rouge are organized in little golden containers in front of the mirror. A rich red rug sprawls on the floor, leading to a walk-in closet at the far end, stuffed with lace and silk.

"Now, you sit here." Deirdre pushes me into the velvet-cushioned chair. Air exhales from the pillow as I sit. "Hair up? Down?" Her fingers lift and play with my hair, and a tingle crosses my scalp. "Half and half?"

Then she attacks my head with a hundred hairpins, transforming my unruly curls into an updo fit for a queen. As she works, I grip the chair and clench my teeth.

My handmaid back home, Elodie, always had soft fingers. Deirdre uses the brutal force of a Frost mermaid, efficiently pulling my hair into position within ten minutes flat.

A fucking ball. This is the king's idea of fun. Better than sex, he assured me. Clearly, I've fallen for an idiot.

But at least I'm out of that room.

With a slow inhale, I push the anger away for now. Tonight could be fun, if I let it. Maybe I'll make new friends with the other ladies. Or dance with so many males, Aethan will boil over and scream like a kettle. That'd be fun to watch.

I'll keep my expectations low and relish whatever comes my way. This room is gorgeous, and I can enjoy a little pampering for a change. Right?

Finally, Deirdre releases my head and steps back to survey the final product. She catches my eye in the mirror and smiles. "You look lovely, my dear."

"You think so?" Softness fills my reflection. My dark eyes are bright, skin flushed, cheekbones full and round. Candlelight kisses my complexion, giving me an ethereal glow. I look happy. Pretty. Adorned with a diamond-studded comb, my coffee-colored hair collects in a loose top bun, with a few ringlets left to frame my face. Pink gloss coats my lips, moving to form my answering smile.

Deirdre squeezes my shoulders. "I *know* so. Simply stunning."

"Thank you." I touch the ringlets, careful not to disturb the curls. "Will there be many people there, did he say? The last time I attended a ball didn't..."

I stare at the handle of a gilded hairbrush. Winona loves throwing balls, the more lavish the better. Like the one she threw for me on the news of my invitation to the Coral Kingdom. I threw a fit and drowned myself in booze in protest of her pageantry. All to escape a land-bound existence tied to the whims of a foreign king. Yet here I am.

"Let's just say my sister wasn't happy with me," I finish. Can Deirdre see the guilt in my eyes?

She laughs. "It was a last-minute plan for me to pull together. I'm afraid it's only the two of you tonight."

"Oh." My shoulders drop in relief. "How unusual."

"The king is anything but usual, Your Highness." Her eyes twinkle for a moment before growing dim. "When he lost his mother, he struggled to find his joy again. It's been quite some time since I've seen that male smile, love." She takes my hand. "Thank you."

I drop my gaze from the mirror as a knot forms in my throat.

She squeezes my hand and pulls me from the chair. "Would you like to pick out your dress? I'm afraid there wasn't time to have one made for you, but I'm sure we can find you something suitable in here."

The closet is stuffed to the gills with ball gowns. Lace, silk, and furs crowd the hangers, abundant frills spilling onto the floor. Most of the dresses are cool-toned. Shades of blues and greens and grays. I trail my fingers along the fabric and inhale their soft scent. A tinge of peppermint hangs in the air.

"What was he like?" I blurt, tugging at a lacey green ribbon. "Before."

"His Majesty was an inquisitive guppy. I wouldn't say he was cheerful—he's always had a hard shell for an exterior, I'm afraid—but he was adventurous. A risk-taker. He loved to explore and have fun. Test the boundaries. There was many a time he pushed me to my limits."

She lifts a hem, rubs it between her fingers, and sighs wistfully.

I smile. "Sounds like me."

"You?"

"Deirdre, I'm a high-class scoundrel, where I come from."

The housekeeper chuckles. "You make a good pair, then."

I pause, grasping a hanger for support as a wave of irritation catches me off guard. "He'll never let me leave. And as long as that's true, we are not equals. There is no *pair*."

She frowns and shakes her head, but Deirdre can't deny it out loud. "His heart's in the right place. Even if his actions haven't caught up. Give him time to surprise you."

I glance at the dress in my hands, a slim silk number in light, glittery blue. Like the color of the sky before snowfall—or the color of Aethan's eyes. My heart lifts, and I pull it off the rack.

"Oh my," Deirdre gasps. She brings her hand to her mouth, eyes glistening with emotion. "That's one of my favorites."

"I think it'll work," I say, holding it up to check the size. It's a little long.

"I can hem it, don't you worry. Now let's get you dressed. We don't want to keep him waiting."

Deirdre holds it out for me. I step into the skirt and slip my arms through the straps. The silky fabric glides over my curves easily, lifting my breasts and flaring away at the knees. Glittery thread embroiders the bodice, adding a subtle silver sparkle.

"It's perfect," I gasp. I spin, watching the skirt lift and twist around my legs. Glitter sheds from the garment, falling to the floor like snow. "Wow."

Deirdre claps. "Oh, that's just darling on you. And a perfect fit, too. I wasn't sure."

"Whose dress is it? Yours?"

"Oh goddess, no. I'm much too…" She gestures to her large bosom and laughs. But the laugh is flat, and her smile falls a little at the corners. "You're in the queen's quarters, love. That dress was Isolde's. She wore it to the midnight dance on Yuletide, when we were young. Before Aethan came along. Oh, she was so beautiful that night. You should've seen her, love." Deirdre's eyes wax wistful, and she chews her bottom lip.

I smooth my hands over my belly, relishing the softness of the silk. "She had excellent taste."

"Yes, well." Her eyes tighten. "I'm glad the dress will get another turn about the dance floor. It's been too long, and I can't bear to clear them out."

"I'm honored." I want to ask more, to learn about his mother. I've only gleaned so much from the history books Perrin brought me. She was tall and pale and, like Aethan, the perfect picture of a Frost siren. Reclusive and prone to mood swings. But that's all I could gather. It's hard to imagine a cold female like that would dance in a gown like this, much less have a closet full of them.

Deirdre fishes a needle and thread from her apron pocket. "Now, this won't take too long. A quick hem so you aren't tripping over yourself." She stoops low and works with the fabric, stitching a few holds around the hem. When she finishes, she clears her throat softly. "Shall we?"

We exit the dressing room, and Perrin's jaw drops. Blush creeps over his freckled cheeks. "Wow."

"Is it too much?" I ask, running my hands over my hips. The fabric is tight. Maybe a little too tight. I should've picked a more voluminous dress from the queen's closet, one that hides my curves.

Perrin shakes his head furiously. "No, you look…" He surveys my appearance at a different angle, then wrinkles his nose. "You look like an icicle."

The pressure in my chest eases. I hike the skirt and shake glitter over his toes. "That was the idea."

"I like it. Sparkly. Make sure to get it in His Majesty's hair." He winks.

"He'll be brushing it out for days," I say.

"I'll walk with you when you're ready." Deirdre touches my elbow lightly.

A fresh wave of nerves hits me, and I take a deep breath. "Ready."

As we descend the stairwell into the parlor, I trail my fingers along the darkwood banister, the train of my dress slithering behind me.

My heart races faster with each step I take. Anticipation twists my stomach into a knot. It'd be a complete waste to look this good and not dance at the ball. How bad could it be?

Deirdre hums happily beside me. "You look beautiful," she assures me. "He'll be pleased to see you."

Light spills beneath the threshold of the throne room doors. Two guards are posted there, standing erect in their uniforms. Their eyes slide over me, then dart away.

"The king doesn't think of me in that way," I mutter.

Deirdre pauses, her hand resting on the door handle. She glances at me with a frown. "Is that what you really think? You mean more to him than you realize, Nahla. And if this dress doesn't wring a confession out of him tonight, then you can dunk me in the Rime. Now. In you go."

My knees wobble beneath me, suddenly unstable. *Shit.*

The door opens, revealing a transformed throne room. It glows with candlelight, illuminating a once characteristically dim space. From the center beam hangs a new chandelier with a thousand glittering ice crystals. Flower petals dust the floor. In the corner, a lone violinist positions at the ready.

And in the center of the room stands the devilish Frost King, dressed in a white tuxedo and grinning from ear to ear.

Chapter Fifty

Aethan

She's magnificent. A vision in light blue glitter, Nahla resembles an ice goddess. Like she was made to be here, in the throne room of the Frost Kingdom. She enters with a bold glare, gaze darting about as if looking for a fight.

She won't find one here. I know I fucked up, and I'm at her mercy. *Mission grovel is a go.*

Nahla has never struck me as a fan of royal antics. So it's just me tonight, and judging by her earlier mood, this could either be fantastic or miserable for me.

Goddess, I hope I got this right.

I clear my throat, overcome with the urge to pull at my collar. "Good evening, Your Highness."

She looks right at me, and all the air whooshes out of my lungs. Her glare softens to surprise. A smile spreads over her face.

"Hi," she breathes.

My heart swells, pushing into my throat with an insatiable ache. "Sunfish."

I offer her my hand. She blushes and places hers in mine, her fingers soft and smooth. Gently, I guide them to my mouth and kiss them, lingering for a moment.

"What are you up to?"

I watch her over the rim of her knuckles and raise my eyebrow. "Groveling," I say. "Like a good boy."

Her jaw drops.

Tugging on her fingers, I pull her close, slide my hand around her waist, and lift her hand into position. Her warm scent floods my senses as her hair brushes the underside of my chin.

"Dance with me," I whisper into her curls.

The violinist strikes a sweet melody. Nahla gasps as I whisk her into a waltz, spinning us across the open floor. Her dress hisses over the wooden planks and leaves a trail of glitter in her wake. She clings to me, her short legs working quickly to keep up. But she knows the steps. When I send her twirling into a pirouette beneath my lifted hand, she smiles radiantly, keeping her gaze glued on my face.

My heart squeezes tighter still, and I wonder if tonight will be the night it finally explodes. How ironic, that the female I've kept prisoner would be the one to captivate me so entirely.

As I watch her turn, I play out the future in my mind, where she and I spend many eventides on this dance floor, in this room. Nahla, seated next to me in a matching fur-lined throne. Nahla, answering the requests of my people with exceptional grace and kindness. The leader they've been craving for years. The leader I'll never be able to give them. Except if...

Queen Nahlani of Frost. A chill runs the length of my spine. Yes. That's what I want. Behind her, my throne hides in shadow, and I'm inclined to pick her up right now and see how good she looks on it.

Nahla twirls into my embrace, and we resume the beat effortlessly. "You're good at this," she says, dipping her head as her cheeks turn pink.

I shrug, even as my stomach roils with nerves. "Were you expecting me not to be?"

"What a cocky thing to say." Her lips curl in a coy smile.

"But you like me this way," I counter. My hand splays across her back, pulling her closer still. Her breasts touch my chest, skin warm with a fresh blush.

She peers at me. "Yes," she whispers. Her hand slides up my arm to rest on my neck, warm fingertips pressing lightly into my dormant gills. "Yes, I do."

I swallow against the pressure of her touch. "That's good news. I wasn't sure for a moment."

"Aethan," she says, and her gaze softens. "I'm fine. You didn't hurt me. Not like that."

The Beast's memory floats in, uninvited, and I'm forced to watch the replay of my abuse. The tearing of her soft skin between my claws.

I slow us to a sway, and the violinist transitions into a somber ballad. New music swells around us, matching the melancholy in my heart. *Fuck, I'll never be worthy of her. Never.*

"Nahla." As I cup her face in my hand, my thumb brushes the crest of her cheek. "Nahla, I'm—"

She leans into my touch. "I understand why you did it, but please, next time don't shut me out, okay? Let me help you."

But she can't understand, not until she knows the full truth. I search her eyes, checking for a hint of terror and finding none—she doesn't know I'm a murderer. And she never will.

Relief lifts my stomach for a moment. I still have time to fix everything. Tonight is for her—we'll dance and kiss and fuck, and I'll grovel at her feet until she sickens of me—and then tomorrow I'll go to Lucas. I'll endure the pain, and I'll get the fucking job done, for Nahla. For my kingdom. It's the only way I can ensure their future is safe.

"There won't be a next time, Nahla." My jaw flexes. "I'm going to fix it. I promise I'll try to deserve you."

"You won't have to try too hard." She gazes at me with warm, trusting eyes. Her kissable lips part to reveal the soft glint of her teeth.

Dipping my head, I capture her mouth. The room fades away as I lose myself in her taste, her touch, and her tongue. Her fingers slide up my face, clasping around my neck and deepening the kiss with a desperate whimper.

Our tongues clash together. Every gasp, every shiver—I claim them all. Fuck, she's perfect. I clutch her to my chest as my hands explore her waist, her hips, *that ass*. We mold together, two pieces of a whole.

Her dress is fantastically tight tonight, a delicious slit running the length of her thigh. Tempting me. I hook my hand beneath her knee. She gasps, breaking our kiss.

I waste no time. With a firm grip, I sling her over my shoulder and saunter into the shadows.

"Leave us," I growl from the side of my mouth. The music stops, and the violinist ducks his head and hurries for the exit. Not that I'd mind an audience, but Nahla would, and I am nothing if not bound to please her.

She drops into my throne with a squeal and looks at me with wide, excited eyes. Fucking adorable. My cock hardens, pressing uncomfortably against my pants, but it'll have to wait.

I have a higher purpose in mind.

"Spread your legs, Sunfish."

She obeys wordlessly. Her gaze locks on mine as she pulls the dress higher, tortuously slow, and the slit in the fabric parts over her thighs. My pulse thunders in anticipation. I buckle before her and drop into a kneel. She deserves all the worship I can give her—Nahlani, the queen of my fucking heart. I trail my nose along her thigh, inhaling the scent of her arousal as I nuzzle closer to her center.

"Oh gods," she whispers. Her fingers twine into my hair. "Aethan."

A flash of foreign emotion brushes my mind: desperate, aching lust.

She's ready for me. With a grin, I shove her knees wider, revealing her sex.

Fuck.

Her bare folds bloom before me, pink and glistening with need.

No panties in sight.

"Someone's naughty," I rumble. Tenderly, I press a line of kisses along her inner thigh as she trembles.

"This dress," she gasps. "It's too tight for panties." Her nails scratch the wood as she digs them into the armrests. "I didn't think you'd see. Not like this."

I hover at the apex of her thigh, a scale's breadth away from where she needs me. "Should I stop, then? If you don't want me to see?"

Her pussy is the most delicious thing I've ever seen. A banquet spread before me, beckoning with the promise of a feast. It'd be a shame not to get to taste her.

She squirms, fingernails scraping through my scalp, tugging on my hair. "No," she squeals. "Gods, no. Please, Aethan. Please!"

"No?" I blow air across her folds, and she arches forward, pressing herself to my waiting mouth with a moan.

I reward her religiously, slipping my tongue across her molten core. I taste each delicate seam of her. Her clit emerges for me, swollen and ready, and I suck it tenderly. Again and again, I kiss her until she's melting into me and writhing against my mouth. Gasping sweet nothings.

"Yes, Sunfish," I croon. "That's my girl. Come for me."

With a flicker of my tongue, I worship her sensitive nub, working her hard. Her thighs clench around me. She bucks and rides my mouth, moving me right where she needs me. Desperate.

"Come," I command. My voice rumbles against her heat, and she cries out.

"Aethan!"

Fuck. She's so perfect. I'll never tire of her lips screaming my name.

"Aethan, I'm going to—"

I feel her tension building, blooming beneath my touch. With a hum of magic, I send a burst of cold to the tip of my tongue and plunge it into her heat.

"Ah!" she cries out as her body spasms.

The taste of her pleasure floods my mouth, and I lap it up, dragging my tongue to catch every drop. Her orgasm works through her until she melts against me, soft and satisfied. I press a kiss to her swollen cunt and slip out of her skirts.

Nahla spreads in my fur-lined seat, eyes glazed, face flushed, and hair mussed. Her dress is askew. The picture of a queen. I grin.

"You look so good on my throne, Nahla."

She smiles sheepishly. "You think so?"

"So fucking good." I lean forward, kissing the soft globe of her cheek.

"Mmm." She smooths her hands over the armrests and surveys the empty room. "There's only one problem," she says.

I knit my eyebrows, disliking the sound of that. If there's a problem, I will fix it for her. Immediately. "How so?"

Nahla reaches for me, pulling both of my hands into her lap. Her smile slowly fades. *Oh goddess.* This can't be good. Panic rises through my body, lifting every scale. Something is wrong.

Why did she let me fuck her, if something is wrong?

She squeezes my fingers, takes a deep breath, and says, "A prisoner can only *play* queen. And unless you rescind your rules—all of them—I'm afraid that's all I can be."

I force my eyes shut and inhale, drawing oxygen through to my toes. My stomach twists, that familiar knot of anger threatening to form. I could so easily explode. And two moon-cycles ago, I would have. Her fingers brush my thumb, the only thing rooting me in place.

I search for the anger, waiting for it to hit. Waiting for the magic to burst forth and kill her. She's too close. I've put her in danger, letting her get this close to me.

But the rage doesn't come. I sit before her, an emptied shell of myself. Heat to quench the anger, bran to stave the hunger, darkness to calm the fight—I need none of it as long as she's here. Nahla, my personal antidote.

She's right.

When I open my eyes, she's studying my face. Hopeful.

"Okay," I say.

"Okay?" She grips my hands, grinning recklessly. Her emotions explode through our thin mental connection, fireworks of joy. "Really? You mean it?"

A fissure forms in my chest, cleaving my soul in two—one part, knowing this means she could leave me; the other, wishing for her sake she'll take that chance.

"Yes," I whisper. "I do."

CHAPTER FIFTY-ONE

NAHLA

THIS IS MY CHANCE to run. Finally, I can accomplish what I left the Brine to do. I can chase my dreams into the unknown sea. Go where no siren has ventured, do what no merfolk has done, and be somebody *important*. It's what I've always wanted, but when given the choice at last, my feet grow numb and heavy.

Why do I feel so sick?

Aethan walks me to the shore in somber silence. We stop on the rocky beach and stare out over the churning water, watching the ice floes bob beneath a slivered moon in the aethersky. He takes my hand, swallowing mine with his palm.

"Is this okay?" He breaks the quiet with a gravelly whisper, lacing our fingers. "I've always wanted to do this. Figured I'd take the chance while I still can."

I glance at our hands, an ache building in my chest. It feels nice, holding his hand. So simple, yet so sweet. "Yes, that's fine."

"Good."

Tidewater washes over the stones, reaching our feet.

I've spoiled the mood. One minute, Aethan was lapping at my clit, and the next I'm dropping a bomb on him and blowing the whole evening apart.

When I asked him to break his final rule, I didn't mean I wanted to leave the Rime *now*. I thought I'd stay a while longer and have time to say my goodbyes. Finish some of those books he so chivalrously picked out for me. But then he nodded, so sure of himself, and led me away. To the edge of the Rime.

Have I ruined everything? Does he want me to leave that badly?

He tightens his grip on my hand, tight enough I'd have to chew my arm if I wanted to be free.

Maybe not, then.

"Aethan, I'm sorry," I start. "I didn't mean right *now*, but if you want me to go, I will."

He blows out the air from his cheeks, turning to peer at me. He wears a sheepish smile. Snow falls around his face, sticking in his hair and eyelashes. "Really?" he says.

Godsdammit, he's like an overgrown cuddlefish, way too cute for his own good.

"Really." With my free hand, I reach for his cheek. Trace his sharp cheekbone with my thumb. A snowflake melts. "I just wanted to be equal with you. That's all. I'm not ready to go yet."

"That's all?" His brow furrows, and he drops my hand to clutch my face between his palms. "Is *that* what this is about? You think I've kept you here as part of some sick power play?"

I nod, cheeks squished between his hands.

"Dammit, Nahla. I'm an asshole, but I'm not that heartless." He presses a kiss to my forehead. "Don't you see what you've done to me?" A kiss to my cheek. "What you do to me every time you enter the fucking room? I can no longer exist without you." To my nose. "I have never known peace like I do when I'm held in your gaze." My chin. "You've upended me, completely, entirely, and I am nothing without you close." Lips. "You've been inside my head, Sunfish. I thought you already knew how much I love you."

I've never heard anything so fucking beautiful in my life. Aethan, the grumpy, temperamental, ravenously loyal king—he *loves* me.

Me.

I surge onto my tiptoes and kiss him. His mouth envelops my whimpering sobs, and his hands slide into my hair. He tastes like peppermint snow, cold and delicious. Perfect in every way. With a gasp, he pulls me impossibly closer. I thrill at the joy of our kiss, at the truth of his proclamation. He loves me, and my heart will sing his praise until the day I dissolve.

The tide washes over my bare feet, cool and crisp. Something bumps into my leg. Driftwood, probably.

Clinging more tightly to Aethan's face, I ignore the driftwood. More. More. I need more.

The driftwood bumps me again, cold and soft. I glance down to find a stiffened siren face floating in the water, frostbite speckled across graying skin, jaw frozen in a permanent scream. Hair spreads in the currents like glacierweed. His eyes are white glass, unseeing, as he bumps against my leg. It's Orson, the young hunter who joined me in the snowball fight against the king.

Dead.

I scream.

Aethan scoops me into his arms in an instant. I can hear his rapid heartbeat through his shirt, where my ear rests as he runs. The world has a hollow sound, echoing as though from a distance. The rush of water. Clacking stones beneath his feet. My scream, ringing in my ears as if it belongs to someone else.

The hunter is dead.

I just saw him last week, on the hunt. He was hooting excitedly as the woollygoat charged, as his arrow made its skillful mark.

Dead.

How can he be dead?

Aethan's chest vibrates, turning cold beneath my touch. Before my eyes, I watch the blue scales crawl over his chest and up his arms. His fingers turn to claws, digging into my flesh.

He sets me on the ground near the gate and bends down to look me in the eye. His claw brushes beneath my chin, tilting my face. Dark blue eyes. Sharp teeth. Horns sprout through his hairline, spiraling toward the sky. "Stay," he growls. "I will fix this."

As he turns, charging toward the sea, long quills burst out of his spine and shred his shirt. The moment his feet touch the water, he howls. His head snaps back, his body expands to twice his size, and his tail slithers out.

The clawbeast hunches over Orson's dead body, grasping at it with panicked hands. But his claws only make it worse. Fresh blood washes into the Rime. His fear crashes over me—Aethan is drowning in it.

Shit.

"Help!" I screech. There's gotta be a guard around here. Someone who can figure out what's going on, why this happened. "Someone help!"

The gate flies open on shrieking hinges. Guards hurry onto the shore, stopping short when they see Aethan.

The clawbeast looks up. The guards raise their weapons, point them at their king. His face falls.

No. Not him. Can't they see the dead hunter in Aethan's arms?

"Beast!" They charge instantly, battle cries rising.

"No!" I scream, but my voice is lost on the wind. I scrabble for stones and lob them toward the guards, to get their attention. What the fuck are they doing, charging their king?

Aethan turns to face them, seething. A guard stabs him in the side, and he howls, dropping the body to clutch the wound. He swipes his paw, knocking the guard into the air. The guard lands with a sickening crunch and moans.

Emboldened, I run down the beach. Tears sting in my eyes and freeze in the wind. "Don't hurt him!"

One guard turns, finally noticing me. His face is stern, reprimanding. "You shouldn't be here," he says. "Get back inside, Your Highness. We'll deal with him."

"But—"

He wraps his arm around my waist, dragging me back the way I came. "You don't want to see this."

"Let me go! You don't understand. He's not an animal, he's your king!"

The guard hesitates. "What?"

Aethan roars. Water splashes. Stones rattle. I glance behind me in time to see him charge. With outstretched claws, he rips the guard away from me and pins him to the stones, snarling. Drool dangles from his pointy teeth. The skin on his face shifts, patches of white peeking through.

His emotions slam into me: jealousy. Anger. Hate. For a moment, he locks his gaze on mine, and I hear his voice ring in my head: *No one touches you, Sunfish. Are you hurt?*

I shake my head. This has all gone terribly wrong.

He will pay, all the same, he says.

The Beast lifts his paw, claws glinting wet, and aims for the guard's face. Before I can stop him, before I can scream, a burst of golden light flashes across the shore. Glowing tendrils wrap around the Beast's body, wrenching him away from the pinned guard.

Aethan writhes in the magical grip, but he can't break free. The light plunges beneath his skin and weaves until it grasps every inch of him. He's dragged through the stones. Feet kicking. Snarling. I turn, following the line of light to its origin.

Lucas stands in the open gate, hands outstretched, singing. His eyes illuminate with matching golden light.

Relief hits me like a punch in the gut. Finally, someone who can help. Lucas will guide Aethan through this and calm him down enough to function again. He will heal the guards, attend to the dead.

"There's a dead body down there, Lucas. And a wounded guard. Can you do something?"

The healer swivels his gaze to me, and he smirks. "If you're going to leave, Princess, now's the time to do it."

Aethan scrambles in the grip of Lucas's magic, collapsing at the healer's feet. Lucas frowns at him. "My, my," he says. "You can imagine my disappointment when you didn't show up to our session tonight, Your Majesty. Pity. You could have prevented this."

Then he raises his fist and knocks the king out cold.

Chapter Fifty-Two

Aethan

"Begone, dark spirit! In the goddess's name, I cast you out!" Lucas barks.

My surroundings come together in pieces: the frostcat glaring. The dim light of a fire. A tidy desk. I'm sitting in Lucas's office.

The sting of magic courses through my body, and I flinch against leather restraints. My hands are bound to the arms of a chair. Dark scales recede from my wrists, evidence of the Beast relinquishing his control over my body.

How the hell did I get here? Only the past few minutes elude my memory this time. I remember every detail before that—Nahla's request, our kiss, Orson's body, and the rage. Guards touching her. A guard putting his hands on my Sunfish. I was going to hurt him.

My rage burned so hot I wanted to rip the world apart, but then Lucas appeared, and everything went black.

I search the room wildly, looking for the healer. He stands out of my reach, eyes glowing with the light of his spell. In his shadow, with her knees tucked to her chest on the floor, is Nahla.

Nahla?

My stomach somersaults. This isn't right. Her panicked gaze pierces me as I drink in the sight of her. She widens her eyes and shakes her head, tears streaming down her cheeks. Her beautiful dress is torn. A cord of golden light wraps around her head and slips between her lips; another cord wraps around her wrists—Lucas's magic, holding her hostage.

I narrow my eyes. He's gagged her. *He's touching her.* She grimaces and twitches, shrinking away from the brush of his spell. What the fuck is the meaning of this?

"Release her!" I bellow.

Rage returns with a vengeance. My veins swell, ice surging to the extremities of my body. The Beast bursts through his cage, ravenous for justice, and our minds fuse, forming one thought only: *Nahla isn't safe.*

I thrash against the restraints and roar. I fight Lucas's spell with mind and body as the magic sears through me—as it caresses her—as if I could absorb all the fear and set her free.

The healer chuckles from the shadows. "Good," he croons through the tune of his Voice. "You want to protect her? Come out and fight me, Beast."

A twist of pain, sharp behind my eye. *Fuck.* I throw my head back. Howling. Panting. Sweat slicks my skin. Nahla screams and snaps her head, clenching her teeth as she faces the ceiling. Ice curdles my blood.

"Let. Her. Go."

Lucas clicks his tongue in disapproval. "Oh, but she's being so *helpful*. Aren't you, Princess? You like to be helpful." A golden tendril splits apart to stroke the length of her throat. Reverently. Seductively.

Mine, roars the Beast.

She struggles against the gag and moans. The sound of her struggle cuts straight to my heart. The Beast fills my limbs, lending me strength. With a flex of muscle, I pull out of the chair, cracking it in half as I rise.

"Yes!" Lucas cheers. "That's it, Your Majesty! We'll get him out this way! Give me all your anger. All your rage. I will cure you once and for all!"

Before I can take a step, his magic stiffens my body, immobilizing me. I stand rigid and seething, caught in yet another of his snares.

"Ah, ah!" he warns. "Don't get too close. She may not want you near her, given your history."

I hesitate, searching her face for confirmation of the healer's suggestion. Her brow puckers with confusion.

"Have you not *told* her, Your Majesty?" Lucas circles me. Golden tendrils thread from his fingers like a dark puppeteer, snaring us both. "*Why* you agreed to this treatment?"

No.

His magic yanks Nahla closer, dragging her before me. She slams to her hands and knees with a cry of pain. She strains her head to lift it slowly, tears streaming down her cheeks, as she looks me in the eye.

It's reminiscent of the first time we met: Nahla forced to bow before me as I stood over her like an over-powered asshole. Regret twists in my gut. How far we've come since then, only to end up in the same position.

"Agreed?" she mumbles around the thread of magic in her mouth.

"I didn't agree to *this*, healer. I agreed to your cure—" More pain sears through my system, and I fight to finish my thought. "Get her out of here."

"As you wish," Lucas says. His magic withdraws from Nahla's body, and she collapses onto the floor, coughing. Blood speckles the floor. He hooks a hand beneath her arm and hauls her up, her body as limp as reedgrass. Her knees knock together as she wobbles unsteadily on her feet. "Go on, now," he says. "Out you go, Princess."

As he lets go, she takes a shaky step forward and stumbles. I press against the magic, but I can't catch her fall. She lands with a thump.

"What have you done to her?" I demand.

"Do you know what it feels like, Your Majesty, to have the one person you love incapacitated?"

Nahla moans on the floor, trying and failing to push herself onto her hands. My muscles burn with power as they grow, every fiber of my being itching for violence.

He hurt her.

With a sharp cry of my Voice, ice explodes from my fingertips. The stream pierces the air as it slices toward Lucas's face. I narrow my eyes, focusing my aim.

He HURT her. He must pay for her pain.

Lucas smiles.

Suddenly, I lose my grip. The ice splinters into a million pieces, shards flying in all directions. I watch in horror as they slice toward Nahla instead, missing the healer.

Her eyes grow wide. She raises her arms to protect her face, hunching to make herself small before me.

"No!" I scream.

But I can't cut the spell. I've lost control of it.

Panic.

Fear.

Regret.

With a flick of his light, Lucas melts the shards inches from Nahla's face, turning them into soft powder. Snow dusts her dark hair and melts on her cheeks. She looks up with a gasp.

"Did you think you were safe from him, Princess? You would have lost your life if I hadn't stepped in," Lucas bellows, peering down at her with a snarl. "Don't you know he's brutalized his subjects for years, and he's done *nothing*? That brave hunter, Orson? His death was the king's fault. His mother. My *sister.* Perrin's gimpy fin. All. His. Fault."

Nahla touches her cheek gingerly, wiping away the snow. Confusion swirls her expression for a moment before the pieces click together. "Aethan, what does he mean?"

Shame.

Shame.

Shame.

I slump against the restraints of Lucas's magic and let him hold me upright. The Beast screams, washing us in agonizing sorrow as I brace for her anger. But the look in her eyes is closer to disappointment. Like I should have known better.

"Aethan?"

I should have told her myself, about all of it. She didn't need to find out like this. Tears slide down her face. Would it have been any different if *I* told her? Would the news not have hit the same way?

"Someone's been keeping secrets. She knew of the Beast, but not of the monster. A shame. The truth will save us all, goddess willing. Let us bring it into the light."

I close my eyes, wetness pooling in my eyelids. He's right. There's no *we*—no Beast versus king. It's all me. Me, the rampant murderer. Me, the heartless king. My two selves merge, and I can no longer tell them apart. I'm all rage, all monster.

I didn't hurt her. But I almost did.

"Shall we continue? Or would you like to keep the clawbeast inside you?" Lucas glares, holding me in the tight grip of his magic. His mouth quirks in a smile. "Better hurry, before your little sunfish becomes your next victim."

His words drop like an anchor on my soul, dragging me into the dredges of my torment.

I will *not* let that happen. Not on my fucking watch. If it's a choice between Nahla and the Beast, there's no contest. I would rather spend my life torn in two than live in a world without her in it.

My eyes fling open, finding hers. She stares with open dismay. "For you," I whisper through the pain. "This is for you."

She shakes her head, but she does not know what she's refusing. I will give her safety, a future. Everything she will never have if I let my power continue unchecked.

This is for her. For my kingdom. For the life we will build together.

I look the healer straight in the eye. "Do it."

Lucas grins. Magic glints off the white of his teeth. His hands clench into fists, wrapping the cords of his magic tight, and he yanks the tether between us.

Pain.

Searing pain.

Tearing me in half.

CHAPTER FIFTY-THREE

BEAST

I SEE HER.

Through his eyes.

Blurry face. Curled up on the floor.

Crying.

She looks at him—at me.

My Sunfish is sad.

Because I lost control.

I almost hurt her.

Again.

Again!

How could I let it happen twice?

I am a monster.

Monster.

Unworthy.

Beast.

I cower in the back of his mind, where I can become small.

Invisible.

Maybe, if I disappear, she will be safe from me.

Maybe I should let the healer win.

But his magic hurts.

Pain.

Searing pain.

He finds me in the depths of the king's mind, wrapping around my core, and rips.

Through the king's mouth, I roar.

I clamber to hold fast. Sink my claws into the darkness. Maintain my grasp.

The healer pulls harder.

Harder.

Pain.

Tearing me in half.

Nahla opens her mouth and sings.

I feel the brush of her mind, barely.

Don't do this, she says. Her voice is like sunlight through mist on the Rime, breaking me apart.

I ache to hear it.

Why not?

Doesn't she want to be safe?

"Aethan, stop!" she screams with mind and mouth.

She pushes from the floor. Legs weak. Wobbly.

The healer has hurt her.

No. I did that.

I brought this upon her.

This is my fault, like the healer said.

The blame is mine and mine alone.

She stands. Braces her hand on the wall. Lifts her face to meet the king's gaze. I stare at her, drinking in her beauty. Memorizing it to store deep within my memory.

Don't say you're doing this for me.

But I am. This is for her. I need her to be safe.

Because you think you're a murderer? Aethan! Tell me, when did you make the kill? You were with me all evening!

I can't answer her. I shove at her presence, pushing her away.

You are kind. Loyal. A little rough around the edges, sure, but you have compassion and love. I cannot believe you're a cold-blooded killer. I will not believe it. Stay with me. Please.

No. No. She means the king. The king is all those things. I am not. I am the monster.

You. Will. Stay. Her eyes burn. Glint with fresh tears.

Crying for me or because of her pain?

I can feel the king's turmoil. His self-loathing mixes with mine.

His love for her.

Our love for her.

Mine.

For a moment, I can't tell where I end, where he begins.

For a moment, we are one.

We consider her words. Maybe she's right. Maybe—

"BEGONE!" Lucas rumbles.

Then the magic floods us.

Drowning.

Washing me out.

Bright, searing wave.
Burning.
Pulling.
Crushing.
Pain—

CHAPTER FIFTY-FOUR

NAHLA

Gone.

The moment our mental connection severs, I feel it like a dagger through my heart.

The Frost King hangs limply, suspended in the glow of the healer's magic, and I can't meet his eye.

The Beast is gone, snuffed out like a fucking candle, and the king agreed to this outcome.

"What have you done?" I choke. I'm asking the king, the healer, the gods above—anyone who will answer. But my ears are ringing, and I can't hear the reply.

The Beast was *good*. He wasn't some creature haunting his thoughts, as Aethan seemed to believe. His emotions, his fears, his memories—all lived within the Beast. And the more I connected with that side of him, the more kind and joyful the King became.

He was improving. Without the Beast, Aethan would never have brought me books or that cloak, or asked me to dance, or played in the snow. I'm sure of it. Without him, I'd still be locked in that fucking cage.

Doesn't he see it? He needed the Beast.

I needed him.

This kingdom needed him.

And now he's gone.

Because of Lucas, the so-called healer. How is it helpful to sever Aethan from a crucial part of his identity? A healer should know better than to inflict harm wittingly.

Lucas's Voice cuts off and the glow of his spell disappears. Aethan slouches as the restraints leave his body, his shoulders rolling and his head sagging. His knees wobble.

A chill traces my spine. What kind of healer is he, anyway? One who inflicts pain? One who can shatter the Beast entirely? He seized me from the beach and dragged me here, tied me up and gagged me with his magic, all to torture Aethan and lure the Beast into the open.

I flick my gaze to the nearest exit. *This is so fucked.*

And Aethan was in on it. He agreed to the treatment, as Lucas said. Did he know Lucas would kill the Beast? That he would gag and restrain me? Hurt me?

Steeling myself, I glance at Aethan's face. Weariness gathers in dark pockets beneath his eyes, and the usual sparkle of humor is absent. He searches my face as I study his, and his eyes tighten. Waiting. Like a petty thief expecting his punishment.

My chest squeezes until I can't breathe. Why didn't he fight harder? Why didn't he protect me? The Beast? Why did he stand there and take it?

"Nahla," he whispers. He takes a shaky step toward me.

I back away. My hands meet the flat of the door, and I slide them along the damp wood until I find the knob.

From the darkness of the room, Lucas chuckles. His words come flat and seething. "Where are you going, Princess? Come, don't you want to enjoy your king, risk free? He did this for you, after all. No more accidental dismemberments in the library. Isn't that wonderful?"

I turn the knob as my breath quickens.

Something is wrong with Lucas. Something either the king knows already or is too blind with loyalty to see. He cannot be trusted. Even now, the healer steps forward. His lips move, revealing the subtle glow in his mouth. His eyes flash as he looks at me, dragging his gaze over my body head to toe.

Panic rises, forming a heartbeat in my throat.

I have to get out of here.

My feet sting with each slap on the cold stone as I stumble into the hallway. Darkness shrouds the bottom reaches of the castle. The air hangs heavily, smelling of must and wet earth, making it harder to breathe. I limp forward on weakened legs.

Fuck, what did Lucas *do* to me? My body moves sluggishly, like I'm swimming in a dream. No way can I climb the stairs before Lucas snares me with his magic again. Or worse.

Somewhere behind these stairs is a beast-sized hole in the floor. As I stumble around the corner, praying to the gods I'm right, my heart lifts. It's still here. The floorboards crack open around a glistening pool of water, churning with current. That'll work.

Unfastening what's left of my dress, I slip out of the ruined silk and dip my toes in the water. My bones crackle and rearrange, my legs merge, and my golden fin sprouts. I peer over the rim. The stone foundation hollows out, giving way to a long tube of ice that plummets into the depths below. A tunnel, as I suspected.

From the other room, Aethan groans. The floorboards squeak under his weight as he shifts and stumbles, likely trying to come after me. As I slip further into the hole, water laps at my golden scales, beckoning me into its depths.

"Nahla!" he cries out. "Wait!"

I strain my ears for a second set of footsteps, the light patter of a thin ghost of a male.

Tears roll down my cheeks, and I swipe them away. There was a better way to tame his inner Beast. I could have used my magic. Helped him train. Helped him learn to control himself. It could have been painless. Therapeutic. Fucking *romantic*.

Betrayal punches my gut. Aethan was *with me* when the murders occurred. He's fucking innocent, but he took the blame and let Lucas have his way. How deep are the healer's hooks?

"Sunfish, please! I'm sorry!" Aethan's voice bellows, rattling through the hall.

I take the icy plunge.

The current sucks me down, down, down. My scales skim the ice as I gain momentum, slipping into darkness faster than I expected. I pump my tail to slow my descent, but it's useless. The water whooshes and churns. Propelled through the tunnel, I careen along its path, slamming into the ice at every turn. My shoulders jostle and bruise. I bite my tongue to tamper my screams.

I trusted Lucas, and I trusted the king. Who else was part of their plot? Deirdre? Perrin? Sure, let's capture a beast-tamer who can expose the weakness of a gentle creature we all needlessly hate, then use her as bait to get rid of him. I can picture them now, chuckling over hot chocolates as they plan the Beast's demise. And I swam right into the snare.

How could I be so naïve? Fuck, it's all so *obvious* in hindsight. Is everything I thought I knew about this kingdom a lie?

I should never have come here. It's my fault the Beast is gone and Aethan is a shell of himself. I fucked everything up, like I always do. If I had listened to Winona and married that prince... *Gods*, she was right about me. My powers are useless, and my meddling only brings trouble. Someone should nail my fins to the floor, or better yet lock me in... *Ice*.

I shake my head to clear the thought before Aethan's face can appear.

With a final twist, the tunnel ends abruptly, and I spiral head over tail in a cloud of bubbles. A few kicks of my tail and I stabilize. The bubbles settle, clearing the view of my surroundings.

I'm in a bedroom, of sorts. Walls of ice form a small dome. Shelves are carved in the far wall, littered with the knickknacks of a hatchling. Small stone toys lay scattered across the floor. A hammock hangs in the corner, the knotted ropes aged and frayed. Glacierweed grows from cracks in the floor.

On the desk perches a painted image of the former Frost Prince—short, white hair sprouts from a younger version of Aethan's face, his piercing blue eyes playful. He has a tail, just like mine. Dark blue with a feathered fin. No claws. No horns. He looks happy. The surface is scratched, marring the image where his smile should be.

Not just any bedroom. His. When Aethan was still a guppy.

Scales rise on my neck. I must be in the old royal city.

Above me, I spot the tunnel I came from. Deep claw marks gouge the ceiling, scarring the ice with evidence of the clawbeast. Is this how he's been getting in and out of the castle, all this time?

I brush my thumb over little Aethan's face. "I'm so sorry," I whisper as my throat tightens. "You deserve better."

Memory pierces the moment: Ramona's retreating form, diving into the deep without me. My sister's scowling face, as I imagine she'd looked when the news reached her that day. Her voice, forming the words that echoed through my head as I left my world behind: *Deserter. Traitor. Disappointment.*

My eyes prickle with salt. I'm a deserter. Not an adventurer, as Keen said. Not a queen, as my sister wanted. Not even a way-maker, as I dreamed I'd be. When the tides get rough, I don't stay for the fight. I fucking leave, like the coward I am.

Princess Nahlani of the Brine, Deserter Extraordinaire.

This is what I do.

As I tilt the image, Aethan's eyes shift, and his playful gaze turns pleading. *Like he needs me.*

With a gasp, I drop the image, and it sinks to the floor face-down. Then I kick my tail and slip through the doorway, following the path to the center of the abandoned city. As I enter the central chamber, recognition dawns. This is where Aethan took me to make love that night. If I follow the tunnel to my right, I'd find the library.

My chest tightens, and I turn the other way, following the wide channel out of the city. I squeeze my eyes closed as I pass the pike-whale statues that guard the entrance, relying on scent and current to lead me into the open water of the Rime. Aethan said I'm free to leave, and I should have gone sooner. I let myself become too attached.

With a burst of magic, I send out a signal. My Voice ripples away from me, spreading through the water as it carries a simple message for Ramona: *Come find me.* A few fish stir as the spell passes over them. They stiffen in attention, turning toward the open sea.

At the murky edge of my vision, the glaciers converge. A dark chasm cuts through the rock, lined with iron spikes, and beyond it, open ocean. It's the one place Aethan never wanted me to go. The final rule, and I'm about to break it.

I'm leaving him behind.

Regret sinks in my stomach like a rock as I fight my instincts to flee. What am I doing? I can't *leave* him. Aethan, the grumpy, royal pain in my ass who stole my entire heart—what if he needs me? I was so afraid of what Lucas might do, I didn't stop to consider his safety. I should turn back and punch that motherfucker Lucas in the face.

From the distant waters, a faint chirping melody floats to me. I squint, and my heart lifts as I spot the pod of glosswhales racing toward me. Their slick gray bodies cut through the water, and their chirps grow louder as they approach. Their minds glow with the thrill of a chase, inviting me to play.

Come find me, they chirp, reprising my message for Ramona, and my stomach sours. No. I can't desert him. I won't.

I latch onto a glosswhale's dorsal fin. *Swim,* I command, imprinting an image of us playing in the shallows. Eagerness sparks in its mind, and the glosswhale kicks its tail, dragging me along as the pod speeds for the shore. My muscles relax, grateful for the respite.

Aethan, I'm sorry. I'm coming.

A boom shakes the sea. The water trembles. The glosswhales screech as panic floods their minds. Scales rise along my spine, tracing an icy path over my scalp. The glosswhale I'm holding twists out of my grip and tears away with a burst of speed.

Something's not right.

A mass of fish soon follows, rushing past me, hundreds of slippery bodies whipping their tails as fast as they can go.

What the fuck?

I stop short, treading water as I peer into the endless stream of fish ahead of me. My heart drops.

A wall of ice presses through the water. Grating. Rumbling. Sliding toward me from sea floor to surface. Fish bolt away from its reach, the unlucky ones caught and suspended in the ice. Frozen solid in an instant.

If I don't reach open water in time, I'll be consumed by it, too.

I slap my tail, adrenaline burning through my muscles. With furious pumps, I dive for the exit, still several paces out of reach. Slick bodies press around me. Glosswhales and pikewhales fight through the crowd, slapping smaller fish out of their way as we all funnel through the same tight spot.

I glance over my shoulder. The wall of ice rumbles, pressing closer. Too close.

Shit. I'm running out of time.

I angle my body against the flow of fish, fighting toward the surface. If I can breach the waves, I can get on top of the ice before it crushes me against the glacier. The skylights dapple through the waterline. I stretch my fingers, kicking harder.

A desperate, shrieking cry echoes around me. For a moment, the fish cease their movement. Stunned.

My body alerts as a shadow rises from below. I can *feel* its presence, all around me—like a god among the fish—before I spot its form in the dark waters of the night. The blue-scaled body, a long thrashing tail between powerful hind legs. Long, white hair parting around gnarled horns. A chiseled jaw. Sharp and glinting white teeth.

Then the fish renew their vigor around me, growing more frantic, their bodies wriggling with impossible speeds, as I stay still.

The clawbeast.

Relief courses through me. Aethan is here. Aethan has come after me. The Beast survived, somehow. I've been a fool to think he'd give up. I left him behind, but still he came to my rescue.

With a stir of my magic, reaching for his mind. *Aethan!* I call out, pouring all my love into his name as part of my mind spirals in his direction.

But I smack into a mental barrier, cold and calculating. Foreign. Female.

Not him.

In the water, the clawbeast cocks her head. Her eyes snap to my face, locking onto me with a predatory gaze.

CHAPTER FIFTY-FIVE

AETHAN

How could I lose sight of her? She was with me not twenty minutes ago, and now... *She's gone.*

I charge into the Rime, leaving the shore behind me. Icy water swallows my bare legs, but I push forward. My knees lift and fall as I cut through the tide, and I scan the water for signs of her—a flash of golden tail or a splash of water. But the ice floes crowd the surface, monotonous piles of snow blocking my view in the darkness.

Gone.

I plunge deeper, wading to my waist as panic rises in my throat. I should have gills by now, and a thrashing tail. I should be gliding through the water, racing to bring her home. To explain everything so she understands.

But the Beast is gone, and I do not transform. My bare skin grows numb from the cold, refusing to sprout scales.

No.

My feet slip on the stones as a wave rolls, lifting me in its crest. I float off the seafloor. Water rushes over my head, and I submerge in the icy current. Muted sound thuds in my ears. Gills sprout along my neck, filtering well enough, thank goddess. Still, no tail. My feet hang like clubs, useless. I paddle wildly, ineffective with unwebbed fingers. My vision is dim, and I can't see farther than the reach of my hand.

With an awkward flail of limbs, I haul myself to shore. Heaving and spluttering, I crawl onto the stones. Water beads on my skin, evaporating in a cold hiss of night wind. My chest expands with every rush of panicked breath. The aethersky swirls above me, bright colors mocking the moon.

Even if she comes back, Nahla won't want me like this. What siren can't swim? I'm broken.

Rage twists in my belly, desperate for an outlet. My limbs grow cold and stiff as the residual chill of my magic leaks from my body. I'm fucking useless. No mer-form. No magic. No Nahla.

After all I did for her, after all I went through to make sure she could be safe with me. She fucking left me. The longer I lie here, the farther she speeds out of reach.

Fuck.

Nahla is gone. The Beast, gone. But the rage remains.

"NAHLA!" I roar her name until my throat grows hoarse and the sound of it echoes across the Rime.

She does not appear.

I slap the ground and shards of ice splash into the frothy water. I scrutinize the path of shards. Did I just...?

A tingle forms in my throat, centered on my voice box.

Magic.

It's not gone. Lucas managed the impossible, after all. He destroyed the Beast and kept my Voice.

Stones bite into my palm as I slap my hand down again. More ice shoots from my fingers. With a growl, I roll upright.

Nahla is never coming back. The truth will spread with her, and soon the kingdoms will turn against me.

It won't matter to them I've resolved the Beast, only that I'm a killer. I've killed them. How many, by now? How many more will fall, by my stupidity?

I am not a good king, and I never will be.

Why shouldn't I succumb to my power?

Rising to my feet, I face the churning water. Focus my intent. With a growling Voice, I shoot ice from my hands. No one will enter the Rime again. I will seal it, as I should have done twelve years ago. No water? No unwelcome guests.

The Rime freezes over, crackling and stiffening at the touch of my magic. The spell courses through me until I've formed a wall of solid ice. Then, clenching my core, I shove it away. Ice spreads, freezing everything in its path. The crust ripples, swallowing the ice floes and waves, holding them in place. Glosswhales shriek and thread the surface, skipping away from the incoming ice.

In the distance, a flick of a golden tail reflects skylight. Her face surfaces moments later, and she looks around wildly. When she spots me, she screams. My name spirals out of her mouth in a desperate plea.

Behind her, a dark shadow rises.

Dread flips my stomach, and my breath hitches. My spell stutters and stops. There's a clawbeast in the water with Nahla.

She screams my name again, moments before the clawbeast pulls her under.

I run.

My feet pound over the frozen sea. I push myself faster. Faster. The ice creaks as I weave through the fixed peaks of paralyzed waves. Not fast enough. My lungs burn. My feet grow numb. The Rime stretches before me, endless and taunting.

There's another clawbeast.

No, that can't be right. I am the only Beast in the Rime. I've checked a thousand times over. I've scoured every inch of this basin to make sure of it.

How could there be another?

Pressure builds in my chest, threatening to absorb my frantic heart. *It can't be true.*

But the clawbeast was there, before my eyes, seconds ago, and it took her. It fucking *took* her, while I stood here and watched.

Goddess fucking dammit, what a fool I've been. All this time I thought I was acting alone.

And I destroyed the half of me that could save her.

What the fuck am I going to do? Jump into the Rime in my bare skin and punch the damn thing? She doesn't need *me*—she needs my Beast. My teeth and claws. Fighting for her. Protecting her.

I've ruined everything.

And now I'm going to lose her for good. Soon enough, her body will wash up on my shore, like the others, and it will be my fault.

My feet slip on the ice. I go down. Hard. Pain explodes through my shoulder. I push to my feet through gritted teeth. Run again.

The beast can't have her. It cannot haunt my waters any longer—I will not allow it. My kingdom, my future, my love—everything is at stake. I have never claimed to be a good king, but I can try.

I have to try.

Chapter Fifty-Six

Nahla

The clawbeast cages me against her chest as we tear through the water. I thrash within her claws, my tail smacking a fury of bubbles.

She's smaller than Aethan, but she still dwarfs me easily. A goddess among the fish. One twist of her hands, and I'm dead.

Shit. Shit. Shit.

My face is smothered against her rock-solid abdomen. Claws dig into my skin as I try to wriggle free, and pain flares through my muscles. Her admonishing growl rumbles through me, and I grow still. Scales prickle along my spine, rising in fear.

She doesn't eat me, yet, and I can't decide if this is a good thing or not. I glimpse the water passing beneath her arm, darkening as we plummet into the depths. She must be taking me somewhere, then. To feast in private? To feed me to her young?

Shit. I know little about clawbeasts, besides what I've learned from Aethan. But he's an anomaly of the species—part merfolk, driven by more complex instincts. This female is a mystery.

I can't fight her. Not physically. But I could persuade her to let me go. My magic worked on Aethan. Why not her?

Magic churns in my stomach. I place my hand flat against her stomach's rough scales. I won't have much time to subdue her once I make mental contact. She could become violent. I could push her to the brink. As my heart pounds, I suck oxygen through my gills to steel my resolve.

The beast twists, angling us through the gap in the glaciers. The sea floor drops away, and we pass into open water.

Now or never.

With a low note, I lift my mind and spiral towards her defenses. Dark mist swirls around the outer shell of her psyche. They rise at my approach, coiling as if to spring.

I press my fingers into her abdomen, strengthening the connection.

An opening appears in her defenses, a small crack in the outer wall. I slip through and plunge into a sea of emotions.

Chaos greets me. Rage. Pain. Frustration. I weave through, planting a new emotion: disgust. Revulsion. I warp her thoughts to my will.

The beast snorts and shakes her head. Can she sense me? Is it working?

Let go, I urge. *You don't want to eat this vile, disgusting meat. Too much fat on the bone.*

She snarls, tightening her grip. Her claws cut into my skin, and the scent of my blood wafts into the water.

Her thoughts converge, swirling to form a single thought: irritation.

With a kick of her feet, she angles toward the glacier. A cave is carved into the rock, the mouth just large enough for her to fit through. The water darkens as she slips inside.

Let go, I press. *Abandon the meal. You're not hungry.*

The tunnel into her lair twists like a labyrinth. We weave and turn until I no longer recall the path we've taken. I couldn't find my way out if I tried.

This is where I die, in some nondescript cave at the edge of nowhere, as food to a beast. My flesh will tear, my bones will dissolve into the foam whence I came, and no one will be the wiser. Beasts don't care if you're royal or low-born. You're either food or foe, and tonight I become both. It seems right that I should die to an animal, after I spent so much of my magic to bring about the demise of other fish. The gods will even the score of the sea.

At least I won't taste good, when she finally eats me. Meat tastes best when the prey dies happy.

Disgusting meat. Unworthy of your taste buds. You'll get indigestion.

Her hand wraps around my throat. My song falters, and our connection wavers. She slams me against the cave wall. Stars explode across my vision as the impact rattles my skull.

Quiet. Her command rumbles through my mind, enraged and raspy.

I freeze.

She releases her grip on my neck and crouches in front of me, dark blue gaze steady on my face. Intelligent, searching eyes. Her thick tail curls around clawed feet, the barbed tip flicking. She's gorgeous, in a shocking kind of way. Sharp cheekbones. Jagged teeth. Small breasts. An athletic body with broad, muscular shoulders and an angled waist. She'll kill me in a second, if it comes to a fight.

I slide my hand against the wall behind me, grasping for any loose bit of stone to clobber her with. I find a decent sized piece and secure it in my hand. As I drag it closer, it catches on something, and shale clatters in the silence.

Her eyes flick down, then back to my face. I bite my lip to stop it from trembling. She reaches for me, hooking her first claw, and trails it down my cheek. Slips beneath my chin. Tilts my head for a clear shot at my neck.

I brace for her killing blow. A slice through my gills would be the quickest. Easy. It'll only hurt for a few seconds as I bleed out, and then I'll be dead.

The color of her eyes reminds me of Aethan's. Blue as midnight with small flecks of white. A small piece of him to comfort my final moments.

I shouldn't have left him like that. I should have stayed. Should have been braver. Smarter. More forgiving.

He fucking needed me, and I left him at his worst. We'll never have a proper goodbye. His last memory of me will be my face, covered in tears as I ran away.

The beast's claw slides lower, grazing the soft hollow of my throat.

What's taking her so long? She should have finished me already.

I squeeze the stone in my hand to channel my anger. Isn't she a beast? Am I not her prey?

Her lip curls, and a deep rumble emanates. Raspy. Chortling. Her eyes glint with dark humor. Is she *laughing* at me?

Fuck it.

Hefting my rock, I swing out and smack her in the temple with all my might.

It bounces off her head like a pebble.

The clawbeast blinks. Her rumbling stops. Then she rolls her eyes and launches away, leaving me stunned against the wall.

Alive.

Chapter Fifty-Seven

Aethan

I LAUNCH ACROSS THE ice, faster. Faster. I jump from the edge without hesitation, plunging into the dark, frigid water.

Nahla needs me, and I will tear the world apart if it means keeping her safe.

Cold pierces my heart. I squint into the blue expanse, searching for any sign of her. A trace of blood or the scent of her fear. The clawbeast's howl. But my senses are dull now, and I can't mark her location among the turmoil of the sea.

The water is packed with panicking fish. They swarm through the gap between the mountains, scales flashing as they flick their frantic tails, crowding my view.

Their eyes whiten as they spot me, but otherwise they pay me no mind. Irritation crawls up my spine. Predators scare fish away, every damn time. But as I kick my feet and flail my arms, moving sluggishly through the water, they ignore me. Indifferent to my presence. Focused on escaping a threat far stronger than me.

My skin crawls at the touch of cold water, like a warm-blooded guppy who hasn't grown into his scales. Useless.

Fuck. I've lost my touch. I can't find her scent. Can't hear her screams. I can't frighten a fucking silverfish. How can I fight a claw-beast in this weak body? No claws. No teeth. No tail. Nothing but my soft siren skin and an abhorrent amount of delusion.

I grit my teeth, clench my abdomen, and kick. I'll figure something out. I have to. I'm the fucking King of Frost, this is *my* domain, I am its protector, and I won't abandon Nahla over a bite of cold.

It's my fault she's been captured. My fault she left to begin with. I tried to protect her, to protect my kingdom, and she ran.

I force my way through the frantic crowd of sea life as dread twists in my throat.

What else should I have done? My people were dying, and I had to protect them, as a king should. I rid them of their villain.

I push my body harder. Kick faster. Regret roils me, its sour tinge coating my tongue. I was misguided and oblivious, and I chose wrong. I picked the wrong villain, my kingdom is vulnerable, and I could lose Nahla forever.

Water churns behind me, and I turn—a lone Frost Guard plunges into the Rime. He's equipped to the gills. Knives are sheathed at his hips. Leather armor encloses his chest, too large for his small frame. His tail is damaged at the end, where half of his fin is missing.

As the bubbles clear, I recognize the young guard's face. Perrin.

My stomach drops. What is he doing here? I should warn him of the danger. The clawbeast is out there somewhere, and he could get hurt. Or worse.

The young guard orients himself in the water, twisting upright with a flick of his tail. The damaged flesh of his tailfin hangs loosely, frayed around the scar my magic left behind.

My throat tightens. I did that. I've already hurt him.

He swims forward, a fierce set to his expression, heading for the gap between the mountains.

"What are you doing?" I grab Perrin's forearm, stopping him.

"Saving Nahla, Sire. I saw the clawbeast take her." His whiskers twitch, and he flicks his gaze over my useless, naked form. "I thought you're afraid of the water."

Annoyance warms the tips of my ears, but I ignore his comment. "You shouldn't be here. It's not safe."

He pulls out of my grip. "Yeah, and Nahla's out there. I'm her rescue party."

"Go back," I snap.

"But Deirdre would kill me," he whines.

"The *clawbeast* will fucking kill you!"

"You don't have to protect me, Your Majesty. I'm a Frost Guard, remember? I protect *you*." He puffs out his chest, touching his gills in a sign of respect.

I swallow hard. Perrin's got his shit together more than I do, it seems. Such bravery. Such innocence. He's the best of us all, through and through.

He narrows his eyes as our silence stretches. "Here." He unhooks a knife from his belt and presses it into my hands. I curl my fingers around the bone shaft. "We're wasting time. Are you coming or not?"

I push the knife away. "No, you keep that. I have magic."

He flares his nostrils, inhaling before he nods and sheathes the blade. "This way." With a kick of his tail, Perrin speeds into the fray of fish, leaving me to flounder.

Fuck.

I stir the magic in my belly with a quick spell and pray to the goddess this works. Summoning two blades of ice, I spin them at each of my hands with a push of my magic. Water stirs. My body propels forward, and I chase Perrin between the mountains.

We swim out of Frost Kingdom territory and into the open sea. I ignore the eerie rise in my scales, and the significance of this moment passes without consequence. I can't remember the last time I left the Rime. My sight-pool doesn't reach this far, and without good enough reason to risk it, I haven't dared venture out of my domain.

My throne. My kingdom. My safety. I'll risk everything for the chance to hold her one more time.

Ahead of me, Perrin dives and arcs gracefully into the depths with the confidence of a merman who's done this before. He follows the mountain's jagged edge, the tip of his tail disappearing into the dark fathoms below.

I angle my spinning blades and kick my feet as I descend. Too fucking slow. She could be dead by now. Torn to shreds by the clawbeast's claws. Her bones, used as toothpicks to clean her own flesh from its jaws.

Rage burns in my stomach, fueling me. The blades spin faster. I speed up, vision darkening, pulse racing, teeth clenching. I will tear that beast apart one scale at a time if it puts a single hair out of place on her head.

Perrin tucks into the mouth of a tunnel, and we regroup at the entrance. Jagged rocks hang like spikes from the ceiling, leaving a space wide enough for the beast to fit through. He signals with one hand, using traditional hunter motions to convey his meaning without sound: *Nahla's scent is strong here.*

I'll take the lead, I signal.

Perrin huffs, and bubbles spray from his mouth. His hands move with irritation. *This is my rescue mission. I'll go first.*

I hold out my arm, blocking the young guard's path. *Sorry, squirt. Can't let you do that. I need you in the back.*

He pouts but obliges. Silently, we glide deeper into the tunnel with Perrin taking the rear. Near-darkness descends, the only light coming from the quiet flicker of glowmites clinging to the stalactites. The mites stir into wakefulness with our passing, glowing brighter and dimming. A signal of our presence.

Fuck.

Will the clawbeast see us coming? Are we swimming into a trap?

The path is winding, the walls twisting and curving until I can no longer determine which direction we face.

Before me, the rock bends sharply to the left. I follow its curve, trailing my fingers along its rough surface, and end where I started. A dead end.

I bump into Perrin to get his attention. My hands sign: *It's a labyrinth.*

He frowns and nods, pushing in front as he taps his nose. He's caught her scent. I follow his lead back the way we came, taking a right turn at the main chamber instead of left. The water feels colder here. More sinister. I inhale, trying to place her scent among the cold stone.

There. Faintly. A thread of her warm vanilla scent, doused in fear. The tunnel curves left. We follow. Faster now. I kick my legs hard, gaining speed. The blades of ice whirr at my sides and propel me faster still.

She's so close I can feel it.

I'm coming, Nahla. I'm going to get you out of here if it kills me.

A roar trembles through the tunnel, freezing the blood in my veins. The glowmites snuff out, and the tunnel plunges into shadow. I slam into the wall, rough rock gouges my skin, and pain bursts through my shoulder. *Fuck!*

The sharp scent of fear permeates the water as we fumble in the darkness. I can't call out to my companion, or else I'll give away his position.

Pebbles clatter to my left. I strain to hear moving water. Someone slips past me. A kick of bubbles. Perrin?

The clawbeast roars again, louder this time, bouncing around one final curve in the tunnel. With numb fingers, I grip the hard rock and prepare to spring.

Chapter Fifty-Eight

NAHLA

THE CLAWBEAST IGNORES ME, squatting at the mouth of her cave without a backward glance. She stiffens into a watchful stance and surveys the darkened tunnel beyond. Her tail is the only part of her that moves, flicking back and forth.

Shock tingles through my body as I process the turn of events. I'm still here, heart beating, mind reeling, watching her as if through someone else's eyes. When I asked the clawbeast not to eat me, I didn't expect her to listen. Now I don't know what to do.

Try to escape? Too difficult. She blocks most of the entrance with her body, leaving minimal room for me to slip through.

Call for reinforcements? I could sing. Summon a nearby animal to create a distraction. And then what? Hope she eats them, giving me enough time to get away? The beast is clearly not hungry.

Kiss her ass? That might work. Every lonely girl has a praise kink.

I reach for her mind, brushing the periphery of her psyche, as I sample her emotions: annoyance reigns, tinged with impatience, boredom, and anticipation. She's waiting for something to happen, something she's wanted for a long time.

Gently, I slip beneath her defenses and project my Voice: *Hey, pretty girl.*

The clawbeast snorts, whipping her head to glare at me. Her eyes burn hot, and annoyance flares in her mind.

Shh, shh, it's okay. I lift my hands in surrender. *I just wanted to say how lovely you look today. Has anyone told you what beautiful eyes you have?*

She cocks her head. Her lips curl in a snarl as she blinks—long, white eyelashes, like Aethan's. Beautiful.

Aethan. I swallow against a knot in my throat, trying to ignore the sharp pang. But I can't. I close my eyes, and his face fills my mind, crowding out all other thoughts. Blue eyes, glinting with mischief. That cocky, lopsided smile. His jaw flexing irritably.

I fucked up.

I feel the spiral coming, the dark emotions threatening to suck me under. My heart beats faster. My chest tightens. A prickle forms in my throat.

What was I doing? I should focus on my task. Come up with better compliments. Operation Kiss Ass is slipping. I'm failing.

The clawbeast launches from her post. Her hand wraps around my throat, and she slams me into the wall, our faces mere inches apart. Nostrils flaring. Eyes blazing. Her thoughts swirl with exuberance and intrigue. Curiosity.

My body tenses. She doesn't eat me. Just crouches, holding me in place. Waiting. Wanting more.

More what?

What do you want from me? I press.

Her eyes widen as she stares at me expectantly. *More.*

So helpful. She's like Aethan when I first met his Beast form, simple thoughts trapped in a complex sea of emotions.

She tightens her grip. *More!*

Aethan? I cock my eyebrow, and she nods. *You like him, too, eh?* I project my memory of Aethan's handsome face for the clawbeast to see.

Her tail slaps the floor. Her smile spreads, revealing pointed teeth as satisfaction colors her mind. Fucking figures. What's not to like about him?

More, she rasps, fingers tightening around my throat. My gills flutter feebly beneath her grip, fighting to draw oxygen. I gasp, vision speckling.

If this keeps her from eating me, so fucking be it. *Okay, but let go of me first.*

She loosens her grip, and my gills flutter freely. Oxygen rushes in.

Thank you. I wait for her to release me, but she maintains her hold. Rough fingers brush the skin of my throat. Her brow furrows, and impatience washes through our connection.

I roll my eyes and sigh. *All the way, please. You can do it, pretty girl. Then I'll show you some more.*

I will *not* be her bitch.

She lets out a low whine but complies, dropping her hand. *More,* she echoes.

Fine.

I skip through my memories of him—running past the intimate moments—and settle on my favorite: our second night on the Frosted Plains. He has me pinned in the snow, and he's leaning in for a kiss. His eyelids droop, half-closed with lust. He never sees it coming—my snowball, smacking into his face. Slush slides down his cheek. Snow clumps in his eyelashes and hair, and he shakes his head to clear it. *Got him.*

The clawbeast chortles, glee sparking through her mind. *More!*

I show her Aethan in the throne room, a devilish grin on his face. He kisses my hand, pulls me into his arms, and twirls me around our private dance floor. My dress wraps around my legs as I pirouette and glitter flies.

The clawbeast startles. Snorts. Hot bubbles wash over my face as she leans closer, eyes wide. *Again.*

How long are we going to play this game? I sigh, flicking to another memory. She growls, the sound rippling out in warning.

No, she says. *Again.*

Clenching my teeth, I rewind and replay our ballroom scene, slower this time. I show her the violinist. The crystal chandelier. The soft weave of his tuxedo, resting beneath my cheek. Feeling his hands as they trail down my dress, lifting me, carrying me to the throne—

I cut it off there, and she rumbles her disappointment. *Look, I'm not going to show you that part. That's private.*

She rolls her eyes and pushes away from me, returning to her perch at the mouth of her cave. With restless energy, she paces back and forth, tail lashing, claws grating against the rock. What the hell is her problem?

Fine. Be that way. I didn't want to be friends with you, anyway.

I sigh, settling against the cave floor once again. Cold seeps from the rock into my scales, and I shift into a more comfortable position. I can't stay here forever, playing memory-dealer for a clawbeast. I need to get out of here. Find Aethan and tell him I'm sorry. Before the beast decides she's hungry enough to end me.

I track her restless movements, praying for an opening. If I could squeeze through while she's on the other side, maybe I can make it. Maybe I can fit.

Quietly, I glide on my stomach toward her, keeping out of her peripheral vision. My hands grasp the rocky floor, pulling me along. She turns, angling right. My opening appears.

But before I can launch, the clawbeast freezes. Her head snaps up. She faces the darkness and opens her mouth, arching her tongue as she inhales. Checking for scent?

Her mind sparks with eagerness. The thing she's been waiting for is close, now. She can smell it. Cool peppermint, like falling snow.

My heart drops into my stomach. I'd recognize that scent anywhere, as I'm sure he'd recognize mine.

As I watch the clawbeast crouch on all fours, her haunches lifting in readiness to spring, everything clicks: I'm not her meal.

I'm the bait.

She's waiting for Aethan to rescue me, and I have to warn him before it's too late. When she glances to the right, I take my chance.

With a hard kick of my tail, I glide through the gap between her body and the wall. My stomach grazes the jagged rock. A few scales tear free, trickling blood. She snorts, a growl reverberating through the water, and her claws descend.

In a final burst of speed, I evade her grasp, barreling into the labyrinthine cave beyond. The clawbeast roars, but I don't look back. I swim into the darkness, weaving out the way we came.

I'm coming home, Aethan, and I'm going to fix everything.

Chapter Fifty-Nine

Aethan

A MONSTER EMERGES FROM the shadows, crouching at the lip of its cave. Glowmites illuminate the sharp planes of its face. Jaws made to kill its prey. A sneer parts its mouth, showing the jagged teeth beneath. Dark villainous eyes. Long white hair. A thrashing, barbed tail.

A clawbeast crowded in a cave, holding a princess hostage within—it feels like looking in a mirror.

The beast I've chased for years, finally now before me. My nightmare. My villain. I can't stand the sight of it.

Fury churns in my gut, feeding my magic as it grows. My hands raise, ready conduits for a spell. There will be collateral damage, once the rage takes over.

I flick my eyes away, looking for the treasure I've come to save. I will not live with myself if I act too soon, if I destroy Nahla in my rush to save her.

As I wait for her to call out my name, I search for a glint of her golden scales.

But the room is empty. A quick scan confirms my worst fear—piles of bones, molted scales, a nest built with stones—but nothing more.

My heart plummets to the floor.

The beast has already swallowed her.

"You motherfucker," I snarl. My vision narrows onto the beast. Its armored scales are speckled with frost. The quiet flutter of its gills, vulnerable at its neck.

I must kill it now. Pierce it with a thousand shards of ice. Or freeze its brain and shatter it against the wall. All along I've thought I was a ruthless killer, why not embrace it now? I'll avenge them all.

With a cry, I send a blade of ice hurtling toward its throat. Sickened glee fills me as I wait for the slice of skin, the scent of its blood. The beast will pay for the life it's taken—my people, picked off one by one while I drowned in the guilt. My sweet Sunfish, gone forever.

She was *mine*.

The beast throws out its paw, stopping my ice blade inches from its gills. The shard shatters into dust as it lunges forward.

Claws curl around my wrist. I'm yanked up, dangling before its face, its glassy eye inches from my cheek. A puckered scar pulls the corner of its eyelid. It assesses me with a longing gaze, drawing its stare over the length of my body.

I punch at its eyes, connecting with the side of its nose. I will not be its fucking dessert.

Did Nahla fight the clawbeast? Did she struggle and bleed? If I had arrived sooner, could I have saved her?

I thrash harder, clawing at its jaw. Gills. I will not die until I avenge her.

The beast growls and shakes me until my vision doubles, lowering its head. It grips my body in both hands, making it impossible for me to move. Its hands wrench tight, wringing me like a wet rag.

Playing with its food.

I sing another spell, sending ice slicing toward its face. A gash blooms across its eyebrow, trickling blood. Another missile cuts its ear.

The beast opens its mouth and roars. The raspy sound of its voice vibrates through my body, rattling my bones. Its hot breath smells of sour meat.

I try to recall her scent, that warm sunshine smell, like sweetnut milk and vanilla cream. But I can't. The thick scent of the beast crowds out her memory.

It's my fault she's dead, and now I can't remember the smell of her.

The beast takes its time lowering me toward its mouth. Sharp, double rows of glinting teeth. White hair floats around its head, tangling around its twisted horns. It stares deep into my eyes, as if trying to burn a hole through my skull.

Blue eyes staring, near-lifeless. Her white hair spreading out. Caught in the currents of her blood. Her hand stretches out toward me. Reaching. I reach for her, and our fingers brush.

My mother. I've killed her. I couldn't control my rage, and it's all my fault.

What's the point in fighting now? I could not save Nahla. I can't save my kingdom. Everything I've ever loved has been taken from me, and I have nothing left to give. My heart shatters, and I let my body grow limp as I brace for the clawbeast's teeth. One monster consumed by another, how fucking poetic.

My mother is dead.

Nahla is dead.

And I will join them both soon enough.

CHAPTER SIXTY

NAHLA

I SWIM IN DARKNESS with my hands stretched out. My palms sting with fresh cuts from the sharp walls. Fucking labyrinth. The tunnel twists in a complicated pattern as I struggle to retrace my path. Is it left after the large stalagmite or right?

Bubbles stir nearby, and I hear the soft flutter of a tailfin. *I'm not alone.*

The person gasps. My face smacks into soft blubber. A brush of whiskers. Flailing arms. An elbow punches me in the ribs.

Then a familiar voice comes, muffled in my hair. "I can't see... fucking... shit!" *Perrin.* He tugs my hair from his mouth and spits.

"Perrin!" I backpedal. "What are you doing here? It's not safe."

"Everyone keeps saying that," he grumbles. "I'm rescuing the damsel in distress. What else?"

My hands find his cheeks, and I pull him close, resting our foreheads together. Godsdammit, Perrin. "I'm fine," I breathe. "Except for this new bruise from your elbow."

His cheeks grow limp between my palms, the tremble of his lip vibrating through. He lets out a choked sob and clutches me. "Shit. I thought you were dead."

I fold him close to my heart as he hiccups again. "Shh, shh. I'm here." Poor youngling must be terrified, coming to rescue me.

He's an idiot, but he's my idiot. My eyes sting and my chest tightens until I can feel the heavy beating of my heart, echoing through every bone. I've got him. He's safe with me. We're going to find a way out of here together. We'll find Aethan and swim home.

"His Majesty is gonna flip," Perrin mutters. He lifts his head off my chest, glancing around as if he's expecting the king to emerge from the rock wall.

Scales rise along my neck. "Perrin," I say. "Where is the king?"

"He went to find"—the clawbeast's yowl echoes through the tunnel—"you."

Perrin's final word sinks between us like a rock and so does my stomach.

"Shit." I have to go back. I have to save him. "I can't ask you to come with me, Perrin."

He snorts. "And you can't stop me, Princess."

We swim deeper into the labyrinth, weaving through the dark tunnels as the sounds of fighting float toward us. The beast growls. Aethan cries out.

My heart thunders as I push my body faster, twisting around the curves with reckless speed. Rocks scrape my skin where jagged edges catch my limbs, ripping scales off to bleed. Perrin is fast on my tail. We turn the final corner, and my heart stops.

The beast holds Aethan in her hands, halfway to her mouth. Claws clamp around his body—not his Beast form, but the soft-skinned form of the king. His legs dangle in the water, those muscled thighs bare and motionless. He stares listlessly at her, limp as reedgrass. Like he's given up.

"No!" I shout.

Godsdammit. He can't give up. He is Aethan Nastrond, King of Frost. A brutal and powerful ice-wielder and lover of hot peppermint tea. Diligent leader and loyal friend. He's fucking *mine*. He can't *give up*.

Aethan turns. Blue eyes lock on mine. His face morphs from blasé acceptance to confusion to anger. "Nahla?"

He squirms in the beast's grip without effect.

Perrin's instincts are faster than mine. With a war cry, he launches at the beast, grasping a knife tight in his fist. He slices at her neck, nicking her gills. Blood trickles out.

The beast screams. A swipe of her arm knocks Perrin away, he flies into the wall with a sickening crack, and his body sinks to the floor, limp.

Perrin!

He doesn't move. His tattered tailfin floats aimlessly in the low current. Is he...?

She'll pay for that.

My blood warms as magic stirs. I snap my gaze to her and clench my gut. With my Voice, I launch my mind toward her defenses.

I punch through. Magic pours out of my mouth, strengthening my attack. Her mind fills with emotion, a chaotic swirl of colors. I don't stop to take inventory. I snuff them out one by one. Wrestle them into submission. Slash them to pieces.

A piercing screech cuts the water. The clawbeast lifts one hand to cover her ear, and she digs her claws into her temple as she screams and shakes her head.

I press on, spiraling toward her center. A small orb glows brightly in the middle of her mind, the fragile blueprint of her psyche. It hums and vibrates as her innermost thoughts thrum beneath the surface in a world of color. I hesitate, staring at the swath of color. So pretty. So fragile.

To enter an animal's center of self has serious repercussions. It's taboo for good reason—but Keen never told me what would happen if I broke it.

I assume it means death. How can a creature survive without a psyche?

Could I kill her? Do I have it in me to take this creature's life? I've assisted so many times in the death of other creatures. What's the difference, really? I brush against the orb. It's warm to the touch.

The beast snarls. Her glare finds me, and she thrashes her tail, lifting from her perch.

Aethan howls as her hands crush his body. "Nahla!" he screams, agony twisting his face. She's hurting him. Killing him before my eyes.

She tucks Aethan against her chest and launches toward me. Her bulk crowds my vision until I see nothing but a wall of flesh and muscle. Trapped.

Through clenched teeth, I strengthen my spell. I grasp the orb inside her mind and squeeze until it fractures like glass. Veins splinter across its surface. Color leaks out, hissing through the cracks. Building in pressure.

The icy grip of panic wraps around my spine. I squeeze my eyes shut, crushing the orb with all my strength, and wait for whatever comes first—her teeth or her demise.

The orb bursts.

The clawbeast stops short, teeth snapping shut. Her eyes widen, and her grip loosens.

Her memory erupts with a rumbling force, flinging me to the far reaches of her conscience. Emotions pour out. Sadness. Longing. Loss. They churn and grow, washing through her mind like great waves. Grief crashes over me, plunging me into her tumultuous sea of memory.

Pieces of her life flash before me, too fast to grasp them all.

A home built within the ice. Chasing silverfish through the Rime. Catching them with bare hands. She was forced to marry young. Too young. He wanted a son. She tried to give him one, but she wasn't fast enough. Beatings. Blood. Her only solace the comforting caresses of her handmaid lover at night, where he couldn't see. She let her rage build for years, kept it close to her heart.

Finally, a viable hatchling. A male. She feared for his life, with a father like that. She plotted the king's demise. Poison in his rum. It was easy. Old age, she said. The kingdom believed her.

Her loving handmaid helped her raise the guppy. Her son would be king someday, and he would be a good king. Better than the last.

I gasp as Aethan's young face floods her mind.

Hatchling Aethan watching her with big blue eyes from the crook of her elbow. Tiny hands. Tiny tailfin. A larger Aethan rolling in glacierweed. Adolescent Aethan in the library, surrounded by stacks of tomes. Asking question after question. Eager to learn. Eager to rule.

Her son.

Memories intertwine with her mood. Her mind grows rapidly, expanding past its shattered defenses. Building new ones. I find myself inside an intelligent being's mind, bursting with color and complexity of thought. I tumble to the edge, pressed out.

When I broke her center of self, I didn't kill the beast—I freed her.

In shock, I cut my spell, landing back within myself. Every scale rises along my body. We stare at each other, both dumbfounded. She blinks, all traces of aggression fading from her features.

The clawbeast thinks she's Aethan's mother.

Fucking hell. If that's true, why was she trying to kill him? Her actions don't add up to reason.

Aethan twists out of her grip, reorienting himself in the water. With a strong arm, he pushes me behind him, placing himself between me and the beast. He growls and raises his hands. The water around his fingers crystallizes with the beginning of his spell.

Sharp blades form in the water, hovering. Ten. Then Twenty. Thirty. He builds them rapidly, collecting a deadly arsenal of ice. His back flexes before my gaze as he prepares to attack. A vein protrudes from his skin, running the length of his neck.

My stomach twists in a hard knot. "Aethan, wait," I whisper.

The shards whir, gaining speed as they spin. The beast shuffles away, hands reaching behind as she backs into the wall.

Gone is the fight in her eyes. Her shoulders slump.

Is it all an act? To trick me into trusting her? The bitch flung Perrin against the wall. She nearly crushed Aethan in her claws. And I'm supposed to throw that all away because I read her memories?

Maybe they were fabricated somehow. Maybe she's been stalking him his whole life, waiting for the right moment to spring.

Aethan growls. His Voice alters the note of his spell, and the projectiles take aim. The beast raises her hands, covering her eyes with a whimper. She peeks between her fingers, watching Aethan with a sad, proud look in her eyes.

"Wait!" I shout.

As Aethan barks with intent, I wrap my arms around his waist and yank. We fall.

Ice flies off course. The shards batter the wall, shattering on impact. A few graze the clawbeast's flesh, shredding her skin in bloody tatters along her ribs. But not deep enough to kill.

Aethan's legs twist around my tail as we tumble. He wraps me in his arms, cushioning me against the impact of the sharp rocks beneath us. Protective. His mouth finds my ear.

"What are you doing?" he hisses. "I had it!"

"I read her thoughts. She thinks she's your mother." My bottom lip trembles. It sounds whaleshit crazy when I say it out loud, but there's a shred of truth to it. And if I'm right, then he'll be glad I stopped him from killing her.

"Impossible. My mother is dead." He plops me onto the cave floor and twists to face the beast. "It's a trap."

I latch onto his ankle, fingers wrapping around smooth skin. "But what if it's true?"

He glances between me and the clawbeast, who watches us both in silence. "I will not risk your life to find out. I have to kill it, Nahla. I have to end this. For the future of my kingdom."

A fissure splits my heart as I look into his face. His expression crumples in pain, eyes searching mine with rapid flicks, as if he's trying to absorb every detail. Just as I'm doing to him.

"No, you don't," I whisper. When I push off the floor, he blocks me. I push past him, approaching the beast.

She opens her eyes as I draw near. She lifts a paw to her mouth and licks a wound between her knuckles. Maybe she is lying. Maybe it's a trap, as Aethan believes. But I'll never forgive myself if I don't find out the truth.

Reaching out my hand, I swim within inches of her. She doesn't move.

Aethan's fingers graze the edge of my tail. "No!" he barks.

I ignore him, focusing on her. "May I?" I ask, stretching my fingers closer. "To strengthen the connection? I want to understand you."

She cocks her head and blinks, then dips her chin. This is not the same beast I fought moments ago. Emboldened, I place my hand flat on her hard stomach and tune my spell.

CHAPTER SIXTY-ONE

AETHAN

NAHLA SLIPS OUT OF my embrace and swims right up to the beast. I kick my legs, trying to swim, trying to reach her and pull her out of its grasp in time. I fail, fingers slipping on the slick edge of her tailfin.

The clawbeast must be a lying trickster, and Nahla falls right into its trap. That beast can't be my mother. It's impossible. I was there the day she died. I saw my own claws rake through her soft face. I swam in her blood.

I'd rather be sliced apart than let that beast within a scale's breadth of Nahlani of the Brine. I want to fold her into my body until every inch of my being shields her from its claws.

I thrash in the water, drawing closer. Almost within reach. My soft-skinned form is fucking useless. Instead of cutting the water with ease, my fingers slip through it, unable to find purchase. My legs kick, pathetic and clunky without a tail to steer my path. Why the fuck did I get rid of my Beast?

I draw within myself, searching the reaches of my mind for any sign of him. Maybe Lucas's magic isn't permanent. Maybe, if I beg him, he'll come out of hiding. But there's nothing there, only the echo of my desperation. My Beast is gone.

"No!" I shout. If I can't reach Nahla, maybe she'll listen to me. I can convince her to see reason.

She ignores my protests, reaches out, and places her hand on its fucking stomach.

If I can snare her waist, I can pull her away before the beast attacks. I can save her from its deadly grasp.

Nahla sings. Her magic releases, and the beast grows still as ice. Its eyes glass over, staring straight through me. It does not lash out, does not fight. Only crouches, motionless, as Nahla's song fills the cave.

The beast is letting her touch its stomach.

Nahla's song takes on a melancholic quality, rolling like a lullaby. The beast curls its tail around its feet and settles to the floor, like a frostcat before a fire. Its eyelids droop closed. I stop short and stare in disbelief. What the fuck is happening right now?

Is she *charming* it?

Nahla has always been powerful. She thawed my frozen heart, after all. I've seen her work on the hunting trip, enchanting a whole herd of woollygoats at once. She's more powerful than I'll ever be; her talents are more useful to my kingdom than I could dream of.

A clawbeast whisperer—Nahla is two for two.

The beast chirps. A smile spreads over its face. Gently, it takes her into its arms, cradling her like she's a newly hatched guppy while Nahla continues to sing.

A lump hardens in my throat. Such a tender touch from a dreadful creature. Is this part of the trap? Or is the beast somehow sincere? Maybe...

I cock my head, studying the beast from a new angle. There's a slight curve to its waist I didn't notice before. A feminine flare to the shape of its cheeks and mouth. Long, white eyelashes. The jagged pull of the scar on its eyelid where I marred her that day.

"She's been stuck in this form for more than a decade," Nahla says. "After a while, she lost herself and became fully animal. She said she's been trying to draw attention, leaving gifts at the castle to entice someone to come after her." Nahla turns to look at me, her eyebrows knitting. "Does this mean anything to you?"

"Gifts," I murmur.

All the killings were hers. The corpses appeared on my shore with the same pattern of scars, never a missing limb. Each one laid out like a present on Yuletide. Like she wanted them to be found. Why else wouldn't she eat them?

I close my eyes against the truth as it hits me. The curse of the clawbeast is generational. I have it. My mother has it. I should have guessed this could happen. I should have known better, should have studied harder, worked harder to solve the mystery. If I had realized it sooner, many of my people could be alive.

I could have rescued her. She needed me, and I didn't save her.

Twelve years.

Trapped in her animal mind, stripped of her memories. She was trying to reach me in the only way she knew how. And I, too full of self-loathing to realize, took the blame.

I've been so focused on destroying myself, consumed with my hatred and rage, to realize the truth. And Lucas fucking sat there and watched.

He must have known. How could he not? He's been the royal healer longer than I've been alive.

Nausea rolls through me, washing away all desire to fight.

I've been deceived.

The beast is watching me. Her head is bowed, her eyes sparkling beneath thick lashes. Waiting to see what I'll do.

It's the same way my mother used to look at me when I was up to no good. The same mix of pride and irritation, the same witty glint. A sly curl to her mouth.

Fuck.

"I thought I killed you," I whisper.

My mother snorts, and bubbles stream from her nose. Nahla laughs. She leans into her mental connection, scrunching her nose with humor.

I let my shoulders drop. My muscles pinch along my neck as tension uncoils and drains. She's laughing.

She's okay.

"She said, 'Fat chance,'" Nahla says. "I like her."

"Yeah." My mouth tugs in an answering smile. "Me too." Slowly, I reach out to her. She lifts her hand, and I tentatively trace the curve of her claw. It's smooth. Sharp. She blinks, eyes crinkling at the corners.

A low moan emanates from the back of the cave, where a dark shape curls against the floor. In the chaos, I'd forgotten about Perrin.

How could I have forgotten? My stomach twists with fresh guilt.

He sits up, wobbling upright. With groggy eyes, he squints into the light of the glowmites. "Shit, did we win?"

The lucky guppy lives.

He rubs the top of his head, and fresh blood trickles into the water. When he spots my mother, his face pales.

"You're bleeding!" Nahla darts to his side, frantic. "Any pain? Where does it hurt?"

"There's a clawbeast behind you," he whispers.

"She's fine. I'll tell you about it later." Her hands flutter as she assesses the damage, careful not to jostle him. "Where does it hurt? What's your name?"

"Just my head, Nahla."

"Wrong. That's my name. Yours is Perrin."

He gives her a toothy grin. "Nice one."

"Watch." She holds up two fingers, and he tracks them slowly with his eyes. "Concussion, likely. Nothing permanent. We need to get you to the surface and Lucas can—" She bites her lip, glancing at me. "We'll get you sorted, okay?"

She pulls him into her arms and faces my mother. "Can you lead us out of here?"

Chapter Sixty-Two

Aethan

The wind cuts sharply across the frozen crust of the sea. My knees plant on the ice as I help my mother out of the water. Nahla and Perrin are already two-legged, hobbling to the distant shore in the light of the dawn.

Weariness settles heavy in my bones, and my body screams for respite. It's been a long fucking night, and I'm glad to see the sun.

The clawbeast hesitates, her mouth set as she treads beneath the surface.

"It's okay," I tell her. "Take my hand."

She nods curtly. With tentative claws, she reaches for my outstretched hand. Her rough palm slips into mine, and I pull her bulk onto the ice. She crouches low, water rolling off her slick scales. Her claws curl into the ice. The spines along her back flex and quiver as she glances around.

As the wind hits her body, her scales shift in color. Dark blue fades to light, then white. Her spines retreat. Body shrinks. Claws retract. Horns coil into her skull. With a final whip of her tail, it disappears into her tailbone, leaving my mother naked and dripping wet on the ice. Her long, white hair falls into her face, covering her torso and shielding her expression from view.

She gasps and gulps the air like a fish struggling to breathe. A fit of coughing takes her as she hacks up seawater, spitting it onto the ice with a moan. Then she draws a shaky breath, shock written across her face. She lifts her hand and twists it before her face, her soft white skin catching the light of the rising sun. She flutters her fingers.

"Are you okay?" I whisper.

My mother snaps her head up, and she takes in her surroundings, glancing first to Nahla, then Perrin. When she sees me, she cocks her head. She has piercing sky-blue eyes, just as I remember.

"Aethan?" she asks, her voice raspy and raw.

"Hey, Mama," I whisper. Salt pricks in my eyes.

"You're so *tall*." She smiles, and my chest tightens. *It's really her.* "Where am I?" She presses her fist to her forehead and scrunches her face. "I can't remember. Everything is so fuzzy."

"You've been trapped in this form for a while, Your Majesty," Nahla says, several feet away. "Can you walk?" She stands with Perrin, her arm looped around his waist to support him. She's found his cloak and draped it around him. The young guard shivers, teeth chattering audibly.

My mother stares at Nahla. "I remember *you*," she says. "You were in my head. You shared memories with me. I saw..." She shakes her head, rises to her feet, and takes a step with wobbly knees. I catch her elbow before she falls.

"Let's get you home," I say.

We hobble across the frozen Rime, Nahla helping Perrin as I support my mother. I watch Nahla's form ahead of me, my chest growing warm at the soft sway of her hips. Despite all my efforts to the contrary, she is safe. Shooting irritated glances over her shoulder, but alive.

It's the best I can ask for.

She's mad at me, still. I can feel the tension rolling off her body. But mad I can handle. I'll take her anger over her absence any day, because it means she cares enough to stay in the fight. I'll spend the rest of my life making it up to her, if she'll let me.

Ahead of us, several figures huddle on the shore. I make out their faces as we grow closer—Deirdre, worried; Lucas, scowling; and the captain of the Frost Guard, cold-stone unreadable. My mother stiffens in my arms, and her fingers curl into a fist. She misses a step, and I haul her onto her feet.

"Nervous?" I chuckle.

"That's him," she growls. "I remember his face. The healer who trapped me."

Ice crawls the length of my spine. "Lucas?"

"He said he could heal me of the curse. He wanted to help. We did several sessions where he entered my mind and..." She shudders. "It backfired. I got so angry, I chased him into the sea. You were there in the shallows. Once I transformed into the clawbeast, I couldn't shift back."

I glance toward the shore. Lucas shifts his weight, eyes darting between our faces. Sweat clings to his brow, despite the cold wind.

I squeeze my mother's shoulders. "I'm stuck, too," I mutter. "But like this."

She grabs my chin and yanks it to get a good look at me. Her gaze roams over my features as her frown deepens. "Useless chum. I should've fired him when I had the chance." Then her eyes soften, and her grip releases. "My handsome little prince, all grown up."

Her face has aged, too. Wrinkles line the corners of her mouth and eyes, and two lines form a V between her eyebrows. Signs of time passing through my grasp. I swallow past the lump in my throat. Twelve years lost. How will we make up the time?

The clatter of shifting rocks snags my attention. Nahla marches to the scowling healer and jerks her chin.

"Check him for concussion, Chumwad," she barks, her touch gentle on the young guard's back.

The healer obeys, touching Perrin's forehead with two fingers. Magic glows beneath his touch, swirling around his head. The tendrils sweep through Perrin's hair, dissolving the blood and leaving his sandy curls standing with static.

Deirdre flutters nearby, wringing her hands with worry anew, until the healer releases his spell.

"There," Lucas says. "Good as new, m'lady."

Nahla relinquishes her hold on Perrin, narrowing her eyes at the healer. Tension rolls off her form as she clenches her hands into fists at her side.

Deirdre rushes forward, pulling her nephew into a smothering hug. She presses a million kisses to his hairline, and the young guard squirms.

"Stop," Perrin whines. "I'm not a guppy."

Deirdre ignores his protests, pulling him in for a tighter hug. When she looks up, she spots the figure next to me and her face pales. Her mouth drops open, and her eyes fill with moisture.

"Isolde?" she whispers, choking on my mother's name. "Your Majesty, I thought you were..."

My mother breaks from my support, stumbling forward on her wobbly legs. Deirdre meets her halfway, and they embrace with a wild sob. Deirdre cups the queen's face, smoothing away her tears with frantic thumbs. She pulls off her own cloak and wraps my mother's naked form.

"I thought I lost you forever," Deirdre cries, burying her face in my mother's hair.

"No, my sweet. I'm here." She presses a kiss to the top of Deirdre's head, keeping her glare steady on Lucas.

The healer shifts uneasily under the queen's penetrating gaze. He glances between Nahla, the queen, and me as he reaches for the sheath at his hip. His fingers curl around the hilt.

Lucas, trusted healer to the royal family, fucked us both over. He promised he knew the "cure" to our family's legacy. Promised he could fix us. Then he banished my mother to an animalistic murder spree, ravaged my kingdom, and left me soft and vulnerable to defend it. Not to mention how he bound and gagged Nahla, *hurt* her, to trigger my Beast's final appearance.

The healer has outworn his welcome.

He glances at me, and his eyes widen. He backs away from the scene. Three steps backward. Then he bolts.

I send ice streaming after him. My magic wraps around his legs, crawls up his waist, and secures him in a solid block of ice.

"Lucas," I bellow, prowling toward him. He wriggles in the restraint, as if he could wrench free. As if he could avoid the full weight of my wrath. He should know by now—I am not decent; I'm dangerous.

"Your Majesty, have mercy," he blubbers. "I healed the young guard, as she asked. I did my duty to you. You *asked* for this. Why do you punish me so?"

I stop before him and stare into his cold, dark eyes. They swim with fear. *Good.* "What did you do to my mother?"

"She was cursed, Sire. Cursed like you. I did as you asked. You wanted the Beast gone, and gone he is! That dark spirit haunts you no longer. Aren't you pleased with your humble servant?"

"You tried the same trick on her, didn't you? You used that spell on your queen."

"She asked me to," he stammers.

"She's been stuck as a clawbeast for twelve fucking years, Lucas. And you act like you didn't know. This whole time, I believed my mother was dead, when it was *you*. Your spell that separated her from me. Your spell that caused her to turn wild and wreak havoc on my people. All those hunters, dead on my shore. And you fucking *stood there* and said nothing of this. You let me believe it was *my* fault. For. Twelve. Years."

His lips press together in a thin line. "Hurts, doesn't it," he says. "To have the only one you love ripped from your hands."

Anger rises from my core. I let it roll through me, reveling in the feeling, daring him to speak with the force of my glare. All my hurt and pain finally has a reason—and he's glowering before me. It'd be so easy to reach out and snap his neck. To take his life for all the pain he's caused my kingdom and my family.

"I could have you flayed for this," I hiss.

"Surely not for performing a request of the king." He jerks his chin defiantly. "You'll forgive me someday, when your rage has cleared. You'll find Audrina's grace in your heart, as I have. We both wanted to make your kingdom safe again, and we've done that. You can't hurt them anymore. I believe what you're looking for is gratitude."

"You vile, writhing *snakefish*. You have not found Audrina's grace," I hiss. "You used forgiveness as a ploy to gain my trust so you could get inside my head and ruin me."

He smirks. "And?"

"You tortured me, taunted me, and ripped me apart. You framed my mother. You gagged and hurt the only female I've ever loved. You tried to destroy my kingdom, my family line. For this, you must pay."

He snarls and spits. "You have not suffered *enough*, Aethan, Terror of the Rime."

I could have him stand trial, pin him as the monster we've been searching for. He's a villain, and my kingdom deserves justice for their dead.

It's what a good king would do. A fair king.

Or I could banish him. Sink him to the bottom of the Drink where he belongs. The dark-dwellers don't think kindly of siren heritage. I could let nature take its course, and his death would be out of my hands.

Or I could separate his head from his shoulders and send it rolling into the sea. A sick sense of satisfaction twists in my stomach. Yes. That's what I want.

But the honor doesn't belong to me.

"Mother?" I say. "Do your worst."

Stones shift as she steps forward, chin held high. All color drains from Lucas's face. She grabs him by his hair, leaning close enough to bite him. She snarls, and the healer whimpers audibly, flinching away from her.

"You vile scum of the sea," she spits. "Fish will feast on your bones, and it still won't be enough to satisfy your crimes against me."

With a quick bark of her Voice, she summons a blade of ice, and runs it clean through his neck. She lifts his severed head from his shoulders, dangling it by his hair as she turns to face me. His mouth fixes in a permanent snarl, not unlike his beloved frostcat stuffed above his mantel.

Blood speckles my mother's pale cheeks and hair, dripping from her chin as she smiles.

"There," she says, dissolving her blade with a flick of her wrist. "Now, let him rot."

CHAPTER SIXTY-THREE

NAHLA

THE BEACH IS EMPTY tonight, just me, the Rime, and the moon. Waves frozen in time form a crust over the sea, the remnants of Aethan's spell.

Odd that the sea could be this quiet. Snowflakes float through the air, aimless on the wind. I sit on the shore and soak in the silence. If the waves aren't moving, is time standing still? So much has changed since they became frozen. The former Frost Queen now returned. Aethan absolved of his self-suspected crimes. Lucas beheaded. And me back on the shoreline, wondering where I'm going next.

I suppose that's nothing new.

Pulling my knees to my chest, I tuck my chin on top. Apprehension twists my stomach as I consider the future. I could stay here, if he'll let me. I'm still angry with him for the way he ended the Beast, but the feeling has dulled—I wish it wasn't so permanent.

I miss him.

But not the tough-shelled world-on-his-shoulders version. I miss the version of him that would bring me hot chocolate right about now, pull me into a hug, and tell me it's all going to be okay.

I miss the Aethan I fell in love with, and I'm afraid he's too far gone.

Life will be different for him now. His responsibilities will shift. He'll be focused on restoring the kingdom and refilling the Rime. What role could I play in that future?

I *want* it. Badly. I want the snowbears, the aethersky, the morning tea chats with Deirdre. I want the guppies screaming as they pummel each other with snow. I want Aethan tucking me into a bed of soft furs. I want the Beast ravishing me in the library.

But it can't be that way. He's made it impossible, and now we both have to live with that.

The clack of stones grounds me, and I turn toward the sound. Aethan's shadow falls over me, blocking the moonlight.

He says nothing for a moment. Just stands there. I close my eyes as his scent catches in the wind, and my heart aches, missing him even as he stands so close.

"Sunfish, I..." He stops, shuffling his foot through the stones. A few trickle down the slope and skitter onto the ice. With a sigh, he sits, folding his large frame next to mine. "I'm sorry."

"Yeah, me too."

"I fucked up. I shouldn't have asked Lucas to..." He runs a hand down his face, rubbing his jaw. "I was trying to protect you. Protect everyone. And when I hurt you... Nahla, I hurt you. You trusted me to care for you, to give you pleasure, and I *hurt* you. I couldn't live with myself. So I fixed it in the only way I knew how. And I'm sorry it's not what you wanted."

Tears bead in my eyes, and my chest tightens. I reach for him, curling my hand around his bicep. "I know why you did it. I just wish you would have talked to me about it first. I could have figured something out, but it's too late now."

"Is it too late for you to forgive me?" he whispers, turning to look at me. His eyes are moist. The Frost King, getting teary for me. "Please, Sunfish. I don't know what I'd do without you. My world is so much colder without you in it."

Sadness pierces my heart with its icy rod. Pretty words can't undo what he's done. I cannot make him whole again. How can I pretend the Beast—and the emotional intimacy that came with our connection—isn't *gone*? How can we move on from that?

He searches my face. "I have known nothing but frost and snow, yet since *you* wandered in, I'm the warmest I've been all my life. You've thawed my frozen heart, and I'd melt the Rime if it'd make you mine again."

I flick my gaze away, landing on the frozen sea. "Well, go ahead then."

His brow knits in confusion. "Pardon?"

"Melt the Rime for me, Aethan, and I'm yours."

I cross my arms. The wind kicks up, whipping through my hair. He reaches out, snatching a strand and tucking it away. He lingers on the shell of my ear as his eyes tighten.

Then he clears his throat. "All right."

Aethan stands to his full height and removes his cloak, draping it over me. The warm leather interior rests heavily on my shoulders, soft fur brushing my cheeks. I fold into it as my heart races.

I was kidding. He doesn't need to prove himself to me. But Aethan doesn't know that.

With a serious glare, Aethan faces the frozen sea, plants his feet into the stones, and raises his hands. A deep, rumbling note emanates from him as his song builds, ricocheting through the night.

The earth trembles beneath him. A loud crack splits the ice, splintering out from where he stands. A chasm forms and water rushes in, swallowing the ice as it breaks into smaller and smaller pieces.

His arms grow rigid and flex with the strength of his spell. Veins ripple across his forearms, straining. He frowns with deep concentration. His Voice thunders louder still, vibrating through my body.

Shit.

He's like a god, bending the sea to his will. My insides soften and warm until it takes all my restraint not to race across the beach and climb him like a sweetnut tree. I grasp the rocks to hold me in place as he finishes his spell.

He fucking did it.

As the last of the ice collapses, waves rush upon the beach with a hush of silver bubbles. Aethan turns to face me. Sweat dapples his brow. His shoulders sag with exertion. He searches my face for something, and when he finds it, a slow grin spreads on his lips.

"For you," he whispers, "Nahla, I'd do anything. I hope you know that."

I can't contain myself any longer. I jump to my feet and tackle him with the full force of my affection. He catches me with a grunt and swallows me with his arms. His nose tucks into my hair and he inhales deeply.

I tip my head back so I can see his face. The depth of his eyes, searching mine as I search his. "You love me?" I breathe.

"With every crystal of my cold, bitter heart. I love you, Sunfish. I fucking love you."

"I love you too—"

Before I can finish, his lips capture mine with a wild growl. We gasp and moan, devouring each other like starving animals. His hands twist in my hair as mine tangle in his. I pull him closer, needing more. My heart swells with passion and my skin cries out for his touch everywhere all at once.

We tumble to the ground, and I land on top of him. My fingers hurry to undo his shirt, hands sliding beneath the hem across the hard plane of his abdomen. His chest. He sits up and I tear the shirt away from him.

He kisses the length of my neck, the valley between my breasts. My shirt goes the way of his, soon forgotten. My skirt is next. His pants. I straddle him, naked, as his erection presses against my stomach.

He leans back and grins, shifting his hips so that I slide closer, and my wetness slips against his shaft. "Goddess, you look good up there," he moans.

I grind against him, slipping along his length. "I've never been on top before," I admit. "I don't know what I'm doing."

"I'll guide you, Sunfish." He grips my ass and lifts me into position. The tip of his cock nudges my entrance. "Now sit."

I do as I'm told.

His thick cock slides inside me, filling me to the brim. I gasp as a wave of pleasure rolls through me, and on instinct, I rock my hips. His cock angles deeper, nudging the sensitive spot within me. *Mmm, that's good.*

"Like that?" I ask.

His eyes flutter closed for a moment. "Fuck."

I rock my hips again, working him slowly. He shudders beneath me.

"That's it, Sunfish," he growls. "Sit on your throne."

I straighten my spine and spread my legs, sinking deeper still. My clit nudges the base of his shaft. And then I ride.

"Good," he rumbles. "Look at you. You're a natural queen."

I roll my hips. Faster. Deeper. Toss my head back into the light of the moon. My hand splays on his chest, grounding me where his heart beats heavily beneath my touch.

Pleasure spreads deep in my stomach like lava unfurling from the maw of a mountain, foretelling the devastation yet to come.

His fingers wrap around my wrist, guiding my hand to where we connect.

"Now touch yourself," he commands. "Use your pretty little hands where I can see you."

I obey. Frantic fingers tease my clit mercilessly as I continue to ride him. My body becomes as light as the aethersky above us, rippling with color and starlight as I approach the edge of bliss.

"Fuck me, Nahla," he orders.

So close. I'm so fucking close. With a final buck of my hips and a flick of my fingers, I tilt into bliss. I come hard.

Aethan bucks beneath me and cries out with a shudder as we come in unison. Gasping for breath, we wring out the threads of pleasure until my body becomes weak and soft.

As he moans, I feel a foreign brush of emotion. Desperation. Desire. Deep, bottomless devotion.

I gasp. "Aethan, I can *feel* you."

He chuckles, and the laughter rumbles beneath my seat. "Is that another dick joke, Nahla?"

Humor. Pride.

These aren't my feelings. They're his.

"No, I can feel your thoughts." I bend forward to grasp his cheeks, pressing our foreheads together.

I don't know how it happened or why it worked, but somewhere inside that head of his, the Beast has awakened.

I weave my spell, pouring all my hope into the intent, and sing. I lift from my body and mingle with his mind.

Gone are the impenetrable outer defenses. He sucks me in with sudden force, straight to his center of self. The golden orb glows and sparks. Something slithers beneath the glass-like surface, clawing for my attention.

My heart thunders, all air drains from my lungs, and an idea takes root. A tantalizing idea formed on reckless hope.

It's dangerous. But it worked on his mother. Why not him?

"Aethan," I whisper. "What would you say if I could get our Beast back?"

Wrapping his arm around my waist, he sits up. Our breath mingles between us, clouding in the cool night air.

Gently, he cups my face and looks deep into my eyes. "Do it."

"It might hurt." I bite my lip. "I'm not positive."

He traces my lip with his thumb. "I trust you, Nahla. You can do it."

I sharpen my spell. With the force of my will, I grasp the glowing orb and squeeze.

At first, it resists. Small cracks splinter across the surface. The colors beneath darken and stain dark blue. I squeeze harder. Harder.

Aethan flinches, then shakes his head. "Keep going."

I clench with all my might, and with a tinkling shatter, the orb breaks into a million pieces.

Emotions pour out. Joy and pain. Love and despair. Rage and wonder.

Where he grips my face, Aethan's fingers grow cold. Blue scales crawl up his arms. From his scalp sprouts two twisting horns. His eyes darken, deep as midnight. The king and the Beast, one, as he was meant to be.

"It worked," I gasp. "You're back."

I kiss him, joy flooding my heart and I feel the shifting of his mouth beneath mine, the sharpness of his teeth as they emerge. He picks me up and walks me into the shallow waves.

His feet splash. His body grows. And in my head, I hear the rolling thunder of his voice. *Hello, Sunfish.*

CHAPTER SIXTY-FOUR

AETHAN

TWO WEEKS LATER

The castle is quiet. I sit at my desk, rolling a gold-banded ring between my fingers so the diamond catches the light. The stone is the size of my pinky nail, bedded in a brilliant halo. The diamond reminds me of Nahla—it catches and bends the light to bring the best colors forth, in the same way she captures the best parts of me.

It's my mother's ring, and I intend to use it to ask Nahla to be mine. If she'll have me. Already, the nerves split my stomach, and I tuck the ring into my pocket.

The future is looking bright.

Last week, I had my room stripped of its iron casements, which uncovered the traditional darkwood paneling beneath. Two windows frame my bed with a view of the courtyard, and for the first time in ten years, light streams through the glass, cutting sharp lines across the slat floor and illuminating the dust. A roaring fire crackles in the fireplace. My door has been replaced with a sturdy darkwood feature with a single lock from the inside, and I've propped it open to draw a cross breeze from the hallway.

The guard is gone—I sent him on recess with the rest of the staff. As of an hour ago, the Rime was reopened for swimming, and the whole Frost Kingdom turned out to celebrate.

A smile tugs my lips as I dip my fingers into the sight-pool on my desk and activate its magic. The image ripples and zooms into the open water, revealing the crowds of Frost merfolk gathering there. My breath catches in my throat at their beauty. Their blubbery tails show off shades of blues and grays, blacks and whites. Dark browns. Silver. Some are dappled like the hide of a pikewhale, others smooth monotone. Beauty once concealed by a decade of wearing their legs.

I spot familiar faces among the crowd. Cyrene is surrounded by a group of hunters, several of whom accompanied our hunting trip across the Frosted Plains. They speed off with harpoons at the ready, chasing a shiver of pearlsharks. No more hunting regulations. No more danger. They're free.

Perrin swims with a group of young guards nearby. The males take turns circling around a smaller group of females, showing off their somersaults and flips in the water. Perrin out-skills them all. With a slap of his tail, he pulls off a triple twist, then dives in to plant a quick kiss on a young blonde's cheek. She blushes and dips her head. As Perrin speeds away, he glances over his shoulder with a tusky grin.

Around the edges, guppies cling timidly to their parents. They stare with wide eyes, taking in the new surroundings. Most of them have never been underwater until now. A brave few venture forth, turning slowly as they experiment with the change in gravity. When a silverfish slips by, the guppies clap their hands in delight.

My chest tightens, filling with an odd mix of sadness and pride. The younglings have missed out on so many beautiful things. They have so much to learn about the sea and their place within it.

"You should be with them." Nahla's voice sounds in my ear as her hands slide over my shoulders. Her thumbs press into the muscle, easing my tension with small circles. Her scent washes over me, warm and welcoming, and I inhale. The Beast purrs his approval.

I catch her hand, passing my fingers over her soft skin.

"Not yet," I say.

"You're their king." She presses a kiss to my hair but doesn't push the matter. I squeeze her fingers in gratitude.

"Is this what you want, Nahla? Where you want to be? We can make it work. I could spend part of the year in the Brine, return here when duty calls. It'll be difficult, but I'd make it work. For you."

She chuckles and rests her chin on my shoulder. "You? In the Brine? I'm not sure the traditional garb would suit you."

My ears grow warm. "And why not?"

She trails her fingers across my chest, circling my nipples through my shirt. "How do you feel about starfish, clinging right about here?" She lays her hands flat and laughs.

"I'm more of a fur cloak kind of guy," I grumble. "But I like them on you."

She ducks close, sneaking a kiss on my cheek. "Aethan, you'd be miserable in the Brine. Besides, I like it here. With Deirdre and Perrin and"—she taps my nose—"my grumpy Frost King. I think I could make a difference. Use my powers for good. I can help people."

I relax at her words. She's right. She will make a difference here, and under her leadership, the Frost Kingdom will thrive. We're lucky to have her.

I'm lucky to have her. "You won't get homesick? We can visit often."

"You are my home," she whispers.

My heart swells until I can hardly speak. We watch the sight-pool together in silence for a moment.

Soon enough, the water stirs, welcoming two newcomers to the festivities. I adjust the view, panning out to watch as Deirdre and my mother dive in. Deirdre shifts into her tail-form, a vision in midnight-blue scales and unpinned silver tresses. As my mother transforms, her claws lengthen and her horns twist out. She grows in height, filling out her intimidating form.

The onlookers pause their activities, staring. A few parents hide their guppies beneath their hair.

My mother grasps the tip of her tail, wringing it between her hands. But Deirdre reaches out, smiles, and takes my mother's hand. Together, they enter the fray, as newly named Duchess and former Frost Queen.

It will take time for my kingdom to rebuild their trust in me and my mother. To undo years of terror at the sight of a clawbeast. But with Nahla, I no longer fear their rejection. With her at my side, we can heal this kingdom, turn it into something magical, the way it should have always been.

"What is that?" she says, peering over my shoulder to point at a shadow on the edge.

I adjust the spell, panning out. She gasps and grips my arm, leaning closer to see the image better.

There, at the entrance to the Rime, treads the largest creature I've ever seen. Its shoulders are too broad to fit between the gap in the mountains. Giant paddle-fins stir the water, keeping its mammoth form afloat. Through the sight-pool, I glimpse an armored under-belly and a large snap-jaw mouth.

Fear tingles along my scalp. What *is* that thing?

Several merfolk tread the water around the creature, their scales brightly colored, their skin shades of deep bronze. One is female, re-sembling a taller, sharper version of Nahla with a pale green tail. Her companions include an older male siren and several well-adorned guards. Each one of them looks cold and out of place.

Fuck. More uninvited guests.

"Winona!" Nahla exclaims. "Keen!"

She squeals in my ear and bounces on her heels. I turn to face her, grinning despite myself. She's beautiful when she's happy. Her face radiates joy, infectious, and I can't help the warmth that spreads through my chest.

Nahla launches into my arms, encircling my neck. "Ramona got my message!"

If these visitors are her family, I suppose I can welcome them warmly. Deirdre will enjoy the bustle of a full house, and it'll be good to chase out the dust once and for all. If Nahla wants them here, then that's all I need.

She's happy. Who am I to ruin it?

Slowly, her words sink in. "Your message?"

Her cheeks stain a delightful pink. "I summoned them, when I was thinking of running away."

My smile falls. She notices my expression and her brows pucker with worry. Fuck. How long will this be a sore spot for us?

My gut twists as a new thought crosses my mind. She could still intend to leave me. Her family's sudden appearance could mean more than an unexpected visit—what if she departs with them, when they go? What if she asked them here to take her home?

What if she hasn't changed her mind?

"I see," I grunt, carefully choosing my next words. "And are you still trying to run away, Sunfish? Do I need to chase them off?"

Because I would. I'd fight that giant paddledrake if I had to—as unlucky as my odds may be. I size up its mouth and swallow hard. It would end me in one bite, one smack of its flipper, or one lash of that barbed tail.

Her eyes glint with mischief. "No," she says, ducking to kiss my cheek. She tugs my arm, pulling me out of my chair. "Come on. Winona's going to *love* you."

***

THE BRINE QUEEN STARES at the severed head mounted on a pike before my gate. Hoarfrost has mottled the healer's skin, frozen his blood around the iron post, and formed a crust over his stringy hair, giving him an eerie blue cast. Her guards eye it warily, keeping proximity to their queen. The older companion ignores the head altogether, instead inspecting me with the intensity of a mother pikewhale. A smug smile tugs the corner of his mouth.

I posted Lucas here in retribution for his damage to the kingdom. Now each time one of my subjects passes by, they spit at the stones beneath him. I didn't consider how a severed head would look to an *outsider*. It must be intimidating.

"Thanks for making the journey all this way, Your Majesty." I dip my head and touch my gills in the sign of respect.

With a bland look on her face, she returns the gesture.

The queen tugs her travel robe tighter and crosses her arms, the stones clacking as she shifts her weight. The family resemblance is obvious—she has Nahla's fierce brown eyes and matching hair, the same slant to her jaw. I'd recognize that stubborn pout in her bottom lip anywhere. It's like the goddess Audrina formed them from the same sheet of ice. And when she speaks, her voice rings with a matching alto timbre.

"Nahlani," she says, glaring at Nahla where she's tucked under my arm in her frostcat cloak.

"Winona," Nahla echoes in the same flat tone. I squeeze her shoulder, rubbing my thumb in soothing circles, and she leans into my side.

"You know, when Keen translated the message from Ramona, I thought this was a rescue mission." She flicks her gaze over my form, to my arm slung around Nahla's shoulders, then to the castle behind us. "A land-bound nation. What an interesting choice for a getaway."

"Look, Win, I'm sorry," Nahla mumbles. She curls in on herself, her shoulders sagging by the minute as if caving under her sister's reprimand. I grit my teeth, not liking that one bit.

The queen's expression sours. "Yes, well, we came all this way at your request, so why don't you come on board and we can *catch up* where it's not so..."

"Cold?" I offer with a smirk.

"I'd prefer not to impose on Your Majesty's hospitality." Her gaze flicks once more to Lucas's severed head.

"Understood," I say, squeezing Nahla's arm.

"Excellent. We'll see you for dinner then." The queen whirls on her heels and moves toward the surf. She drops her cloak, which her guards hurry to pick up and store within a transport satchel as she dives into the water. Her green tail flicks and submerges with a splash.

The older male shrugs. "I believe she means now. Which is a pity. I would have enjoyed gleaning from your hospitality, if it meant getting the story behind the poor headless fellow," he says. He touches his gills and bows before me. "Keen, lead way-maker of the Brine, and very pleased to make your acquaintance, Sire."

Nahla laughs. "I'll tell you all about it on the way over, Keen."

The male brightens and spreads his arms in welcome. "Splendid, my girl."

Nahla drops her cloak and steps toward the sea with the way-maker, preparing to dive.

She means now. I swallow hard as a flurry of nerves batters my stomach. As in, swim *with* them to that colossal paddledrake. What will Nahla's family think of me when they see the Beast? What will my *kingdom* think, as I swim right through their celebration?

Not even the plump curve of Nahla's bare ass can soothe my anxiety.

She splashes into the water, then breaks the surface with a timid smile as she looks back at me. "Let's go, Beasty," she says. My resolve crumbles at that name alone. "Don't make me do this without you."

How can I say no to her?

With a brisk inhale, I step forward, drop my cloak, and submerge.

CHAPTER SIXTY-FIVE

NAHLA

WINONA LOOKS GAUNT AS she slumps in her chair at the head of the Brine table, her face pale like she's seen a ghost. A stray piece of her hair falls across her forehead and she doesn't smooth it away. Her fingers are steepled, eyes weary, as she surveys the dining room, staring mostly at the space above my head. She flicks her gaze around the table occasionally to disguise her glare—to our chattery mother, our frowning father, the old way-maker Keen, and Aethan next to me, then to my forehead. My sister can't look me in the eye. But she skips Ferrell entirely, her king husband, so that's points in my favor. However minimal.

I'm bursting with questions, but I keep them locked tight behind my lips. I'm sure my actions put her through the political wringer. How long until she discovered I was missing? What did she do when she found out? She hasn't been sleeping, that much is obvious. My stomach twists into a knot as the guilt settles in.

We've run out of things to say. Mother and Father rolled out their performative welcome party already, showering me with hugs and compliments and assuring their forgiveness of my *big mistake*. Nobody mentions it specifically. Nobody tells me what came of the Coral Prince and his mother's arrangement of matrimony. It hangs above us like a cloud of whaleshit waiting to sink.

The only one who seems genuinely excited to see me is Keen. He watches me from the far side of the table, wiggling his eyebrows and darting glances at the hulking Frost King sitting next to me. About an hour ago, Keen saw Aethan's Beast form, and the way-maker hasn't stopped giving me googly eyes since. "A beast-tamer," he'd whispered when we surfaced. "That's my girl."

Aethan finds my hand beneath the table and gives it a cool squeeze. His palm is sweaty. Poor thing is probably melting in the heated dining room.

Keen clears his throat, dispelling the awkward silence. "So, Nahla. The Frost Kingdom. That's a far cry from Coral, don't you think?"

I rearrange my expression into blank politeness. "I'm sure Her Majesty already sent them my deepest regrets. How was the weather?"

Keen's eyes twinkle. "Sunny and splendid, as you'd expect. A real treat for my withered bones."

Winona bends her fork, curling it in half. The metal squeaks, then clatters to the table.

And here I thought this reunion would be pleasant. "What's for dinner?" I ask, filling the silence before it can fall.

"Sunfish."

A deep rumble fills the room. Aethan splays his hand flat on my thigh and tilts his head back, a glorious grin on his face. Laughing. The whole table slides their gazes to him.

"Excellent," he says with a sparkle in his eye. "My favorite meal."

A flurry of eels squirm in my stomach. Winona's careful mask cracks, revealing a shred of surprise. "You've had it before?"

"I enjoy Sunfish thoroughly. When the occasion arises." His hand slides higher on my thigh, pinky finger straying dangerously close to my center. I clench as arousal floods through me. Heat burns my cheeks and ears.

Oh gods. He didn't just say that to Winona, fucking Queen of the Brine.

He's trouble. A pure, untamed *animal*. His hand rotates, and that damn pinky slides right across the seam of my legs. I'll get him back for this later as soon as that finger finishes...

"Am I missing something?" Winona asks.

I cross my legs, trapping his hand between my thighs. "Nope. Just a little joke between me and His Frostiness."

Aethan wiggles his finger, unable to move it any closer. His disappointment brushes the fringes of my mind.

I shoot him daggers with my eyes. *Later.*

"I'd like to hear the punchline." Keen raises an eyebrow, flicking a knowing look my way.

Fucking hell.

The servants pick that moment to enter the dining hall, carrying trays of roasted sunfish. Tension breaks as my family receives their plates, their attention at last diverted.

My meal sits on a bed of salted reedgrass, garnished with a lush-fruit and chilibean sauce. The rich, familiar scent wafts and my eyes close briefly. My stomach rumbles. Before I can lift my fork and dig in, Winona opens her mouth.

"Isn't that lovely." She sniffs. "You've been off making jokes instead of doing your duty."

What low chatter started around the table snuffs out. I hear the pain in her voice, thick with betrayal. Everything she did that bothered me was for the sake of her kingdom—the generosity, the carefully cultivated words, the tight protocols with no room for error. I see that now. I understand it deeply, having watched the male I love sacrifice so much to protect his own people. I was wrong about her. Maybe someday, I'll tell her that.

I smile. "It's good to see you, too, Winona."

"You don't know the hell I went through to cover up your mess. Imagine my embarrassment having to explain to the Coral Kingdom we lost his bride in transit."

Ferrell fidgets with his collar. "Well, he was already married when we got there, though, Nahla. So it's not a big deal, really."

"What?" The breath sucks out of my lungs from the shock. A thousand questions bubble up behind my lips.

"Yes, it seems the invitation you received was already two moon-cycles too late. Lost in transit, if you will," he says. He gives me a small smile. "The prince married an Abyssal, of all things."

"*What?*" I repeat.

"Ferrell!" Winona hisses through her teeth, blushing dark red. Caught in her lie?

"Were you not going to tell her?" he asks.

The room narrows in an instant as I'm swallowed by the sudden emptiness in my gut. Sound distorts until all I can hear is a distant ringing. Like I'm watching myself from third-person as I sit in my chair, balling my hands into my skirt to feel something. Anything. I'm numb.

The answer is clear on my sister's face: I wasn't supposed to know the truth. She would have kept it from me until the day she dissolved. The whole reason for my rebellion was moot from the start.

I should never have summoned Ramona, should never have brought her here, and I already can't wait for the moment she guides the city out of our waters. I'm staying in the Rime, where I'm *happy* and *loved*. Where I belong. I found love; Winona fucking settled. She wouldn't know love if it sat on her face.

Aethan finds my fist and unwinds it from the silk, lacing our fingers together. Holding his hand, I feel grounded. I was never lost. Not really. I was just finding my way to him.

What if my *big mistake* wasn't a mistake, after all? What if running away is what I was meant to do?

Winona scrambles for control, turning to address Aethan instead. "Your Majesty, I cannot express enough how grateful we are to you for harboring my lost sister these past several moons. We're happy to take her off your hands, and deeply apologize for the..." She flicks her gaze over me with unfiltered disappointment, trying to fix her expression and failing. "...inconvenience."

It's the lowest insult imaginable, coming from my sister. To be inconvenient is to be unwanted. Problematic. Like a blemish on her forehead before the big ball. All she wants is convenience. Her marriage—convenient. Her rise to the throne—convenient. I'm the piece that never quite fit into her elaborate puzzle, and she's always resented me for it.

Sometimes I think she wishes she was an only child. It would have been better for her that way.

Aethan's anger rolls through our mental connection, burning hot as the sun. He braces both hands on the table and stands. His knuckles pale from the strength of his grip. Veins rise from his forearms.

"Inconvenience?" he thunders.

Winona flinches—a minute twitch in her eye, imperceptible to an untrained observer—but I see it. She's afraid of him.

"Nahla is a fucking *delight* to all who know her, and I will not have you soil her good name by suggesting otherwise." Aethan's voice rumbles across the room, and his face contorts with rage. His fingers stain blue against the table, scales crawling up the backs of his hands. "You will not take her off my hands, nor will you be taking her anywhere. I do not concede her, not now, not *ever*. You can't separate a king from his queen. I'll fucking drown you first."

Silence falls.

Winona's jaw drops in muted disbelief. Mother stares hungrily and licks her lips. Father looks like he's swallowed a lushfruit whole. Ferrell picks at his napkin, ignoring the tension altogether.

When Keen meets my gaze, he grins from ear to ear, shoots me a thumbs up, and winks.

My heart pounds in my ears, heavy with hope. Never has anyone stood up for me like that. In one fell swoop, Aethan put Winona in her place.

Aethan. The grumpiest sourfish I know. Called me a *fucking delight*.

I grasp the hem of Aethan's shirt, and he turns to look at me. His anger fades the moment our eyes meet, replaced with a warmth reserved only for me.

There's one thing he said that I'm desperate to confirm.

"Your queen?" I whisper. "Is that what I am to you?"

He blinks, confused. Then realization dawns.

"Fuck. I was going to…" He rubs the base of his jaw. "I had a more romantic proposal in mind, I swear I did, Sunfish. I have the ring and everything."

He grins, sheepish and devilishly handsome all at once, and my heart nearly bursts. He drops to his knee, fishes around in the pouch on his hip, and holds out a glinting diamond ring. "Nahlani Mahelona, Princess of the Brine and the sun of my heart, would you do me the immense pleasure of becoming mine?"

I launch out of my chair, throwing my arms around his neck. "I'm already yours," I gasp. "Always and forever." He catches me and hooks my legs around his hips as he stands again.

"Is that a yes?" he grunts.

I drink in the sight of him. The glint in his ice-blue eyes. The crooked slant to his smile. The sharp planes of his cheeks. That tiny dimple at the point of his chin. He's glorious, and he's all mine.

"Of course it's a yes," I say, and I kiss him hard on the mouth. He responds with a groan, and our lips slide together.

Somewhere behind us, Winona clears her throat. I wave my hand in her direction, dismissing her protests. I'm kissing my Frost King, and Winona can fucking wait.

"I thought you didn't want a land-bound king," my sister mutters.

I break from the kiss just long enough to say, "This one's different."

Aethan grins, and we pick up where we left off.

BEAST

EPILOGUE

SUBMERGE.

Swim.

Scent.

Today, we'll reopen the royal city of Doloch. A new era begins.

The Rime vibrates with anticipation, and I can taste the excitement in the water.

Electric, almost.

The same excitement runs through my body, from horns to tail.

My muscles flex with ease and my body revels in the slick glide of water over my scales.

I missed this form. That my king-self ever sought to destroy it feels blasphemous now. Unthinkable. This body is as much mine as the soft skin I wear on the shore.

The king's memories are as clear to me now as the water before my eyes—our shared memory restored, thanks to Nahla's spell.

I am the Frost King, I am the Beast, and I burst in gratitude for the siren who made me whole.

Nahla squeezes me, small fingers curling around my thumb. Her hair sprawls in a voluminous halo around her face, eyes bright and happy. Her lips part, letting the tune of her spell flow as she maintains the soft connection between our minds.

Nahla's emotions mix with mine—nervousness, delight, and hope. We pass them to each other as easily as water through our gills.

How did I get so lucky?

My Sunfish.

My mind-mate.

My queen.

She's everything I dreamed of and more.

And I'm bringing her home.

The gates to the city have been cleaned up for the celebration. The pikewhale statues on either side of the gate are free of glacierweed, buffed and shined to their former glory. A wide ribbon stretches between their horns.

The whole kingdom is here. They line the entrance, treading on either side to clear a path for us to swim through. Cheers break out as they spot our approach.

Nahla's grip on my finger tightens, and a wave of nerves brushes against my mind.

I speak to her, *Are you ready for this?*

Yes, she says. *It's all so beautiful. I can't believe it's mine.*

I focus on her face, memorizing the soft crest of her cheeks, the tiny bubbles clinging to her eyelashes, the curve of her mouth. I pass my gaze over the length of her golden tail. My stomach clenches, cock hardening each time she flicks her hips.

Mine. I echo her sentiment, relishing the word as it soaks through my being. She's so beautiful, and she's mine.

Nahla gasps as the strength of my thought enters her mind. She glances sideways, catching my eye as she blushes deeply.

Shit, she says. *You can't say that right now. We have an audience.*

I rumble my disagreement. The sound ricochets through the water, and the crowd grows silent, oblivious to our mental exchange.

We stop before the ribbon. I'm supposed to cut it with my claws, signifying the opening of the city. Nahla rests her hand on my wrist as I move into position. One snip of my claws, and I can whisk her away to our new bedroom. I can tie her into our hammock bed, secure her as I ravish—

They're waiting on you, she prods with amusement.

I shake my head, dismissing the tempting thoughts. Right. That comes later.

As I turn to address the crowd, I clear my throat. I've been practicing speaking aloud in this form, teaching my tongue to form the words. I'm still clumsy, but it will get better with time.

"Welcome," I bellow. My voice rumbles across the crowd like wind on the waves. "Welcome back to your home."

I snip the ribbon with my claws, and the crowd cheers. The gates open, and we swim through, hand in hand.

How did I do?

Pride floats through our connection. She's bursting with it. *You did great, Beasty.*

I sigh, flipping onto my back, and I tug her onto my stomach. I paddle us backward, lazily meandering through the open spaces.

Above us, sunlight filters through the ice, like glitter falling from above.

Nahla curls up on my chest, humming her quiet content. With a gentle claw, I tilt her chin so I can look into her eyes.

Welcome home, Nahlani, Queen of Frost.

ALSO BY LIESL WEST

The Sirens of Adria Series:
Giving fairytale princesses a mermaid tail and a good rail.
Interconnected standalone fairytale retellings—read them in any order!
Of Song and Scepter: it's The Little Mermaid, but she's stabby
Of Rime and Ruin: Beauty and the Beast x Jekyll and Hyde, with mermaids

ACKNOWLEDGMENTS

First thanks goes to my husband, my real-life book boyfriend. Thanks for showing me the fairytale moments in our every day world. I couldn't do this without you.

To my mom for being my number-one cheerleader always. And to my sister for answering all my marine biology questions and helping me fact-check the science of mermaids. It's harder than you think.

Thanks to my critique group and writing partners, Caitlin Mazur and Laura Graham, for your support and encouragement for this book start to finish.

To my editing team for working your magic! To Wren for your wealth of worldbuilding knowledge and constant support. To Zee for your shouty-caps love and expertise finding those tricky typos. And a huge shout out to my beta readers. All your enthusiasm and critique helped shape this book into the best version of itself, and I'm so grateful for your roles in making it happen.

Finally, to all the girlies who cringed when Beast turned into a blond man, this one's for you.

ABOUT THE AUTHOR

Liesl West is a deep sea mermaid disguised as a romantasy author, hatching spicy plots and hissing at daylight. She spins fairytales into ocean fantasy romance books that delight and destroy, ripping out your heart with her teeth before kissing it better with an HEA. She lives with her husband, child, and fluffy feline overlords in Virginia, where she devours the souls of lost sailors and watches way too many ocean documentaries.

Find her on social media @authorlieslwest or join her Newsletter: lieslwest.com/newsletter to stay connected.

CONTENT NOTES

THIS BOOK IS INTENDED for mature audiences and includes content not recommended for readers under the age of 18. *Of Rime and Ruin* contains: profanity, explicit sexual intimacy, blood, gore, descriptions of corpses, past death of a parent, slight suicide ideation, medical malpractice, young person's loss of limb, and hunting of animals.

Please read safely. If you have any questions, or you're wondering about the presence of a trigger not listed here, please contact me by email: author@lieslwest.com

Spicy scenes and where to find or avoid* them:
Chapter Thirty-Six
Chapter Forty-Four
Chapter Fifty
Chapter Sixty-Three

*Find a spice-free summary of each chapter on lieslwest.com/content-notes

9 7 9 8 9 9 9 0 0 4 8 2 4 9